For Gemma.

Enjoy!

Carlie Cullen x

HEART SEARCH

Book One: LOST

Carlie M. A. Cullen

Happy Birthday darling.

Love Dad xx

2015

Copyright © 2012 Carlie M. A. Cullen

All rights reserved. Except as permitted under the U.S. Copyright Act of 1976, no part of this publication may be reproduced, distributed or transmitted in any form or by any means, or stored in a database or retrieval system without the prior written permission of the author or publisher.

This is a work of fiction. Names, characters and incidents are products of the author's imagination or are used fictitiously and are not to be construed as real. Any resemblance to actual events, organizations, or persons, living or deceased, is entirely coincidental.

ISBN-13: 978-1-939296-60-3

ISBN-10: 1-939296-60-9

Myrddin Publishing Group

Credits:

Editor: Maria V A Johnson   Cover: Nicole Antonia Carson

www.myrddinpublishing.com

DEDICATION

To my beautiful daughter, Maria, the light of my life, whose love, support and encouragement knows no bounds; and for pushing me ever harder to keep the writing going.

Also, to Jakki, my wonderful friend, for always being there - every step of the way - and kicking my butt when the doubts set in.

Finally, to Terry and Marina, who gave me everything they could including my love of books and writing. I miss you.

ACKNOWLEDGMENTS

Every author has some special people behind the scenes who make priceless contributions to the finished product and it would be terribly remiss of me not to give them due credit.

First, and most importantly, my unending thanks to my awesome editor, Maria V A Johnson, who whipped the raw first draft into incredible shape and supported me through the whole process – I couldn't have done it without you! (And yes I know I owe you a bottle of wine or 3.)

Thanks also to Jakki Draper, my alpha reader, Alison DeLuca and Rachel Tsoumbakos my beta readers, whose insights and feedback helped make the story much stronger. To Nicole Antonia Carson, my thanks for designing the beautiful cover – you've got talent, girl! To Connie J Jasperson, who made my book trailer, my thanks and admiration – you promised perfection and boy did you deliver!!

Thank you to all my friends and colleagues at Myrddin Publishing for their encouragement, support and help getting my novel published. To all my friends at Writebulb, my writing group, for their support – thank you.

To everyone who participated in the Blog Tour launch, thank you for your support and keeping the momentum going when I couldn't.

Finally some special friends, peers and colleagues for their unending support and encouragement, who deserve an extra special mention; Jakki Draper, Connie J Jasperson, Alison DeLuca and M G Wells – thank you from the bottom of my heart and I love you all dearly.

An empty highway, pinprick stars.

Silence; no favoured song clouds her sight.

Pictures; sunlit journeys

now dead and gone, obscure the road.

The seat beside her

cold, missing his warmth;

a glorious sun burning.

Tears streak her cheeks.

She curls up, hugs her knees

pulls a blanket tight –

her heart search done for the night.

© Maria V A Johnson

Prologue

His hiding place was perfect; darkness surrounded and comforted him and he became one with it. He had chosen well. The ancient ruins were totally hidden by overgrown shrubs and trees. From this place, he could venture out before dusk, completely obscured by the dense canopy of the primordial trees; the sun struggled to break through even at midday.

He was close, closer than ever before; so close the flavour of the human's essence coated his sensitive tongue. The one sought was nearby – he could sense him. He had searched for a very long time to find someone this special. Sure he'd found talent along the way, but this one, this human was something else entirely.

The excitement was building inside like a volcano preparing to erupt. His tongue ran over his teeth; venom pooled in his mouth and he savoured the taste. There would be a new flavour to add to it soon. Very soon.

He first detected the scent two days ago. Unfortunately, an opportunity had not presented itself and he had become frustrated to the point of anger as strategy after strategy was thwarted by the most stupid and pointless of reasons. He was tenacious when there was something he desired and right now there was nothing he desired more than this human. There was a plentiful supply around to quench his thirst – that was not his aim.

His reverie was interrupted – a familiar scent wafted on the air that permeated the shelter. It was the human – the one he sought – and so near, too near to be allowed to escape again. Once more venom collected in his mouth.

He moved swiftly through the darkness with perfect vision towards the exit hidden amongst the foliage. The closer he got to the outside, the stronger the scent, and the more eager he became.

It was time.

Chapter 1 – Joshua

The sun, a ferocious golden orb, burnt into his skin as Joshua wandered aimlessly through the country park. He was vaguely aware of the voices from families enjoying the early evening warmth and the shrieks and giggles of excited children playing games, but the noise was too distant to permeate his consciousness. He felt a twinge of discomfort, the edge of the plaster where he had donated blood earlier that afternoon pulled on the delicate wispy hairs framing the inside of his elbow, but he ignored it. Perspiration formed diamond-like droplets on his forehead and his thin polycotton shirt became glued to his back. He gazed around to get his bearings and then headed towards the wooded area off to his right.

South Weald Country Park attracted thousands of visitors every year. Its 550 acres of wide-open grassland and wooded areas were beautifully kept and steeped in history. It was once the site of a great hall with formal gardens and had been a Royal Hunting Estate. Remains of an Iron Age Settlement had been discovered on the site. The wildlife was wonderful: the squirrels darting across the grass from one area of trees to another and the rabbits peeking out on occasions. There were ducks and swans down by either of the two lakes and myriad varieties of songbirds, but also a paddock housing deer. Its' numerous ponds and network of pathways winding through the park made it a firm favourite, not only with residents, but others from neighbouring counties. Joshua visited the park for many years and loved the place, especially in summer.

He entered the shade of the arboreal canopy and welcomed the relief. It was a beautiful sight. Different shades of emerald, jade and olive dappled with a heavenly radiance, sporadic shafts hit the bracken covered earth like overlarge fingers. He tore his eyes away with some reluctance and continued his stroll. He heard an object drop to the ground beside him and glanced down to see; his car keys had fallen from his pocket. As Joshua crouched to retrieve them his eyes drifted to the key fob which contained a photograph of Remy taken last summer. His mind began to wander.

He wasn't by nature a romantic type of guy and hadn't really considered the subject of matrimony, until he met Remy, that is. His thoughts paused for a second; in his peripheral vision he noticed a bench seat tucked away. He walked over and sat. Once again his thoughts returned to his fiancée. With her collar length bobbed strawberry blonde hair, round face and the warmest and most gentle eyes he had ever seen, he was unreservedly and irrevocably in love with her. He wanted to protect her; despite her having an inner strength and the self-confidence to be assertive; she often teased him about his "knight in shining armour" mentality. Joshua chuckled softly to himself as he pictured her face when she pretended exasperation at his 'needless worrying'; both of them knew how much she enjoyed it. His smile broadened as he contemplated their forthcoming wedding. He had no reservations whatsoever about marrying Remy, no second thoughts, no cold feet, nothing. He was thrilled at the prospect of this wonderfully warm and sexy lady becoming his wife, and the corny cliché 'a match made in heaven' jumped into his mind, which made him chuckle out loud. Joshua closed his eyes as he remembered the first time he saw her nearly three years ago . . .

It was a Saturday in August and I was with some mates at the Basvegas Leisure Park in Basildon. As we walked towards one of the American-style restaurants, a small cluster of girls came out. I nudged Simon and we cast admiring glances at the party then my eyes met Remy's. It was like . . . SHAZAM – a thunderbolt straight to the grey matter. I was totally blown away – she was . . . stunning! My mouth gaped and I was rendered totally speechless.

As I propped up the bar at BB's club later that night, I spotted her on the dance floor. Finishing my drink in record time, almost choking on it, I negotiated my way through the gyrating bodies. I asked her to dance, tripping over my words a little making me feel a total prat, but she just smiled and nodded.

The shade among the trees gradually darkened as he lounged on the bench daydreaming about Remy. He was totally oblivious to the dark suited stranger who had noiselessly approached him, stopping a few yards from where he sat, partially concealed in the trees. The stranger sniffed the air, the sweet smell of blood from under the plaster on the man's arm drew him forward, the thirst threatened to overwhelm him as he licked his lips in anticipation.

This was a different type of thirst for him – there was a . . . *uniqueness* about the flavour – he could taste it in the air and he knew he would not drain this special one. He listened intently to his surroundings, hearing nothing save the musical trill of birdsong high in the trees and the pounding of his victim's heart; he glided silently forward noting Joshua's eyes were closed. This distinctive thirst was so intense it caused him physical pain; he could contain himself no longer and pounced, like a cat after a mouse, sinking his incisors easily into Joshua's flesh.

The last thing to cross Joshua's mind was his plan for Remy's homecoming the following day, before the pain rendered him unconscious.

Chapter 2 – Remy

The seatbelt sign flashed on as the announcement came over the address system: "Ladies and gentlemen, we will shortly be landing at London Gatwick. Would you please return your seats to the upright position, put away your tray tables and ensure your seatbelts are securely fastened. Local time is 09:43am and the forecast is for an extremely warm and sunny day. On behalf of Captain Heathwick and the crew, we thank you for flying with ABA. We trust you have had a pleasant flight and look forward to seeing you again soon."

I complied with the instructions as the stewardess cleared away my glass and empty carton of orange juice. I kept my headphones in place as I watched the end of 'New Moon' – I'd read all 4 of the books in the saga and loved them, so was thrilled to find the latest film on the flight, it wasn't due out in the UK for another couple of weeks. As the movie ended with a proposal, I smiled as I thought of my forthcoming wedding. It was so exciting to think that in two weeks' time I would be Mrs Joshua Grant; it was a dream come true.

As a teenager, my friends and I would speculate about 'our perfect man' and would make endless lists of physical attributes as well as personality traits we all found appealing. It was comical how many times the physical attributes closely resembled the latest heartthrobs from films or bands, or the boyfriend of the moment. It was even more hilarious how the lists changed when one of us broke up with a boyfriend, or another new boy band was catapulted onto the music scene. It seemed so long ago, but it was only 6 years. I wondered what happened to the lists I penned, and whether any of the attributes actually resembled Joshua. In some ways I'd like to think they did, but how much had my taste in men changed? I'd certainly become more discerning towards the end of my teen years and as I entered my twentieth year, I discovered I had a yearning to find my 'soul mate', someone who would love and accept me for who and what I am, who wouldn't try to change me; *someone special and wonderful and loving; someone just for me.*

The stewardess walked down the aisle of the 747 checking that all the passengers had fastened their seatbelts. I stared out the window, a smile on my face and saw the stewardess reflected in the glass. A smile lit her face as she saw mine. I heard the landing gear being lowered. It wouldn't be long now. I wanted to see Joshua and the anticipation of being in his arms caused a fluttering in my chest. The last two weeks in the USA had been quite exciting, my first trip overseas due to my recent promotion, but I'd missed him terribly. My colleagues at the Washington office had been really friendly and showed me around; but as lovely as they all were, it would have been so much more special if he'd been with me.

The ground started rushing up as the massive jet came in to land; the wheels touched down on the runway with a bump. The engines roared as the brakes were applied and within mere seconds we were taxiing towards the terminal. I fervently hoped there wouldn't be a delay collecting my luggage or getting through Passport Control, as Josh was waiting in Arrivals.

At last the jet stopped and the cabin crew opened the heavy door allowing us to exit. I knew there was no need to hurry - it would take time for the luggage to be unloaded and sent through to baggage reclaim - so I gathered my belongings and moved out into the aisle when a gap appeared.

As I walked into the Arrivals hall, I eagerly scanned the ocean of faces until I found the soft, coffee-coloured eyes I sought. Moving towards him as fast as my cumbersome suitcase would allow I launched myself into his waiting embrace. I turned my head to look at his face and his lips found mine – his ardent kiss feverish as if he wanted to devour me on the spot – and he was completely oblivious to the fact we had an audience. As the depth and pressure of his lips on mine began to send sizzles of pain into my jaw, I tried to gently extricate myself, but his arms were so strong I found it impossible to pull away. I felt a small wave of panic and a cry erupted in my throat as I renewed my efforts to push him away. He withdrew his lips from mine and looked questioningly into my eyes, his expression changing in response to what my face portrayed. Joshua took a deep breath.

"Sweetheart, I'm so sorry if I hurt you. I've missed you more than you can imagine and I just got a bit carried away. Forgive me?"

I let my eyes drift up to meet his and was shocked to see the pain in them.

"Of course I forgive you." I reached up and cupped his face in my hands and gently pressed my lips momentarily to his. "I've missed you too, darling," I whispered.

His face relaxed and a small smile of relief replaced the hurt. "Phew!" he grinned at me. "Come on, let's get you home."

He grabbed my suitcase and took my hand in his, leading me out of the terminal and towards the car park.

As we pulled onto the M23 heading towards London, the traffic was flowing quite well; as opposed to the journey we would have had only an hour earlier. Although I'd spoken to Joshua nearly every day while I was away, I hadn't gone into much detail about the places I'd been taken to and the things I'd seen, so while I had him as a captive audience, I filled in the gaps. Before I knew it, we were on the M25 and queuing at the tolls for the Dartford Tunnel. Thankfully, the vehicles were moving through steadily and we were through the tunnel in a matter of minutes. Twenty minutes later, Josh pulled the car onto the driveway of the three bedroom home we'd bought 3 months ago. It was so good to be back - I was gasping for a decent cup of tea.

Thirty minutes later, my case was unpacked. Joshua came into the bedroom and walked purposefully towards me, his smouldering eyes never leaving my face. I smiled at him enticingly and in moments I was in his arms. His lips travelled from my collarbone, up my neck and across my cheek to meet my lips with a passionate caress. My body grew warmer as my desire hit fever pitch and I returned his kisses with fervour. I started pulling at his clothes at the same time as he began to undress me and we were soon naked, our hands re-acquainting with each other's bodies. We sank onto the bed and journeyed to our own unique corner of heaven.

Chapter 3 – Remy

I opened my eyes and squinted against the brilliant light pouring through the window. I peeked at the alarm clock next to the bed and was amazed to read 2:40pm on the digital display. Oops – I must have fallen asleep. I smiled to myself then reached to the other side of the bed, expecting to find Joshua lying there, but the sheets were cool, indicating he'd been up for some time. I arose slowly, feeling an unaccustomed soreness between my legs, and padded to the bathroom thinking a shower would freshen and wake me a bit more. I glanced at the mirror over the sink as I passed by and gasped in astonishment at the sight of my body. I retraced my steps so I could fully see my reflection and my jaw dropped when I noticed the mass of bruises beginning to show on my upper arms and torso. I looked down at my legs and discovered more purple marks on my thighs. My fingers lightly traced the maze of blotches; I winced once or twice when I exerted more pressure than I intended, but I wasn't in any pain. None of it hurt unless I touched it.

I thought back to when we made love earlier: it was wonderfully passionate and yes, he had been a bit more demanding and dominant than usual, but I put it down to us being apart for two weeks. I hadn't noticed any pain at the time, caught up as I was in the 'moment', but seeing my body now……words failed me. Perhaps I'd inflicted a few bruises on him too, I reasoned. I determined not to mention it to him. I hurriedly had my shower, got dressed carefully so as to hide the marks he'd left behind, and walked downstairs to find him sprawled on the sofa rifling through the recently received wedding invitation replies, and marking them against the master list.

He looked up as I entered the room and smiled at me.

"Well, hello you," he chuckled. "Are we feeling a bit better now?"

"Just a lot! And in more ways than one." I responded, grinning back at him, my eyes twinkling mischievously.

He laughed out loud at the expression on my face, a rich deep chuckle that some might call a 'dirty laugh', and I laughed with him.

I pointed to the cards and list on the seat beside him. "How's it going then? Have we had all the replies in yet?"

"Not quite. We're three missing. – the cousins in Sunderland, Uncle Alf and Matt and Keira. But get *this*," his voice rose in his excitement. "Anna and her crew are coming from Canada AND my Auntie Joan is making the trip over from Australia. I'm totally blown away."

"Bloody hell!" I exclaimed, my eyes wide with surprise. "I really didn't expect either of that lot to come – I only sent them invitations out of courtesy. That's *amazing*!" I agreed.

I walked over to the magazine rack, pulled out a folder and manoeuvred myself onto the opposite end of the sofa, being careful not to disturb his neat piles of cards and letters. Opening the file, I pulled out a list of my own and glanced at the items which still hadn't been crossed off.

"We've still got quite a few last minute things to take care of yet. Me thinks we'd better get cracking – we've got less than 2 weeks now."

"I know. What do you need me to do then?" he enquired, the false exasperation in his voice not really masking the underlying excitement.

I raised my eyebrows and smirked at him. "Well……I think we should have a list for this week's jobs and a separate list for next week. Does that sound okay?"

He nodded. "Yeah, so what's on for this week then?"

I consulted my master list again. "Right, we need to finish the schedule for the day and make sure everyone in the main party has got one. Next we need to give the hotel the approximate number of guests for the reception." I put a small mark against each item as we went through them. "We need to reconfirm everything and check all the suits and bridesmaids dresses will be ready for collection two days before the big day….." I trailed off, checking to make sure I hadn't forgotten anything.

"What about the place cards and table plan?" he asked.

"Shoot, I *knew* there was something. That's my mum's job. We need to get all the acceptance cards round to her so she can get weaving. We can pop them round sometime tomorrow can't we?"

"Don't see why not."

"Great. I'll give her a ring later. In the meantime, can you start reconfirming everything while I speak to the hotel and the dressmakers?"

"Yep. Let's get started. The sooner we start the sooner it's done," he confirmed.

I nodded and reached for my mobile phone.

The day whizzed past and by 10pm I was yawning my head off.

"I'm going to bed, babes," I announced. "It must be all the travelling and jet lag, but I feel completely wiped out."

"Not to mention the physical work-out earlier," he chuckled.

"Yeah, that too." I grinned. I got up from the sofa and kissed him softly. "You coming?"

"Yep. I've been waiting a whole two weeks to cuddle up to you. I'll turn everything off and check the doors and I'll be up in a min," he replied.

"Okay." I turned and walked out of the room, dragging my feet wearily towards the stairs.

I went into the bathroom, washed my face and brushed my teeth before going into the bedroom to get ready for bed. I peeled off my jeans and placed them neatly on the floor beside the wardrobe, then dragged my t-shirt over my head and dropped it at my feet. As I reached behind me to unclasp my bra, I heard a sharp intake of breath and then a groan of anguish. I whirled around to see Joshua standing in the doorway looking absolutely distraught, his eyes clouded with such agony, I instinctively reached out to him. To my utter astonishment, he took a step back away from me.

"Babe? What's wrong?" I asked confusion evident in the timbre of my voice.

"*Oh my God*! W-what… where did those bruises come from?" he whispered. I relaxed a little, understanding what had caused his reaction.

"Hey, it's fine. They don't hurt. Don't worry about it."

"I don't understand," he exclaimed.

"We just got a little…carried away earlier – it's nothing." I tried to reassure him.

"How can you say it's nothing? It looks so painful, so…awful" he cried.

"Honestly, babe, I'm not in any pain. I'm fine." I asserted. "C'mon let's get in bed – I'm shattered."

I finished undressing and climbed under the duvet, the bedding cool against my skin. He pulled his clothes off, dropping them in a heap and carefully got into bed, staying resolutely on his side of the bed. I turned to face him and stroked his cheek.

"I'm *so sorry* Rems – I feel gutted…disgusted I've hurt you like this."

"I told you, I'm fine. Please babe, don't beat yourself up over this. It really doesn't hurt."

I kissed his cheek and snuggled up to him, snaking my arm across his chest. He lay there stiffly, as if he was afraid to move in case he hurt me some more.

"I don't know what to say," he moaned, anguish still apparent in his tone.

"I told you, I'm fine. Please babe, don't beat yourself up over this. It really doesn't hurt."

I kissed his cheek and snuggled up to him, snaking my arm across his chest. He lay there stiffly, as if he was afraid to move in case he hurt me some more.

"I don't know what to say," he moaned, anguish still apparent in his tone.

"There's nothing you *need* to say. Let's get some sleep huh?"

I moved so he could put his arm around me and laid my head on his chest. His fingertips gently stroked up and down my arm as I listened to his heart. My eyelids were so heavy I let them close and was asleep within seconds. I didn't even hear him whisper, "I love you and I'm so sorry."

* * *

Time flew past and before we knew it, we only had four days to go before our big day. I was in the kitchen preparing dinner when Joshua arrived home from work. He walked straight into the kitchen and kissed me on the cheek.

"Hey, gorgeous. How you doing? Did you have a good day? What's for dinner – I'm starving."

I laughed. "Which question should I answer first?"

"The food one!" he chuckled.

"Steak, chips, mushrooms and salad," I replied, grinning. "Typical bloke, only interested in his stomach." I grumbled good-naturedly.

"Great. I'd like my steak very rare please. I'm going to change – back in a min."

"Hold it mister. Since when do you have your steak rare?"

"Dunno. I just fancy it that way today – okay?"

"If that's the way you want it – your wish is my command, oh master!" I cheeked him.

"Glad you're finally remembering your status," he retorted, chuckling, then ducked as I threw a mushroom at him and ran up the stairs laughing.

After spending the evening reviewing last minute wedding arrangements, we decided to have an early night, climbed into bed and cuddled up close. I lightly dragged my fingernails across his chest, drawing shapes and swirls around his sparse chest hair, kissing his neck softly. I heard his breathing change just before he put his hand under my chin and lifted my face so our lips met. Our mutual passion and longing rose together, our kisses deeper and more sensual. His arms crushed me into him and his lips became more demanding, exerting more pressure, making my lips tingle. My body was on fire as we sped once again into paradise.

The alarm clock woke me for my last day at work before the wedding. I reached over and hit the snooze button then rolled onto my back. I winced as my back and shoulders rubbed against the sheet, so I lay still and waited for the discomfort to pass. I couldn't think what had caused the soreness, but then again, I wasn't fully awake yet.

All too soon, the alarm sounded again and I knew I didn't have time to lie here any longer so I rolled over again and switched it off. I got out of bed and headed straight to the bathroom, noticing stiffness and aching throughout my body as I moved. I paused in front of the mirror and gasped in horror at my reflection. I was covered in bruises again, but more of them and long scratches snaked down my arms and around my thighs. I inhaled deeply and winced again, turning so I could see my back in the mirror. I stifled a shriek when I noticed more abrasions running from my shoulders down to my waist.

I was so immersed in what I was seeing I didn't hear Joshua's footfalls approaching. He popped his head around the door to greet me, but the words died on his lips and a low moan escaped instead. He sank to his knees as if his legs weren't strong enough to support his body and put his head in his hands. I was in too much shock to go to him and remained where I was, motionless, staring at him. His body heaved like he was crying, but all I could hear was the whispered words,

"Oh my God. Oh my God. Oh my God."

"Josh?"

"Oh my God. Oh my God. Oh my God," he kept repeating.

"Joshua?"

"I feel sick!"

"YOU feel sick? Not as sick as I feel," I snapped at him.

"No. Oh No. What. Have. I. Done?"

"I would think the answer to that one is *quite* obvious, wouldn't you?"

"I'm so sorry, Remy. I don't remember doing it…..I wouldn't hurt you for the world, you know that. Well, not on purpose, I mean. I don't know what to say. I'm so disgusted with myself," he cried into his hands then raised his face to look at me, huge fat tears rolled down his face, drained of colour.

The anguish in his eyes softened my heart and my anger dissipated as smoke on a breeze. I knew him. He wouldn't hurt me on purpose. He loved me like I loved him.

"It's okay. I know you didn't mean to do it. I'm alright – just a bit sore," I tried to reassure him.

He looked into my eyes and shook his head in denial. "No you're not!" he said vehemently, "I can see you're not."

"Yes I am." I insisted. "Honestly, I'm okay."

He shook his head again, and before I could say anything more, he got to his feet, albeit a little unsteadily and ran from the room.

I heard him moving about in the bedroom and then he ran down the stairs. I called out to him, "Josh?"

"Erm, I've gotta go. I'll see you after work. I'm so sorry babe. I love you," he replied, tripping over the words in his haste. Before I had a chance to reply, I heard the front door slam shut behind him, the engine roaring in his Audi and the screech of the tyres as he hurriedly pulled away.

I stood there, rooted to the spot, totally gobsmacked. I couldn't believe he'd run out on me. I was confused by his reaction – it was so out of character, but so was the violent lovemaking.

In all the time we'd been together, he'd never hurt me, not even when we'd been play-fighting, and to up and leave…I could only deduce he needed time to comes to terms with what he'd done to me. I walked back into the bedroom, grabbed my mobile phone from the bedside table and dialled his number. It must have been switched off because it went straight to voicemail. I hesitated, and then decided to leave him a message.

"Hey babes, it's only me. Just want you to know I'm not angry with you – I know you didn't do this deliberately, and there was no need to run off. I love you with all my heart, Josh, and I still can't wait to become your wife on Saturday. We can work this out, so don't worry. Call me later? Love you. Bye."

I hung up and tossed the phone onto the bed. I glanced at the clock and groaned – I was going to be late for work – and ran back to the bathroom.

Joshua

Around 10:30am, Joshua returned to the house. His mouth was set in a grim line, his eyes hooded and his skin pale grey. He climbed the stairs, using the banister rail to drag himself and entered the bedroom. He didn't seem surprised to find it a mess; the bed wasn't made and dirty laundry was still on the floor. Moving automatically, he quickly straightened the duvet, picked up the washing and dropped it into the laundry basket in the corner of the room. He opened his wardrobe, grabbed a holdall from the top shelf and started pulling clothes off hangers to stuff into it, not caring if they got creased. Hangers were flying off the rail, but he ignored them in his haste. He yanked open his underwear drawer, pulling it completely off the runners, the contents tumbling to the floor. He snatched handfuls of socks and pants and chucked them into the top of the bag before going into the bathroom and seizing toiletries off the shelves.

When the bag was full, he picked it up and without a backward glance, marched down the stairs. He dropped it by the front door and walked into the lounge. On the coffee table was the pad and pen they'd been using to make the wedding lists. He sat on the sofa and pulled the coffee table closer so he could lean on it. He seized the pen, and sat with it poised over the blank sheet, trying to marshal his thoughts. The first sign of emotion crossed his face as he wrote 'My darling Remy,'

An hour later, wearing a desolate expression of absolute grief, he drove away from the house.

Chapter 4 – Remy

I pulled onto the drive and glanced at the clock on the dashboard before switching off the engine. It was only 5:25pm – I'd made good time getting home for once. I grabbed my bag, climbed out of the car, locking it remotely as I walked to the front door and let myself into the house.

As soon as I crossed the threshold, I knew something was not quite right, but couldn't think what it could be. I walked into the kitchen, but it was exactly as I'd left it that morning – a mess. I wandered into the lounge and let my eyes drift slowly around the room, searching for anything amiss. I didn't spot anything at first, but then I noticed the coffee table was out of place. I moved towards it meaning to put it back when I saw a letter addressed to me lying on the surface.

I recognised Josh's writing on the envelope and a chill shivered down my spine. I reached for it, my hand trembling. I picked it up and managed to extract the contents on the third attempt; I unfolded the sheets and began to read.

My darling Remy,

It's hard for me to put into words how disgusted I am with myself right now. When I saw what I'd done to you, I felt so sick inside and I hate myself for it. I really don't remember doing it, which makes it really weird and scary. I'm obviously not safe to be around, I'm a monster and I can't risk hurting you like that again, so I have to go away. I don't want to leave you, but there's something wrong with me and I couldn't bear it if I injured you again.

I'm in so much pain right now – my heart is shattering into a million pieces at the prospect of never seeing you again, and my sight is blurred with tears. I never thought I would meet anyone who could make me feel like you do.

When I'm with you I'm so vibrant, so alive, you make me feel so loved, so wanted and needed and I feel 12 feet tall. I can't put into words how much I love you Remy, but it's because I love you so much that I have to give you up.

I know it's a terrible cliché, but you do deserve someone so much better than me, someone who will cherish you, love and adore you and put you on a pedestal where you belong, someone who can make your heart sing, someone who won't leave awful marks on your body after making love to you. You need someone who will always be able to protect you, as I now know I can't.

Beautiful lady, you are my life and always will be, but you have to let me go. Please don't try to find me – I don't even know yet where I'm going to end up. I only know I have to go to protect you. I need you to find someone who can be what I can't, and to move on from the here and now. I need you to find happiness and I have to believe that you will, or I could never find the strength to walk away from you. You are strong enough to get over me and carve a new life for yourself, so go do it with my blessing.

I will always love you – I will never love anyone else, my heart will always belong to you.

Please, please forgive me my darling for everything I've done and am doing to hurt you. I wish there was some other way.

Be happy!

                      Love always,

                      Josh xx

I could feel my face drain of colour, my knees buckled and I collapsed onto the sofa. A scream built inside me as my heart splintered into billions of shards which cut me from the inside out. The pain in my chest so intense I couldn't breathe properly. My head filled with an angry wasps nest. Fat, pearl-sized droplets fell from my eyes and down my ashen cheeks; a small waterfall had taken up residence on the tip of my nose. I wailed in grief, the pages slipping from my fingers.

My whole body heaved with the strength of the sobs that escaped from the back of my throat, making me wince again and again as the very action stretched and pulled on my already bruised and battered body. I couldn't think straight, couldn't reconcile his reasons for leaving me. It felt like a bereavement and my entire body gave the impression of being alien to me. I don't know how long I remained crumpled on the sofa weeping; all I knew was that my world had exploded beneath me, carrying the particles far, far away as dust motes blown by a sudden gust of wind. Why hadn't I exploded too? Why didn't the same current of air which had so cruelly snatched my universe waft me away?

My eyes were stinging and my throat was raw; what was left of my heart was pounding and the agony was unbearable; my stomach churned making me nauseous and my whole torso shivered as if aflame, but I couldn't move. I didn't think I had the strength to move, so I didn't even try. The room appeared to be spinning, like an out of control fairground ride, all the colours blurring into a kaleidoscopic rainbow. A heavy darkness descended on me, crushing the breath from my already painful lungs.

* * *

Sometime later, I eventually opened my eyes and was surprised to see the sun had gone down and the sky had turned a purplish-grey. The upholstery was sodden where my head was laying and it felt grainy and scratchy against my skin. Using my hands, I pushed myself into a sitting position and got an immediate head rush. I closed my eyes and sat perfectly still until it passed.

Denial started to set in and I was suddenly galvanised into action. I got up from the sofa and ran upstairs to our bedroom; the sight which greeted me was as unexpected as it was horrifying. Joshua's wardrobe doors were open, empty hangers were strewn across the floor and drawers which had housed his underwear and t-shirts were lying upturned on the carpet, a couple of stray socks the only evidence of what they'd once contained. A sob escaped my throat and my hands flew to my mouth. Staggering out of the bedroom and into the bathroom I found all his toiletries were also missing. I couldn't deny the facts any longer and unbelievably more tears began to stream from my already stinging eyes. The thought of going back into the bedroom tore at my already battered spirit so I slowly walked back downstairs, gripping the banister rail so hard my knuckles turned white with the pressure. My face was a fixed mask akin to waxwork dummies, except I was still crying silently. I trudged back into the lounge, moving zombie-like and sank down onto the sofa once more; without thinking I reached for my phone and dialled a number.

"Hiya hun, what's up?" said the cheerful but wary reply from the other end.

I tried to speak, but nothing came out except a small, strangled cry.

"Remy? You okay?"

I took a deep breath and forced what miniscule amount of energy I had left into saying one word, "Becky…" I croaked, my voice sounding completely different to normal.

"I'm on my way, sit tight, okay?"

I managed to whisper one more word. "Hurry!"

Chapter 5 – Joshua

Joshua pulled off the motorway and into the car park of a service station. He turned off the engine and sat unmoving. The heat of the sun was baking his skin through the tinted glass of the vehicle; his back felt stiff and he knew he needed to get out and stretch, but he had so many thoughts diving around in his head that he wanted to try and calm himself first.

He knew he hadn't been sufficiently concentrating on his driving and didn't want to be responsible for an accident, so this was obviously his most sensible option.

He leaned back onto the headrest and closed his eyes behind the dark sunglasses balanced on the bridge of his nose, the nearby traffic sounding uncharacteristically loud, and began to try and sift through some of the disturbing images darting in and out of his mind.

All of a sudden, it resembled sitting in a cinema watching a film - the images were so *clear*... He could see himself as if looking at video footage and allowed the memory to resurface, the episode which for some reason had got buried in his subconscious – until now.

He regained consciousness in South Weald Country Park, still sprawled on the bench under the trees, the darkness all-encompassing. He glanced at his watch, unable to see the hands but knowing it must be really late. He arose, stretched, and tried to get his bearings before making his way to the exit.

His left arm felt extremely heavy as if his hand had morphed into a lead weight, and there was a great deal more discomfort in the crook of his elbow than was normal after donating blood. He started walking towards the exit, hearing owls hooting in the trees around him and rabbits scampering away frightened by the sound of his footfalls on the stony and twig strewn pathway.

Ten minutes later he arrived at his car to find the main gates padlocked. He swore under his breath as he pressed the button on the key fob, opened the door and climbed inside. He switched on the interior light and carefully peeled off the plaster, taking great care not to pull too many hairs out with it. He was stunned to find two puncture wounds and they were much larger than he was used to seeing. He rubbed his hand gently across the area – it was rather tender and bruised. He didn't know what to make of it.

A rustling noise outside diverted his attention. He stared out the windows, twisting in his seat to see out of the back screen too, but couldn't detect anything. He suddenly felt extremely tired so he reclined his seat as far as it would go, locked the car from the inside and made himself as comfortable as he could. He closed his eyes and within minutes was snoring lightly.

A tapping sound on his side window aroused him. He rubbed his eyes then peered out, finding an amused park ranger standing there grinning at him, the early dawn light surrounding him like a giant halo. Joshua turned the key and partially lowered the glass.

"Good morning, sir," greeted the ranger. "Comfortable was it?" he chuckled, inclining his head towards the reclined seat.

"Oh, er, no, not really." Joshua admitted. "And good morning to you."

"How in God's name did you get locked in here last night then? We always check around the Park before we shut up shop," the ranger asked curiously.

Joshua gave an embarrassed grin, shrugged his shoulders and replied.

"To be honest, I'm not really sure. I remember sitting on a bench under the trees and the next thing I recall is waking up in the pitch black and after finding my way back to the car, I found the gates padlocked. I feel a right wally I can tell you."

The ranger chuckled again.

"No harm done – well except to your back maybe, ha ha ha. Well I guess you'll be anxious to get on your way now then?"

He glanced at the clock on the dashboard and nodded.

"Oh crap, YES! I've got to be at Gatwick by 9:45 to pick up my fiancée and I don't think it's a good idea if I turn up looking like I slept in a car all night, do you?"

"Not if you wanna keep your ladylove sweet," he agreed, chortling.

"Well thanks for waking me up and sorry to have been a bother."

"No bother son," the ranger confirmed. "No bother at all. You take care now."

"You too. Bye." He quickly started the ignition and after raising his seat back to its original position, manoeuvred the car towards the exit, waving to the ranger as he pulled away.

He glanced in the rear view mirror; the ranger was going about his business, but he couldn't tear his gaze from his reflection - beneath his eyes were dark smudges and his face was much paler than usual. A sense of being totally washed-out and tired made him uneasy. He shook himself; I need to get more sleep tonight, *he thought.* He checked the clock again and realised he only just had time to get home, have a shower, change and grab a quick bite before he needed to leave for the airport. He drove out of the gate and sped down the road.

Joshua sat bolt upright with an electric shock as the memory finished playing. His eyes snapped open and he stared at the barely visible scars of the puncture wound inside his elbow – he could see them as clearly as if they were freshly made that day. He examined them more closely, running his index finger over the skin, and a small quiver of disbelief tingled at the back of his neck.

He could suddenly understand matters so much more clearly, but he couldn't give credence to the insane idea at the forefront of his mind. It wasn't possible. It was a myth – something Hollywood had glamourised from the vivid imaginations of countless novelists, to entertain, amuse and frighten. They didn't exist – they weren't real for God's sake. But what if they *were*…..?

A sign in the window of the service station advertised an Internet Café inside.

* * *

Joshua walked into the motorway service station and headed straight for a free terminal at the back of the Internet café. He made himself comfortable then paused for a moment staring at the search bar; having decided what to type, his fingers flew over the keys and in the time it took to blink, the results appeared on the screen. He carefully read each item before selecting the one he thought would give him the information sought, and clicked on the link.

He read the page through carefully then pulled a small notebook and pen from his pocket and started listing the changes he'd undergone since the day in the park:

Eyes sensitive to light, especially the sun

Skin much paler than normal

Incisors much sharper and more pointed

Eye colour changing

Excellent night vision

Normal food makes me sick

Prefer uncooked or barely cooked meat

Hearing so much sharper

Much stronger

He laid the pen next to the keyboard, put his hand on the mouse and moved it to click on another page. Cross-referencing the information on the screen with the list he had compiled, a new understanding swept over him, a huge wave crashing onto a cliff face in a storm. Now he knew what he was becoming . . . a vampire.

He looked down at the hand holding the little notebook and wasn't altogether surprised to see it tremble a little. Picking up the pen, he stuffed it in his pocket along with the notebook and leaned back in the chair, staring at the screen, unexpectedly unruffled after his realisation. How did he feel about it? Astonishingly he wasn't that upset – it hadn't really sunk in yet that he would crave blood and wouldn't be able to exist without it, or immortality was part of the package, but he could feel a new strength, a new *'power'* surging through his body. At the same time his senses heightened to the extent that, without trying, he could clearly hear conversations from the other side of the service station, ants marching along the floor wearing hobnail boots and the furious fluttering sound which came from the wings of a tiny fly.

He looked around with his 'new' eyes and detected little things which would have gone unnoticed before; the minute particles of dust which lay on the desk around the keyboard and monitor, a single eyelash on the tiled and grubby floor. He felt a weird fluttering feeling in his chest and then an acute pain which flashed like a lightning bolt from the top of his head through to the soles of his feet. It was so unexpected and fierce it made him gasp and he shoved his fist in his mouth to prevent him crying out; he knew he couldn't stay where he was so he quickly closed the tabs so only the search engine remained on the screen, got up from the plastic seat, rushed through the door and stumbled to the Gents toilets as fast as the pain would allow, not noticing his pen drop from his pocket.

The room was mercifully empty as he entered and he had his pick of cubicles. He moved to the one farthest from the entrance and locked the door behind him as another wave of agony blistered through his torso, buckling his knees with its ferocity. He sat on the floor knees up to his chin and arms tight around them, as if afraid to let go and straighten himself out. His heart was pounding so fast he couldn't discern the individual beats and just when he thought the agony couldn't get any worse, it escalated to a point that he felt he would surely die. It took every single ounce of his strength to stay quiet and not scream – which he wanted to do more than anything.

He was only vaguely aware of the comings and goings of people using the facilities and thankfully no one attempted to gain access to his cubicle. He clenched his teeth together as the torture increased by another couple of notches on someone's sick joke of a scale. He was slipping into a strange sort of unconsciousness where he could still feel each nerve ending throbbing with the torment yet the urge to vocalise his woe subsided and he wondered if he was actually dying – a thought that was not unwelcome.

How long he lay there was a mystery to him, people came and went, cleaning staff performed their duties then left; there was no change in the lighting to indicate day or night. As sudden as the onset of the torture was, it dissipated as swiftly; his heart slowed to a crawl in comparison and as the pain subsided to nothing his heart pulsed for the last time.

Joshua became gradually more aware of his surroundings and gained in confidence that he could straighten himself out. He slowly uncurled from his scrunched up position on the floor, expecting to feel stiff and uncomfortable, and was pleasantly surprised at how limber he was. He could hear the fluttering wings of a moth heading towards the fluorescent light and conversations going on all around the service station. He exited the cubicle and looked around the room seeing where the cleaning crew had missed areas and the bacteria feeding off the dirt which remained. He could see all the imperfections in the wall tiles too fine to normally be seen, the full colour spectrum in the fluorescent light tube; all of this in the time it took to blink.

He was somewhat awed, more so than he had been before the tortuous experience. The power he'd experienced earlier surging through his body was a mere tickle compared with how strong he felt now – so invincible . . .

Comprehension dawned; all the peculiar aches which had plagued him, the appetite changes, mood swings, increased sensitivity to sunlight, even the aggressive lovemaking – it was all part of becoming what he now was. It seemed he'd suffered a form of amnesia since being bitten, but he could now recall everything with exquisite clarity, even the face of his maker, although he had only glimpsed it for a fraction of a second. He had to find him.

He sniffed the air. The smell of blood made his tongue tingle, his throat felt parched and a craving to taste it ripped through his system leaving behind a palpable throbbing. He left the toilet and moved into the main area; he travelled so fast that no one saw him pass. He knew he couldn't remain there – it was much too dangerous; he slowed his pace so as not to draw attention and returned to his car.

His transformation was complete.

* * *

Joshua sat motionless in the car until the throbbing and craving had subsided to a manageable level. The traffic on the M6 thundered past and he could hear snatches of conversations and music from inside the vehicles. He knew he couldn't remain parked there much longer – the CCTV cameras by the entrance and exit recorded the comings and goings, and large notices attached to lampposts advised that charges applied after 2 hours. He had been there so much longer than 2 hours and was surprised there wasn't a ticket on his windscreen; perhaps something would arrive in the post instead, although he wouldn't be around to receive it. He didn't want to think about it now – he had more important things on his mind.

Joshua had no idea where to go from here, but he knew he wasn't alone – he couldn't be. After all, *someone* had turned him and again he recalled the memory of briefly glimpsing the face of the one who bit him. He reached for the keys to start the car, when out of the blue he heard a strange voice in his head.

Head south. You will find me, the slightly accented voice commanded.

What the…? He looked around but there was no one nearby. He spoke aloud.

"Am I hearing things?"

No, my child. Trust me. Use your new senses – they will lead you to me. We are connected now – our minds can converse as if we were in the same room. You don't need to use your voice – if you think it, I will hear it.

Who the hell are you? Joshua thought.

He heard a chuckle. *All will be revealed in good time, my child. Now do as I say – trust me and head south.*

Peace stole over Joshua. If asked, he wouldn't be able to explain why he felt he could trust this unusual voice, but he did. He started the car and headed for the exit so he could return to the motorway. He would have to continue travelling north until the next junction; he could then loop back onto the southbound carriageway.

Fifteen minutes later he was heading back down south. He was astounded how far north he had travelled; he hadn't paid any attention to the signs and junction numbers earlier, nor had he noticed how long he had been driving, but his journey had taken him as far as Preston before he turned back.

As he thundered down the motorway, he didn't concentrate on the signs, he *knew* where he needed to exit and he manoeuvred the car accordingly onto the various motorways. In what appeared to be no time at all (although it was nearly four hours later), he was on the M25. Even though he didn't possess an address for his destination, his direction was more clear and defined to him than if he were following a map or SatNav; it was as if he had a homing beacon planted in his skull.

About an hour later, he found himself on the A307 and could feel his arrival was imminent. He turned onto a single-track country road, flanked by farmer's fields on one side and a wall of bushes and trees which appeared to form an impenetrable barricade on the other. Its potholed surface bounced the vehicle around, although he didn't feel it; it twisted and turned for a couple of miles before he slowed and turned right onto a private concrete track. There were huge, plain, black wrought iron gates four feet onto the track; as Joshua approached the gates swung slowly open.

Chapter 6 – Remy

I was vaguely aware of a hammering on the front door but I ignored it; I didn't want to see anyone. I was sitting in the exact same position as when I'd phoned Becky – I hadn't moved at all, but I wasn't really aware of that. The hammering continued and I tried to tune it out, but I thought I heard my twin's voice calling me. I shook my head to disperse the intangible fog I had surrounded myself in and listened more carefully. Then I heard it again, much clearer than before.

"Remy? It's me, Becky. *Please* open the door, hun."

I wearily dragged myself to my feet and shuffled to the door like a geriatric crippled by arthritis, grabbed the handle and slowly, carefully, I pushed it down to release the catch. Becky must have heard me or seen me through the translucent glass in the door as she'd stopped trying to smash the door down. I opened it just wide enough to peer through the gap and there was my own face staring back at me looking incredibly worried.

"Remy? Let me in," she said softly.

I opened the door wider and heard her gasp in shock at the sight of me; my clothes were creased and dishevelled, my hair was unkempt, my make-up had smudged and run leaving black streaks down my face. But it was my eyes which had shaken her most of all – they were dead fish eyes, blank.

She stepped over the threshold; putting her hands on my shoulders she gently pushed me backwards so she could get herself clear of the door, which she then kicked shut. I didn't really notice her intent gaze as she scrutinized my face, nor did I see her frown with consternation.

"Talk to me – tell me what on earth's happened." Becky said, her voice loaded with worry.

I didn't react at all – as if I was totally immersed in water, unable to hear the words but recognising some sort of sound.

"Remy?" she tried again, a little louder this time. "What's wrong?"

I heard her that time, heard the words but I couldn't answer. I couldn't say the words. I shook my head.

She slid her hands from my shoulders to either side of my face and gently moved my head so I was looking directly at her.

"I want to help you. What hurts you hurts me, right? C'mon hun, tell me, *please*."

There must have been something I heard in my sister's voice which struck a note deep inside me; I reached up to my face, took hold of her hands and lowered them. I released one then slowly turned and walked into the lounge, pulling her behind me. I moved closer to the sofa and pointed to the floor in the direction of where Joshua's letter had landed earlier. I didn't allow my eyes to look down and glimpse its' exact position, instead I gazed at some distant point not focussing on anything in particular. Becky gently squeezed my hand before letting go and retrieving the letter.   Her eyes scanned the contents quickly. She sank onto the sofa and read it again more slowly, ensuring she absorbed it entirely; she gazed up at the mask pretending to be my face with ill-disguised anguish.

"Oh my God, Remy. I'm so sorry. I can't believe he'd do that to you."

I didn't answer, shrugged my shoulders and continued to stare at nothing. I didn't trust myself to speak. Becky put the letter onto the coffee table, rose from the sofa and came over to where I stood. She gently caught hold of my hand and led me back to sit down beside her.

"Hun? Can you tell me what happened?" she asked softly.

I looked at her, my eyes finally in focus and shook my head.

"Yes you can," she affirmed. "We've never had secrets before. C'mere." She pulled me closer and wrapped her arms around me. It didn't register whether or not she'd noticed me wincing.

I laid my head on her shoulder and a torrent of fresh tears erupted as I howled for the loss of the man I adored. She stroked my hair, holding me tight and murmured, "Let it out hun. It's okay. It'll be okay. I'm here."

Time means little when you're in such excruciating pain, so I have no idea how long I cried on her shoulder; she cuddled me and crooned soothing words until I literally had no more tears left. My heart felt like an egg which had been cracked open and my body ached all over, yet I was also numb. I pulled away from Becky a little and sat upright. My throat was dry and sore so I instinctively rubbed the skin on my neck, not even thinking about what I was doing.

"Fancy a cuppa?" Becky enquired, "I sure as hell do," she continued.

I nodded my head and tried to smile a bit; don't know what it looked like, but I felt I had to try for Becky's sake. She smiled back at me, so maybe it didn't look as horrendous as I imagined. She got up and walked into the kitchen. I heard her fill the kettle, but unexpectedly, I was dreadfully vulnerable and lonely, so I followed her. She turned at the sound of my footsteps on the tiled floor and smiled.

"You okay hun?"

I nodded. "Yeah… no… I don't know…of course I'm not," I croaked, sounding more frog than human.

Becky smirked at the sound – trying to keep a straight face but failing miserably – so she turned away in case it upset me further. She made the tea and carried the steaming mugs back into the lounge; I trailed behind her like a lost puppy, and after putting the tea on the coffee table, we flopped back onto the sofa.

"Do you feel up to talking now?" Becky asked tentatively.

I shrugged my shoulders. "Wouldn't know where to start…" I responded, still croaky.

"At the risk of sounding flippant – how about at the beginning? When did you first realise something wasn't quite right?"

I sat and thought for a few minutes, and then I remembered that first kiss in the airport on my return from America.

* * *

I was exhausted. With the shock of finding Joshua gone, the crying and having to relive the ordeal to Becky, I was totally wiped out. When I showed her the bruises and scratches, she uttered a small cry, her hands flying to cover her mouth. Despite her best efforts, she was not able to hide the shock and horror she felt. She turned her face away in the hope I wouldn't see her expression, but it was too late; what made it worse was I had seen that same look, or similar, only a few hours previously on Josh's face.

I hung my head as a sharp pain shot through my temple and a large lump in my throat threatened to cut off my air supply. I tried to get some air deep down into my lungs, but the obstruction in my airway prevented it. My breathing became rapid yet shallow as I struggled to get enough oxygen; I began to gasp and my body started to tremble; the room was spinning once again and my eyes couldn't focus on anything. I didn't know what it was and I felt the fear mounting towards a crescendo, as the colour drained from my face and my lips took on a blue-ish tinge. Becky recognised the signs of a panic attack and acting quickly, spotted a brown paper bag. She ran to get it and was beside me once more, so fast I barely had time to blink. She held the bag over my mouth with one hand, the other she placed on my shoulder.

"It's okay, Remy, don't panic. Just breathe. Slow it down now. Concentrate on your breathing, Remy. That's it – good. Keep concentrating. Slow it down. Slow. Slow," she crooned softly, encouraging and trying to calm me at the same time. This continued for another five minutes before my breathing was close to normal and the peachy tones had returned to my face. With concern still evident in her bright blue eyes, Becky asked, "Hey. Are you okay now?"

"Uh-huh. I…think so." I responded, my voice still a bit shaky.

"You *sure*?"

"Yeah, I guess so. That frightened the hell out of me!" I exclaimed.

"Hey. Me too. Me too," she gushed, a look of relief on her face.

I smiled weakly at her; in some ways I was glad she'd saved my life, yet in others I felt cheated. I didn't want to live without Josh. I had no future if he wasn't part of it and I couldn't see past that fact. My entire body was foreign to me. It felt empty, hollow, and numb, yet the ache from the bruises and scratches coupled with the engulfing heaviness in my chest and the searing heat in my throat, were totally at odds with each other. On the outside I appeared calmer, but inside I was screaming, and I didn't think I'd ever be able to stop.

Chapter 7 – Joshua

As Joshua drove through the gates, they gradually closed behind him, and he continued down a densely populated tree-lined driveway. After a couple of minutes he followed the road around a bend and was astonished at the sight which greeted him. The rear of a magnificent 18th century mansion lay before him. He continued round the house and stopped the car in front of the building, got out and gazed in awe at the glorious Corinthian-style columns which flanked the stone steps of the tetrastyle portico, topped by a pediment featuring a single sculpture of a pair of griffins. The large solid oak door surrounded by an ornately carved architrave, was adorned with brass fixtures and a huge, weighty doorknocker.

Although Joshua didn't know what to expect on his arrival, in his wildest dreams he didn't imagine anything as grand as the sight before him. He mounted the steps slowly admiring the architecture along the way and as he advanced to the top, the door swung open to admit him. In normal circumstances he would have hesitated or not entered at all, but his legs carried him over the threshold without pause.

He found himself in an elegant marble entrance hall with an unusual design on the highly polished floor, more Corinthian columns and elaborate plaster mouldings, cornices and a ceiling rose which was partially obscured by a voluminous crystal chandelier. There were several more heavy-looking oak doors leading off the entrance, as well as a staircase carpeted in a rich blood red weave and bordered by a white balustrade decorated in gold leaf. The wall on one side of the stairs had small plaster niches evenly spaced along the cream-coloured expanse, each one containing a vase or ornament, the niches interspersed with oil paintings depicting people from bygone eras dressed in the finery of the day.

Joshua was so immersed in studying the grandeur of the entrance hall that, even with his greatly enhanced hearing capabilities, he failed to notice he had been joined there by someone else. Then he heard the accented voice in his head again. *Welcome.*

He turned his head sharply and on the other side of the hall, standing before one of the doors, was a man. It was his maker.

The man standing across the entrance hall from Joshua looked quite imposing, but had a welcoming smile on his handsome face. He was over six feet tall, slim and rangy, with long dark brown hair.

"Greetings. My name is Samir. Welcome to my home," he said, in his accented voice.

"Er, hi. I'm Joshua."

"I'm glad to meet you." Samir replied sincerely. "Come. Let me introduce you to the rest of my little family," he extended his hand towards him.

Joshua drifted over to where Samir was standing and found himself being escorted through one of the doors.

The room they entered was a bibliophiles' paradise – floor to ceiling bookcases on three walls crammed with leather bound volumes, some obviously exceedingly old and probably priceless, some with simple gold tooling on the spines, a few more modern ones with shiny colourful jackets.

The floor was a highly polished wood which looked similar to oak and another massive chandelier dominated the centre of the ceiling. The view from the massive windows was unexpected; the vista would be a shadowy landscape with even darker shapes to humans, but to Joshua was an artistic blend of dark greens, dark blues and purples which revealed manicured lawns, imaginatively shaped flower beds resplendent with colourful blooms, ancient trees, neatly trimmed bushes and a large raised pond featuring a fountain.

In the room itself were a number of large comfortable-looking leather armchairs, each having a small table at its' side with a reading lamp on, a couple of old fashioned writing desks with chairs in front and a small wooden trolley containing a few books which hadn't been returned to the shelves. It was an impressive room with original fittings and very in keeping with the age of the house. However, the occupants, who sat silently appraising him, claimed Joshua's attention.

Samir took Joshua's elbow and steered him towards the nearest armchair, which was occupied by a short, slightly plump yet extremely attractive young woman, with sad eyes and extremely long dead straight mousy brown hair.

"This is Jasna." Samir enlightened him, then facing the woman said, "Jas, this is Joshua."

"Hello, Joshua, welcome," Jasna said in a jolly-sounding voice.

"Hi, Jasna. Pleased to meet you." Joshua responded, smiling at her.

"Jasna has the wonderful gift of telekinesis," Samir reported, sounding proud.

"Wow, that's amazing!" Joshua enthused, obviously impressed.

"It comes in handy." she laughed.

Samir once again took his elbow and escorted him to the next nearest chair. The man sitting in this one had male model looks most women would drool over. His natural blonde hair was swept away from his face; he was of medium build and looked to be reasonably tall. As the duo approached, his crooked smile lit up his face.

"Hello, Joshua, I'm Farrell," he jumped in, not waiting for Samir to do the introductions, and extended his hand.

Joshua shook his hand and smiled back. "Hi, Farrell, good to meet you."

"Farrell also has a wonderful, if somewhat unusual gift," Samir informed. "He can see and read auras."

"Oh, that's a new one on me. Sounds impressive though," Joshua replied, grinning.

"We'll have *plenty* of time to teach you about it." Farrell chuckled.

"Sounds good to me," he chuckled in response.

Samir turned towards the gorgeous lady sitting right next to Farrell.

"This is Erika," he introduced. "She's Farrell's partner."

The woman who smiled up at him was breathtakingly stunning. Her midnight black shoulder length hair framed her alabaster skin; her slim frame and long legs deceptively gave the appearance of being taller than she actually was; her smile gentle in her relaxed face.

"Hi, Joshua, it's lovely to meet you. We're going to be great friends." Erika said in a musical voice.

"Hi, Erika, Farrell's a lucky man!" Joshua replied grinning then turned to wink at Farrell, who chuckled.

"Erika's an exceptionally talented empath," stated Samir, who sounded like a proud parent.

"Isn't that difficult to cope with? I mean, if you feel someone else's pain…" Joshua trailed off.

"It would be extremely difficult as a human, but as a vampire it's not so…invasive, or debilitating," Erika explained, struggling to find the right words.

"Why is that?" Joshua asked, confused.

"I'm not really sure," Erika admitted. "Maybe because we are so much stronger, physically I mean."

He nodded thoughtfully, considering her response.

"Come, Joshua," Samir interrupted, putting his hand on Joshua's shoulder, gripping it slightly. "I have not finished introducing you yet."

Joshua nodded apologetically at Erika and allowed himself to be led further into the room towards the final chair which was in use. The occupant didn't look exactly pleased to see him, which he found somewhat disquieting, but did his best to conceal it. She was tiny – obviously less than five feet, slim, with short curly blonde hair and what looked to be a perpetual sneer on her hard face.

"Joshua, meet Dayna," Samir said.

"Hi Dayna," Joshua greeted.

"Hello," she responded, but not in a particularly friendly tone.

"Dayna has a magnificent gift – she is pyrokinetic," Samir continued.

"That's something to do with fire, isn't it?" Joshua inquired.

Dayna laughed derisively. "That's one way of putting it, I

suppose," she sneered.

"Now, now Dayna, be nice for once!" Samir instructed.

Dayna shrugged and pouted, but said nothing.

"Dayna's a grade one bitch," Farrell piped up. "She's got a chip on her shoulder the size of Ben Nevis and seems to take great delight in trying to make life difficult for everyone around her. When she's like this, we tend to ignore her."

"I'm NOT a bitch," Dayna replied vehemently, her temper flaring instantaneously.

"Yes you are," Farrell confirmed. "You could have been more gracious to the newest member of our family, instead of being contemptuous. He only asked a question – it's not exactly an offence."

"My children, let's not fight, especially today of all days," Samir commanded gently.

Farrell grinned, but held up his hands in mock surrender, Dayna nodded then looked away.

Satisfied that calm had been restored, Samir turned back to Joshua.

"It will be interesting to see what gift you develop," he mused.

"What if I don't develop a gift?" Joshua asked nervously.

"Don't worry – you will," Samir assured him.

"How can you be so sure?" he persisted.

"One of my gifts is to be aware of these matters, even before a human has been turned." Samir explained. "We call it 'Vamp Radar'. A bit crude, I know, but it serves a purpose. This particular gift is…multi-faceted, you could say. Not only can I tell that a human will be gifted if turned, but I can also track other vampires over quite large distances."

"You said 'one of your gifts' – how many do you have?" Joshua inquired, his curiosity piqued to the extent he failed to consider his question may be inappropriate or construed as rude.

Luckily Samir didn't appear offended – in fact he was rather enjoying himself.

"I have three main gifts in total: as well as the 'vamp radar', I am also telepathic as you have already discovered," he chuckled before continuing. "And I can astral project myself," then without waiting for any further questions from Joshua, he demonstrated his ability. "You see?"

"Bloody hell!" he exclaimed, his mouth gaping like the entrance to a tunnel.

Everyone in the room laughed at Joshua's expression, and as Samir finished showing off, Joshua laughed too.

"Enough frivolity for now. Let me show you around your new home – there is much to see, as well as much to learn, but your education can wait a little longer. Come," Samir invited.

"See you later," Joshua said to the others, then turned and followed Samir out of the room.

It took quite a while for Samir to show Joshua around his beautiful manor house; he was intrigued by the tunnels and walkways connecting the main house to some of the outbuildings, and impressed by the beauty and majesty of the rooms and their furnishings. The last room they came to was in the west wing on the second floor. It was obvious by Samir's demeanour he had left this room until last for a reason.

"I hope you'll be comfortable in this room," he said, turning to gaze at him. "This is yours now." And with that, he opened the door with a flourish and stepped back to allow Joshua to enter ahead of him.

The room was huge, and dominated by a large four poster bed with midnight blue heavy lined drapes held at each corner with a gold plaited tieback; the same curtains were hanging at the massive window. The furniture was solid, rather old-fashioned and a dark cherry mahogany colour; beneath their feet the polished floorboards matched the furniture. A woven rug lay on each side of the bed, the colours faded with age. It was a typically masculine-looking room and Joshua was immediately comfortable in it.

"Thank you," said Joshua, turning towards Samir. "I feel very…at ease here."

"I'm glad," Samir replied simply. "You left your bags in the car so I suggest you collect them, unpack and then meet us back in the library. There is much you need to learn and I'm sure you must be thirsty by now. I will leave you to settle in and see you shortly." Samir turned, silently disappearing out of the room.

Joshua returned to the library having completed his task and found the coven assembled awaiting his return. Samir smiled and gestured towards an empty chair between Jasna and Erika, waiting until Joshua was seated before speaking.

"We are all relieved you didn't take too long, my son," he began. "We are all rather thirsty and anxious to hunt. However, before we go, there are a few things you need to know."

Samir paused to ensure he had Joshua's full attention, and then continued.

"I'm sure you realise there are many things we need to tell you and in turn we acknowledge you must have numerous questions to ask, but the majority of these can wait until later. You are a new-born vampire and will not be complete in your…*transformation* until you have hunted and tasted blood. Only then will you become a fully-fledged member of the coven. We will be going shortly and you will hunt with me until you have er…what is the expression? Oh yes, *learned the ropes* as it were. Now listen carefully," he commanded then flashed his eyes at the others as they began to get restless and fidget in their seats. Silence and stillness pervaded.

Samir turned back to Joshua. "The best place to bite your victim is on the neck." He pointed with his fingers to the area he was referring to.

"There are two main sources of blood so if you miss one you have an excellent chance of hitting the other. If you bite but only taste and don't drink the blood, you will be turning them into one of us. This you must NOT do. You must always consult with me beforehand – do you understand?" Samir demanded. Joshua nodded solemnly.

Samir, satisfied by Joshua's reaction continued.

"The most important thing to know is when to stop drinking; you must listen to the heart beating as you feed and as you hear it start to falter you MUST stop. If you keep feeding after the heart stops, the taste becomes bitter and is like poison to us - not that we can die of course," he chuckled, and then grew serious again, "but it will sap your strength instead of feeding it and your gifts will grow weak or disappear for a time. This would make you especially vulnerable because you are a neophyte and haven't got your full strength yet."

He paused to ensure he still had Joshua's full attention, aware the others were getting extremely restless as their thirst grew.

"The rest of the family will hunt wherever they choose, but you," he pointed at Joshua's chest, "you will stay by my side," he commanded.

Joshua bowed his head in deference. "Yes Master," he replied.

Turning to face the rest of his coven, Samir smiled benignly and said, "Go feed, my children, you have been patient long enough."

They didn't need telling twice and in the blink of an eye they had vanished from the room; their voices a soft echo coming from afar.

"Come Joshua, let me teach you how to live," he said softly, reaching for Joshua's hand, and together, with feet like swift wings, they left the house and journeyed out into the night.

Chapter 8 – Remy

We chatted a little about panic attacks. While we talked she'd prepared a snack, but I couldn't manage more than a couple of mouthfuls – I pushed the rest of the food around my plate.

"Remy?"

"Uh-huh?" I put the fork down.

"Have you tried to phone him?"

"No. Why would I? I think the letter says it all – don't you?" I replied in a resigned tone.

"Maybe, but I know how much *you* love him and I *know* how much *he* adores *you* – isn't that worth fighting for?"

"Of course, but don't you understand? That's why this is so damn hard. We're soul mates; we're sooo good together and so in love. We have an almost perfect relationship. We're happy . . . or were," I cried.

"Precisely! All the more reason not to take this lying down. Fight for him!" she bit back.

I sat in silence trying to digest the conversation while she watched me nervously, wondering if she'd pushed me too far too soon. I was so tired and couldn't think straight. My head was stuffed with cotton wool; I was in some form of dissociative state. I could see, hear, speak and walk, but nothing appeared real. My brain was in a bath of Novocain, my body partially anaesthetised. There was a cocoon surrounding me; sense and reason were unable to pierce it, all I knew was my misery. On some level deep inside I knew what Becky was saying made sense, but I didn't have the strength to deal with it – not now anyway. My eyes drifted shut.

"Remy?" she called. No response.

"REMY?" louder and this time she shook my arm.

I forced my eyelids back open and although I could see her outline, the rest of her was blurred. "Yeah?" I mumbled.

"Are you okay?"

"Tired. So, so tired."

She came over to my chair, put her arm around me and helped me onto my feet. "Can you make it upstairs?"

I had a vague recollection of the room in a mess and it wasn't exactly appealing. There was another reason too, but I forced the thought away before it had time to register. I shook my head.

Becky led me to the sofa, sat me down then lifted my feet and positioned them on the seat. I lay down and she adjusted some cushions under my head. My eyelids were so heavy I couldn't keep them open any longer. I didn't feel her cover me with a blanket or hear her talking to Mum on the phone; I had plummeted into a dark and dreamless abyss.

* * *

Distant sounds of someone pottering in the kitchen penetrated my unconscious state and I began to gradually claw my way up the walls of the chasm towards the light. My eyelids still felt heavy, but I knew I could command them now; as the aroma of fresh coffee and toast assaulted my nostrils, I slowly forced my eyes open. My back was stiff, my whole body ached and my head was still fuzzy. I got to my feet, stretched until I'd worked some of the kinks out of my back then padded into the kitchen.

On the table was a cafetiere of steaming black coffee and a plate of buttered toast, which Becky was munching her way through. She looked up at me and smiled. "Well, good morning. How're you feeling hun?"

I sat opposite her and reached for the coffee. "Erm, weird. Like I'm in a waking coma or something."

"Oh. Are you feeling *any* better?"

"Maybe? I guess so. I don't feel so tired now, but I do feel quite drained. You okay?"

"Yeah I'm fine thanks – just worried sick about you. Anyway, do you want some toast?"

"It's okay, I'll do it." I replied, starting to get up.

"No. You sit there and I'll make some for you. I can't do much to help, but this I can do so please let me look after you a little, okay?" she pleaded.

I raised my hands in mock surrender and smiled. "Okay. Okay."

She laughed at the expression on my face then bustled around preparing my breakfast.

I managed two slices of toast and marmalade and was on my third cup of coffee before either of us spoke again.

"Remy? I don't suppose you've thought any more about what I said last night, have you?" she asked tentatively.

"To be honest, I don't remember much of last night at all. What did you say then?"

"I was saying you should fight for Joshua, for your relationship," Becky said gently.

My eyes clouded over at the mention of his name and an icy breeze whipped itself around my torso; I shivered but didn't answer her.

"C'mon hun. You can't take this on the chin. I know it's hard to even think about, but you have to do *something*," she stated.

I shrugged my shoulders and remained silent.

"REMY HARMAN!" she shouted and startled me. "Why don't you answer me?" then more softly, "c'mon sis, you must snap out of this. You owe it to yourself to fight for him, for the love you shared, for the life you had, for the future you are meant to have together. You can't just sit there and let this fly over your head – you've got to do something, anything. I'm here, I'll help you. You're not alone."

I glared at her, mouth agape. She reached across the table and squeezed my hand.

"You'll never forgive yourself if you don't even try," she said in a softer voice. She then produced a photograph of Joshua and me from our holiday last year, and held it up in front of my eyes. It was one of my favourites. I started to turn my head away as my eyes filled with tears.

"Hun? Look at me," she commanded.

I turned my face back towards her, trying to keep my eyes averted from the photo which carried a mixed bag of memories.

"I pulled this photo out on purpose – I needed to get a reaction from you, and it worked. You've shown the anguish you are suffering, but you don't seem to be willing to do anything about it. You *can* do something – you can FIGHT for him. You know I'm right."

I'm not sure if it was what she said, how she said it, the photograph or a combination of all three, but it plucked a string or two. Although my head still appeared to be wrapped in cotton wool, it wasn't nearly as substantial as before; maybe Becky's tirade had penetrated the fog and stripped some of the layers away, leaving me a little more alert. Did I have the fortitude to do what Becky demanded? Did I want to let him go without so much as a token protest?

She was right, of course. Why should I wallow in my grief? Why haven't I done something already? God! I was so stupid. I loved him. I adored him. He was my life.

"But, how? Where do I start?" I asked.

Becky grinned at me. "That's more like it."

I smiled back. "Thanks sis. You're so right and I'm not going to give up on him. We can sort this out – I need to find him, but I haven't got a clue where he's gone or where to start looking."

"You just said the magic word."

"Huh?"

"Clue. We need to see if he's left anything behind which might give us an idea where to start," she replied excitedly.

"Of course. Let's start in the bedroom, shall we?"

She nodded, and we tore up the stairs.

* * *

After rummaging around through drawers and cupboards for a while, Becky discovered a leather bound book concealed under Joshua's side of the bed.

"Remy – look at this."

She handed me the tome. I'd never seen it before and I turned it over and over in my hands. There was nothing on the cover so I opened it gingerly. It was a diary. I started to flick through the pages, not reading the contents – I felt I was invading his privacy – but then I reasoned there might be something in there to help me. I sat on the bed and flicked to the first week I was away in the States. Becky sat beside me and I positioned the pages so she could read it with me.

1st June
Remy flew to the USA today. Dropped her at Gatwick. She's only been gone for 5 hours but I'm missing her like crazy already. How am I going to get through the next 2 weeks?

2nd June
Remy rang. She's arrived safely. Her body clock is out of whack but she's coping. She said the people are nice. I'm glad about that. God I miss her.

There was more of the same until.......

14th June
One more day and my beautiful lady will be home - I can't wait! Giving blood today so will probably go for a walk in my favourite park after.

15th June
Don't know what happened yesterday – I fell asleep in the park. When I woke up it was dark & the gates were locked. Had to spend the night in the car. My arm was hurting – they must have really messed up when taking my blood, there were two marks. Gotta pick Remy up from airport & I'm going to be late.

Boy did I get carried away today. I hurt Remy when I kissed her at the airport – I didn't mean to, I was so pleased to have her back, but when I was kissing her I sort of lost control. She smelled so good and I wanted to taste her. I don't know how else to put it.

Oh my God. What the hell happened? That was the most AMAZING sex we've ever had but I felt totally out of control. It's hard to describe how I felt but it was like I had to be completely dominant. I felt powerful, even aggressive but strange. Perhaps it's coz I've missed her so much and we've never been apart for that long before. Yeah that must be it.

16th June

Do I feel shit or what? Remy is covered in bruises. She keeps telling me it doesn't hurt and not to worry about it, but how can I not when I know I did that to her? I would never hurt her – so why did I? How can I put this right? How can I make this up to her? I love her so much.

My head is all over the place now. I've got a peculiar throbbing feeling in my body, perhaps I'm coming down with something. I hope not.

17th June

Still feel awful for what I did to Remy & I still don't know why I did it. She's been wonderful about it, which is more than I deserve.

Still got this aching problem & my moods have been all over the place today. My eyes have been stinging a bit & I've been off my food too. Defo think something's not right.

Again there was more of the same about his mysterious aches and pains, talking about how most foods were making him sick and how sore his eyes were until…….

Every time I've tried to eat today I've been sick. Pains seem to be getting worse. I don't want to say anything to Remy – I don't want to worry her, especially so close to the wedding. Perhaps it's nerves – who knows?

Things are getting weirder. I never eat meat almost raw, the thought of it's always turned my stomach before, but the steak I had for dinner tonight was the first thing I've been able to keep down for a few days. I couldn't eat anything else on the plate — just the very rare meat. I don't understand it.

27th June

What's happening to me? I must be some kind of monster! We had fantastic sex last night but Remy is covered in horrendous bruises and scratches. I feel sick to my stomach. I thought last time was a one-off but this is even worse. She couldn't hide the pain she was in and the way she looked at me — it was like she's scared of me. How can this have happened again? I must have been so out of control but I don't remember. I can't bear this. I can't risk hurting her again — I love her too much. I don't want to leave her but how can I stay? How can I look her in the eye, knowing what I've done to her? I know it's going to hurt her if I leave but I'm more afraid of how much damage I could do to her if I stay.

What am I becoming? I don't think it's nerves about the wedding that's caused my symptoms and it doesn't explain the abrupt change in my behaviour when we make love, so what the hell is it? I'm frightened. What's next?

Oh God. I feel so shit about all this. It's no good — I've got to leave. I hope one day she'll forgive me. I will always love her.....

I turned to Becky with tears streaming down my face and was shocked to observe wetness in her eyes too. I knew now Joshua really didn't want to leave and that he was trying to protect me, but it still didn't make it any easier to come to terms with. However, it did make me more determined to fight for him. "I've got to find him." I declared, sniffling, "will you help me? Please?"

"You know I will – I'll do as much as I can," she agreed.

"Thanks sis. Oh God. The *wedding*. I better phone Mum and tell her."

"No need. I phoned her when you were sleeping – she's pretty shocked, to put it mildly."

"Have you phoned anyone else?"

"No, not yet," she replied.

"Okay. I guess I'd better talk to his Mum first. She might know where he's gone. If she doesn't, we can start ringing round his mates. Okay?"

"Sounds like a good place to start. I'll make a list of his friends while you're talking to his Mum."

I nodded, reached for my phone and dialled a number. It was answered on the third ring.

"Hi Grace, it's Remy…"

My first move after talking to Joshua's mum was to call his mobile phone. Perhaps I should have tried that first, but my brain wasn't exactly in gear. I prayed he would answer, but it went to voicemail. I wanted to leave a message, but as I went to speak, my throat closed up and all I could manage was a croak. I took a deep breath to calm myself and then tried it again; this time when the voicemail message had finished I was better prepared.

"Hey babe, it's me, Remy. I know you're upset, but you didn't need to run away. We can work this out together - you know we can. Please, please don't give up on us. I love you Josh – you are my life. Please let me know you're okay. Please call me. I'm not giving up on you – on us. Please babe, come home…" my voice pleading at the end, ended with a sob and tears began to trickle down my face.

Becky put her arm around my shoulders.

"I'm okay," I told her, wiping the droplets away with the back of my hand.

"You sure?" she asked, kindly.

"Yeah," I replied, my voice a little stronger. "I've got to be resilient now Becky – I can't let myself fall apart again or I won't stand a cat in hell's chance of finding him, and I've GOT to find him."

"Okay. Well I've done the list of his friends that I know of, we just need the numbers," Becky stated.

"No probs. I've got his address book – so let's get started, eh?"

Becky and I started going through Joshua's address book and phoning everyone in it. He hadn't kept it as current as I'd hoped and some of the numbers were no longer recognised; I guessed his mobile phone contained the most up-to-date details, but he had taken it with him. A couple of hours later we had drawn a complete blank. Even Joshua's older brother, Todd, didn't have any idea of what was going on. In fact, he was as shocked as we were. He was Josh's Best Man for the wedding and was normally especially tactful, but on this occasion the shock of his brother's disappearance became apparent when he made a comment about not needing the speech he'd laboured over. *Rather poor taste*, I thought, but I was sure he didn't mean to be insensitive or hurtful.

About three hours later, we'd reached the end of the address book and drawn a complete blank. I sat and wracked my brains as to what my next move should be, while Becky was in the kitchen making us something to eat; we hadn't eaten a thing since breakfast. I let my gaze wander around the room, my eyes stopping to linger on anything which was special or brought back memories of happy times, in the hope it might provide some inspiration.

Then I spotted his laptop propped up on edge beside the magazine rack. I reached for it but it was too far away so I tutted to myself, got up and retrieved it. I opened the lid and switched it on; it was so slow firing up. I was getting impatient so, deducing the battery was probably running low, I grabbed the mains lead and plugged it in. The laptop log in appeared instantly and I typed in the password. I was surprised when a dialogue box appeared telling me the password was incorrect. I knew Josh used two main passwords on all his online accounts so I entered the second one and was relieved when it was accepted. It took two or three minutes for the system to complete the start-up procedure and another couple for the wireless LAN to connect. I drummed my fingers impatiently on the casing while I was waiting.

At last it was ready and I double clicked on the email icon. It opened quickly and started to receive mails. My eyes scanned down the page at the subject lines, but there was nothing which immediately captured my attention. What did, however, was his Contact list. I snatched his address book from the seat beside me and started to cross reference the two sets of names, making a separate list of the people not yet contacted. To my chagrin, the resulting list was short, but at least there were a few names I could try; two of the eight names didn't have phone numbers attached, only email addresses, which was a bit of a bummer, but it was better than nothing.

Before I had the opportunity to make any more calls Becky appeared with a plate of sandwiches and two large mugs of tea. I wasn't feeling particularly hungry, but I knew that without food to keep my energy levels up, I'd soon start flagging. I smiled at her in appreciation and tucked in.

Half an hour later I was rather full and had to admit it gave me renewed energy. I made the six phone calls first, but again it produced no results. I moved the laptop onto my knees and opened up a blank email; at first I couldn't think what to write, but then I had a sudden brainwave and my fingers started to move over the keys. I re-read the message and once satisfied, flagged it as urgent and clicked on the 'send' icon. I now felt distinctly lost. What would my next move be? I needed inspiration, but didn't know where to start. I made an impatient kind of snort and frowned.

"Hey – what's up?" Becky asked, trying to hide her smirk at the expression on my face.

"Brain dead," I responded huffily.

"So what else is new?" she joked, giggling.

I grimaced at her. "There's nothing like kicking a person when they're down, is there?"

"Oh, come *on* Rems, you know I was only joking," she retorted in an exasperated tone. "So, what can I do to help?"

"It's okay, I know you were," I smiled conciliatorily, "I'm frustrated and out of ideas of what to do next – don't suppose your brain is in gear for once?" my mildly sarcastic tone making her raise an eyebrow at me.

"Oh, I see. Getting our own back are we?" she asked.

"Told you before – there's only one way to get your own back."

"Ha ha!" she pretended to laugh. "Do you want me to put my brilliant brain at your disposal or what?"

"Yes please, but perhaps you'd better sit down first – I don't want you to strain yourself," the sisterly banter continued.

"Wow-wee, the gems just keep on coming."

"You love me really, Becky."

"Yeah and don't you know it," she laughed.

"Yep. Just like you know I love you to bits too," I responded, laughing with her. It felt strange, in poor taste, to laugh and joke about, as if we were being sacrilegious, but in other ways it was a good experience – it certainly relieved some of the tension.

"Right missy – enough of this," she said sternly, but still with a grin on her face.

"Okay, okay. What have you come up with then?" I enquired.

"Well, you've got a computer on your lap haven't you?"

"Yes," I replied, a frown wrinkling between my eyes, not quite sure what she was alluding to.

"So why not use Google to get some ideas?" she asked smugly.

"Mmmm" I pondered. "Not a bad idea that, sis." I clicked on the relevant icon and waited for the Google home page to display on the screen. I hesitated for a moment then typed 'search for missing person' in the dialogue box and hit the 'enter' key.

* * *

Becky and I made copious notes from the different websites we visited, searching for ideas of how to find my man. There were things like developing a small website (which I thought was a great idea), distributing posters with Joshua's photograph and description on and talking to people like neighbours, chemist, dry cleaner, newsagent, publican, – in fact anyone who spoke to him on a fairly regular basis, so the biggest part of my list was taken up by the latter.

All the ideas had merit and we decided anything was worth a try, so we'd go for all of them. The other thing, of course, was to report him missing to the Police. As we weren't married I wasn't sure if I could make the report or whether it had to be his parents. This was something which needed a bit more research and I'd need to discuss it with Grace and Theo before I did anything.

I could design the posters – that bit was easy, I'd already got digital photos of Joshua on the laptop and I was competent with most of the standard operating systems and software packages, plus there was a small colour laser printer in the spare bedroom I could print the posters on. My biggest problem was the website – I wouldn't know where to start. I started wracking my brain trying to remember who I knew that could design a website for me, but I kept drawing a blank – it was damn irritating.

Becky arranged to take a few days holiday from work and volunteered to start working through my list of people, so it would leave me free to concentrate on designing and distributing the posters.

I glanced at the clock on the wall, the one with dolphins as the pendulum Josh and I had bought at the Epcot Centre in Florida two years ago, and was astounded to find it was 7pm. It was still so bright and warm outside I thought it was still afternoon. We decided it was a bit too late to start cooking and elected to have a takeaway. I went into the kitchen and rummaged through one of the drawers until I found a menu for one that delivered and took it back into the lounge for Becky to make her choice. We had such similar tastes in food it only took her a matter of seconds to decide what she wanted – the same as me. I phoned the order through and while we waited for it for arrive, we chatted - reviewing the day's progress. I was feeling awfully drained and emotionally wrung out – it had been the most unbearable 24 hours of my life; I was trying so hard to portray a brave and positive demeanour, but in reality I was drowning in unshed tears and a quicksand of despair. The energy expended by attempting to maintain an optimistic facade was not sustainable in my current state and, for Becky's sake as much as anything, I wanted to continue with my 'deception' a bit longer.

By the time we'd finished tweaking our notes and adding to our list, the food had arrived. We didn't bother with plates; we opened the pizza box and dived in. Although I was peckish, I wasn't really very hungry, but I knew that to keep up my ruse, I would need to stoke the fire which drove me on, so even though my stomach signalled it was full after only two slices, I continued to consume the contents of the box. Becky remembered seeing a bottle of wine in the fridge, she walked into the kitchen grabbed the bottle and two glasses and placed them on the coffee table. She took another bite of pizza, opened the wine and poured it.

"I think we deserve this," she stated, as if she had to justify her actions.

"We not only deserve it," I responded between mouthfuls, "I think we bloody *need* it."

We picked up our glasses and clinked them together.

"Cheers," she toasted.

"To finding Josh," I responded sadly.

"To success then," she continued.

We drank and ate until everything was consumed, by which time I was yawning so much my eyes were watering. The combination of the days' events and the strain of hiding my misery had culminated in an exhaustion which was all consuming; I needed to be alone and I needed to sleep. Becky observed my eyelids were growing heavy.

"Time for bed, I think," she stated. "Don't worry about this mess – I'll clear up."

"You sure?" I asked, feeling a little guilty.

"Course I am. Go on hun – you get to bed and I'll see you in the morning," she replied, stroking my arm.

"Okay," I managed. I gave her a hug and kissed her on the cheek.

"Thanks for today hun, I don't know how I would've coped if you weren't here. I love you sis."

"No probs. And I love you too. Night hun," she replied.

I smiled wearily and headed for the stairs.

Chapter 9 – Joshua

Joshua lay on the bed, his eyes staring at the canopy above him as he re-lived his first kill. He really hadn't known what to expect, whether it would be easy or difficult, if he would find the act itself repulsive or exciting. He didn't realise how natural his taste for human blood was; part of the transformation process was the removal of guilt or qualms about hunting humans and feeding from them. Samir had taken him to a large village about 10 miles east of the manor house; it was a little olde worlde in most places, picturesque, but on the outskirts there were some more recent dwellings which were in stark contrast to the character of the remainder of the village. It was a great shame.

There was a party in full swing in the village hall next to the church; the music wasn't blaring out as the windows and doors were shut, but the *boom, boom, boom* of the bass rattled a few windows in nearby properties. Samir and Joshua stealthily moved closer to the hall, taking care to stay in the shadows; they didn't really need to take much care – they were chameleon-like in the way they blended into their surroundings. They only had to wait a few minutes before a lad of about 19 staggered out of the hall, obviously quite drunk – he wouldn't have been able to complete a sobriety test if his life depended on it. He was carrying a bottle of beer in one hand and swigged from it as he weaved down the path away from the hall.

"Watch me closely. It will be your turn next," Samir instructed and without pausing to wait for an answer, he moved as fast as lightning, crossing the distance between himself and his victim in less time than the shortest of breaths. He appeared behind the drunk and grabbed the teenager by the throat sinking his teeth into the pulsing vein in his neck. He drank thirstily and within thirty seconds it was over. Samir disappeared with the fresh corpse and re-appeared by Joshua's side without it mere seconds later with a self-satisfied smile on his face.

"Did you see how easy it is?" Samir asked, his voice gloating.

"Yes." Joshua replied, simply.

"It's your turn next," Samir stated. "Are you alright with that?"

"I...*think* so," the reply was a little sheepish, "I'm a bit nervous, but most of all I want to get it *right*. I don't want to...let you down."

"I'm sure you will be fine – I have every confidence in you," Samir's response was sincere and he smiled at his young one as if to prove it.

They remained in a companionable silence while they waited for someone else to exit the hall; they only had to wait about fifteen minutes before the door opened and a man and woman stumbled through, holding hands and giggling like a couple of children.

Joshua looked at Samir in consternation. He couldn't handle two at once – *one* was going to be enough of a challenge. Samir chuckled softly – too softly for the drunken couple to hear – then keeping his voice low said, "Of course I wouldn't expect you to try and take down two at once. You pick which one you want and I'll take the spare."

Joshua smiled sheepishly, and then matching the volume of Samir's voice replied, "I'll take the man."

"Good. Whenever you are ready then..."

Samir watched him carefully then at the first sign of a movement that was so subtle it wouldn't have been visible to humans, they flashed across the road and came up behind their victims. Like a synchronised ballet they grabbed their prey at exactly the same moment, and without any hesitation whatsoever, they sank their teeth into their necks, drinking the torrent of blood which flooded from the punctured arteries. Joshua listened carefully for the heart beat to slow, remembering what Samir had told him earlier. He cast an inquiring glance towards Samir to check he'd reached the right point to stop and was rewarded by a nod and smile.

Joshua slowly ran his tongue over his lips, savouring the honey-sweet taste. He was feeling rather proud of himself and raising his eyes, noticed an expression akin to pride on Samir's face. Obviously they couldn't leave the bodies lying on the pavement, so picking them and holding them like rag dolls, they blended once more into the shadows. Dissolving into the trees, they sped through the dark until they were far enough away to be able to dump the bodies, before returning to satiate their thirst yet again.

* * *

Joshua was unaware of the passing of time while he lay on the bed. The house was eerily silent in human terms, but he could hear so much more; there were insects in the walls and woodwork - ruminating and building nests, the birds chirping in the trees using amplified microphones, he could hear the cars traverse the nearby roads - even noting every pothole or bump they drove over, all manner of small creatures in the surrounding countryside he'd been totally oblivious to before.

He was stunned by how quickly things had changed in his life and even more so, by his ready acceptance of who he now was and the lifestyle he would be living from now on. In thinking back to his first hunt, he felt no sorrow or remorse for the lives he had extinguished, and paid no mind to the devastation this would leave in its wake. Why was that? As a human he'd always been a caring person who went out of his way not to hurt other people if at all possible, and on the odd occasions where his actions did cause pain, he'd always felt so awful about it. That was why he made the decision to leave Remy – he couldn't bear the idea of inflicting more pain on the woman he adored, even though he wasn't actually aware of doing so at the time.

Remy. This was the first time in many hours he'd even thought about her and the guilt enveloped him like a shroud.

Remy. He still loved her and always would, but he was not part of her world anymore and she could never be a part of his, so perhaps it was better this way. How would he have found a way to reconcile any sort of existence, human or otherwise, if he finished turning while still with her and she had become the first victim to quench his thirst? He shuddered at the thought. Thinking about her this way was screwing with his head and, although he missed her, he knew he must put aside the love they shared; forget the joy she brought to his life. She was better off without him now, *especially now*, and besides, he had a new and exciting future to embrace.

He got up from his bed, wandered out through the door and made his way leisurely down the long corridor towards the stairs, admiring some of the works of art ceremoniously displayed on the wood panelled walls, his eyes able to discern each individual brushstroke and all the different hues which were previously unnoticed. He reached the head of the stairs and slowly descended, letting his fingers trace the smooth varnished wood of the banister rail; he could feel every inconsistency of the grain in the wood and the places the varnishing brush had missed. As he reached the bottom, he marvelled at the beauty of the marble floor, the miniscule cracks and fissures which created pictures of their own.

He continued across the hall into the library, pausing to glance out of the huge window and out across the spectacular landscaping. He could tell it was late afternoon or early evening by the position of the sun peeking through clouds, and was sure it wouldn't be long before the rest of his coven started to appear. In the meantime, he was enjoying being able to explore, and now he planned to investigate the magnificent library. Who knows, he chuckled to himself, I might even learn something…

As before, he had no concept of the time passing as he ploughed his way through the tome he'd chosen, but in no time at all, the others joined him. This time he felt less an interloper and more like he actually belonged with them. With the exception of Dayna – 'The Bitch' as Joshua thought of her – he was greeted warmly by his new family and they were all raving about how accomplished he'd been on his first hunt. The clouds were lower in the sky and thunderstorms had been forecast, so night descended much earlier than it had the previous evening. The coven were pleased. They could start hunting that much earlier.

Samir floated into the room and greeted his 'children' one at a time; Joshua was surprised to see how Dayna related to him compared to everyone else – there was a warmth in her touch and a smile which reached her eyes when she looked at him – but as soon as he passed her and moved onto the next person, the smile faded and her face adopted its' usual scowl. Joshua thought it was such a shame, because Dayna was so much more beautiful when she smiled. After Samir embraced Farrell last of all, he turned so he could see all of them. Before he could say anything, Farrell glanced at Joshua, and with a hint of a grin on his lips, he turned to Samir. "As Josh did so well last night, can he hunt with me and Erika tonight?"

Samir paused in thought, he looked a little torn then as he made his decision, his handsome face returned to its' normal inscrutable mask.

"It is up to Joshua. However, I would advise perhaps one more hunt under my tutelage first. What do *you* think Joshua?"

He looked first at Farrell's eager face and then the patient mask of his maker; he was not stupid and rapidly guessed which decision he should reach regardless of what he actually wanted. Turning to Farrell and winking, he delivered his choice.

"Hey Farrell, thanks for inviting me, but can I take you and Erika up on your offer another night? I think I should stick with Samir again – just to be sure, you know. Is that okay?"

Farrell smiled at him, no trace of disappointment evident in his face.

"That's fine – I totally understand. Another night it is then."

Joshua turned to face Samir, whose face lit up by the smile on his lips.

"I am pleased you are being sensible about this, my son. It is all too easy to get excited and carried away with our power and strength, but you do need to learn caution and to pick your prey carefully. We must not be exposed now, must we?" It was apparent Samir did not expect a reply to this last rhetorical question.

"I'm famished – shall we go?" Samir held out his hand towards Joshua.

"Oh yeah," Joshua responded enthusiastically, as he moved towards him. And once more they all dispersed into the night.

Chapter 10 – Remy

I was strolling down a tree-lined lane and as I rounded a bend, there was a tunnel in front of me. As I continued to move closer to it, I noticed a man standing by the entrance; he looked rather familiar, but I was too far away to see him clearly. Something from the depths of my soul resonated and I knew I had to go to him; I quickened my pace. About 80 yards away, I realised it was Joshua and started running towards him screaming out his name, but he was moving backwards into the tunnel. I started sprinting trying desperately to catch up to him, but no matter how fast I ran he still appeared as far away. I could feel despair mounting along with the physical agony of pushing my legs to their limits; tears coursed down my cheeks in frustration and my throat burned from yelling his name.

I was surrounded by shadows which appeared to be closing in on me as I pelted on towards him and fear began to ripple through me like a major earth tremor. Abruptly, I collapsed on to my knees, my poor tired legs unable to sustain the extreme effort any longer; I started to sob and extended a hand forward to him, but he was still too distant. I cried his name again and again; a mantra I hoped would bring him back to me . . .

Through the pain of my dream I became aware of another's angst and was shocked to discover it was Becky. At first I couldn't understand where her pain came from and then it seemed to meld with mine; we shared each other's pain and it was difficult to distinguish where mine ended and hers began. I felt her slide into bed beside me and envelop me in her arms; her whispered words of comfort penetrated the fog of my nightmare and I sank, finally, into a deep dreamless slumber.

I awoke to find a cup of tea on the bedside table; it obviously hadn't been there all that long as steam was still spiralling from the top of the mug. I lay there staring up at the ceiling, not really wanting to move, knowing once I got up I would have to continue with yesterday's charade and not convinced I had the strength for it. I heard Becky approaching and shut my eyes quickly feigning sleep; the longer I stayed in bed the better as far as I was concerned.

Of course I wanted to find Josh, I wanted it with all my heart, but I wasn't confident I could. It was the doubt and denial as well as the anguish of his disappearance which caused the disbelief in my ability to succeed. She walked into the bedroom, came over to the bed and softly called my name. I knew it was wrong to do so, but I ignored her and pretended I was still asleep. She called me again, this time gently shaking my shoulder; I couldn't disregard her this time so I sleepily fluttered my eyes open and smiled up at her.

"Hey, sleepyhead. How're you doing? Did you sleep okay?"

"Mmmm, I think so, but I'm still tired though" I mumbled.

"Well you've slept for thirteen hours straight so I'd have thought you'd be raring to go," Becky stated.

"Th-thirteen hours? No way."

"Yes way. It's just gone ten o'clock. There's a cuppa on the side for you and I'll do your breakfast when you come downstairs, okay?"

"Thanks sis," I replied. "I think I'll jump in the shower first, I feel all yucky and I could fry chips in my hair."

"Well…I didn't want to say anything, but yeah you could," she laughed and stepped away from the bed rather sharpish as my arm swung out, my hand heading towards her bum. "See you in a bit." And with that, she flitted from the room and back downstairs.

I sat up, rubbed the sleep from my eyes then grabbed the mug of tea and started to drink it. It wasn't as hot any more so I was able to finish it quite quickly; I dragged myself out of my pit and wandered into the bathroom, grabbing my bathrobe en route.

Twenty minutes later, I emerged from a somewhat steamy bathroom wearing my bathrobe and with a towel wrapped around my wet hair. I had to admit I certainly smelled a damn sight sweeter now than I did before I went in there. I went into the bedroom, pulled on some clean clothes, rubbed my hair as dry as I could before dropping the damp towel into the laundry basket. I noticed the room had been tidied; all traces of Joshua's hurried departure absent. I pulled a brush through my tangled hair then traipsed downstairs to the kitchen to find Becky buttering toast for me. A fresh scalding mug of tea was already sitting on the table, as was a jar of marmalade. She placed the toast in front of me, grabbed her tea from the worktop and sat opposite me, one leg curled beneath her, silently waiting for me to finish eating.

It didn't take me much time to polish off breakfast, nor did it take Becky long to start talking once I had.

"What's the game plan for today then?" she asked.

I paused to gather my thoughts before answering her. "Well, if you can pick up where you left off yesterday that would be great."

"That's fine. What are you planning to do then?"

"Well . . . first off I'm going to talk to Todd about doing the website, then I'm going to talk to Grace and Theo and see if they want to come to the police station with me then, if there's time, I want to start on the posters." I reeled off.

"Busy day ahead then," she retorted. "If you want me to help with any of it, let me know won't you?"

"Course I will. Thanks Becky," I smiled warmly at my twin, genuinely grateful for her help and support, then got up and walked into the lounge, grabbed the phone and started to dial Todd's number.

* * *

Another demanding day had left me exhausted again. Firstly there was an exceedingly long and painful phone conversation with Todd; he agreed to construct a website and we spent ages discussing what we wanted on there. Some two hours later with a plan of action agreed the phone conversation ended. So much for fair usage policies I chuckled to myself. That was the easiest task of the day.

My next undertaking was much more difficult; the visit to the police station with Grace and Theo became unbearable. Grace could hardly talk through her tears – she looked like she'd aged ten years in the last couple of days and wasn't anywhere near as well-groomed as normal. Theo *did* answer all the questions put to him by the officers, but in a monosyllabic tone, his facial expression sombre, eyes dead, zombie-like as his anxiety overwhelmed him.

As for me, I struggled to *not* fall to pieces, and for the most part managed to succeed until the police started to ask me why Joshua had left the way he did. How could I tell them about the aggressive lovemaking which left me bruised, battered and scratched in front of Josh's parents? It would break their already fragile hearts to think their son was capable of such brutality. Yet I didn't want to hide this crucial piece of information either. The strain of this was emotionally excruciating; from the expression on the officers' faces, I knew they could tell I was hiding something but they didn't pressure me – I got the impression they understood my predicament and were willing to wait for a more 'convenient' time for me to enlighten them.

Nevertheless, thinking about the reason for Josh's disappearance opened up the chasm in my heart even wider. I felt more vulnerable than ever; the physical and mental torture of this memory tore at what little sanity I had left. Soon the questioning came to an end and as we were escorted out of the room towards the exit, one of the officers whispered in my ear. "You have something more to tell us."

This was said in such a manner it was unclear whether it was a statement or a question. I merely nodded. "We'll be in touch later today," the whisper came again.

I said nothing, lengthened my stride to catch up with Grace and Theo, and we departed with heavy hearts.

After taking Joshua's parents to their house and making sure they were all right, I left and returned home to begin my final major task of the day – the posters. I knew this would take at least an hour or two – after all, I had to get them just right.

As I was about to begin looking through the photographs there was a knock at the door. Although I wasn't expecting anyone, I guessed who it might be. I opened the door and found the two police officers

I'd seen earlier standing there.

We sat in the lounge, Becky by my side holding my hand.

"Miss Harman, we need to clarify a couple of points with you." The younger officer began. "When we asked you earlier if you had an idea why your fiancé might have gone missing you hesitated. What are you holding back?" his voice was not accusatory which made it easier for me.

"There were things I didn't want to say in front of Grace and Theo – I didn't want to upset them any more than they already were." I explained. The officer nodded so I told them about the two lovemaking sessions and the injuries I sustained. I recounted Joshua's reaction to seeing the bruises and scratches and how it seemed he couldn't get away from the house fast enough.

As I was telling the officers, tears streamed down my face and I had to stop several times to regain my composure. I answered a few more questions for them until they were satisfied and left.

I was sapped of all energy and wanted to curl up in a ball and shut out the world. Becky kept throwing glances in my direction, but said very little. She made us a light dinner, but I couldn't finish it despite the small portion she dished up. As soon as she finished eating I made my excuses, kissed her goodnight and went to bed.

It was a long time before I drifted into a deep sleep.

In the morning I woke in a deep funk. I glanced at the bedside clock and a wave of misery surged through me, but at first I couldn't make a particular connection. And then it hit me. Today would have been my wedding day, the happiest day of my life. Now the groom was missing.

I dragged myself out of bed, too depressed to even cry. As I strolled across the landing I heard Becky bustling around in the kitchen and soft voices in conversation. I didn't even stop to speculate who it might be. I had a quick shower, dressed and went downstairs. Today I *had* to get the posters done. I wandered into the kitchen and as my eyes settled on a different face a gasp flew from my lips. She walked over and swept me into a huge hug.

"How're you doing, hun?" whispered my best friend, Jakki, sympathy dripping off every word.

"Ok, I guess. This is a lovely surprise - what're you doing here?"

"Take an educated guess," she replied flippantly as she drew away and studied my face.

I stuck my tongue out at her and her laugh bounced around the walls.

"Right, missy, breakfast for you and then we crack on. Where do I start?"

The hardest part was looking through lots of recent photographs of Joshua to find one which we deemed appropriate for use. Each one I perused drove another scorching blade through my already shattered heart as I remembered where we were when the picture was taken and the happy memories we shared at the time.

I finally found one we thought suitable and copied it into the document. As I typed the words 'MISSING' and 'HAVE YOU SEEN THIS MAN?' onto the page at the top and bottom of the photo, tears began to sting my eyes. My eyes were drawn to the photo once more; Josh looked relaxed and had a small smile on his lips as he faced the camera. He was sitting on the shore besides the most glorious body of water in the Lake District.

In the background were the large hills covered for the most part with foliage, grass and natural country blooms, whose seeds had been blown on the soft breeze or fallen from the claws of one of the many species of bird that frequented the area. The sun sparkled off the smooth surface of the water like lightning hitting a pylon, the rainbows and prisms of colour in the 'sparks' couldn't be easily described, except perhaps by accomplished poets who had a way with words. The scenery was absolutely stunning and made you think you had found your way to heaven.

This had been one of our more recent trips – Joshua had surprised me with it when I'd first got my promotion only a couple of months ago – in some ways it seemed a lifetime ago now. I steeled myself, tearing my eyes away from the face I adored, and determinedly set about finishing. Becky loaded the printer and after printing off a test one to ensure it looked right, we set it to print the first one hundred copies.

While I'd been occupied, Becky and Jakki had been phoning around our friends and lining them up to distribute the posters door to door, to shops, bars and anywhere else they could think of. They had printed off local maps and marked each one up, transferring the details to a master copy, so every person had their own area; what a stroke of genius this was. It meant no one would cover the same ground twice thus diluting the effort to get as wide coverage as possible.

As the first set of posters finished printing, Becky reloaded the paper and set it printing again as Jakki phoned the first person on their list.

Chapter 11 – Joshua

Joshua sat in one of the armchairs in the library, an ancient tome in his hands. This wasn't a normal book – there were no printed pages neatly numbered – this was handwritten in a flowery old-fashioned script which would have made it difficult to read if you were doing so through human eyes. The pages were thin, like tissue paper; if they hadn't been bound within an animal skin cover even a small breeze would have scattered them like confetti. The author, Pavel, had quite a unique way of telling his story, or maybe it was the language which made it seem so different.

Pavel was a vampire who had been born to his new life around 800 years ago. He was the son of a nobleman in Burgas, in Bulgaria. His father, an austere man who ruled his domain with an iron hand in a soft glove, idolised his only son and indulged him more than was normal for the times.

Pavel was showered with expensive gifts of clothes, jewellery and horses, and his armour, swords and bows were encrusted with precious jewels. Despite being showered with gifts and affection, he still had a rebellious streak; his father was paranoid that jealous neighbours or disgruntled servants would attempt to abduct or murder him and so Pavel was never allowed out of the grounds alone. Pavel, being a high-spirited young man of twenty, felt aggrieved he was constantly followed by 'babysitters' and often used his considerable intelligence to outwit them and thus gain some independence and freedom, even if only for a short while.

Pavel, and his father Vasili, loved to go hunting together and often had small wagers on who could bag the largest or most beasts. They never went entirely alone; after all, they couldn't be expected to dirty their hands with their kills, so they were normally accompanied by four serfs.

Just a week before Pavel reached his twenty-first birthday another hunting party had been planned. However, at the last minute his father had to cry off. A message had arrived regarding a land dispute between two tenant families on his estate which was threatening to turn ugly. Not wanting his precious son to be disappointed, he arranged for the hunt to proceed as planned, with the promise he would join in as soon as he could.

Pavel set off with the usual four servants in tow and, as was normal when his father was not about, he schemed to get the freedom he craved. After about an hour of riding through dense forests, he came upon a clearing where a herd of majestic-looking fallow deer were grazing. He came to an abrupt halt and, as quietly as he could manage, removed an arrow from the quill strapped across his back. He inserted it into the bow and carefully took aim at the biggest buck there. His shot was swift and true, the beast fell to the ground without making a single sound and the rest of the herd scattered into the trees in fright.

He sent all four of the servants to collect the massive beast; one was reluctant to leave his master, but the cunning Pavel argued it would take all of them to lift his trophy and he was anxious to take the magnificent animal back to his father. They didn't dream he would use their distraction against them so they complied with his command. As soon as they were all surrounding the fallen deer and discussing the best way to transport such as large beast back home, Pavel moved his steed into a gentle walk away from the clearing, hoping they wouldn't make any noise which would alert his servants to his plan. As soon as he was out of sight, he urged his glorious chestnut stallion to gallop deeper into the forest and well away from his protectors.

He rejoiced as the wind caressed his cheeks and blew through his wavy hair, making

his eyes sting a little in the process. The sense of freedom was a heady experience and not one he wanted to give up any time soon. He rode until he came to a river which snaked its way through the undergrowth and stopped to allow his horse to rest and drink. He dismounted and tied the reins to a tree on the bank of the river so his horse could easily quench its' thirst and removed a package wrapped in cloth from a bag tied to the saddle.

He leaned back against the tree and chuckled, proud of the way he'd escaped, then ripped a chunk from the half loaf of bread and began to chew. When he finished eating his meal, he tipped his head back, closed his eyes and allowed the sun to embrace the contours of his face. He began to feel drowsy in the heat and was soon softly snoring.

When Pavel opened his eyes it was dusk and the heat had drifted away with the sun, leaving a coolness nipping the air. He wasn't afraid being so far from home as night approached and didn't give a single thought to how worried his father would be. As he readied his horse, he heard a rustling in the foliage nearby. He paused and turned to face the direction the sound had come from.

After a few seconds a beautiful young woman emerged from the bushes. She was simply attired in a white cotton dress, her ebony hair hung in waves down to her waist and her face had the innocence and beauty of a heavenly deity. He was rendered speechless at first, but then recovered and spoke more gently than he was accustomed to and bid her good evening.

She smiled shyly and modestly at him, as was the custom of the day, and returned his greeting in a voice which sounded like the most exquisite melody. He could tell she was a lady of breeding and felt compelled to continue the conversation whilst his eyes feasted on the delicate planes of her face and the more voluptuous curves of her tantalising body. The scent emanating from her was intoxicating and totally addictive; he felt himself drawn to her in a way which left him powerless to fight it – yet he didn't want to resist, quite the contrary.

He moved gradually closer until they were only inches apart. He reached out and stroked her crowning glory, letting it run through his fingers. It felt like the softest, most delicate silk. He looked into her glittering jade eyes and started to lose himself; he placed a finger under her chin to lift her face further up. Her lips, with the softness of down, a perfectly drawn cupid's bow and a delicate rose pink were slightly parted and a little moist. Those lips were too inviting and he lowered his lips onto hers, brushing them gently at first and then with an ardour he'd never felt before. He was delighted when she returned his passion, her lips moving with his.

A burning heat started in his loins and travelled through his entire body. He thought he would explode with the force of the passion which consumed him and he wrapped his arms around her body and crushed her to him. Her lips parted and her tongue flicked into his mouth and caressed his as her own excitement took hold. They sank onto the mossy grass and suddenly her lips were everywhere; under his chin, along his jaw line, his chest, down the side of his neck – her teeth nipping and scraping against his skin; some sharp enough to draw blood.

He knew he couldn't contain himself much longer and started to peel her clothing away as quickly yet carefully as he could. When she was naked in all her gloriousness, he stripped quickly and joined her, letting his hands and eyes caress the exquisite form beside him, marvelling that he had found this most wondrous creature. Their lips met again, and with their fervour growing in intensity, they embarked on a remarkable loving journey way beyond the stars.

When he awoke it was daylight once more; she was still naked and his head was lying in her lap. She was leaning against a tree and teasing her fingers gently through his hair. He opened his eyes to look into her beautiful face and she smiled. The sun was beginning to blaze down from the azure vista above, but in the deep shade of the trees where they lay there was some respite from the heat.

They spoke for a while and he learned her name was Iskra, she was a year younger than him and her father had been a nobleman before he'd died. She told him she was alone in the world and her uncle had taken over the family estate and made her leave with only the clothes on her back. Pavel was angered by the way she'd been treated and vowed he would care for her forever. He knew he was already insanely and irrevocably in love with Iskra and wanted to spend the rest of his days with her.

He kissed her softly then nervously declared his feelings for her. He sat silently watching the expression on her face, impatiently yet apprehensively awaiting her response. Then the corners of her mouth sprung upwards into a heartbreakingly lovely smile and declared she felt the same.

His joy knew no bounds, his heart was pounding so hard and fast he could imagine it bursting out of his chest. He pulled her into his arms, wrapping them around her and kissed her with wanton abandon. As she returned his ardour, the passion rose as a phoenix rising from the ashes; once more they travelled as only they could, to their own special part of the universe.

They spent the day wrapped in each other's arms, talking about so many different things. He was totally fascinated by her and loved listening to her musical voice which sounded like a choir of angels had inhabited her larynx. He glanced up to the cloudless sky; surprised to see the sun was in the west. They hadn't eaten a thing all day and he found himself suddenly famished.

The only item he had left in the bag he'd brought from home was two apples – they would have to suffice until he could hunt for something more substantial to cook. He got up, walked over to his horse and retrieved the bag. He removed the apples, returned to her side and offered her one, which she politely refused stating she didn't want them. He shrugged, took a large bite, and as he began to chew, the taste of it soured on his tongue and he spat it out in disgust.

He looked at the apple and could see nothing wrong with it. He lifted up to his nose and sniffed it, recoiling from the sour odour. He was obviously puzzled by this and his brows knitted together in dismay; he held the apple at arm's length and offered it to his faithful steed who didn't hesitate to demolish it. Pavel then brought the second apple towards his nose and again the smell forced him to extend his arm away from his face; he fed it to his horse once again.

While all this transpired, Iskra's eyes never left him and a small smile of amusement danced on her lips. He was beginning to hurt *deep inside and he noticed he could hear things so much more clearly than he ever had before. He could hear the wings of the tiniest flies flapping as they cavorted above his head, he could hear the ants as they traipsed about the forest floor looking for food, he could hear his heart beating in time with a new drum, much faster than ever before. His eyes began to observe tiny creatures as they bustled about in the foliage, he could see the most minute veins in the leaves on the trees and bushes, he could see all the different hues of colour surrounding him so much more clearly – it was as if he'd been blind and now his sight was restored.*

He marvelled at the acuity of his senses yet was still puzzled by what had caused it. He glanced at Iskra, noticing how she observed his every movement with an enigmatic smile; she even looked different. Her skin appeared to be made from the most perfect white marble; there was not a single blemish anywhere on her stunning body or face. Her eyes glowed they were so bright.

The pain escalated in a nanosecond; in that single moment it had gone from a bearable pain deep in his core to an unimaginable agony which cleaved through him from head to toe. He cried out in surprise and curled up into a foetal position, hugging his knees to his chest. Iskra moved closer to him and wrapped her arms around him, cradling him like she would a large infant. Her silky skin felt soothingly cool on his burning hot body, for which he was deeply grateful, but the pain was such he couldn't talk – it was all he could do to hiss her name through his teeth.

Just when he felt he was getting accustomed to the level of agony inside him, it got worse and he began to shake all over as wave after wave of new torture tore all the way through him. His heart was pounding so fast it was a continuous single note, and he wouldn't have been surprised if it had throbbed its way right out of his chest. He knew he couldn't take much more and he wanted to die.

He managed to hiss three words through his teeth, although he was unable to open his eyes to look at her. "Kill. Me. Now." She continued to hold him comfortably in her arms despite the convulsions which added insult to injury with everything else he had to endure, and crooned softly in his ear, secure in the knowledge he could hear her even if the words didn't penetrate into his brain.

For the next few hours it continued; the sun began to set and the air became cooler, but to Pavel it was midday and he was roasting alive in the scorching sun. His writhing became more and more violent; he thrashed on the carpet of the forest floor while Iskra observed, until it stopped as suddenly as it had started. She cradled him in her arms again and listened as the drum of his heart got slower, slower, slower, stuttered and then stopped completely. Pavel didn't move a muscle for at least five minutes then she perceived a slight fluttering of his eyelids. A huge smile lit up her face as he slowly opened his new eyes.

Joshua was totally engrossed in Pavel's story, so didn't notice he was no longer alone – Jasna had floated in and sat across the room gazing adoringly at him. Dayna followed a few minutes later and seeing the way Jasna gazed at Joshua, she snorted derisively. Jasna looked up, startled, and would probably have blushed if it were possible; meeting Dayna's eyes she bared her teeth and a low growl escaped from between her lips. Joshua raised his eyes from the tome as the sounds penetrated his concentration and was surprised there were others in the room.

Just at that moment Samir entered the library, closely followed by Farrell and Erika; unusually everyone sat, staring expectantly at Samir. Joshua searched all their faces, and then he too looked at Samir, waiting expectantly. To an outsider, or human peeping through the window, they would have appeared to be mannequins or wax dummies - they were so still.

Finally Samir smiled softly and turned to face Joshua.

"Joshua, my son, you have done so well in such a short time and we are all incredibly proud of you."

A negative-sounding grunt came from Dayna's direction, and when Joshua looked over at her, she sneered at him. Samir turned to glare piercingly at her and hissed through his teeth. The effect was instantaneous – a contrite expression flittered onto her face like a butterfly dancing around a sweet-smelling rose, and curiously, a pained look flashed into her eyes. Satisfied he would suffer no further interruptions, Samir turned back to Joshua.

"I see you have found Pavel's book – are you enjoying it?"

"Very much," Joshua admitted. "His story is totally fascinating."

"I'm glad you think so. How far have you got?"

"I had reached the part where he'd opened his eyes to his new life for the first time, when . . ." he tailed off.

Samir nodded his head sagely.

"If you hadn't found that book by yourself, I would have given it to you to read, " he stated, still nodding his head. "I want you to finish the book and you only have 2 days in which to complete it – there is something you need to be prepared for."

Chapter 12 – Remy

Becky and I ran off over two thousand copies and had numerous friends around to collect their allotted share. By the time the vast majority had stayed to offer words of sympathy and caring, murmuring platitudes like, 'stay strong', 'I'm sure he's fine', 'try not to worry', 'keep your chin up', I was ready to scream. I knew in some ways I was having ungrateful thoughts (though I thanked them all for their help – and I was truly touched by how many people were ready and willing to pitch in), but if I heard one of those platitudes again in the next week it would be far too soon.

It was bad enough hiding my true feelings from Becky, but to have to put on a show for all these friends was even harder in some respects and I felt more drained than ever. As soon as Jakki, the last person had left, I collapsed into an armchair and closed my eyes. Becky came straight over and knelt beside me; she took my hand in hers and squeezed it gently.

"Hey hun – you okay?"

I nodded not trusting myself to speak and trying desperately not to let the smarting in my eyes develop into full-blown tears. I was fooling no one. She knew me too well.

"You've done so well today and I'm really proud of you, but you don't have to put on a show for me, especially now we're alone. I do have an inkling what a strain today has been for you, you know."

I merely nodded, not believing my voice wouldn't give me away, but I *did* press her hand in response.

"I don't know about you, but I've drunk *so* much tea today, I think I'm going to wake up tomorrow resembling a teapot," she said chuckling at her own little joke, all the while eyeing me surreptitiously to see my reaction.

I tried to smile, but I was sure it came across as more of a scowl.

"Fancy a glass of wine or three?" she walked away towards the fridge where she'd placed a bottle earlier in the day. "It's your favourite, by the way."

I swallowed then cleared my throat before trying to speak. "Sounds perfect."

Now that didn't sound too bad – maybe a little shaky - but apart from that, passable.

As I watched her unscrew the bottle of White Zinfandel and pour it into two oversized wine glasses, I caught sight of one of my favourite photos of Josh and I which had been taken on a weekend break to Norfolk. It was on the polished timber shelf over the mock coal fire we'd bought last winter; the frame a beech coloured wood with delicate carvings showing off the colourful photograph to good effect.

Josh had hired a pleasure cruiser for a few days and we'd spent the weekend travelling along the Norfolk Broads; we'd laughed so much – neither of us had ever been on one before and negotiating the locks was an absolute scream. A kindly older couple had taken the photo of us on the boat soon after we'd pulled into Beccles and Josh had almost fallen in trying to tie it up to the bollards which were evenly spaced along the jetty.

I could feel a pricking sensation in my eyes, my throat started to close up and a sharp pain thundered across my chest like a stampeding herd, making it difficult to catch my breath. The bittersweet memory was crushing in its clarity. We were so happy then. Was it only a couple of months ago? The weight of my desperation and anguish threatened to conquer me again. I couldn't articulate how much I missed him and how utterly empty I was feeling. Yet I knew if I stood any chance of finding him and bringing him back home where he belonged, I would *have* to be strong. I would have to discover an inner strength and a single-minded determination if I were to have a possibility of succeeding.

I raised my eyes to see Becky sitting opposite me, the two wine glasses sparkling as hundreds of tiny stars from the condensation formed a blanket around them, sat on the coffee table between us. Her brow was furrowed with concern and an unspoken question floated in her eyes. A tentative smile came to my lips. Whatever she now saw on my face made her relax and she lifted the goblet to her lips, taking a long swallow. I copied her actions, the cold wine easing the discomfort in my throat and a sound of appreciation escaped my lips. Her smile broadened as she sensed whatever crisis I was having had begun to disperse.

As we sat in companionable silence, a germ of an idea began to form in my overloaded and fragile brain. I stared again at the photo which had caused the near meltdown only minutes earlier and the seed that had been planted began to take root. Abruptly I arose and walked to the cupboard where I'd returned the photo albums after my search for the 'right' picture for the 'Missing' poster, and pulled some of them out again, bringing them back to the sofa. I sat back down, putting the albums on the seat beside me. I kept one hand on top of the pile as if holding them down in case they sprouted legs and ran away, my other hand reached for the ice-cold glass and I drained the contents without pause.

Becky raised her eyebrows staring bug-eyed at me in surprise – she had no notion what I was thinking or intending to do with the photo albums – the shock for her was watching me empty a large wine glass which was three quarters full in one hit. She looked so comical that, despite the trepidation I noticed creeping through me as I prepared to open the albums and see his wonderful face staring back at me, I couldn't keep a straight face and erupted into paroxysms of laughter.

As Becky looked on, obviously confused by my jollity, her expression changed and it appeared as if her eyes were crossed. That did it for me, I clasped my arms around my stomach and doubled up laughing, tears streamed down my face, my sides and jaw began to ache and I thought I was going to fall off the chair. It was totally alien to me to be laughing, I was sure I'd forgotten how – it had been so long since I'd tried, or that was my perception, but I couldn't stop.

In a strange way it felt kind of good, *cathartic*, like a release of steam from the unscrewing of a tightly closed valve, but in another way it was so wrong. How could I be so…*amused* by something so daft at a time when I was really depressed and desolate?

These conflicting emotions were confusing to say the least, but I let nature take its course. She knew she wouldn't get any sense out of me while I was like this, so she arose and walked into the kitchen to get the wine bottle so she could top up our glasses. By the time she returned and sat back down, I was a little more in control although still chuckling. I wiped the last few droplets from my eyes with the heels of my hands.

"Care to share?" Becky asked huffily as she filled my glass again.

"Sorry hun. It's just the look on your face was so funny, it cracked me up."

"What look?"

"The surprise on your face when I knocked my wine back," I replied starting to giggle again.

"Oh. Well I'm sooo glad you find me amusing and entertaining," she said snippily, obviously not that happy being laughed at.

Her body language echoed her sentiments, which was actually quite strange for her – she was usually so easy going and laid back. In fact she didn't normally have a problem laughing at herself, especially when it was me who started it. My hilarity evaporated fast in the wake of her reaction. I gazed at her open mouthed trying to imagine why she was being this way. She glared back at me, resentment in her features, and remained silent.

A light bulb suddenly switched on in my brain, I understood. Since Josh had left, she'd put her entire life on hold for me. She'd stayed with me, cried with me and for me, helped me with posters, organised the search effort, supported me, cooked for me, in fact she'd done everything for me and she was feeling stressed, tired and perhaps a teensy bit unappreciated right now.

The enormous weight which had temporarily evaporated from my shoulders during my amusement at Becky's expense, descended once more like an out-of-control elevator and it hit me hard. I got up from the sofa and rushed to her side. I bent down and put my arms around her, squeezing her as tightly as I could from this awkward position. She sat stiffly and silently, ignoring my attempts to comfort her. I kissed her on the top of her head, gently but firm enough that she could feel it; her hair tickled my nose and I had to release my hold on her with one hand so I could stop myself from sneezing all over her. I didn't think she would appreciate that somehow. I tilted my head to the side and moved my lips closer to her ear.

"Becky, I'm sorry," I whispered contrition evident in the timbre of my voice even through the whisper. "You *know* how much I love you *and* how grateful I am for all your support."

She turned her head slowly to face me and as our eyes connected I saw the hurt there. I hoped I looked as remorseful as I felt. She must have seen the apology and sincerity on my face as her lips curved slightly upwards at the corners and her eyes softened.

"It's okay, Rems, I know," she sighed. "Perhaps I over-reacted a little."

"It's not okay," I argued my lips set in a firm line. "You've been *so* great, so supportive and you've done *everything* for me and all I can do is laugh at you when you unknowingly pulled a funny face. I'm *really* grateful for everything you've done and are doing for me – even if I don't show it much, I don't know how I would've got through the last few days without you. I'm pretty disgusted with myself right now," my voice cracked a little with emotion. I hung my head; my guilt a thick dense fog enveloped me.

She now wrapped her arms around me and pulled me close.

"Hey. Enough of that missy. I *know* how grateful you are – you don't have to say anything, and you have no reason to be disgusted with yourself."

She was trying to make me feel better, I told myself, but I knew I'd hurt her. My tear-filled eyes directed towards the carpet, but not really seeing anything. The silence stretched on while she waited for a response from me. I said nothing.

"Hey. Look at me," her voice was soft yet commanding.

I paused then raised my head a little, but not enough to actually look her in the eyes. She put one hand under my chin and tilted my head upwards; I didn't resist. She gasped at the expression of agony on my face and her own eyes filled with tears. Suddenly we were both crying in each other's arms as the emotion and strain of the previous few days overwhelmed us.

After a few minutes, our tears and sobs faded, as a hot morning sun burns mist from fields. It took a little longer for our ragged breathing to return to normal and we were able to speak. Our arms loosened from each other's bodies and we both reached for our wine glasses at exactly the same time, prompting giggles to escape from our lips. As we drank, my eyes drifted once more to the photo albums and I recalled the notion which had started this whole episode off. I pulled the album from the top of the pile and placed it on my lap before reaching for the pad and pen on the coffee table. Becky looked at me curiously but said nothing, waiting for me to enlighten her.

I sat for a minute marshalling my thoughts into a semblance of coherency then took a deep breath.

"I've had an idea," I announced. "It might be a bit wacky, but hear me out before you comment – please. Okay?"

"Yeah, sure." I could tell by her expression her level of interest was now off the chart.

"Okay. When I was looking through the photos earlier to find one we could use for the posters, a passing thought flitted into my head. It didn't register at the time, or so I believed, but then it came back to me. The majority of the photos were taken either on holiday or one of the many weekend breaks we took. Then it occurred to me that maybe Josh has gone to stay at one of the places we'd visited together, somewhere which brought back happy memories. I know it's a long shot and maybe I'm paddling up the wrong creek, but it's as likely a theory as any and I sure as hell haven't come up with anything better. Sooo . . . my *brilliant* idea is to visit those places and see if I can find him . . ." I shrugged my shoulders at her and waited for her response.

She sat quietly for a few minutes digesting and cogitating then a small smile lit up her face.

"I think that's a pretty good idea actually. At least it's a plan and it's much better than sitting here twiddling our thumbs. I can only see one small flaw. . ."

"What?"

"Have you any idea how long it will take? You *do* have a fantastic job – are you willing to throw away all the hard work you put in to get the promotion?"

Her remarks, whilst having some validity, had irritated me. "I'm not stupid, you know," I snapped.

"I know you're not. I wanted to make sure you'd considered all aspects. . ." her gentle tone trying to placate me, fearing I was about to lose control.

I took a few breaths to calm myself, before continuing. "Well, I'm supposed to be about to embark on a three-week honeymoon, plus I have another two weeks holiday owing and, on top of that, they owe me about twelve days in lieu for all the weekends I've had to work this year, so if I take them all at once, I'm only taking what's owed to me. However, you do have a point and I'll ring them to explain and get authorisation before I go anywhere. Okay?"

"Sounds good to me."

The smile on her face dropped and I knew she'd had another negative thought. I concentrated on keeping my breathing even – I really didn't want to snap at her again; I knew she only had my best interests at heart. I waited for her to speak. Twice she took a breath and went to speak, but both times she closed her mouth, stopping herself.

"Spit it out, Bec."

"I don't want to burst your bubble or anything. . ." she blurted out.

"I know you don't. It's okay – I'm not going to go into one, tell me what's on your mind, *please*."

She hesitated a moment as if still unsure what my reaction would be, then spoke quickly.

"What if you haven't found him by the time your leave runs out? What will you do then?"

"To be honest, I don't know," I admitted, "I guess I'll have to deal with that if it happens. All I can do is hope I find him before then."

"Don't take this the wrong way, hun, but do you honestly think you're strong enough for this – emotionally I mean?"

"Honestly? I can't say for sure, but I've got to find the strength. I love him too much to let him disappear from my life."

"Remy, you're one of the strongest women I know. You *can* do this – I have every faith in you," Becky said earnestly.

I smiled at my twin and nodded. It was time to start making my list.

Chapter 13 – Joshua

Samir and Joshua arrived back at the Manor House just before the first of the sun's rays appeared on the horizon.

"Another successful hunt. You have taken to this life as if you were born to it – I'm very proud of you, my son," Samir clapped Joshua on the shoulder and smiled.

"Thank you." Joshua replied simply.

"Oh, by the way, how are you getting on with the book?"

"I've almost finished it. There are only a few more pages left to go. It makes mesmerizing reading," Joshua enthused.

"I'm rather glad you're enjoying it so much. Will you finish it today, do you think?"

"Yeah, sure. Hey, can I ask you something?" The somewhat offhand question was delivered in a respectful tone.

"Of course," Samir smiled, mildly amused, guessing what was coming.

"Why is my reading and finishing the book so significant?"

"Ahhh!" His smile broadened; teasingly he hesitated, as if deliberating whether to share a secret. He could sense an air of anticipation and decided not to prolong the agony.

"We will be receiving important visitors tomorrow, *exceptionally* important visitors. . ."

Joshua gasped as the realisation hit him and his eyes widened in surprise.

"Not. . .?" he left the question open.

"Yes, my son," Samir confirmed. "Pavel, Iskra and some of their . . . *family*, the 'Commissioners', will be arriving at dusk tomorrow." He announced in a proud yet reverent tone.

"Wow," Joshua whispered in awe. He stood there for a moment processing the information.

"May I ask why Pavel is coming? And who or what are the

Commissioners?"

"Why? To meet you of course," Samir appeared surprised by the question. "To answer your other question, the Commissioners are the principal body of all vampires – sort of akin to a government. The Commission is made up of the five oldest vampires still in existence, of which Pavel is the Head Commissioner."

"T-to meet me?" Joshua stammered, utterly gob-smacked that Pavel was travelling such a great distance to meet *him*.

"Yes, dear boy. Pavel and the Commissioners always choose to meet with new members of our . . . *fraternity*. As you know by now from reading his book, Pavel has a special gift or two of his own, and as such he prefers to visit and ensure we have chosen well."

"But what if he doesn't like or approve of me?" A trace of fear was evident in Joshua's voice.

"You have nothing to fear, Joshua. Trust me."

"I *do* trust you."

"Good. Now go and rest, then finish reading. I'll see you later – we'll meet in the library before we hunt, I need to tell the others about Pavel's visit."

Joshua nodded, then turned and headed towards the stairs as Samir moved off towards another part of the house.

* * *

Joshua was sitting in what was becoming his favourite chair in the library, and had read the final line of the tome when the door opened. Farrell and Erika glided through the door hand in hand, closely followed by Jasna. Before they had a chance to strike up conversation Dayna entered, with Samir immediately behind her. Samir gestured towards the chairs and they all sat expectant and silent, waiting for their maker to begin.

Samir stared at them, one by one, to ensure he had their complete attention, before making his announcement.

"My children, I am happy to tell you we have some important

visitors arriving tomorrow." The expression on Samir's face was akin to that of a parent imparting exciting news to his offspring, yet there was a twinkle of mischievousness in his eyes as he held back, hoping someone would ask the obvious question.

Dayna, scrutinising Samir's expression, and being eager to please, spoke quickly.

"Who's coming, Samir?"

He was delighted his little ruse had produced the desired result and his smile lit up the room. He paused for effect before continuing proudly, "We will be welcoming Pavel, Iskra and the rest of the Commissioners to our home."

A few surprised gasps traversed around the room; Joshua pretended to be as astounded as the rest, and waited for the inevitable question which would follow. Again, it was Dayna who enquired.

"Why are they honouring us with their presence again?" Whilst sounding respectful, she also came across as sycophantic and Joshua inwardly cringed. He glanced across the room and observed Farrell rolling his eyes, a disdainful expression on his face and he stifled a chuckle. Farrell caught a glimpse of the fleeting smirk on Joshua's face and grinned at him – they were definitely on the same page.

Whether or not Samir noticed this brief exchange, he continued as if he was unaware.

"They are coming to meet the newest member of our family, of course, just as they did when I made each of you. I'm sure you must remember that," Samir saw them all nodding in agreement, so he carried on.

"They will be arriving at dusk tomorrow, so I suggest we hunt well tonight in case we don't get the opportunity to do so after they get here. Joshua, you can hunt with Farrell tonight if you wish."

Joshua looked over at Farrell, who grinned in agreement.

"Thank you, I will if you're sure you don't mind?"

"No, that's fine. Shall we depart then?" Samir responded.

They all arose and made their way to the exit, leaving the manor behind to disappear into the ebony night.

* * *

Joshua lay on his bed in the darkened room thinking about the visitors who would be arriving soon. His eyes could trace every hairline crack in the plaster of the ceiling, but he wasn't really paying any attention to them. Although Samir had said it was to be more of a social occasion, Joshua knew that if Pavel found him wanting or, for some reason did not approve of him, he would be destroyed – literally. He knew he needed to make a good impression, but what did Pavel expect of him? Did he expect to find him with useful talents? Was he going to be tested on the cleanliness of his kills or his ability to conceal the wasted bodies of his victims?

All these thoughts and more tumbled around in his head like autumn leaves blown in a park. The more he thought about it, the more his anxiety grew. He arose from the bed and started pacing around the room. Without realising it, his movements sped up faster and faster until he was a blur crossing back and forth.

A knock on the door halted his frenzied movements and he walked over to open it. Samir stood there with a grin across his face.

"May I come in?"

Joshua pulled the door open wider and stepped back. "Of course."

As Samir entered, he glanced down at the floor and chuckled when he noticed the scorch marks across the huge rug. He looked into Joshua's face and was unsurprised to see the consternation etched into his features. What Samir was surprised to see, was the amount of fear in Joshua's eyes. He put his arm around Joshua's shoulders.

"What is troubling you, my son?"

"I'm worried about Pavel's visit" Joshua replied, trying to keep his voice even.

"But why?"

"What if he doesn't approve of me or finds me inadequate? I'm beginning to enjoy my new existence."

Samir turned Joshua to face him and looked deep into his eyes.

"Pavel knows I only choose the best to join our way of life – you have nothing to fear."

"But I don't have any talents to demonstrate so. . ." Joshua began, but Samir interrupted before he could finish.

"Just because you haven't displayed your talents yet, doesn't mean you don't have any. Whilst I don't know what you can do yet, I *do* know you have special gifts. If you remember back to your first night here, I told you one of *my* gifts was the ability to detect talents in others, my 'vamp radar'. I have never been wrong yet and I know without any reservation you possess a talent which is strong and powerful. Trust me, Joshua, you have nothing to fear."

Whether it was the tone Samir used, or the unwavering conviction in his voice, Joshua was not sure, but he suddenly felt calm and more confident.

"Thank you, Samir," he said, "for your confidence in me. I *do* trust you, I was doubting myself," a sheepish smile played on his lips.

"You're welcome, Joshua. Anyway, it's nearly time to start our preparations. Take a few minutes to compose yourself further, then dress smartly and meet me in the library. I'll see you shortly." Samir smiled, turned and glided out of the room, the door clicking softly shut behind him.

Chapter 14 – Remy

The suitcase stood in the hall near the front door. Upstairs, I had finished packing toiletries and make-up into my vanity case; I only needed to put my toothbrush in and I was done. The last time I'd used this case was when I'd been in the States – it seemed an age away instead of just two weeks. Now I was setting off to find him and I was more miserable than I'd ever been. My eyes drifted to the locked cupboard on the landing which housed my beautiful wedding dress and all the carefully selected accessories; I stared at the door unmoving for a minute or more then dragged my eyes away determinedly.

I felt my eyes start to sting as the tears pooled across my lower lid before sliding gracefully down my cheeks. The pain in the centre of my chest radiated throughout my body and I felt my legs grow weak and wobbly; I manoeuvred myself so I could collapse on the bed rather than the floor as the urge to scream my anguish nearly overwhelmed me. My throat constricted and a low moan escaped from my lips. I grabbed my pillow and hugged it tight to my chest, burying my face in it as the sobs tore through my aching body and exited between my trembling lips.

I sat there, rocking back and forth, for several minutes. My sobs muffled by the pillow. A voice from downstairs broke through my grief and I swallowed back the next sob which threatened to escape.

"Rems? Breakfast."

I cleared my throat so I could respond. "Coming."

My voice sounded a bit off, but it wasn't too bad considering. I put the pillow back in its place, arose and walked swiftly into the bathroom. The face gazing back at me was red and blotchy; the agony in my eyes still all too apparent. Running the cold tap onto a flannel I placed it against my face for a few seconds. Repeating this a couple more times before checking out my reflection, I was satisfied that enough of the redness had subsided for me to go down to breakfast; I squeezed the excess water from the cloth, put it on the side of the sink, dried my hands and taking deep breaths to calm me, walked slowly down the stairs.

Becky greeted me with a huge smile. She'd ignored my normal breakfast of cereal or toast and cooked me a lovely plateful of bacon, sausage, eggs, mushrooms and beans, with a plate of buttered toast on the side. I raised my eyebrows in surprise and she chuckled.

"Hey. What's all this? Since when do I eat cooked breakfasts?"

A huge grin spread across her lovely face. "Since I cooked it for you, of course."

"And I'm very grateful, but why?" a teasing smile on my face made her chuckle again.

"I didn't want you to leave here without a decent breakfast inside you," Becky explained.

"Thank you," I responded sincerely, then sat and started eating.

I didn't feel particularly hungry, especially since it was taking a lot of effort to hide what I was really feeling – yet again, but she had gone to so much trouble I didn't want to hurt her feelings. I polished off the breakfast and the toast, washing it down with a cup of tea. Being honest with myself, I did feel a bit better and it made good sense to have a reasonable quantity of food in me to start the day off. After all, I had a good seven-hour journey ahead of me, and that was assuming I didn't encounter any traffic problems en route. I leaned back in the chair and looked up at my twin. She was smiling down at me, obviously pleased I'd cleared my plate without any fuss.

I returned her smile. "Thanks, Becky, that was yummy."

"You're welcome," she replied simply then set about clearing everything away.

"I'm going up to brush my teeth. Back in a mo." I got up and left the room.

"Okay," her voice followed behind me.

I did a final check in the bathroom while I was in there to make sure I hadn't forgotten anything, took my toothbrush and toothpaste into the bedroom, placed them in my vanity case and zipped it up. Without looking back, I grabbed the handle and took the case downstairs, placing it next to the suitcase.

Becky heard me come down the stairs and came into the hall.

"Have you got everything?"

"I think so…can't think of anything I've missed," I racked my brains just to be sure.

"Where's your handbag and keys? Have you got your phone charger?"

"Phone charger packed. Handbag and keys are on the coffee table. I was about to get them, actually."

She walked into the lounge and I followed behind. My bag was exactly where I said it would be. I moved towards the table, but she beat me to it; she picked it up and handed it over.

"Oh. Trying to get rid of me now are you?" I pouted, pretending to be hurt.

She looked at my face and burst out laughing. "Sure am. I've arranged a wild party for tonight and I need time to set it all up."

I laughed with her, knowing full well she was jesting. I wandered slowly back into the hallway, all levity forgotten. Now it was time for me to leave, I was strangely reluctant to take those final steps out of the house. As much as I desperately wanted to find Joshua, I was scared of what I might find and even more scared of not finding anything at all. Out there, I would be alone.

Here it was safe. Here it was known. Here I had my family to support me. The task ahead of me was incredibly daunting, but I couldn't allow myself to fall at the first hurdle. I took a really deep breath to calm myself before turning back towards Becky. She was standing behind me, trying very hard to keep her expression neutral.

"Well, I guess I'd better get on the road," I tried to smile, but it didn't quite reach my eyes.

She nodded then flung her arms around me, enveloping me in a huge hug.

"You take care, okay? If you need me, call me," her voice was muffled against my shoulder.

"Of course I will. I'll ring you every few days, I promise."

"Okay. Love you, sis," Becky's voice broke on the last word.

"I love you too. Thanks for everything, Becks," the emotion in my voice was evident.

I took another deep breath and gently pulled her arms away, stepping backwards in the process. She was trying so hard to blink back the tears which were threatening to fall, just as I was. I knew I had to move now – this was prolonging the agony for both of us. I turned away and picked up my cases; Becky squeezed past me, opened the front door and followed me out to the car. I loaded the cases into the boot and put my handbag on the front passenger seat. I grabbed Becky for one last hug and then swiftly got into the car. I started the engine and pressed the button to lower the driver's side window.

"Drive carefully," Becky called as I backed off the driveway.

I waved back as I pulled away, not trusting my voice, and as I drove down the street, the tears flowed once more.

* * *

The journey heading north was a lonely one. Last time, Josh had been in the seat next to me, sharing the driving and chatting nearly all the way – when we weren't singing along with the radio. So far, I'd been driving nearly four hours in silence –in case the radio played one of 'our' songs. I wasn't sure what would be worse, hearing a special song or listening to the thoughts running roughshod through my mind. Doubts plagued me. Was I strong enough for this? What if I couldn't find him? What if I found him and he really didn't want me anymore? What if he's met someone else? How would I cope if this was all for nothing? Could I go on without him? How would I handle it if he were with someone else? Am I setting myself up for even more anguish?

All these notions were swirling round and round in my head, like a whirlpool gaining momentum. I realised I wasn't concentrating on my driving as much as I should on a busy motorway, so I decided to pull into the next service station and take a break. After all, it would defeat the whole exercise if I ended up as the jam in a lorry sandwich. About ten miles further down the road I saw the sign for the next rest stop; five minutes away. The time and distance passed very quickly and before I knew it, I was pulling off the M6 and onto the filter lane.

I sat at the little table and slowly sipped my tea. I wasn't really hungry after the large breakfast I'd consumed, but I thought perhaps a sugar hit might liven me up so I ate a chocolate chip muffin. My eyes drifted around the café area, not looking for anything in particular. A family sat at a table not far from me - a mum and dad with two small children. The little girl was adorable with blonde curls which brushed her shoulders and huge bright blue eyes. She saw me looking at her and smiled tentatively at me. I smiled back, unable to resist that lovely face, and a huge smile was returned. The dimples in her cheeks became more prominent – it made her face even more beautiful. It took my breath away for a moment as a realisation hit me like a blow to the stomach – she resembled the little girl from my dreams of how Joshua's and my daughter might look.

The pain returned then, but strangely in a good way. My resolve returned. Yes, I still had doubts however my determination to find him came galloping back, a wild stallion running free. I gulped down the rest of my tea, grabbed my bag and arose from my chair. The little girl looked a tad disappointed I was leaving so I smiled at her once more, waggling my fingers in farewell. Her smile returned and she waved back. I turned away and strode purposefully towards the exit, not looking back. As I passed the internet café I caught a glimpse of something glinting on the floor. Normally I would have ignored it yet some inexplicable intuition told me to look at it. As I moved closer I saw the silver tip of a pen protruding from under a workstation. I bent down and eased it out, brushing some dust from it as I straightened up. An audible gasp exploded from my lips as I looked at the pen; engraved on the shank was *'Joshua T Grant'*.

I was soon on the motorway, resuming my steady progress north. I was now fuelled with a determination to succeed, all thanks to that lovely young girl and my amazing find. It was strange how life or fate sometimes threw a few crumbs for you to follow and I wondered what I would have been shown if the girl hadn't been there or I'd not seen the pen tip. Who knew? I knew I was feeling more positive about my direction knowing without doubt Joshua had stopped at the same service station. But I had to keep in mind all the reasons for this journey, even though some would be unbearably painful and I couldn't afford to let doubts get the better of me.

At least I knew I had the support of my wonderful family, Jakki and especially Becky, who would drop everything and rush to my side if I asked her to. I thought about my twin for a moment or two. She was one of the most caring and unselfish people I'd ever known. She'd put her life on hold to get me through the last few dark days; with no mention of how it might have inconvenienced her, or what plans she'd had to cancel. She'd looked after me, made sure I'd eaten something, offered a shoulder to cry on. The list was endless, I owed her *big* time. 'Thank you' seemed so inadequate . . . what could I do to show her how grateful I was? Being the sort of person she is, she wouldn't expect anything, so it was all the more reason to do something nice for her, but what? I had a sudden epiphany and knew what I would do.

I glanced at the huge sign on the motorway and was pleasantly surprised to see I had only one more junction to go before I left the M6. I found myself getting a little impatient and pushed my foot down a bit harder on the accelerator pedal, noting the speedometer notching up to 85m.p.h. I didn't want to push my luck, or get pulled up for speeding so I didn't allow my speed to creep any higher.

Within a few minutes I left the motorway and was making my way through the small towns and villages towards my final destination. As I drove through another small town, a sign caught my eye up ahead and I looked for somewhere to stop. As luck would have it, a parking space became available opposite and I pulled into it gratefully.

Ten minutes later I was in the car and en route once more. I only had about another five miles to go. The scenery was beginning to look more familiar now. And then I saw it. The sign in the small car park at the front of the building read "Amble-Rose Guest House". I pulled in and found a space. I had arrived.

* * *

I got out of the car and stretched, before getting my bags out of the boot. I walked slowly through the door and into the familiar reception. Mrs Kirk, the owner, was sitting at her desk in the little office behind the counter. As she heard me enter, she lifted her head and smiled, rising from her seat she moved towards the counter to greet me.

"Hello, my dear and how are you? It's so lovely to see you again."

"Thank you, Mrs Kirk" I replied, returning her smile.

"Where's your nice young man? Isn't he with you this time?"

My face must have betrayed my emotions, although I tried to keep my composure; before I could answer, she spoke again, contrition in her voice.

"I'm sorry if I've said something wrong – I didn't mean to pry."

"Don't worry, Mrs Kirk, you haven't. I'll explain a little later, but first I would love to get settled in my room and freshen up."

"Of course, dear. When you're ready, why don't you come back down and I'll make us a cup of tea and we can have a chat. Only if you want to. . ."

"That would be lovely, Mrs Kirk. Give me about half an hour or so and I'll be back down."

"You take as long as you need dear – I'm not going anywhere. Oh, and by the way, please call me Pat – Mrs Kirk sounds awfully formal." She pulled a key from one of the hooks behind her and handed it to me. "I've put you in room 5, Miss Harman. It's on the first floor to the right of the stairs."

I took the key from her hand and put it in my pocket. "Ok, Pat. Thank you. And please call me Remy."

"Remy. What an unusual and very pretty name. Where did that come from?"

"I'll tell you when I come back down. Okay?"

"No problem dear – I'll see you in a little while."

I nodded, grabbed my bags and made my way up to my room.

After texting Becky to let her know I'd arrived safely and unpacking part of my case, I had a quick shower and changed my clothes before going back down to reception. Mrs Kirk was sitting in her office, shuffling papers which covered the blotter on her desk. I leaned against the counter watching her for a few seconds before calling out.

"Hey, Pat. Is the kettle on yet? My throat thinks my lips have been sewn together." She chuckled as she turned to face me.

"It's in the pot brewing and about ready to pour out, cheeky miss," I laughed with her.

She came out and lifted a section of the counter so I could pass through, then replaced it before leading me into her office and round the corner into a small lounge area, where a couple of floral covered armchairs and a small settee were placed around a coffee table laid with tea and a plate of biscuits. She gestured for me to sit so I sank into the soft squidginess of the settee. She perched on the edge of one of the armchairs, and after enquiring how I took my tea, poured it and gave it to me in a cup and saucer. I admired the Royal Worcester pattern on the side. It reminded me of a set my grandmother had owned.

Pat settled back into her armchair with her own cup and saucer, before speaking.

"So, how did you get your lovely name then?"

I smiled as I remembered the story my mum had told me.

"When Mum was carrying me, she used to watch a series on the TV about London firemen. Apparently one of the main characters had a brief fling with a girl called Remy and Mum fell in love with the name. Of course, she didn't know she was carrying a girl at that time, let alone twins, but the name stuck with her and when I was born, it was the only name she'd considered."

"Ahhh. That's nice. Twins did you say?" she smiled, a sort of dreamy look on her face.

"Yep. This is the funny bit. She had no idea she was carrying twins and her and Dad got a real shock when my sister came out five minutes later. They hadn't considered any other girl's names so it took them a whole week to decide on Rebecca's name." I laughed when I remembered my sister's reaction when she was first told the story – the look on her face was hilarious. Pat chuckled with me.

"Are you identical?"

"Yes. The only difference between us is the colour of our eyes. It's the only way to tell us apart. Rebecca's eyes are bright blue whereas mine are brown."

"That's unusual. I've never heard of that before!" she exclaimed in wonderment.

"Neither had the midwives at the hospital," I pronounced with pride.

Pat shook her head a little and we lapsed into companionable silence. I looked around at the décor before my eyes drifted back to Pat. She looked as if she wanted to say something, but wasn't sure where to start.

"Are you okay?" I asked a little concerned.

"What? Oh, yes dear, I'm fine," she smiled softly, but fidgeted on her seat. I moved to the end of the settee, nearer to where she sat and gazed into her kindly face.

"You were going to say something and then stopped yourself. What is it?" I asked her gently.

"I-I didn't want to risk upsetting you," she stammered a little, dropping her eyes to stare into her almost empty cup.

Instantly I knew what she'd wanted to ask me, and understood why she was reticent. She wanted to know where Josh was. My stomach churned a little; my intestines tying themselves into knots. I took a couple of deep breaths and worked hard to try and keep my voice even.

"You were going to ask me about Joshua." It was a statement, not a question.

She nodded, still keeping her eyes down. "I-I don't want to pry. You don't have to tell me if you don't want to," she mumbled.

I wasn't sure I would be able to tell her about it without breaking down – it was still so raw and painful. I drained my cup and placed it on the table. Perhaps it would be easier telling a stranger. Perhaps not. I didn't know, but one thing I was sure about was my emotions were suddenly closer to the surface than they had been all day – well since leaving home. I glanced at my hands and was surprised to see them trembling. I clasped them together in my lap, took a deep breath and started to speak.

I struggled with my composure on several occasions. She could not miss the little catches of emotion in my voice, and as she was watching me intently, could see the pearly droplets escaping from my eyes despite my curtailing efforts. I left out the intimate details and the scratches and bruising – it was too personal to discuss.

By the time I reached the end and was explaining my plan to find him, she was sitting on the edge of her seat and had taken my hands in hers.

When I finished, I glanced at her face and, to my surprise, saw my sorrow etched into her features and her glassy eyes. We sat in silence for a few minutes while we both recovered some self-control before attempting to speak further. It was Pat who broke the silence.

"Oh. You poor, poor dear," she said softly, consolingly, gently squeezing my hands in hers. "So that's why you've come here?"

I nodded. I couldn't bring myself to ask the obvious question, but Pat knew. She arose from her seat and came to sit beside me. She put her arm around my shoulders before apologetically saying, "I'm so sorry Remy, but I haven't seen or heard from him. He *may* be in the area, but I honestly don't know."

I cleared my throat before replying.

"Oh. Okay. Well I'm here so I'm going to do the job properly. Do you have a list of all the local Guest Houses and Hotels I could borrow please?" my voice gained in strength and my resolve became stronger once more.

"You are a truly remarkable young woman," she stated in awe. "I'll sort the list out for you for breakfast tomorrow. Is that soon enough?"

"Thank you." I replied simply, nodding.

We sat there a little longer in comfortable silence until I noticed the time. I still needed to eat dinner – after all, I hadn't really eaten much since breakfast. I thanked Pat for her hospitality and made my way into the dining room. I ordered a main meal and a glass of wine and had soon despatched the lot. As I made my way up to my room I determined I would try to get a good night's sleep, so I would have plenty of energy for tomorrow. Something told me I would need it.

Chapter 15 – Joshua

The coven assembled in the library awaiting the arrival of the visitors; the ladies dressed in elaborate gowns which would not look out of place in a ballroom. Jasna and Erika had swept their hair up into stylish arrangements, while Dayna's short curls were more artfully arranged than usual. They all wore stunning jewellery which, by Joshua's estimation, would have cost many thousands of pounds. Samir and Farrell were wearing tuxedo style trousers, dinner shirts with silk cravats and embroidered velvet smoking jackets. Joshua felt somewhat under-dressed as he didn't possess anything that grandiose, but nevertheless was debonair in his dark suit, silk shirt and tie.

There were half a dozen slightly dusty, ornamental bottles on a silver tray and an assortment of Edinburgh crystal wine glasses on a table by the window. Everything was in readiness.

The light outside was fading fast and a sense of anticipation and excitement was building within the Manor House. It wouldn't be much longer now. Joshua was still nervous, but after his earlier conversation with Samir, was not feeling the fearful anxiety which had gripped him before.

They chatted amongst themselves to pass the time; even Dayna was being less of a bitch than normal. Samir cleared his throat loudly to get their attention.

"My children, Pavel and his family will arrive momentarily. Let us all move to the hall so we may greet our guests properly." He gestured towards the door as he spoke and they all arose and followed him into the hall.

They took up their positions in a receiving line of sorts, in order of seniority. Joshua was placed at the very end, being the newest member of the coven.

Just then, there was a loud rap on the door. Samir was already standing right next to it and opened it immediately. On the porch stood a collection of ten men and women; all elegantly attired and all very beautiful in their own way. At the head of the group was a young looking man with wavy chestnut hair that reached his shoulders and warm chocolate coloured eyes. He smiled warmly at Samir; arms open in invitation.

"Samir, my dearest friend, it is such a pleasure to see you again."

Samir smiled in response, embracing Pavel like a long-lost brother. "Pavel, it brings me joy to welcome you once more to our abode. Please come inside and make yourself at home."

Pavel crossed the threshold followed by an exquisite woman with waist length ebony hair and compelling jade eyes. Behind them, four more couples filed into the hall.

Pavel didn't need to be introduced to any other member of the coven, except for Joshua. He moved down the receiving line shaking hands with each member, as did all his companions, but when he reached Joshua he halted. Samir, knowing what was expected of him, rushed to Pavel's side and gesturing at Joshua said in a very formal tone, "Pavel, may I present the newest member of our coven. This is Joshua."

Pavel looked at Joshua carefully, his face an inscrutable mask as he examined the neophyte before him. Suddenly his lips broke into a smile and he grasped Joshua's hand.

"A pleasure to meet you, Joshua," his heavily accented voice sounded warm and friendly.

"I can assure you Sir, the pleasure is all mine," Joshua replied with reverence and sincerity, bowing slightly as he spoke.

Pavel smiled wider, obviously pleased by Joshua's response. He indicated the woman standing by his side.

"Joshua, this is Iskra, my wife."

Joshua bowed his head towards her before shaking her proffered hand gently. "An honour to meet you, Madam Iskra."

Iskra smiled in response and replied, "Likewise," in her melodic voice.

Next Joshua was introduced to Luka and his wife Amaranta, then

Sophia and her husband Costa, then Dragos and his wife Stela and finally Emile and his wife Oleana. Once all the introductions had been completed, they adjourned to the library where Dayna was handing around what appeared to be glasses of red wine, poured from the decorated bottles which had been on the table. It wasn't until Joshua had been given one of his own he realised it was actually blood. When everyone had been served, Dayna drifted to Samir's side to await further instructions and the chatting slowly faded away until only silence remained. All eyes were on Pavel as they waited for him to speak. They didn't have long to wait.

"My dear friends, what a pleasure it is to be reunited once more and to have the opportunity to welcome a new member to our way of life." Pavel looked directly at Joshua before continuing. "As is our custom, Joshua, you will be examined by each of the Commissioners and then set a challenge. Should you be successful, you will be officially accepted by us as part of our family forever more. Do you understand the procedure and accept the challenge which will be set for you?"

Joshua looked Pavel directly in the eyes and replied firmly and with conviction, "I do, Sir."

Pavel nodded in acknowledgement then walked over to stand directly in front of Joshua. As Samir had briefed him, Joshua knew what to expect so he offered his hands to Pavel and waited. Pavel took Joshua's hands in his and closed his eyes. After a few moments, Pavel re-opened his eyes and stared down at Joshua in astonishment. He said nothing, but nodded to Luka who took his place and repeated the procedure. This happened three more times, with Sophia, Dragos and finally Emile. The Commissioners then wordlessly left the room and disappeared to another part of the house, until they were well out of earshot.

Emile was the first to speak. His voice echoed the astonishment Pavel had felt earlier.

"I have never felt anything so strong as with this neophyte – he is going to become very powerful."

Dragos spoke next.

"I agree with Emile. Does Samir suspect or know what he has made?"

Sophia turned towards the group and gave her opinion.

"I can feel at least three gifts and all will be formidable. He must be nurtured."

Luka nodded in agreement.

"In my opinion, he will be an amazing asset. What is your judgment Pavel?"

Pavel turned to face his colleagues.

"I have no hesitation in recommending acceptance, as long as he completes the challenge successfully. In fact, I can foresee he will soon outgrow Samir and will form his own powerful coven. There will be no animosity when the split comes and they will remain close friends. To answer your question Dragos, Samir knows Joshua is talented, but I don't believe he realises to what extent. But I digress. Are we all agreed?"

Four heads nodded in assent.

"Good. Let us now return to the others and set Joshua his task." Pavel glided down the hallway and back to the library, the others following.

As they entered the room, conversation ceased. All eyes turned towards Pavel and they waited for him to speak. Pavel turned to face Joshua and spoke directly to him.

"Joshua, you may not know this, but I am such a connoisseur of blood that I can tell the approximate age and sex of the victim, without having seen them. Your task will be to take these twelve bottles," he indicated some half-pint sized bottles lined up on a table, then continued, "put a decent sample of blood in each one and bring them back. Now you may think it will be easy, BUT what is required is a sample from each decade starting with teens, one male and one female from each and you have until dawn to achieve it. If you cannot complete the task in time then you will not be welcomed back. Do you understand?"

Joshua stood and in a firm voice answered, "Yes, I understand."

"Then you had better begin – time is *not* your ally. We hope to see you later," Pavel announced and gestured towards the door.

Joshua scooped the bottles into a bag which was lying on the floor and made his way to the door. He turned at the threshold and raised his hand in farewell before he disappeared into the darkness.

* * *

The atmosphere was tense in the Manor as dawn approached without Joshua's return. Samir tried to disguise his anxiety with affability, but as time went on, it became harder to maintain the façade. With half an hour till sunrise, the tension became unbearable; everyone in the library became more still and quiet and increasingly worried. The heavy drapes had been drawn across the window plunging the room into darkness; the only light came from a small reading lamp on a side table. With fifteen minutes left, a sense of desperation clouded the room – even Dayna appeared affected.

Five minutes later, a sound was heard from the main door. The occupants of the library started in surprise and Samir ran to the door, but before he could reach for the handle, the door opened and Joshua walked into the room. Samir was beside himself with joy and threw his arms around his latest protégé. Joshua looked over Samir's shoulder to find everyone in the room smiling at him, even Dayna.

Pavel cleared his throat and Samir, laughing, let go of Joshua so he could officially complete his challenge. Joshua strode proudly over to Pavel and handed over the bag containing the twelve bottles, giving a little bow to Pavel as he did so. Pavel took the bag and removed the bottles, placing them on the table in no particular order. He picked one up at random and removing the top, raised it to his lips and tasted the contents.

"Ahhh. Essence of female teenager," he declared, smiling.

He then reached for the next bottle and repeated the process, continuing until every bottle had been opened, tasted and identified.

Pavel turned to Joshua and clasped him by the hand.

"Joshua, you have successfully completed your challenge and, on behalf of the Commissioners, I have pleasure in welcoming you to our family. We are very proud to have you."

Applause broke out around the room and Joshua basked in his success. He thanked Pavel and shook his hand again. Suddenly he was surrounded; everyone wanted to congratulate him at once. He found his hand shaken repeatedly and lost count of the number of kisses which were planted on his cheek; he did remember one particular kiss which was much closer to his lips and lingered longer than the others though. But now was not the time to reflect upon it. There would be plenty of time for that.

In the midst of the celebrations a powerful emotion charged through him. He now felt, without reservation, that he truly belonged.

Chapter 16 – Remy

I awoke early, much earlier than I normally would. I didn't feel in the least bit groggy as I usually did when I woke up too early – on the contrary, I was immediate wide awake and firing on all cylinders. The sun was beginning to peek over the horizon and the sky was a beautiful shade of lavender. It was much too early to get up, so I lay on the bed with my face turned towards the window and watched the day begin. I let my mind meander down memory lane to when I was here with Josh; in reality it was such a short time ago, but in some respects it was a lifetime away, so much had happened.

We arrived after lunch on the Friday and checked in at the Amble-Rose Guest House. After unpacking, we went out to explore the village of Glenridding, holding hands and laughing about silly things as we strolled. The village had an old world charm; some of the buildings on the outskirts dated back to the 19th century. Most of the original mining village had been rebuilt or refurbished in the early 1930's after two major episodes of flooding and it was now mainly an area for tourists to view one of the most beautiful areas in The Lakes. The locals were very friendly and we chatted to some of them as we ambled into various little shops.

We had a nice meal in one of the local pubs that evening and stayed for drinks in the bar, soaking up the atmosphere and people watching; making a game of creating stories about some of the more colourful patrons. The stories became increasingly bizarre and outlandish commensurate with the amount of alcohol we consumed, until we couldn't talk for giggling. We bade farewell to the landlord and stumbled out into the balmy air; holding hands we weaved through the streets, still chuckling at our little game, eventually arriving back at the guest house.

Trying to negotiate the stairs in our inebriated state must have looked similar to a comedy sketch; Joshua repeatedly staggered two steps forward and then three steps back until he made a run for it and made it half way up before falling flat on his face in paroxysms of laughter whilst I, being perhaps more practically minded, decided to crawl up on my hands and knees – something I was quite successful at – until Josh fell and I found myself paralysed by my own fit of giggling. It must have taken us a good half hour to reach the second floor where our room was located and another ten minutes to find the correct door. Once in the room, we both flopped onto our bed fully clothed and passed out.

The following morning, Joshua awoke with a sore head, but felt a bit more human after a shower and a full English breakfast, although he refused to remove his sunglasses (which I found immensely amusing). I, on the other hand, suffered no ill effects whatsoever (I'd never had the dubious pleasure of shaking hands with Mr Hangover, much to Josh's chagrin), and felt it was my duty to rub a little salt in and poke fun at my fragile fiancé.

We drove to Ullswater – the most beautiful of the lakes surrounded by the most stunning scenery imaginable – and spent the entire time exploring the area and taking photographs. We had a picnic lunch on the shore of the lake and excitedly discussed our forthcoming wedding and plans for after the nuptials. It was an enchanting day; we even found a magical waterfall surrounded by picturesque walks where the water tumbles 70 feet down a rocky ravine to join with Ullswater. We stayed until early evening then drove back to Glenridding, had dinner in our guest house and a few drinks in the bar before going to bed and making love until we fell asleep in each other's arms. The perfect end to the most perfect day.

The following morning we packed our stuff and left.

We drove to Lake Windermere and spent an hour exploring the area. Whilst being pretty and peaceful, I found Windermere disappointing after Ullswater. After all the hype, it didn't live up to my expectations. Josh felt the same way so we left early and decided to visit Dove Cottage in Grasmere, a former home of William Wordsworth. The museum attached to the cottage was a poetry lover's delight; housing an archive of poems, not only by Wordsworth but also Shelley, Coleridge and Byron, and some contemporary works.

We spent a couple of hours drinking in the literary history before beginning the long drive back to Essex. The journey didn't seem as long as I'd expected as we spent the vast majority of it discussing everything we'd seen and trying to create new superlatives to describe some of the fantabulous scenery.

I was jolted out of my reverie by wetness on my face. I brought my hands up, touched both cheeks and found a small stream of tears running down them. My chest felt tight and achy, my throat constricted and I turned my face into my pillow to stifle the sobs desperate to escape. My body heaved as I cried myself out. In another part of my mind I wondered at the capacity of my body to keep producing so many tears in such a short space of time. I turned my face away from the pillow and sat up. I felt very alone and entirely lost. Wiping my eyes with the backs of my hands, I looked out of the window and was surprised at how much everything had changed. The sky was now porcelain blue, with the occasional wispy cloud shimmering in the heat. I glanced at the clock on the bedside table and was shocked to see breakfast was now being served. I dragged myself up, walked into the bathroom and took a shower. The heat of the water pounding on my tense torso began to relax my muscles, making me feel calmer. After a few minutes I turned off the water and wrapped a large towel around my body. I pulled a brush roughly through the tangles, grabbed some clean clothes, got dressed and hurried down to breakfast.

As I was about to leave the dining room, a waitress approached me with an envelope in her hand. "Excuse me, Miss Harman?" she enquired.

I nodded and smiled at her.

"Mrs Kirk asked me to give you this," she continued as she held out the envelope to me. I took it from her. "Thank you." I responded and smiled as I remembered what it was. "Please thank Mrs Kirk for me."

"I will."

I hurried to my room to examine the contents and plan my day.

I mentally blessed Pat Kirk when I looked inside the envelope. Not only had she given me a list of all the hotels and guest houses in the area, but she'd given me the addresses, phone numbers and enclosed a local street map too. In addition, she'd taken the trouble to number each establishment on her list and marked the numbers on the map for me, making it so much easier to create my plan of action. Within half an hour I knew which route I was taking and the establishments I would cover that day. I grabbed my small knapsack, the map, list, Joshua's pen and photo of him and set off with hope in my heart.

Chapter 17 – Joshua

Pavel and Samir sat alone in a small office on the first floor of the manor house. The sun was still high enough in the sky for everyone to be in their rooms, but as the heavy drapes were closed, it wasn't a problem.

The two vampires had been chatting for quite some time, catching up on each other's news before the conversation turned to Joshua.

"Where did you find him, Samir?" there was an element of excitement in Pavel's tone Samir had never heard before.

"In a country park in Essex. I'd been getting ... *urges* to travel in that direction for some time and, as I knew my coven could take care of themselves and be ... trusted, I decided to follow my instincts." Samir explained. Pavel nodded as he listened, so Samir continued.

"To be honest, I've never before detected such a strong presence – I picked him up quite quickly once I arrived in the area and was able to zero in on his exact location. However, finding the opportunity, catching him alone was another matter. It took a couple of days before I got the break I needed. I tracked him to the park and stayed hidden in the shadows while he wandered around in the sun; I had to hope I could get close enough to bite him before he left. My patience was rewarded – he decided to sit on a bench in the shade, a short way from the path, but far enough that it was secluded. I made sure there was no-one close enough to be a problem and seized the moment."

"Yes, I can understand what you mean about his strong aura. He is going to be formidable when his talents present themselves; I admit I was taken by surprise at the strength of them when I touched his hand yesterday. I believe, as Joshua develops, you will have an interesting few months, my friend."

Samir nodded in recognition. He knew Joshua was special – perhaps more special than the rest of his coven – but hearing it from Pavel made it more definite, more conclusive.

As Samir thought about the conversation they'd had, Pavel recalled the conversation he'd had with the rest of the Commissioners, after the celebrations had concluded and before they retired.

Sophia, Dragos, Luka and Emile had all been stunned by the power they had detected in Joshua and also a little concerned, not about Joshua as such, more whether Samir would be able to nurture him in the correct way. Did Samir have the fortitude, the patience and the understanding to cope? Luka and Dragos had expressed serious doubts about his abilities bearing in mind at least three gifts had been identified. Sophia was more positive, reminding everyone how well he had done with the existing members of his coven, and with minimal assistance or support. Emile, ever the diplomat, decided to keep a foot in both camps and echoed what the others had proclaimed, but in addition, he suggested more regular visits, to offer help as needed would perhaps be appropriate.

Pavel, as Head Commissioner, had to make the final decision as to how they should proceed and whether it was necessary for them to involve themselves any further. After all, Samir was an old and trusted friend and the last thing they wanted to do was disappoint, alienate or, in any way, give the impression he was not trusted with this very special task. The other consideration was that Samir alone had found this treasure and had turned him. He hadn't needed any assistance for that.

As they were making preparations to leave as soon as it was dusk, Pavel was running out of time to address this issue. He would have to … what was the expression? Oh yes, he remembered … he would have to *wing it* and hope Samir didn't take offence.

Pavel turned his eyes to look once more at Samir, and, to his surprise, found his friend grinning at him. A puzzled expression crossed Pavel's face as he struggled for a moment to understand why Samir was so amused. Samir chuckled and raised one eyebrow, then winked in a cheeky manner as he waited for Pavel's realisation. Without warning, the silence was broken by a loud booming laugh as Pavel grasped the source of Samir's amusement; Samir was telepathic, so he knew everything which had just gone through his mind.

"Don't worry, my friend," Samir leaned forward and placed his hand on Pavel's shoulder to reassure him. "I'm not offended in any way and I fully understand the reservations of the others. I have to admit, it *is* a daunting task in some respects." The amused expression faded as he became more serious, a slight frown creasing his forehead.

"Dealing with one gift is relatively straightforward – as soon as you realise what you are nurturing, it seems to develop easily and it doesn't normally take much training for the holder to learn to control it. There are always exceptions of course – the temperament of the individual can be a determining factor, someone who is quick to anger takes longer to discover the necessary level of constraint – but in Joshua's case, there are at least three talents and we have no idea yet what we are going to be coping with."

Pavel nodded sagely. "You are quite right. However, I *think* I may have an inkling what one of the talents is …" he paused for effect, but not long enough for Samir to have to ask. "I believe he has what you affectionately call 'vamp radar'. One of his gifts feels totally alien to me – it is something I've never felt before in over eight hundred years – so it will be extremely interesting to discover what that turns into."

Samir digested the imparted information before responding.

"Mmmm, it will be very interesting indeed. I have to admit my curiosity is seriously aroused. I wonder how long it will be before they start to appear …"

"Not too long, I think."

"The 'vamp radar' will be extremely easy to cope with," Samir affirmed, with a small smile playing around his lips.

Pavel returned the smile. "It should be – for you anyway." He chuckled, but then turned serious once more. "What about the other gifts? Do you feel you will need any assistance? I'm not doubting you or your abilities, my friend – I want to assure you of that."

"Honestly? I'm not sure yet." Samir spread his hands wide, palms upwards and shrugged his shoulders. "And I know you don't doubt me, Pavel, I understand your concerns and share them." He continued.

"The best answer I can give you is that if I feel I need some support, you will be the very first person I contact."

Pavel felt a sense of relief, not only because he knew he hadn't offended Samir, but also that Samir would turn to him if need be. He reached towards Samir and clasped his elbow.

"It would be my pleasure to give you any help or support I can – you only have to ask."

"Thank you, Pavel. It is comforting to know I have your friendship and counsel."

There were various miniscule sounds of movements coming from other parts of the house – too small to be detected by human ears – as the others began to move around in their rooms. Pavel glanced towards the window and through a tiny gap where the curtains met at the top near the rail; he could see it was early evening and only an hour or so until dusk.

"I'm so glad we found the opportunity to have this conversation. Iskra will be preparing for our departure and I need to speak with her and the others, before we leave. Therefore, if you will excuse me …?"

Samir inclined his head towards Pavel, a slight bow. "Of course. May I suggest we all meet in the library?"

"Sounds perfect," replied Pavel as he arose from his seat and glided to the door. He raised his hand then without another word, disappeared through the door, leaving Samir in a very thoughtful mood.

* * *

Joshua prowled around his room restlessly. He didn't need to sleep anymore so the daylight hours he spent in his room were too boring for words. He'd asked Samir why they stayed closeted in their dark rooms during the day and he'd explained sunlight was extremely dangerous to them, it would set their skin alight causing them unimaginable pain and prolonged exposure could destroy them, turn them into a pile of ash. The thought made him shudder. So, what were they supposed to do during these long hours? Again, Samir had an explanation. Most vampires were able to achieve a sort of meditative state – to anyone else it would resemble deep sleep, hence the storybook pictures of vampires lying deathly still in coffins – but it took a little practice.

The idea of lying on the bed for hours on end was anathema to Joshua. He wanted to be doing something, anything to relieve the tedium. He continued to pace the floor for a few minutes before making a decision; with his lips set in a firm, determined line, he opened his door and walked out into the corridor and toward the stairs. There was no fear in him as he descended to the foyer, despite the light which streamed in from the windows either side of the front door. He glanced down at his hands and saw they were unaffected – *perhaps it was only direct sunlight which made them burn*, he thought – so he continued on to the library. That would be more of a test, with the huge windows which overlooked the spectacular manicured gardens. He hesitated for a fraction of a second before opening the door and stepping inside.

The sunlight poured through the south-facing windows creating crazy patterns as it bounced off the reflective surfaces and shiny objects. He marvelled at the incredible colours and shapes this effect fashioned; this wouldn't have been as noticeable with human eyes. He moved very slowly into the room, at first being cautious, not allowing the rays to touch his skin, glancing down at his hands again to see if they were changed in any way, but they remained the same. Feeling braver, he decided to push his luck and moved one of his hands directly into one of the shafts of light, prepared to pull it away again at the first sign of pain or damage, but nothing happened. Curiosity got the better of him. He gradually allowed more of himself to enter the light until he was standing completely engulfed by it, turning his face towards the window last of all.

The sun felt warm on his ice-cold skin, but there was no pain, no damage whatsoever. He stood there for several minutes waiting to feel the unimaginable agony Samir had described. Nothing happened. He moved off to the side and sat in his favourite chair, his mind whirling round and round like a mini tornado, trying to process this new development. Had Samir lied to him? Or did he not know? Had Samir been lied to by whoever made him? And if Samir had lied, the big question was why? It didn't even occur to him that maybe he was special, the only one who could go into the light, that this was one of *his* talents. He *had* to speak to Samir about this, and soon. But how to broach the subject? He couldn't blurt it out any more than he could say anything in front of the others. Well, not until he'd discussed it with Samir. Should he mention it while Pavel was still here or should he wait until the visitors had gone?

Joshua didn't really notice the time passing, so absorbed was he in his thoughts, until he heard movement from upstairs. He looked out of the window and was shocked to see it was close to sunset. He heard several people descending the stairs. Having made the decision to keep his own counsel until Pavel and his entourage had left and wanting to give the impression everything was normal (bearing in mind Samir and the rest of his coven were used to finding him in the library reading), he quickly rose and picked a random book from one of the shelves, sat again and started to read.

The library door opened. Pavel and Iskra glided into the room, closely followed by the rest of the Commissioners and Samir. It was obvious the former had prepared for their departure; they were all wearing long dark coats which were fitted into the waist then flared out down to the hem. Joshua surmised this was to enable them to run more freely. Within a few minutes the rest of the coven appeared and the library was crowded with bodies. Samir glanced in apparent irritation at their late arrival, but said nothing in front of Pavel and the others. He would bide his time.

All too soon, Pavel and his party were saying their goodbyes. They all spoke to each person individually, shaking hands with the men and kissing the cheeks of the ladies. When it came to Joshua's turn, Pavel clasped his hand much longer than anyone else's, and leaned in to whisper quickly in his ear, hoping the conversations around him would prevent the others from hearing.

"Joshua, Samir is a wonderful ... person and mentor – let him guide you and you won't go far wrong. However, if you ever feel you need *my* help, you have only to ask." Joshua could feel Pavel slip something into his pocket as he continued.

"I can sense you have amazingly strong gifts, stronger than most immortals I've come across and I can't help being intrigued by how they will develop and manifest themselves. The best advice I can give you is not to let the power go to your head. Be humbled by the gifts which have been bestowed upon you, be generous with others and I can foresee that you will become one of the great immortal leaders. Keep this conversation to yourself – prove to me my faith in you is not misplaced." Pavel leaned away from Joshua, aware that other conversations were coming to an end and Iskra was waiting to say her own farewell.

"It has been a great pleasure to meet with you Joshua," he continued, at a normal conversational volume. "I look forward to seeing you when we next visit."

"The pleasure has been mine, Sir. I wish you a safe onward journey," Joshua replied with sincerity.

Pavel nodded, a small smile playing around the edges of his lips. "Thank you," he replied simply, before moving to the side so Iskra could speak to him.

Soon the farewells had been completed, everyone moved into the foyer and to the front door. At a nod from Pavel, Samir opened the door and saying "goodbye" one last time, they stepped outside and vanished into the twilight.

Chapter 18 – Remy

I arrived back at the Amble-Rose Guest House around dusk, fatigued and a little disheartened. As it was such a warm, sunny day I had elected to leave my car behind and make my enquiries on foot. I'd set out that morning with a spring in my step and hope in my heart, but as the day progressed, and I'd received more negative responses, the optimism had turned to pessimism.

It was probably naïve of me to expect to find Josh on my first day out but hey, hope was a densely populated place, right? I dragged my weary legs and aching feet through the entrance door and crossed reception heading for the stairs. Pat was in her office and she glanced up as she heard my footsteps. The cheery greeting died on her lips when she saw the expression on my face and instead gave me a sympathetic smile. I tried to smile back, but it was probably more of a grimace and kept right on walking.

I'd just got into my room and flopped on the bed when my phone bleeped with notification of an incoming text message. I pulled it from my pocket and unlocked the screen, knowing before I looked it was from Becky.

"Hi hun. How u doin? How did u get on 2day? Luv u xx"

Getting any sort of message from my twin was normally guaranteed to put a smile on my face, but it only served to highlight how alone I was right now and a swell of desolation swept over me like waves crashing into a cliff face. My eyes start to prick with unshed tears and my throat constricted. Drawing on an inner strength I didn't know I had, I shook my head angrily. What the hell was I getting choked up about? If I was ready to collapse in a heap and go to pieces after one day, how could I ever expect to find Josh? Was I such a loser that I would give up at the end of the first rough day? **NO!** It was a shout in my mind. I had to keep strong. I knew it would be difficult when I'd set off from home, just as I knew I would feel lonely at times, but my determination returned in a flourish and my eyes dried without a single tear escaping. A proud smile swept briefly across my lips as I hit the 'Reply' button on the phone.

"Hiya. I'm ok a bit down & missin u. No luck 2day so gonna finish here in 2 days then move on. Don't worry abt me – I'm fine. Luv u 2 xx"

I hit the 'Send' button then waited for the reply I knew would arrive momentarily. I was not disappointed – the phone bleeped again.

"Try & keep yr chin up. I'm here if u need me. Miss u 2. Give mum a call – she's worried! Xx"

Again I pressed the 'Reply' icon.

"Ok, will call mum after I've eaten. Will txt u 2moro & let u know how I've got on. Xx"

I sent the message then placed the phone on the bedside table before heading for the shower; I was icky and my strappy top was sticking to my back.

I felt much better after stepping out of the cool shower; in fact I was suddenly ravenous. I glanced at my watch and saw the dining room would be open for dinner in 15 minutes. I got dressed and brushed my hair before heading downstairs. I still had a few minutes to wait and feeling a pang of guilt about not speaking to Pat when I returned, I decided to stop at Reception while I was waiting.

Pat was sitting at her desk when I approached the counter, so engrossed in paperwork she didn't realise I was there.

"Hi Pat," I called a small smile on my lips.

She raised her head and looked in my direction. When she saw I was smiling, she grinned back at me, got up from her chair and came over to the counter.

"Hello. Coming through?" she gestured towards the back, hopefully.

"If you're sure I'm not disturbing you …" I replied.

"No, of course you're not," she affirmed, lifting the counter for me to pass through. She replaced it and put her arm around my shoulders as she steered me towards her little lounge. "Tea or something a tad stronger?" she asked as we sat.

"Ooo, something stronger I think, please,"

Pat chuckled, opened a little fridge and pulled out a bottle of white wine. She placed it on the table, grabbed two glasses and filled them before speaking again.

"I'm reluctant to ask …" she began, but then hesitated. I didn't want her to feel uncomfortable so took the opportunity the pause afforded me.

"No luck so far, but I've still got a few on my list to try. Thank you so much by the way – the list and map were great. It must have taken you ages."

"You're welcome, dear. And no, it didn't take me that long really – it helps when you're a local," Pat grinned at her slightly flippant response, but then her expression turned more serious and her voice became softer as she continued.

"Are you okay, Remy?"

"Yeah. A bit foot-sore and weary, but apart from that I'm okay."

"Are you sure, dear?" she leaned forward and placed one of her hands on top of mine, giving it a small squeeze. Her voice echoed the concern in her eyes.

"Yeah." I said brightly, but continued when I saw the sceptical expression on Pat's face.

"I was feeling a bit down-hearted when I first got back here, but I've given myself a good talking to and I'm okay again now."

"Okay, if you're sure…" she didn't sound totally convinced, but after searching my face for a long moment, she appeared satisfied by what she saw, leaned back and changed the subject. "Are you eating in tonight?"

"Yes," I confirmed. "I'm starving. Must be all the exercise."

"Well, hubby is out tonight so how about joining me for dinner? I do *hate* eating alone and it's not often I have a chance for some 'girl' time, if you know what I mean?"

"Thank you. I'd love to," I replied simply, lifting the glass to my lips and taking a large mouthful.

"Wonderful," Pat exclaimed, a huge beam on her face. "Let's drink up and go through, shall we?"

I nodded, grinning back at her. I picked up my glass at exactly the same time as her; we swiftly drained the contents then arm in arm, walked through to the dining room.

* * *

After a delicious meal and two bottles of wine, Pat and I were giggling like a couple of teenagers. We were the only ones left and the last remaining waitress looked totally bored and rather fed up. I guess all she wanted to do was go home, but didn't dare while the boss was there. I pointed her out to Pat, who, after checking her watch, apologetically sent her home.

I didn't realise how late it was until then; I'd planned on phoning Mum then having a reasonably early night, so I was shocked to discover it was almost one o'clock. Strange, but I didn't feel in the least bit tired. Or I didn't think I did. I was enjoying an alcohol-induced euphoria; I had wings on my heels and I felt as light as a feather floating along on a soft summer breeze.

The conversation was still in full flow, the wine having loosened both our tongues, but I couldn't be positive it was making any kind of sense. Just the thought we were probably babbling nonsense sent me into a paroxysm of giggles and I found myself doubled up with tears pooling around my lashes. Pat didn't have a clue what I was in stitches about, but one glance at me and she was in the exact same state. We laughed until we were both panting, trying to catch our breath, and our stomachs' hurt. Slowly our breathing returned to normal and we sat there with stupid smirks on our faces. I checked the wine bottles on the table and found they were both empty. My glass was half empty and Pat's only had about a mouthful left. She saw me check them and slurred,

"D'ya wanna open 'nuther one?"

I shook my head. "Nah. Think I need t'go bed."

"Think I do too," she chuckled, her eyes somewhat unfocussed.

I drained my glass and carefully returned it to the table, using both hands to steady it. She made a grab for her wine and only succeeded in knocking her glass over. She chuckled again as she watched the contents puddle onto the tablecloth.

"Oooops. I made a mesh!" she exclaimed between giggles.

"C'mon, bedtime, yeah?" I asked trying to push myself to my feet, using the table for support.

"Yesh pleeease," she replied trying to copy me, but only managing in lifting her behind a few inches off the seat before collapsing back into it, which resulted in another fit of giggles.

Using the table for balance, I swerved around it and dragging her arm around my shoulder, I managed to get her to her feet. We linked arms and weaved through the dining room to the exit. Once into the reception area we hugged and said goodnight – Pat headed in one direction and I headed towards the stairs.

I grabbed the banister rail and looked upwards; the stairs were comparable to a small mountain and instead of steps there appeared to be a smooth slide. I put one foot on the first tread and as I proceeded to move my weight onto it, my foot slid off and I ended up on the floor. I sniggered, before deciding it would probably be safer and more productive to crawl up, so on hands and knees I negotiated the stairs and eventually made it to my floor.

I edged a short way along the hall before getting to my feet, using door handles and the dado rail which ran the length of the wall. I snaked along the corridor, ricocheting off first one wall then another until I finally reached the door to my room. I pulled the key out of my pocket and promptly dropped it on the floor; as I bent down to retrieve it I overbalanced and ended up in a heap. Chuckles escaped unbidden and, despite my drunkenness I must have somehow realised there were people asleep nearby, so I put one finger against my lips and made a shushing sound.

I picked up the key and rolling onto my knees facing the door, I tried to insert it in the lock. I was seeing double and missed it, again the key slipped from my grasp. I slapped my hand over my mouth to stifle the laughter which threatened to erupt; with the other hand I reached for the key. My third attempt was as successful as my first two had been and once more the key ended up on the carpet, causing the exact same reaction. I changed my tactics. Having recovered the offending article, I gripped it tightly in my right hand and using my left, I located the keyhole and kept my fingers beside it to use as a guide. I slipped the key into the lock and gained entry. Success!

I shuffled over to the bed on my knees, after closing the door behind me and pulled myself into a standing position. I suddenly felt giddy, lost my already precarious balance and flopped onto the bed. Another chuckle burst forth; I manoeuvred the rest of my body onto the mattress and gazed up at the ceiling. As if caught in a vortex the room spun and queasiness assaulted my stomach. I shut my eyes firmly and concentrated as best I could on breathing slowly and deeply until the nausea passed; the bed was floating on soft rippling waves and spinning with the current, but too gently to have an adverse effect on my stomach contents. My breathing slowed further and fully clothed on top of the bed, I fell into a deep slumber.

I was standing in front of a window looking into an unfamiliar room; I could vaguely see my reflection bounce back at me, but could also look into the room and see everything clearly.

Joshua occupied an old yet comfortable looking chair, surrounded by books. His skin was very pallid yet his eyes sparkled, at odds with his complexion. He sat motionless, reading an ancient tome, yet the pages turned so rapidly it was as if someone was fanning the leaves of the book, but no one else was in the room with him. I wanted to explore the room further, but I couldn't drag my eyes away from Joshua's face. In my eyes he'd always been handsome, but now he was so breathtakingly beautiful – as one would imagine an angel to be – that I was completely captivated.

At first I didn't notice anyone else had entered the room, not until Joshua looked up and smiled. I reluctantly tore my eyes away from him, curiosity getting the better of me, and was surprised to see five other ashen-skinned, beautiful people join him; two men and three women. One of the women hovered very close to Joshua, a look of longing in her eyes. It was blatantly obvious this extremely attractive woman was head-over-heels in love with him. He didn't seem to notice; this made me irrationally, spitefully delighted.

There was a conversation or two going on as I could see lips moving, but all I could hear was a peculiar burbling noise. I found it frustrating. It was akin to watching a silent movie without the subtitles. I tried to move closer, but the glass prevented it. I turned my head and pressed my ear against the surface, but was still unable to ascertain what was being said.

The light in the room was dimming, gradually at first then it sped up. I was able to see through the windows on the other side of the room and out to the garden where the shrubbery was more black than green in the twilight. Joshua stood. Placing the book on his seat, he turned and sauntered over to join the younger of the two men and his incredibly beautiful girlfriend (they were holding hands so it was easy to make that connection); the woman who was hovering beside Joshua's chair joined the trio. I was only dimly aware of that fact; I was now mesmerised by the way Joshua moved. He didn't appear to walk so much as glide. It appeared graceful and effortless, but strange nonetheless. They were now split into two distinct groups.

The older man opened the door and they all filed into a large hallway with a stunning marble floor. I failed to understand how without moving, I could now see this hallway as clearly as I'd been able to see the library. It was a peculiar sensation and not an altogether pleasant one. The two parties approached the large, heavy wooden door and again the older man opened it. His lips moved, but I didn't hear a sound. Perhaps I'd gone deaf. The next occurrence had me questioning my sanity, as all six of them vanished right before my eyes. One minute they were standing by the open door, and the next, the door was shut and there was no sign of anyone. The hall was completely deserted.

Had I imagined them? No, I *couldn't* have. Could I? I felt an ache in my chest – Joshua was gone once more. Before I had a chance to dwell on this, the light got rapidly brighter as the scene in front of my eyes dissipated like mist burnt off by the hot morning sun. My eyelids fluttered open to greet the new day.

I lay there unmoving for a few minutes as my eyes adjusted to the bright light streaming through the window. In my drunken state, I'd forgotten to close the curtains. I moved slowly to a sitting position before glancing at my watch - it was 9am. I noticed I was still fully dressed and uttered an expletive under my breath; *I must have been totally shitfaced last night to not even get undressed*, I thought.

I arose from the bed and stripped, leaving my clothes in a heap on the floor, and walked into the bathroom. I turned the shower on and waited for the water to reach the correct temperature before stepping into the cubicle. As I washed my hair and body, I analysed how I felt – as usual, there was not the slightest inkling of a hangover despite the copious amount of alcohol I'd consumed – I felt fine in myself, but as I recalled the dream, I was a little troubled. It was too real to be a dream yet it obviously was – I hadn't moved off the bed all night as far as I knew – and Joshua would have seen me if I'd really been there. It was a strange sensation, particularly as I could remember every minute detail; it was as if I'd watched the entire thing on DVD.

I turned off the shower, stepped out of the cubicle and dried myself rapidly with the huge fluffy towel provided. As I dressed, I wondered how Pat was faring; I was actually quite refreshed and optimistic. I grabbed my key and locking the door behind me, made my way downstairs.

As I walked over to the counter in reception, I could see Pat sitting at her desk, head in hands and wearing dark glasses; I could smell the strong coffee in the mug in front of her. I tried unsuccessfully to suppress the grin spreading across my face as I called out, "Morning, Pat. How are you?"

She slowly turned her head in my direction and grimaced, raising one finger to her lips.

"Ssshhhhhh! Not so loud please" she whispered.

I chuckled and she gave me a dirty look; the sort of look which says *I hate you. I'm jealous. Why the hell aren't you suffering as much as me?*

"Want to join me for breakfast?" I asked, in a much softer volume than before.

"Ugh. Not sure if I could keep it down to be honest. I'm feeling rather nauseous and my head has one hundred big burly men marching while banging huge bass drums in it."

"Oh dear," I responded trying to sound sympathetic and not smug. "That's not good. I'm sure you'll feel better with a full English inside you. Everyone I know says that's the best cure for a hangover."

"Yeah? Maybe you're right. I guess it's worth a try. I don't think anything can make me feel much worse right now. Okay then, give me a minute?"

"Sure. Do you want me to get the waitress to put a bucket beside your chair?" I asked flippantly with a huge smirk on my face.

Pat didn't dignify that with a response other than to poke her tongue out at me. She lifted the mug of coffee to her lips and drained it before very gradually easing herself into an upright position. She made sluggish progress as she shuffled across to the counter; I lifted it for her to pass through, but as I went to replace it, the heavy wood slipped out of my hand about six inches from the bottom and crashed loudly as it found the end stop. The sound reverberated, making me jump and Pat grabbed her head in both hands and moaned loudly. Before she had a chance to remonstrate with me, I quickly apologised.

"Ooops, sorry Pat. It was an accident. It slipped. I didn't do it on purpose," the sincerity in my voice must have appeased her and she nodded. She continued in to the dining room with me bringing up the rear.

By the time we'd finished eating, Pat was feeling a little better. The nausea had passed and the headache was not quite so severe. As we'd sat there, I surveyed the room looking for traces of last night's debris, but found nothing. The early morning staff had obviously cleared away the evidence prior to opening the room for breakfast. I vaguely wondered what they had thought when they saw it, not that I really cared. My musing was interrupted by Pat's voice, which sounded a tad stronger now.

"So, what's the plan for today then?"

"Same as yesterday. I've still got about another ten on my list that I didn't get to," I replied evenly.

"Okay. Well good luck. I really hope you get better results today," her sincerity was touching and I smiled gently at her.

"Thanks, Pat. I'd better get cracking and I'm sure you've got things to do as well." I grabbed the key from the table and held it in my hand.

Pat got up from the table and I followed suit. "I sure have, and now I feel a bit more human, there's a reasonable chance I might actually achieve something" she chuckled as we walked out into reception together. She wrapped her arms around me gave me a huge motherly hug, whispering, "See you later then?"

"Yep. I'll come see you when I get back" I affirmed as we broke apart and we went our separate ways.

I ran up the stairs, trying not to recall the embarrassing ascent of the previous night (well earlier this morning to be exact) and entered my room with much less difficulty. I groaned softly at the vague recollection of trying to gain access in my inebriated condition. I grabbed my mobile phone and made a quick call to my mum. As Becky had warned me, mum was worried, but I managed to reassure her I was fine and would call her regularly. By the time we ended the call with the normal "I love you's" and "take care", she was much calmer.

I went to replace the phone on the bedside table when I noticed some writing on the pad it had been lying on. On the paper were three words written in a familiar script;

I'm sorry, Rems.

Positive the paper was blank before, I ran a fingertip over the words half expecting them to disappear. Instead the ink smudged slightly as if it had only just been written. My heart began to race. Had Joshua been here? Did this prove he was in the area? I hurriedly grabbed my small knapsack, ensuring I had everything and dashed out of the hotel very hopeful and positive.

Chapter 19 – Joshua

The vampires arrived back at the manor house shortly before dawn. They congregated in a tastefully furnished and sympathetically decorated large sitting room and chatted for a short while before drifting off to their rooms. As usual Samir was the last to leave and make his way upstairs.

Joshua lay on his bed, countless thoughts swirling around his head. He listened carefully for any sounds in the house and heard when Samir finally entered his room and shut the door behind him. He continued to pay attention to any unusual or unexpected sounds, while he examined the ideas which flooded his head. His little experiment the previous day was still uppermost in his mind and he still couldn't decide whether Samir knew or was deliberately withholding information. He didn't want to think badly of Samir, but the not knowing was even worse. He resolved to try and broach the subject with him later.

Having made the decision, Joshua now had another one to make. His naturally curious nature was driving him to experiment further. The big question was inevitable – would he survive if he went out into the sun and, perhaps more to the point, was he prepared to pay the ultimate price? He wasn't a coward by any stretch of the imagination, nor was he overly cautious, yet there was a great deal at stake here. Was he prepared to take the chance?

He re-examined how he had carried out his experiment previously and concluded that, as long as he progressed *very* slowly, he should be able to control the situation and take appropriate evasive action should it prove necessary. So now he needed to consider the details of his plan; he had to ensure nothing was overlooked and he was adequately prepared for any eventuality before attempting what could be construed as a suicide attempt.

Joshua spent the next hour planning and scrutinizing every detail. He chuckled at the realisation that if things didn't quite turn out as he expected, he could move at such a phenomenal speed, he could probably return to the dark shelter of the house before any major damage could be sustained. That thought alone made him more confident about the whole event.

He still hadn't heard anything unusual; confident the rest of his coven was completely settled down for the day, he felt it was safe to proceed. Soundlessly opening his door, he slipped out and glided along the corridor and down the stairs, his feet barely seeming to make contact with the floor, so noiseless was his movement. He reached the foyer and paused, remembering his first day when Samir had given him the tour of the property then recalling where the kitchen was located, he continued in that direction. As luck would have it, the kitchen was at the opposite end of the house to Samir's room; Joshua decided this was a good omen.

He reached the kitchen and proceeded silently through to what had once been a huge larder. Off to one side was a door which led to the garden. On closer inspection, it appeared the door had not been opened for many years and Joshua wondered if the hinges would be so rusty as to alert the occupants upstairs. He decided to take a chance and after unlocking the door (the key turned smoothly, much to his surprise), he turned the handle and inched the door very slightly open. The hinges, like the lock, had obviously been well maintained and the action was silent.

There was a little porch over the door which created some shade as the door opened. This was a bonus Joshua had not been expecting; he'd thought the sun would come streaming through as soon as the door opened. His confidence level increased a notch and he stepped through the door, remaining in the shade for the moment. The weather was a repeat of the previous day; the sky an azure blue with no clouds marring it and the sun beat down, bleaching the grass yellow.

He felt composed as he gradually and gingerly extended his hand into the light. First his fingertips were exposed, and when nothing untoward happened, he reached his whole hand forward. Still nothing happened. Feeling more confident, he decided to throw caution to the wind and took a huge step forward until he was completely immersed in the sun's rays. Although he was ready to jump back into the shade, it was completely unnecessary. At first he stood motionless, allowing the sun to caress his skin unhindered, but Joshua decided to push the boundaries even further and started to stroll backwards and forwards over the same patch of ground, never allowing too much distance between himself and the open door. There was no difference. He didn't even smoulder let alone burst into an inferno on legs. He slowly and deliberately let his eyes roam over his body, twisting and contorting to try and observe as much as he could, to see if there was the slightest cause for concern (as he didn't feel any different). He was elated to discover he and his clothing were completely unblemished.

At that precise moment he wanted to whoop and holler, to celebrate this new facet of his life, this new freedom of not having to be confined to a dark room all day every day, but he resisted the temptation. He needed time to think this through before he discussed it with Samir, so he decided it was wiser to keep quiet. What was he to do with his newfound freedom? He surveyed the landscape before him, there was much to see and explore, so he decided to do just that – explore.

He began to wander around the grounds, which were quite vast, admiring the landscaping. Someone had obviously put a lot of thought into the design and layout of these grounds and the result was a stunning cornucopia of colours, shapes and themed areas. He strolled over to an area which had been given a Far Eastern theme; it was beautifully laid out with Japanese Maples as the backdrop to an exquisite 'Jade Mountain' Teahouse. The burgundy roof had upswept corners; there were traditional railings and an external veranda leading to an 'Arashiyama' style bridge over a small man-made body of water. The area was populated with bamboo, acers and gingko biloba trees, chrysanthemums, azaleas and a wonderful display of a variety of bonsai trees. There were small and medium size statues of pagodas, Buddhas sitting on lotus leaves and some three-legged lanterns. It was breathtakingly beautiful and very restful.

He didn't know how long he stood there admiring the scene, drinking in the magnificence, but when he finally tore his eyes away, he noticed the sun had changed position in the sky. He glanced at his watch and saw it was mid-afternoon. He would have to pay closer attention to the passing of time if his secret was to remain undiscovered. He ambled away and began a slow meander through the gardens heading back towards the house. He passed an Indian themed area with a boundary wall, geometric layout and a crossing pattern of miniature canals, an herb garden with aromatic plants grouped into small beds, a rose garden containing blooms of different heights and colours and an area with trellises supporting climbing plants; wisteria, clematis and jasmine.

By the time he got back to the house it was nearly 5pm. Joshua silently closed the door behind him and locked it, before making his way back to his room. Once inside, he changed his clothes and without trying to keep his movements secret, went down to the library, sat in his normal seat and picked up the book he'd left on the small table beside it. He was too preoccupied with the day's events to actually read, but wanted to keep up appearances. As the day had progressed, Joshua had given a great deal of thought about what he should do and had finally decided he *would* discuss it with Samir, but he wanted to keep it to himself a little longer, just a day or two. He relished the idea of having a secret. He sat and patiently waited for his coven to arrive.

Chapter 20 – Remy

It took me about half an hour to walk to the first hotel on my list; I didn't rush to get there, but I didn't dawdle either. I walked into the entrance and approached the counter where a middle-aged man was taking a booking over the phone and writing it in a large book. He glanced up when he heard my footsteps and nodded in acknowledgement of my presence. While I waited patiently for him to finish, I looked around the small foyer. Compared with Amble-Rose, this was small and shabby, it wasn't as clean either; I could see surfaces where the dust was much more than a day or two old and there were a few cobwebs at ceiling level and around light fittings. A small shiver of disgust ran down my spine – I was so glad I wasn't staying here.

Finally the man ended his call and replaced the receiver. I turned to face him and smiled tentatively. Although he returned the smile, it didn't reach his eyes; he made me feel uncomfortable and I wanted to leave as soon as possible, but I was here for a reason so I took a deep breath before breaking the silence.

"Hello. I wonder if you could help me?"

"What do you want?" he responded, and not in a particularly friendly tone.

I pulled the photo of Joshua out from between the papers in my hand and turned it around so he could view it.

"Have you seen this man at all?" I enquired then held my breath while I waited for him to respond.

He barely glanced at the picture before shaking his head. "No."

His attitude was beginning to upset me. If he treated his guests in this manner, he wouldn't be in business for very long.

"Please look again," I pleaded, emotion entering my voice for the first time. "Are you sure you've not seen him?"

He searched my face for a long minute then turned his eyes back to the photo. Something in my voice must have touched him, even if only slightly, and he took a longer look. Again he shook his head before responding, "No. I've not seen him," he said gruffly then to my surprise he continued in a softer tone, "sorry."

I returned the picture to the other papers in my hand.

"Thank you anyway. Sorry to have troubled you" I replied sadly and I turned to the exit and rapidly walked out. The man didn't say a word, but I could feel his eyes boring into my back. It gave me the creeps. My pulse was racing and I was holding my breath as I put some distance between that horrible man and myself and it wasn't until I was halfway down the street, the trip hammer that was my heart started to return to its usual rhythm and I could breathe normally. I paused by a wall and leaned against it; holding my breath for so long had made me a little woozy.

After a few minutes I was more myself again. I checked my list and the map then headed for the next one down. It was around the corner from my current location and it would only take a couple of minutes to get there, so I set off at a reasonable pace.

As I approached, I scrutinised the exterior of the building, still feeling the vestiges of discomfort from my last experience. This place looked better kept and had obviously been decorated quite recently, which gave me more confidence. I walked up the path and through the open door into a homely-looking reception area. There was nobody in attendance so I rang the bell, examining the interior while I waited. The chairs were covered in floral chintz with curtains to match, there were decorative plates almost obscuring one entire wall and a collection of vases lined the mantelshelf.

By the time I'd absorbed the surroundings, footsteps alerted me to someone's approach. I turned back to the desk as a middle-aged woman entered through a rear door. She walked up to the counter and smiled welcomingly.

"Hello. How can I help you?" her voice was surprisingly jolly and loud.

I smiled in response and pulled the photo out again, handing it to her.

"I'm sorry to trouble you, but have you seen this man?"

She looked closely at the picture for a couple of minutes before answering, her voice more gentle and the volume moderated.

"I'm sorry, but I'm sure I've never seen this young man. Is he your sweetheart?"

"Y-yes," I stammered, her question catching me unawares.

She glanced at the photo of Joshua once more before handing it back to me.

"He's a good looking fellah that's for sure. If I do see him, how can I get in contact with you?"

I grabbed a pen and a post-it note from the desk and wrote down my name and mobile number then passed it to her.

"Thank you very much for your help."

"No problem. I hope you find him," she replied kindly.

"Thanks – so do I," a sad look passed over my face, as I turned and walked away. "So do I," I repeated under my breath. I glanced back and gave her a small smile before exiting onto the street.

I walked along the pavement feeling a little dejected. I knew this wasn't going to be easy and maybe it was a bit naïve of me to think the first area I searched would bring the results I prayed for, but I had to cling to the hope that I *would* find Joshua. I berated myself mentally (again) and took a deep breath before making my way to the third establishment on my ever- dwindling list.

As the day's events unfolded, it was the same story everywhere I went, negative response after negative response. By the time I returned to Amble-Rose, my mood had deteriorated significantly. I had gone from being a little sad to downright miserable. The mental scolding I'd given myself earlier hadn't lasted the distance, so as well as despondency I was also rather annoyed I was allowing my lack of good fortune in this one location affect me so much.

I walked into reception and, as promised, stopped to tell Pat how I'd fared. I tried really hard to cover my depression by smiling a lot and sounding positive, but I was pretty sure she saw through the façade I was creating, if the expression in her eyes was a good indicator.

"So what's your next move?" Pat enquired.

"Well, I'll be checking out neighbouring towns tomorrow then the following day I'll be driving to the Peak District and starting again there." I responded, still trying to inject some enthusiasm into my voice.

"I'll be sorry to see you leave, Remy – I've grown very fond of you," her voice was as sad as her eyes.

"Likewise. But I have to do this, Pat, I *have* to find Josh." I blurted out earnestly, my voice breaking with emotion as I said Joshua's name.

Pat came out from behind the counter, put her arm around my shoulders and squeezed me to her.

"I know you do dear and I can see what this is costing you, emotionally." At that moment she sounded like mum (apart from the accent, of course) – warm, loving, caring – and I instinctively threw my arms around her and hugged her tight. No words were necessary.

We stood for a couple of minutes before slowly moving apart. I grabbed one of her hands and gave it a gentle squeeze.

"Thank you," I whispered then walked to the stairs without looking back.

* * *

I ate a solitary meal. I wasn't being unsociable; I needed to get my head straight without interruption or interference. Pat was a fantastic companion, she was warm, funny, caring and sincere and I had gotten really quite close to her in a relatively short space of time and there lay part of the problem – it was going to be hard enough to move on the day after tomorrow as it was. I was reasonably sure I wouldn't form the same level of attachment anywhere else on my travels so I had to adjust to being alone again.

After last night's frivolity, tonight was very sober by comparison. Talk about chalk and cheese. I sat there and thought about the last couple of days; was it pure fluke I'd chosen to start at the Lake District, or fate? The fact I'd found Joshua's pen on my way up here was, to me, a sign I was on the right track. Bearing in mind how raw everything still was, how much I was still hurting inside, how much effort it took not to shut myself away from the world and wallow in my misery, I really couldn't have picked a better place to start my search. Pat was so supportive, kind and motherly without being overprotective. She'd helped take my mind off my troubles for whole periods of time and as she wasn't emotionally involved, she brought a new perspective to the situation. I was so incredibly grateful to her and it was probably exactly what I needed.

What were the chances of finding another Pat Kirk on my travels? *The odds must be a hundred to one at least*, I thought. One thing I did know for sure – the friendship Pat and I had built over the last few days was the lasting kind. I would make sure I kept in contact with her and come to visit when I was able. Perhaps she'd enjoy coming south to visit me sometime.

Draining the last of the wine in my glass I wandered up to my room to finish packing. As I hadn't fully unpacked when I arrived, there wasn't much to do. I thought about the dirty washing lying at the bottom of my wardrobe; I would have to find a launderette at my next destination or I would rapidly run out of clean underwear. Unlocking the door, I walked in the room and stopped dead in my tracks, gasping in surprise; lying on my bed was a pile of clothes which had obviously been washed and ironed. I was sure I recognised some of the items as being in the bottom of the wardrobe, so I walked over and opened the door. To my astonishment, the only things there were a couple of pairs of sandals – all the dirty clothes were gone.

Stunned, I turned back to the bed and looked through the pile of fresh laundry. Sure enough, they were the items which had previously been worn. There was a little note on the top. It read,

Dear Remy,

I hope you won't be offended but I've done your washing and ironing for you. You have more important things to do at the moment than spend valuable time in a launderette. I know you will have to eventually, but hopefully this will help you a little.

I really do wish you the best of luck and hope with all my heart you get the result you want, and you find that lovely man of yours. If there's anything I can do to help, please let me know – even if it's just as a shoulder to cry on.

Keep in touch!

Love Pat xx

I was absolutely speechless and moisture sprang to my eyes. I blinked quickly several times; I didn't want to start crying. *What a kind and thoughtful thing to do*, I thought, *but that was Pat all over.* How on earth could I thank her? I would have to give it some serious consideration.

I completed my packing much quicker thanks to Pat's thoughtfulness and was left with about an hour of spare time on my hands. I briefly considered returning to the bar and having a drink, but discounted that on the grounds I would be driving tomorrow and wanted to make sure I was legal. I got ready for bed, laid down and switched on the TV. I flicked through the channels until I found something reasonable – a re-run of Casualty I'd missed – and settled down to enjoy it. When it ended, I turned off the TV and bedside lamp and settled down for the night, quickly falling into a dreamless sleep.

Chapter 21 – Joshua

It was nearly dusk and the coven was assembled in the library, preparing to disperse on their nightly hunting expedition; Joshua was again venturing out with Farrell, Erika and Jasna. Just as they were about to leave, Samir announced he would not be going out for quite a while and suggested Dayna accompany Farrell and the others. Dayna visibly bristled at the idea, stating she would prefer to hunt alone. Joshua could see the relieved expressions on the faces of his party and tried to hide the smirk which crossed his face. If Dayna noticed the looks on any of their faces, she didn't react to it; she looked as sour as she always did, except when talking to Samir.

Farrell took the opportunity to make good his escape and Erika, Jasna and Joshua followed tight on his heels. When they reached the end of the property line about two seconds later, Farrell paused.

"Okay guys and girls, where do you want to go tonight? The usual or somewhere different?"

Joshua spoke up quickly, "How about somewhere new for a change?" an excited edge to his voice.

Farrell looked at the two girls for their opinion.

"Sounds good to me," Jasna replied, matching Joshua's tone.

"Fine by me," Erika agreed, nodding.

"Okay then. Let's go," Farrell grinned and they set off in the opposite direction to normal.

As they ran, or perhaps flew would be a better description, Joshua started thinking once again about being out in the sun earlier. The elation was a heady sensation and he had to admit he liked it. At the same time, despite having made his decision to discuss it with Samir, he was still confused as to whether he was being lied to or not. The two emotions were at odds with each other and his inner turmoil was driving him crazy. His preoccupation did not go unnoticed. Perhaps he'd forgotten that Erika was an empath; she was quick to perceive his distraction and troubled to feel his emotions.

The mixture of feelings which surrounded Joshua puzzled Erika and it worried her. Should she talk to him about it? She couldn't ignore it; she couldn't pretend she didn't feel this turmoil evidently tormenting him. She thought about it some more as they ran, concentrating on Joshua's feelings in case anything changed, or got worse. Should she tell Samir? Perhaps not. After all, technically it was none of her business and she didn't want to put Joshua in an untenable position. She *could* discuss it with Farrell – he would know the best thing to do. She would wait until they were alone – she didn't want anyone to overhear and draw the wrong conclusion. With her decision made, Erika felt much better about the situation, although she did continue to monitor Joshua's mood.

It didn't take long for the hunting party to reach their destination and split up into pairs, Erika with Farrell and Jasna with Joshua.

As Jasna and Joshua prowled around the small town looking for prospective candidates, he began to take more notice of her. He hadn't realised before, but she was really pretty and her eyes were lovely and soft. He'd already discovered she was a caring person and he genuinely liked her. Jasna felt rather than saw Joshua appraising her; she turned to glance at his face and was startled to see him staring back at her. She lowered her eyes immediately less he saw the naked adoration shining from them, hoping she'd managed to conceal it before he noticed. She wasn't quick enough and Joshua was astounded and a little flattered to discover she had feelings for him.

They continued skulking in the shadows until they came across two lone drunks staggering out of a local pub. Joshua and Jasna froze in the shadows and waited to see which direction they would take before following them. The unsuspecting prey conveniently wobbled and snaked their way down an unlit pathway; the predators closed in on them and pounced as soon as they were far enough from the road.

When they'd satiated themselves, Joshua and Jasna picked up the drained bodies now as light as feather pillows and ran for about two miles across the fields, finally disposing of them in a ditch. They decided to start back to meet up with Farrell and Erika and loped carefree and happily back across the fields. As they ran, Joshua kept surreptitiously glancing at Jasna, admiring her gracefulness and began to notice an attraction to her. He found himself unconsciously moving closer to her as they travelled; he enjoyed the proximity of her. He inhaled her scent – something he'd never bothered to do before – and discovered he liked the perfume which exuded from every pore.

The attraction was growing imperceptibly minute-by-minute and although Joshua was a little intoxicated by this new development, a part of him felt he was being unfaithful to Remy. He still loved her wholeheartedly and missed her – when he allowed himself to think of her at all, which wasn't often as it hurt too much – but hadn't he opted to leave his human life behind him and embrace his immortality?

Joshua glanced at Jasna at the exact same time she decided to look at him; their eyes met and held for a second or two before they both looked away again. Jasna was thrilled Joshua was noticing her at last; this whole unrequited love thing was painful although most of the time she tried hard to be her normal cheerful self. She couldn't help the surge of hope and anticipation which coursed through her entire body. Could she really be that lucky? It was too early to tell. She knew she mustn't get carried away; yeah she could keep hoping, but she had to keep herself reigned in. The disappointment and hurt of things not working out as she prayed they would, well it would be too much to cope with. She didn't have the self-confidence the others possessed; she didn't even think she was pretty and certainly not pretty enough for a god-like creature such as Joshua. She had to concentrate on being herself and wait to see what, if anything transpired.

They were now back in the town and instead of running, they were creeping along in the shadows trying to be invisible to any humans who might still be using the streets. They didn't come across anyone, nor did they really expect to bearing in mind the time, but they remained vigilant. Soon Jasna and Joshua reached the outskirts of town and were able to stretch their legs once more. It only took them a few seconds to reach the pre-arranged meeting spot and were surprised to note they had arrived first.

Joshua was feeling carefree and playful; this was even more at odds with the multitude of different thoughts and emotions flowing through his body. There was a clump of trees nearby and Joshua decided he wanted to play monkey. Without saying anything to Jasna, he grinned hugely and ran over to the trees, leaping up the trunk and scrambling through the branches until he reached the very top. He looked down at Jasna. She was gazing up at him and laughing at his antics. He started laughing too, before he disappeared into the foliage for a couple of seconds, only to re-emerge at the top of another tree. He laughed again and was pleased when Jasna laughed delightedly at his silly game. He beckoned for her to join him; she didn't hesitate and was by his side in the time it takes a human to blink. They decided they would play a trick on Farrell and Erika, letting them believe they had arrived first and then jump out at them. Jasna and Joshua knew they were being childish, but it was *fun*. They sat in the top of the tree listening intently for Farrell and Erika's approach, ducking down into the foliage when they heard them coming.

Erika and Farrell advanced into the field holding hands and slowed to a walk. They looked around and seeing no one there, embraced and began to kiss passionately. Jasna and Joshua watched from their hiding place, at first, but began to feel like voyeurs intruding on their friend's private moment, and turned their eyes away. A twig caught in Jasna's hair and as she reached to free it, a quiet rustling noise broke the silence.

Farrell pulled away from Erika and searched the area, sweeping his head from side to side, listening intently. He saw and heard nothing, but was still wary. He grabbed Erika's hand, pulled her behind his body to protect her and slowly moved toward the trees where Jasna and Joshua were concealed. He moved as a predator stalking his prey – ready to spring at a moment's notice – Erika mimicked his stance as she prowled behind him. Joshua and Jasna stared at the scene unfolding before them, smirking. They were trying very hard not to burst out laughing and give their position away, but it was becoming increasingly difficult. Farrell stopped directly below where Joshua and Jasna were hiding, still listening intently and continuing to explore his surroundings. His instincts were screaming that someone or something was nearby and he was prepared to defend Erika and himself, to the death if necessary.

At that moment, Joshua nodded to Jasna and they dropped out of the tree and straight onto Farrell's back. The three of them collapsed in a heap and Erika leapt back in surprise. Joshua and Jasna started howling with uncontrolled laughter while Farrell was still entangled beneath them. Once Erika realised who it was, she joined in the hilarity. Farrell pushed Joshua & Jasna off and sat up, rubbing his head as if he were hurt.

"I'll get you both back for that," Farrell chuckled with mock sternness.

"Bring it on, bro," Joshua responded, his eyes shining with devilment. Jasna nodded in agreement by his side, smirking.

"Oh, I will, I *will*. And when you're least expecting it," Farrell shot back.

Erika glanced at the dainty watch on her left wrist – it was time they made tracks back to the manor – besides she still wanted to discuss Joshua's emotional state with Farrell and she couldn't do it in front of him.

"C'mon, you lot. We need to head back," Erika announced. She waited semi-patiently while they picked themselves off the floor; ten seconds later the four of them were bolting through the countryside heading home.

The four of them were the first ones back to the manor; on arrival they headed straight for the library only to find it empty. Much to Jasna and Joshua's surprise, Erika and Farrell made their excuses and disappeared off to their room immediately. Joshua didn't want to go to his room yet so he slouched in his favourite chair; Jasna was overjoyed to have Joshua all to herself, even if it was only for a short while, and decided to make the most of this unusual development. It was the ideal time for her to get to know him a bit better and, she hoped, vice versa.

Jasna lounged on the small settee, tucking her legs on to the seat beside her and positioned herself so she was facing him. He was quite happy to have some company and they chatted comfortably, like old friends, laughing and joking at times, more serious at others. As he got to know her a bit better, Joshua found himself liking this somewhat shy girl more than ever. She had such a sweet nature and was what his mother would refer to as a 'gentle soul' – very open, loving, sincere and giving, but easily hurt. He began to feel protective towards her and the earlier attraction grew in leaps and bounds.

An hour passed before Joshua and Jasna heard another of their coven return; they didn't pay much attention and carried on their conversation as before. Abruptly the door was flung open as Dayna made her entrance; one glance at the cosy scene before her and an evil grin crossed her face.

"What are you making doe eyes at him again for?" Dayna sneered, placing her tiny hands on her hips.

"P-p-pardon?" Jasna stuttered in surprise and a look of confusion marred her gentle features.

"P-p-pardon?" mocked Dayna derisively. "I said, what are you making doe eyes at him again for?"

"I-I'm not. We're only talking – what's wrong with that?" Jasna replied, her voice small, her expression wary.

"Yes you were. Do you really think an ugly fat cow like you would stand a chance with someone like him? Just look at yourself. What on earth would he find attractive about you? He probably wouldn't fancy you if you were the last immortal female left on the planet!" the contemptuous tone in Dayna's voice was shards of glass piercing Jasna's heart.

Before Joshua had a chance to defend her, Jasna's face crumpled in agony and she fled from the room, Dayna's mocking laughter following behind her.

"What the hell was that?" Joshua growled furiously, getting out of his chair to tower over Jasna's nemesis, continuing before Dayna had a chance to respond. "You stinking bitch! Why did you do that to her?"

"What's it to you?" Dayna retorted, unrepentant, staring up at Joshua's enraged face.

"She's part of this coven, a friend and she did nothing to deserve being treated like that," he bellowed, shaking with anger.

"Well it livened the night up a bit, don't you think? A few minutes entertainment to relieve the boredom," a smug smile crossed Dayna's lips at her flippant response – a smile which rapidly faded when Joshua took a measured step towards her, his fists clenched so tightly she thought his knuckles would break through the skin.

"Never before in either my human life or this one, have I *ever* considered any form of violence against a woman – until now. It's taking every ounce of willpower I possess to keep my hands from ripping you to pieces," Joshua yelled, leaning down so he was right in Dayna's face, his eyes boring into hers until she looked away.

Dayna's bravado began to slip a little as she realised that perhaps she might have pushed her luck a tad too far. Would he lose control and attack her? She couldn't be sure and her self-preservation instincts told her maybe it was time to beat a hasty retreat. She shrugged her shoulders nonchalantly, and turned to leave the room, deciding it was probably wise to refrain from making any further comments at this juncture.

As she took her first couple of slow steps towards the door, Joshua spoke again.

"Dayna!" the menacing tone in Joshua's voice made her turn around to face him, the tension in her body evident as she poised to flee. Joshua continued in the exact same tone, "I warn you now, if I ever hear you talk to Jasna like that again, or if I hear from any of the others you have humiliated her, I *will* end you," he was glorious in his fury; his eyes narrowed, lips curled back over his teeth, and his strong chin jutting forward. "Do. You. Understand?"

For the first time since becoming immortal, Dayna felt a frisson of fear worm its way down her spine. Not quite as controlled as normal, she didn't trust her voice to remain steady, so she merely nodded then turned back towards the door. As she looked up she saw Samir standing by the threshold, a grim expression on his face, and she staggered two steps back into the room in horror.

Joshua made the most of Samir's unexpected yet timely arrival. He strode to the door and, brushing past Dayna, he said in a slightly calmer voice, "I'll leave *you* to explain this to Samir."

Dayna blanched at Joshua's words and watched him as he left her to face Samir alone.

Joshua ran from room to room on the ground floor searching for Jasna, but to his disappointment every room was empty. He extended his search to the first floor, looking in all the guest rooms then proceeded to the second floor where all their rooms were situated. He reached Jasna's room and rapped his knuckles on the door. His efforts were met with silence. With his heightened senses he didn't need to put his ear to the door to listen for any movement; it did occur to him she *could* be in there, but remaining completely stationary to avoid discovery, so he knocked again, this time calling her name softly. Again no sound was heard. Joshua turned away, saddened, and made his way down the corridor towards his room.

A sudden epiphany froze Joshua to the spot for the briefest instant, before he rocketed down the stairs and out into the grounds. He raced around the grounds, starting with the outer perimeter and working his way back towards the house in ever decreasing circles, exploring little niches created by the landscaping, checking seats and benches, and, once he reached the house, the outbuildings. Jasna was nowhere to be found and Joshua became anxious. He meandered at a human pace back into the manor and through the foyer to the library door where Samir was seated alone.

"I've looked everywhere I can think of and I can't find Jasna." Joshua stated his forehead creased into a deep frown, his voice ringing with worry.

"I'm not surprised after what Dayna did," Samir responded, sounding extremely disgruntled, his expression mirroring Joshua's. "Although Jasna is obviously and justifiably upset, she's not reckless. She will return when she is ready."

"Has this happened before then?" Joshua asked incredulously, his eyes opening wide.

"Unfortunately, yes," Samir reluctantly confirmed. "However, you frightened Dayna tonight and that in itself is a major feat – I believe she will try to resist the temptation of humiliating Jasna in future. I have also warned her I will not tolerate anyone in our coven upsetting the other members." Samir's tone became first slightly awed then vehement.

"She'd better not demean Jasna again or she'll have me to deal with!" Joshua said darkly, his normally gentle eyes glinting with menace.

"I applaud your loyalty and caring Joshua – it is a rare thing among immortals. Now if you will excuse me, I have some tasks to carry out before retiring. I'll see you later."

Joshua nodded. "Thank you. See you later then."

Samir left the room and disappeared down the hallway to another part of the ground floor while Joshua headed up to his room to wait out his enforced incarceration until everyone was settled and he could escape to the gardens once more.

* * *

Jasna was curled into a foetal position on her bed, tearless sobs wracking her body. The words which had been so cruelly hurled at her had found their mark; Dayna had hit the bullseye. She became dimly aware that some of the decorative objects in her room were hovering in mid-air, some spinning dervishes, some on an invisible track racing backwards and forwards, some floating above their normal perch. This always happened when she was angry or upset – it used to scare her but not anymore, she was accustomed to it now.

Jasna had always had a problem with self-confidence – even more so when she was human – but when she became immortal, the enhanced senses, speed and strength, made her feel better about herself. When she now looked in the mirror, she noticed subtle changes in her face and body; her face appeared prettier, slimmer, with more defined cheekbones and jaw line, some of the puffiness had disappeared and her lips now had the most perfect cupids bow. Her body was slimmer too, more toned yet still voluptuous. Obviously she'd been deluding herself, she thought miserably.

She heard someone ascending the stairs and approaching her room. She remembered the objects floating and whizzing in their frenzied dance and concentrated briefly to restore them to their normal positions. She didn't want to see or speak to anyone – she felt too wretched – so she took a deep breath and forced her body to remain motionless and the sobs to subside. It took a monumental effort on her part, but she just managed to quiet the sobs completely when there was a knock on her door. She ignored it and hoped whoever it was would go away and leave her alone. For one horrified moment she considered it might be Dayna coming to pour ten tons of salt into the incredibly raw wounds she had inflicted, but reason returned when she realised Dayna probably wouldn't bother knocking at all – she would barge her way in with no consideration or respect for Jasna's privacy.

She remained completely still and silent, listening for the person at the door to go away so she could plunge further into her own private hell. Then she heard *his* voice calling her name as he knocked on the door once again. Every strand of her yearned to respond, desperate to be in his arms, wanting to be comforted, but Dayna's jibes echoed in her ears. She didn't want Joshua's pity; she couldn't handle looking into his eyes and seeing sympathy for the fat, ugly, lovesick girl.

Soon, Jasna heard Joshua start to move down the corridor, but she didn't allow herself to relax or move in case he decided to return. She heard him come to a halt and then shoot off somewhere at a tremendous pace. She sat up on the bed confident no one was around now to hear her. She fully expected the sobbing to recommence, but nothing happened. Her throat felt strange though. She arose from the bed and dared to look in the mirror which hung over the fireplace; instead of seeing the pretty face and slimmed down body she had observed when she had first been turned, all she saw now was exactly what Dayna had said, *"a fat, ugly cow"*. She knew in her heart she would never be good enough for Joshua, she'd been deluding herself and this launched her into a bottomless pit filled with profound sorrow. She turned her back on the mirror in disgust and threw herself back on the bed; pushing her agonised face into the pillows, she sank further and further into the depths of despair.

* * *

Erika sat tensely in the large armchair in the room she shared with Farrell thinking about Joshua; Farrell sprawled on the bed, hands behind his head, watching his partner intently. He knew she had something on her mind she wanted to discuss with him – she'd told him as much earlier – and he knew from experience he had to be patient and wait until she had marshalled her thoughts into a coherent stream before she would be ready to talk.

Erika's brow furrowed in concentration as she determined how to begin; she made her decision a few minutes later, her features smoothed out and she sighed. Farrell knew she was ready to start and sat forward bringing his knees up to his chest and wrapping his arms around them, his eyes never leaving her exquisite face.

"Okay," Erika said, taking another breath before continuing. "I'm worried about Joshua. I was picking up a great deal of inner turmoil when we were out hunting earlier. He was elated about something, but also very confused, worried, and conflicted. The latter was causing him such . . . *anxiety* yet there was this strange euphoria which swirled in and around the other, darker emotions. I'm not sure what to make of it or what to do about it," she admitted, the expression on her lovely face showing her consternation.

"O-kay," Farrell began slowly, dragging the word out as he continued to think about what she'd said. "Is it the turmoil of his emotions which has you jittery or the 'strange euphoria', or both?"

"I think it's a combination of all of it. It's just so . . . out of character for Joshua. Normally he's kind of mellow – pretty laid back actually – you know? He's . . . well . . . not exactly *happy* as such, he's . . . *content* I think is a better word."

"Yeah, I think I know what you mean – he *is* pretty chilled virtually all the time," he agreed nodding his head. "So, do you want to talk to him about it or what?"

"I'm not sure," she admitted honestly, shrugging her delicate shoulders. "I don't want to upset Joshua, plus I don't want him to think I'm prying or interfering, but I feel I should reach out to him and offer . . . oh, I don't know . . . maybe a sounding board or a shoulder to lean on – although perhaps *you* would be better suited for *that* task," she winked at him and grinned at her last statement. "What do you see in his aura?"

This question took him by surprise. It wasn't very often they discussed his particular talent; in fact he couldn't immediately recall the last time.

"Well . . . *normally* his aura is a mixture of pinks, browns and white with hints of yellow, gold and green. This basically means he's down to earth, convivial, pure of heart and mind, understanding, loving, creative and intellectual. The hints of gold represent service to others, caring; the green hints signify balance and peace.

"Today his aura changed, but although I noticed it, I didn't really pay much attention at the time – I have to say I was rather distracted by a gorgeous woman and the thrill of the hunt." He chuckled at his last comment, love blistering from his eyes as he looked at Erika. He continued in a more thoughtful tone.

"Today I noticed strands of blue, some red and worryingly, some black interweaving through his natural colours. In order, these signify some sadness and or depression then energy, passion and strength, and finally the black is a blockage or something being concealed."

"Ohhh," Erika sighed thoughtfully, leaning forward towards him. "So what do the changes in his aura actually equate to?"

"I would interpret them as Joshua having a secret perhaps, which is making him quite excited yet at the same time he fears someone around him has been dishonest, resulting in unhappiness. He doesn't want to believe this person could deceive him, but evidence is pointing in that direction." Farrell's expression became more sombre as he explained, and now a mask of furious disbelief painted his face as he guessed who the person might be.

"Wow," Erika whispered admiration and awe cascading from her face in waves. "So now what?"

"Right back atcha," Farrell grinned. "You were the one who started this, remember?"

"Yeah, I know. Well, the other consideration was whether we should mention this to Samir – what's your opinion?" she rolled her eyes, a small smile playing around her luscious lips.

"*Absolutely not*," he thundered, taking her by complete surprise.

"Hey. I was only asking," she retorted, offended by his tone. She shifted her position, leaning back into the chair away from him.

His expression softened immediately, aware his outburst, although not directed at her, had disturbed her.

"I'm sorry, sweetheart. I didn't mean to upset you. I have a strong . . . *intuition*, if that's the right word, that Samir could be the person Joshua believes has deceived him in some way. And, if it *is* the case, the very worst thing we could do would be to alert him to Joshua's beliefs."

"Oh. Yeah, you're right. So, now we've come full circle – what do we do?" Erika seemed appeased by Farrell's explanation; she got out of the chair and went to sit beside him.

He took her hand in his, grateful to see the forgiveness in her eyes.

"I think the best thing we can do, at least for now, is wait and observe. If Joshua's turmoil increases or his aura changes become more significant, then perhaps we should broach the subject with him. I don't want to upset him either; I want to help him if I can. He's a great guy and I like him very much – I already look upon him as a friend, a brother even, so I want to be there for him if he needs me."

Erika was touched by her partner's sincerity and her love for him swelled like a magnificent breaker any surfer would rather die than miss riding. She snuggled closer to him and he wrapped his arms around her so her head was resting on his chest.

"Sounds like a good plan to me – watch and wait ..." she murmured, tailing off as she raised her face to his and kissed the small dimple in his chin.

His brought his lips down to meet hers and their passion ignited like a match to touch-paper. There would be no more discussion for a while.

Chapter 22 – Joshua

Joshua was finding the wait interminable. He could hear voices from further down the corridor, but they were too faint for him to discern what was being said. He also hadn't heard Samir return to his room yet; this meant his enforced incarceration would last for at least another hour. His face reflected his irritation and his fingers moved continuously. He felt agitated, hemmed in; he couldn't think straight cooped up as he was and he yearned to be outside. He wanted to wander through the grounds and do some soul searching, maybe spend time in the idyllic and peaceful Japanese themed area. For now though, all he could do was procrastinate until he could escape this dark and increasingly depressing room.

As his mind crept back from the garden and into his room, his senses returned also and he realised the conversation down the hall had ceased. One down, he ticked off in his mind, one to go. Pacing the floor had become too boring so he clambered on the bed and laid back, hands behind his head, and stared up at the ceiling. Ten minutes passed but it seemed more than an hour. He'd been tracing the cracks in the ceiling with his eyes, trying to make random lines into shapes and pictures – it was quite numbing and childishly stupid really – but even that became tedious.

However, at that very moment he heard footfalls too quiet for human ears pass his room and continue further along the corridor. He heard Samir's door open and close again, followed by a silence so absolute it could have hurt less sensitive ears than his. He only had to wait about another thirty minutes then he could make good his escape and get out into the sun again. The thought placed a small smile on his lips.

As he lay there he inadvertently let his mind drift to thinking about Remy. Generally he stopped these thoughts before they had a chance to take shape, but this time, for some inexplicable reason, he allowed them to form. Perhaps it was as a result of what had occurred earlier with Jasna that he felt the compulsion to open the locked vault he had shut Remy in and examine his memories and emotions. His screwed his eyes shut and cringed, a shudder rippled down from the top of his head to well past his knees, as the first trace of pain returned to claim him once again. He sighed a massive sigh and forced himself calm – he couldn't put this off any longer.

The memory of her beautiful face was the first thing to consume his mind and he dwelled on every facet, examining each one as if he were seeing them for the very first time. Her eyes soft and inviting, her slightly uneven eyebrows and her skin blemish free and gently tanned. Her delicate ear lobes sporting a pair of diamond drop earrings he'd bought her for her birthday one year peeking through her glorious mane of hair which glinted in the sun. The dimple in her cheek when she smiled and her lips so very kissable upturned in a seductive smile he remembered oh so well.

Unconsciously he reached his hand forward as if to comb through her hair with his fingers, and in his mind's eye he could see himself doing it, as if he were in a virtual reality world, but his fingers felt nothing and he was jolted back to reality. He felt a strong pang of disappointment flood through him; a small tortured cry escaped from his lips, he sat forward and cradled his head in his hands, remaining in that position for several minutes without moving.

Abruptly Joshua rose to his feet and moved to the window; his eyes were hooded, his face brutally solemn. He peeked behind the curtains and judged it would be safe for him to escape the confines of his dark room and venture out into the garden. He silently exited, glided downstairs and out through the same door as before. He didn't hesitate in the shade, he didn't need to, and he strode straight out into the brilliant sunlight glorying in elated freedom.

He meandered around the grounds, as slowly as a human would take a leisurely stroll, myriad thoughts now tumbling inside his head like dice across a Craps table. Did his attraction to Jasna mean he no longer loved Remy? An emphatic NO ricocheted around his head. Was this attraction a result of missing Remy so much? A possible, probable, maybe. Did he want to take things further with Jasna? That was the biggest and most complex question of all.

Joshua recalled how Jasna had looked when they were hunting, remembering how pretty she was, how gentle her eyes were, how they had laughed and had fun together. His lips turned up at the corners for a fraction of a second before his face settled back into an unreadable mask. Then, as he recollected how murderously furious he felt when Dayna had ripped into Jasna, humiliating her so absolutely and how protective he felt towards her afterwards, his expression changed to one of pure rage, his hands balled into tight fists and a completely animalistic snarl ripped from between his clenched teeth.

It took him several minutes of striding across the grass for his anger to subside enough to continue with his deliberations; he slowed his steps until he was back to human strolling speed. Finally came the memory of how alarmed he became when he couldn't find her after she'd run from the library to escape Dayna's brutal words, how he'd suffered an emptiness of sorts.

Joshua had paid no attention to his wanderings yet his feet had taken him to the very place he wanted to be – the Japanese garden. He sat on the veranda of the teahouse, leaning his back against one of the support posts and again his eyes drank in the exquisite décor and peacefulness.

He focussed his thoughts once more, his eyes glazed over and his expression became bland. What did that emptiness signify? Were his feelings for Jasna deeper than he'd recognised? If the answer to the last question was affirmative, how could he reconcile it with the love he still had for Remy?

Although it seemed many months had passed since he'd last seen her and held her in his arms, in actuality it was only a few weeks. However, that was a whole different world. Then he'd been human (well, except for the last couple of weeks anyway), he'd been able to love her equally, able to share her life as she shared his, able to make her his bride and spend the rest of his life with her. It had all vanished like wisps of smoke on a strong wind. Joshua's face crumpled in anguish and a cry of pain issued forth from deep in his throat.

He still considered himself engaged to Remy in some respects, but he knew it was utterly ridiculous. He had said goodbye, leaving her a letter, like a coward, but he knew he would never have had the strength or resolve to tell her to her face. He didn't want to go – he loved her too much to want to leave her – but after what he'd done to her, how could he have stayed? The pain he'd experienced the day he drove away from Remy and the house they shared, knowing he would never return, was still very much in evidence, but from a gaping wound of excruciating agony it had subsided to a dull roar; his expression portrayed it so exactly, it was as if it had been painted onto a canvas then transposed on his face.

Actually this was all academic now. He was no longer human, he was a vampire, immortal, and she could never be a part of his bright yet strange new world. So why did he feel he was being unfaithful to Remy because he was attracted to Jasna? The love which lingered in his heart as strong as ever, had to be shut away and allowed to die a natural death. He had to let her go once and for all. His face twisted with pain at the thought, for a part of him would always love her – she was his soulmate – but now it could never be. He'd managed to keep from thinking of her for more than a day at a time now, so if he could manage that, he had the ability to lock away his memories along with his love and not allow them to see the light of day ever again. A look of resigned melancholy settled on Joshua's face yet his eyes blazed with a flash of determination before they blanked out once again. Yes, it would take a lot of effort on his part, but it was for the best.

His eyes came back into focus and he gazed around the tranquil surroundings, permitting the serene atmosphere to penetrate his being and calm his troubled mind. He had resolved one thing, but another remained undecided – Jasna. Still the biggest and most complex question – did he want to take things any further? Essentially this question wasn't as multifaceted as it had been when it first presented itself – his decision about Remy had rendered the question simple. Did he or didn't he? Yes or no?

His mind was abruptly filled with Jasna's lovely face, looking up at him in adoration, the same look she'd tried so unsuccessfully to conceal from him earlier and he knew in that instant the answer was a resounding *yes*. He smiled to himself in satisfaction, content with his decision then remembered Jasna was missing and his heart sank down into his boots, the smile turning to a grimace. There wasn't much he could do about it, but as Samir was so confident she would return, he had to cling to that for now.

* * *

Joshua was so self-absorbed he didn't notice the passing of time; it wasn't until he heard a particularly loud caw from a bird nearby that he surfaced from his reverie and, seeing the position of the sun, realised how late it really was. He would be lucky to make it back to the manor before Samir arrived in the library and he still wasn't quite ready to have his secret discovered. He rose from his perch and raced back at top speed, the grass swaying violently as if a high-speed jet had executed a low fly past. He reached the door, shutting and locking it as before and without making any noise on the uncarpeted floor, dashed to the empty library to take his usual seat.

Phew, he thought to himself, *made it*, as he heard a whisper of movement as someone descended the stairs. *I must concentrate on appearing relaxed*, he considered. He worked hard to smooth his features and changed his position in the chair so he lounged slobbishly rather than sitting upright. The door opened and Samir walked in, a curious expression on his face.

Samir had heard Joshua's last thoughts and was perturbed by them. What did they mean? He appraised Joshua's face and knew instantly that, despite his best efforts, Joshua wasn't fully able to conceal something was troubling him. Samir approached him slowly, his expression changing to one of concern.

"Hello Joshua."

"Hi Samir, how are you?" Joshua enquired politely, still working on keep his features bland and his voice steady.

"I'm fine, thank you. More to the point how are you?"

"Yeah, I'm good thanks." Joshua, not being slow on the uptake, became wary at the way Samir had phrased his question.

"I'm not sure you are," Samir stated gently, the concern more evident in his voice, his eyes staring into Joshua's as if trying to bore through to his mind. "I think we need to have a private chat – don't you?"

"I don't know what you mean," Joshua stalled for time, his eyes widening in faked innocence.

"I think you do," Samir pressed his voice gentle, but firmer than before.

Joshua tore his eyes away from Samir's intense scrutiny and looked at his feet, his shoulders slumped a little but his lips were set in a line.

"Please come with me to another room – we *do* need to talk," Samir's voice was persuasive and he beckoned to Joshua with his hand.

Joshua hesitated. He'd made the decision to talk to Samir about his gift, if that's what it was, but he wanted to be in control and approach him, not the other way around. He wasn't sure he was ready to discuss it yet, or if he could cope with finding out he might have been deceived, especially not after all the difficult decisions and chaos his brain had already handled that day. Did he have a choice now? Could he refuse?

Samir sensed his turmoil and heard the words tumbling around in his head. *Deceived? By whom?* This gave Samir grave cause for concern and he knew he had to be decisive. "Come," he commanded, his expression serious.

Joshua felt he had no choice but to obey; he rose unhurriedly and followed Samir through the open door. They walked across the marble floored foyer and down the hall to the left, stopping outside another heavy door. Samir opened it and gestured for Joshua to precede him over the threshold. It was an old-fashioned drawing room; it had a heavy wall covering which looked a sort of damask in shades of palest blue and pastel green, the floor was a polished wood resembling oak which had lost some of its sheen over the years, the thick curtains were a slightly darker shade of blue with an even thicker lining, there was an antique writing desk against one wall, two large comfortable looking ivory leather sofas facing each other with a long glass topped coffee table in between, some landscape paintings on the walls and odd bits of occasional furniture dotted around the edges. Joshua felt he'd stepped back in time; he expected to see a liveried butler standing unobtrusively in the corner bearing a silver tray.

Samir gestured to one of the sofas so Joshua sat. Samir sat opposite him. Nothing was said to begin with; Joshua's eyes were examining the room so he sensed rather than saw Samir scrutinising his face. Eventually, Samir broke the silence, concern etched on his face and audible in his voice.

"Joshua, I know there is something that vexes you. I want to help you if you'll allow me. Won't you tell me what it is?"

Joshua sat staring at the floor; he didn't want to blurt it out in case he made any false allegations and, as a result, alienate Samir. He decided to stick to the facts, how it started, how he found out and his experimentations, and gauge Samir's reactions. He raised his head to look Samir in the eyes and began.

"I have ... *discovered* something, something strange and I'm not sure what to make of it." Joshua's voice betrayed his uncertainty and his face showed some confusion. Samir merely gestured for him to continue.

"It began two, no three days ago. I was feeling frustrated and bored stupid in my room during the day so I went into the library. I guess my idea was to get a book to read and didn't really pay much heed to the fact that daylight would be pouring into the room. I walked in and nothing happened." There was an edge of excitement to his voice and his eyes lit up.

"It was strange but I had an ... *urge* I guess, to see what would happen if I put my hand in the direct path of the sunlight which streamed through the windows, so I did. It didn't hurt as I expected and there were no marks or anything on my skin, so gradually I put more of myself into the sun until I was standing completely bathed in the light. Again nothing happened – I was absolutely fine. I stayed in the room all the rest of the day and I was still okay.

"I thought about it that day and night and decided I would try the real thing the next day, so I waited until everyone was settled then ventured outside. I was very careful to begin with, first a finger, then my hand and so on, until eventually I was totally immersed in the sun's ray, and I was totally unharmed. I spent most of the day yesterday and today out in the gardens, in the sun, and look at me – not a mark." A large smile beamed out of his face.

Samir on the other hand looked incredulous; his eyes so wide he would have burst a few blood vessels if he were human and his mouth hung open in shock. It took quite a few seconds before he could find his voice, and even then it was a whisper.

"A . . . *daywalker*? Are you *serious*?"

Joshua nodded at him, in some ways pleased by his reaction, but also very dubious. Was this reaction genuine or was Samir a good actor? He still couldn't shake the idea Samir knew it was possible and had been deceiving him.

"I've never heard of one such as you in my five hundred years," Samir whispered in awe, his features still arranged in a shocked expression as he slumped back in the seat.

"Really?" Joshua asked sceptically, one eyebrow rose sardonically.

"Really," Samir confirmed. "I'd heard rumours that it *could* be possible but. . ." he tailed off, lost now in his own thoughts.

Joshua sat and patiently waited while Samir came to terms with the information provided. He could almost see the cogs whirring in Samir's head and had to suppress the desire to chuckle. However, he still wasn't totally convinced by Samir's response – was this part of the deception? Should he say something? The silence stretched between them like a chasm as Samir, caught up in his feelings of astonishment and, to a degree, pride, struggled to find the right words to say. He leaned forward, resting his lower arms across his knees.

"Joshua, I'm . . . *gobsmacked*, I think is the terminology. I knew you had a special talent, but I never *dreamed* it would be something as monumental as this. What surprises me even more is you've managed to keep this hidden from me. Oh, I don't mean in terms of you coming to talk to me about it, I mean your thoughts. How have you controlled your thoughts around me so I was unaware until now?" Samir's voice went from excited to exasperated in one smooth transition, his expression mirroring his voice.

Joshua shrugged and pushed out his bottom lip a little as he considered how to answer.

"I guess I just made sure I was thinking of other things when you were around." Then he realised what Samir had said and his expression changed to one of surprised delight. "Sorry, did you say 'my talent'?"

Samir nodded thoughtfully, not really hearing the last question, just the answer to his – he'd never known anyone who was able to block his mind, until now. Another couple of questions occurred to him and he uncharacteristically blurted them out.

"Does this frighten you at all? How do *you* feel about this?"

Joshua didn't pause at all. His face and voice exuded confidence.

"No, it doesn't frighten me at all – in fact I think it's kinda cool – I love the fact I don't have to stay cooped up in my room all day."

"Yes, I can see the attraction. So, what to do, what to do?" he muttered more to himself.

"Why do you *have* to do anything? The facts are the facts and I'm guessing nothing is going to change so isn't it a case of learning to live with it?" Joshua spread his hands wide as he spoke, his face had darkened a little, and his eyes were less bright than before.

"I *suppose* so - this has all taken me by surprise and if I'm honest, I'm not sure how to handle it." Samir admitted truthfully, his hands were twisting around and around each other as he spoke.

"I don't think there's anything *to* handle. It is what it is and I happen to think it's pretty awesome," Joshua was obviously getting disgruntled now, his expression darker still, annoyance clear in his eyes.

"Oh, please don't misunderstand me, Joshua," Samir pleaded, his eyes filled with remorse. "I didn't mean it like that. You're right – it *is* an awesome gift and I'm ecstatic for you – what I meant was how am I supposed to guide you with a gift this unusual?"

"Oh, okay." Joshua conceded, much more composed than before. "Perhaps we'll have to take this as it comes?"

"Perhaps. Or maybe I should speak to Pavel about it – would you mind?" Samir added, as an afterthought.

"No, I don't mind at all." Joshua agreed. His eyes drifted towards the window and noticed it was beginning to get dark.

Samir saw his gaze and followed it, surprise etched on his face when he realised how late it had become. Samir rose and gestured for Joshua to follow. As they walked together to the door, Samir put one arm around Joshua's shoulders.

"It might be best if we don't mention this to the others yet – at least not before I've spoken to Pavel. Do you agree?"

Joshua glanced at Samir and saw the hope in his eyes.

"Okay, I won't say anything for now. Will you let me know what Pavel says?"

"Of course. Hopefully I will speak to him while you're out hunting and will be able to relay his response upon your return." Samir assured him, the sincerity evident in Samir's voice.

"Fine. Our little secret for now then?" Joshua whispered conspiratorially and yet jokingly.

"Yes, our little secret," Samir agreed also whispering, a small smile playing around his lips.

They reached the foyer and walked together back to the library.

They walked into the room and found Farrell, Erika and Dayna assembled and waiting. Jasna was conspicuous by her absence and a physical throb coursed through Joshua's body as he worried about where she was and if she was all right. How stupid – of course she wasn't all right, if she were, she'd be here with everyone else. His anger reared as he glared at Dayna. She was seated alone, on the other side of the room from Farrell and Erika, seemingly contrite but with a flash of defiance in her eyes. She glanced up as Samir and Joshua walked through the door; she was obviously more confident now Samir was there and a smug expression flickered across her face to be replaced by her normal perpetual sneer. Joshua's fury was on the verge of exploding out of him. He clenched his fists tight, his lips curled back over his teeth and his normally gentle eyes turned lethal and vicious. As he took one step towards her, he felt a restraining hand grip his arm. He whipped his head around to confront the one who was preventing him from ripping the bitch apart, and found it was Samir's hand clutching him tight. Joshua was trembling as the rage overtook him, but the expression of anxiety on Samir's face served to calm him a little and he heard Samir's voice in his head.

Compose yourself, my son. Nothing will be gained from the violence you yearn to inflict – it won't bring Jasna back any sooner. I understand your fury, but I cannot allow this. Please, Joshua, calm down.

Joshua looked into Samir's beseeching eyes and nodded imperceptibly, acknowledging his plea, but he wasn't physically able to turn off his rage like water from a tap; he stalked from the room and charged out of the front door not daring to look behind him as he sprinted across the grounds.

Samir turned to Farrell and Erika, looking anxious.

"Go after him. Let him get this out of his system but watch him carefully – don't let him act rashly – he's not thinking straight," he commanded, his speech so fast it would have sounded garbled to a human.

Farrell grabbed Erika's hand; moving towards the door, he patted Samir on the shoulder as they passed him and then they too shot out of the manor as arrows from a bow to follow Joshua.

Dayna rose from her seat a little unsteadily – she had been shaken by the ferocity of Joshua's rage – and started to walk towards the foyer with her head down, not daring to meet Samir's disappointed eyes. Although she wasn't really repentant for the pain she'd inflicted on Jasna – she, like the others, meant absolutely nothing to her – she *was* sorry she'd made the only person she *did* care about displeased with her, and she couldn't bear to see this on Samir's face. As she reached the threshold, Samir's voice, tinged with sadness and a certain amount of disdain, stopped her cold.

"See what you have done? I will NOT have discord in this coven – do you understand?"

Dayna remained where she was and didn't turn to face him; not trusting her voice to sound right she nodded, her blonde curls bouncing around like coiled springs which had just been released.

"For your own safety, I suggest you give Joshua a *very* wide berth until he calms down again – I may not be around to save you next time," Samir continued in the same tone.

Dayna turned her head so she could glance at Samir in her peripheral vision and replied in a grateful yet slightly defiant tone, "No problem." And with that, she continued to cross the foyer and disappeared through the main door out into the night.

* * *

Samir stood gazing at the front door, a wistful expression gracing his features, thinking about what had just transpired. He wasn't oblivious to the affection Dayna held for him, and maybe if she hadn't deliberately engineered to hurt the most defenceless member of the coven, not once but three times now, there may have been some interest on his part, but now there was absolutely no possibility. On her own, away from the temptation to unleash her bitchy tendencies, she was actually a pleasant and at times, charming companion; she was also very beautiful, especially when her smile was genuine, but he knew she couldn't be trusted to resist her true nature and for that reason alone, he would never return the affection, despite his feelings for her. It did concern him when he considered how truly vindictive she could be if and when she realised she would never become his partner, but at that precise moment he had more important things to deal with. He strolled across the now empty room and lowered himself into one of the chairs; pulling a small black mobile phone from the pocket of his trousers, he hit a speed dial button and waited for the recipient to answer.

"Hello, Samir, what a pleasant surprise. How are you my friend?" Pavel's warm accented voice flowed into Samir's ear.

"I'm very well, thank you. How are you and Iskra?" Samir replied courteously.

"We are also well, thank you. To what do I owe this pleasure?"

The pleasantries concluded it was now time to explain the purpose of his call. Samir took a deep breath before continuing.

"There is something I need your advice on, Pavel, something I'm not sure how to deal with."

"Tell me what is troubling you – I will help you all I can."

Samir recounted the conversation he'd had earlier with Joshua verbatim, leaving nothing out, attempting to sound calmer than he actually felt.

"Is it *possible*?" the uncertainty and awe apparent in his tone.

"Yes," Pavel confirmed, surprise colouring his voice. "I have only ever met one in my eight hundred years and she lived in Egypt. I haven't seen or heard from her for about two centuries, but she was able to walk among the humans totally undetected. I knew Joshua was more special than the other members of your coven – I identified three gifts when I came to visit – have any other gifts revealed themselves yet?"

"Not that I'm aware of. Joshua has only spoken to me about his ability to walk in the daylight unharmed." Samir's shock that Pavel had confirmed the possibility of a daywalker was evident in his tone as he replied. His torso was tense as he contemplated what he might be required to do about this and his features conveyed the anxiety he still felt. "I honestly didn't know a daywalker existed or it was even possible. So what do I need to do about it?" he blurted out

Pavel was silent as he considered Samir's question and the suddenly fearful tone in which it was delivered.

"The only thing you *need* to do is reassure Joshua. Tell him although this gift is extremely unusual, it's not unheard of. I would advise that he should refrain from mixing with humans until he is completely in control of his thirst – after all he *is* still a neophyte – suggest he remains within the confines of the grounds, at least for a while, so temptation does not cross his path."

"Thank you, Pavel. I will do as you suggest," the relief in Samir's voice was echoed in his expression and he felt the tension drain from his body.

"My pleasure. Feel free to call again at any time if you need further assistance."

"Thank you – I will. Please give my best regards to Iskra," Samir replied, happily.

"I certainly will. Take care of yourself, Samir. Goodbye my friend."

"Goodbye, Pavel and thank you again." And with that, Pavel ended the call.

Samir rose, smiling. He was so glad he'd sought Pavel's advice – it had certainly put his mind at rest and he could now allow his excitement of having someone as talented as Joshua in his coven. He was pleased he could also reassure Joshua. Despite being so much more relaxed, there was an uncomfortable ache in his throat as the unquenched thirst reminded him he needed to feed. He unconsciously raised his right hand to his neck and massaged the skin as if trying to ease the ache from the outside. He glided across the foyer and exited the mansion, blending with the dark purples and greys of the night.

Chapter 23 – Remy

When the alarm clock buzzed, I awoke refreshed and alert. I leapt out of bed and walked straight into the bathroom for a shower. Twenty minutes later I was dressed and on my way down to breakfast. I decided not to stop at reception on the way – I would see Pat when I checked out.

Although I would miss her, I was curiously anxious to get to my next destination and recommence my search for Joshua. Just thinking his name brought a lump to my throat and a piercing arrow of pain shot through my chest, making it hard to breathe for a minute or two. I focused my mind on staying calm and gradually my ability to breathe normally returned. I walked purposefully into the dining room and took a seat at my normal table.

While I waited for my breakfast to be cooked, I removed my mobile phone from the pocket of my jeans and unlocked it. I clicked the icon for the Internet and using the search engine, quickly found what I was looking for and placed my order. I smiled to myself, satisfied with my purchase and closed it down as my steaming hot meal was placed in front of me. I didn't realise how hungry I was as I demolished my breakfast in record time then left to brush my teeth and finish the last of my packing before checking out.

Pat was behind the counter in reception as I walked through with my bags; she smiled when she saw me although there was sadness in her eyes and her shoulders were slightly slumped. I could see she was making a great effort not to let it show; I was sad to leave her too – I would miss her very much. I paid for my stay and gave her my mobile number written on a piece of hotel stationery I'd found in my room. She came around to my side of the counter and gave me a huge motherly hug.

"You take good care of yourself, Remy, and remember, if you need to talk or anything, just call. Okay?" she whispered emotion evident in her voice.

I found a lump forming in my throat as I tried to respond in a normal voice.

"Of course I will and thank you for *everything*," I emphasised the last word, my voice breaking a little. Although I felt safe and warm in her embrace, I knew it was pointless to prolong the inevitable, so I gently pulled back hoping she wouldn't see the glassiness of my eyes as I tried to fight back unshed tears. I noticed with surprise her eyes were as shiny as mine and we both chuckled self-consciously. "I'll call you soon and let you know how I'm getting on, I promise."

She nodded, perhaps not trusting her voice, a sad smile on her lips. I grabbed the handle on my case and made my way to the exit, turning at the last minute to call back.

"Bye Pat, and thanks again," I didn't wait for her reply and walked straight out into the parking area. I got into the driving seat, connected the SatNav and prepared to drive out. Just as I was about to pull onto the road, a florist's van pulled into the car park and a satisfied grin dashed onto my face – my thank you present had arrived. It was a pity I wouldn't be able to see her reaction, but it was enough for me to know I'd been able to do something nice for her. I pulled out onto the road and didn't look back. If I had, I would have seen Pat rush through the main door with a huge bouquet of flowers in her arms and tears streaming down her kind face.

It didn't take me long to get onto the M6 heading south, or maybe it did, but I was concentrating more on listening to the SatNav than I would on the motorway, so wasn't as perceptive about the time passing. I was so focussed on the first part of my journey I hadn't allowed any other thoughts to intrude, but now I was on the M6 it was a completely different matter and memories of Josh came flooding into my mind like a river which had burst its banks, causing a torrent of agony to rampage through me.

My hands were shaking on the steering wheel, my eyes blurred and there was a white-hot fire burning in my chest. I pulled one of my hands from the wheel and dragged it across my eyes, wiping the tears away so my vision was no longer compromised. I knew I was a danger to other road users in this debilitated state and searched the verge for signs announcing a service station. Luck was on my side as I spotted what I wanted about thirty seconds later – I just had to hang on for another mile and a half. I gritted my teeth against the waves of torture which ravaged me from the inside out and tried to focus on keeping my wheels within the markings delineating my lane until it was time to exit.

I pulled into the parking area of the service station and stopped in the first free space as great heaving sobs ripped out of me and I collapsed sideways onto the passenger seat, wrapping my arms around my body. My entire torso shuddered as each new sob thundered its way up and out of me, the desolation was too much to bear – I wanted my Joshua back. Loneliness engulfed me. A massive solid black cloud of deep depression settled over me, crushing the breath from my lungs with its weight.

After what seemed hours, but was only about forty minutes, the sobs transmuted into small gasps and my body became immobile apart from the small rise and fall of my chest. I squeezed my eyes tightly shut until they ached and I saw multi-coloured stars dancing on the insides of my eyelids. Easing the pressure changed my view to a solid inky blackness then Joshua's face appeared in my mind's eye, smiling in that gentle sexy way which had always made me all gooey inside and putty in his hands; this time it made me even more miserable, if that were possible. A part of me wanted to keep staring at his loving face as it made me feel closer to him somehow, but the pragmatic part of me knew the longer I stayed here incapacitated by my anguish, the longer it would take me to complete this part of my journey and consequently move another step closer to finding him.

I shook my head rapidly from side to side before slowly opening my eyelids. The brightness stung my eyes and I blinked a few times until I became more accustomed to the light. I sat up, noticing I was actually rather uncomfortable. I leaned back and stretched, easing the kinks out of my muscles. The depression remained, shrouding me like a hooded cloak and the feeling of isolation was the scarf, gloves and boots.

Once more, doubt overwhelmed me and I again questioned the strength of my resolve. My desperation to find Joshua was all encompassing yet I really didn't believe I was strong enough to go the distance, to do whatever it took to find him. There was a battle being waged inside my head; on one side was my irrepressible love for Joshua coupled with the frantic need to bring him home where he belonged, and on the other, was my pervasive self-doubt joined with depression, pain and grief. *What a combination* I thought, a cynical smirk flashed across my face and was gone again as soon as it arrived. The biggest, most humungous question of all was *which side would win?* Damned if I knew. I knew what I wanted with every part of my being, knew what I was prepared to sacrifice to get Joshua back but . . . *geez a little word with such a big meaning,* I thought.

I glanced at my reflection in the rear view mirror; the normally sparkling eyes were sad and dull with dark smudges underneath where my mascara had run. I looked like I'd aged ten years and it shocked me. If Joshua saw me in this state, he would be horrified and most likely frightened – I had to admit it, I was a mess. I couldn't let him see me in this condition. I reached for my handbag and placed it on my lap. First, I pulled out my brush and stroked it through my hair until it was smooth and silky looking. Replacing it, I then pulled out a small pack of hand wipes and dabbed at the black smudges until they disappeared. I checked my reflection once more and was relieved to see I looked less scary than before, although still melancholy.

I glanced at the clock on the dashboard and was dismayed to discover how much precious time I'd wasted with my 'mini breakdown'. I took a deep breath and let it out slowly before restarting the engine. After checking it was safe to move, I pulled out of the parking space and was back on the motorway within two minutes.

As I continued on my journey, I knew it was imperative I didn't lose my concentration or allow my emotions to run amok again; I needed a distraction. I mentally reviewed the CD's I had within my reach and remembered one with no real connection to Joshua. Luckily it was in the side pocket of my door and I was able to grab it without compromising the safety of my driving; I inserted it into the CD player and turned up the volume, immediately recognising the first track I began to sing along with the lyrics as the black tarmac flew by swiftly beneath my wheels.

I arrived in the picturesque conservation village of Winster within the Peak National Park around three hours later and quickly located Redow House, the beautiful 16th Century Grade II listed country house where I was staying. This was where Joshua and I stayed when we visited last year - although it had changed owners since then – but from the outside, it looked completely unchanged apart from a couple of large ceramic tubs containing a colourful array of blooms.

As I walked through the door into an elegant hallway, I gasped in surprise at the magnificent sight before me. The new owners had obviously spent time and serious money restoring the property, uncovering some of the original features and bringing them back to their former glory. I was mesmerised by the carved plaster cornice with its' intricate detail, the picture and dado rails, the stunning ceiling roses with their elaborate patterns and an antique chandelier which sparkled like diamonds as the sun bounced off the crystals and created prisms of rainbow lights that shimmered against everything they touched.

My feet moved slowly forward as I gazed enthralled by the changes. A heavy door with bevelled glass panels was open to reveal the dining hall - if anything this room was even more beautiful than the hallway. My jaw dropped and I stared around with my mouth hanging open. The original beams had been exposed – it was criminal to have covered them up in the first place – along with a part stone floor and a wood burning fire place, all of which combined to give an impression of warmth. The huge Georgian sash windows complemented and balanced the room with just the right amount of light and the room had been tastefully decorated to highlight all the wonderful features. Beyond the dining hall was the guests' lounge where more unique and decorative plasterwork had been uncovered as well as some huge beams which ran the length of the room; there were large comfortable sofas, a wealth of paintings and off to one side, an honesty bar.

I wandered back out into the hallway where I was met by Marcia and Justin, the new owners, surprised by how young they were. They both greeted me warmly and gave me the key to my room. Justin insisted on carrying my case up the stairs while Marcia told me where to find everything I would need during my stay. I thanked her and followed Justin up the curving staircase admiring the décor as I went.

We chatted on the way to my room and I complimented him on the renovations. He explained he'd grown up in a place similar to Redow House and loved the history and architecture of old buildings with a passion; he was horrified when he saw what the previous owners had done to cover up all the original features and it was a labour of love to restore it. By the way he spoke, he was obviously immensely proud of what he and Marcia had achieved here, his face glowing and animated as he spoke.

We arrived at my room and I took a deep breath as I walked in, letting it out with a whoosh as I saw the elegantly appointed bedroom. It was huge, vibrantly colourful without being gaudy and featured a large bed, a deep sofa and chair to match, large Georgian windows which let in a great deal of light and overlooked a pretty walled garden, a deep plush carpet and solid wood furniture.

As my eyes feasted on my surroundings, I'd forgotten Justin was even there until I heard a discrete cough. I turned around to face him, slightly embarrassed, but he had a massive grin on his face – he appeared to enjoy my appreciation of the fruits of his labour.

"Thank you for bringing my case up, Justin, and for giving me such a beautiful room. I love it!" I exclaimed, my eyes shining bright and a beatific smile on my face.

"You're welcome. Seeing your reaction has made it more of a

pleasure," he insisted, grinning like the proverbial Cheshire cat. "Anyway, I'll leave you to settle in and see you later," he continued, moving towards the door.

"Okay, and thanks again," I called after him.

He raised his hand in acknowledgement as he disappeared through the door, shutting it on his way out.

I walked over to the window and looked over the garden below. The walls looked ancient but solid and housed all manner of summer blooms, artfully planted to form patterns and shapes using colours and varieties to achieve the end result. I opened the window wide and leaned on the sill; poking my head out I inhaled deeply and became intoxicated by the fragrances which drifted on the air. I closed my eyes and breathed slowly and deeply, enjoying the warmth of the sun on my face, the scent of the flowers and the sound of the birds serenading each other in the trees. For a few minutes I forgot my purpose here – I was so wrapped up in the spectacular rooms and hallway downstairs, my striking bedroom and the exquisite garden – but then, unexpectedly, thoughts of Joshua stormed into my head like a bull charging a matador. He would have adored this place now it had been renovated and been just as speechless, as enthusiastic, as . . . *blown away* as I was.

I opened my eyes and wasn't surprised my vision was a little blurred. Joshua should be here with me not God knows where. I shook my head angrily – I AM going to find him!

Moving over to where Justin had left my case, I hefted it onto the bed and started unpacking, putting my clothes away neatly in the wardrobe and chest of drawers. I grabbed my toiletry bag and wandered into the spacious bathroom, dominated by an enormous bath big enough for two people. I placed my bag on the glass shelf over the basin and touched the towels draped over two towel rails by the shower cubicle. They were soft and fluffy with a new, luxurious feel to them. I pulled a small one off the rail and buried my face in it, inhaling the scent of the fabric conditioner it had been laundered with. It felt squishy against my skin, like a brand new teddy bear given to an infant and it was oddly comforting in a way. I reluctantly replaced it and strolled back into the bedroom. I glanced at the delicate watch adorning my wrist – the one my parents had given me for my 21st birthday – and noted it was a little too late for lunch, but much too early for dinner. I was peckish and needed a small snack to keep me going. I grabbed my handbag and the key and left the room, walked along the corridor then downstairs and out through the front door.

It was a pleasant walk down to the village shop, with hardly any traffic to spoil the idyllic afternoon. A small smile played around my lips as I admired the scenery. My hair was ruffled by a gentle breeze as the sun blazed overhead, the wild flowers growing by the side of the road swayed in rhythm with each other, a formation dance team in perfect harmony. It was a day for sweethearts to share, to exult in their love and togetherness, to make plans for their future, as Joshua and I had once done. A pang of regret and sorrow swirled around inside, filling me up until it became an all-encompassing ache as I remembered all the times we'd shared similar days; picnics, long walks holding hands, even longer kisses, talking, planning and rejoicing in each other.

Having reached the shop, I hesitated, staring at my reflection in the glass. The vision which stared back was not the real Remy, the happy, bubbly, extrovert who loved life and was always laughing and smiling. No, this person was a mere shadow of her former self, sadness being the most dominant feature, with the edges of the lips down-turned, shadows under the eyes (which had nothing to do with cosmetics), a little drawn around the edges, but the biggest change was in the eyes themselves – the spark had gone. I thought back to how I felt seeing my reflection after my mini breakdown in the car earlier and forced my lips to turn upwards into a smile, all the time watching my face in the glass. I noticed the smile didn't really reach my eyes, but it did make a bit of an improvement overall. Trying to force the smile to stay in place, I entered the shop.

Fifteen minutes later I was walking back towards Redow House. I had purchased a low calorie snack bar and a bottle of water and was consuming the bar as I strolled. The lady in the shop had been pleasant and chatty – I got the impression by the amused expression on her face, that she'd witnessed my embarrassing self-examination – and I'd taken the opportunity to show her the photo of Josh and ask if she'd seen him. She said she vaguely remembered him from quite some time ago, but hadn't seen him recently. I wasn't really surprised by her response but nevertheless I'd hoped . . .

I arrived back at the guest house and ran up the stairs to my room. I pulled a spiral notepad and a pen from the drawer and returned back to the entrance hall. I found a telephone directory under a table housing brochures of local attractions, grabbed it and proceeded into the guest lounge. I didn't want to be alone in my room – it was too depressing, lonely and I wasn't sure my fragile emotional state could handle it at the moment – so even if there wasn't anyone else in there, chances were someone would be around soon, even if it was Marcia or Justin.

I chose a large and comfortable-looking sofa to spread out on with the directory taking up one seat and me another. I started making lists of Bed & Breakfast establishments, Guest Houses and Hotels in the vicinity, using a new page for each town where there were quite a few to list, and another for the small villages where there were only one or two places.

It took me about two hours to list all the establishments and their addresses – I was surprised how many there were – my hand was aching and my fingers were a little stiff. Looking at the lists, I realised I would have to extend my stay here to cover every one of them. I stood, stretched to ease the kinks in my back and strolled back into the entrance hall, replaced the directory then headed up to my room to get ready for dinner. I was going to have an early night – I had a lot of ground to cover tomorrow.

Chapter 24 – Remy

After breakfast the following morning I set off to Matlock loaded with my list and a local map. The list of establishments in Matlock alone covered nearly 4 pages in my notebook – I estimated it would probably take me about four days to check them all out and that was without Bakewell and the surrounding villages. Geez I had my work cut out here.

As I drove, I recalled my last trip to this area. Josh and I spent ten days exploring the picturesque villages, all of which had some amazing history; like Eyam, the Black Death plague village or Matlock Bath with its' cable cars and the Heights of Abraham or Birchover with a pub housing a 30ft well in the main bar and Rowter Rocks where Druids practised their magic. We'd left the Peak District at the end of our holiday with a deep affection for the area and a desire to return.

Yet again, as I remembered the wonderful time I'd spent here with Josh, a lump the size of a golf ball settled in my throat making it hard to breathe and swallow and my eyes started pricking with the unshed tears which threatened to spill over and run in torrents down my face.

Would I ever be able to think of Joshua or recall trips and holidays we'd shared without breaking down, or suffering physical pain like an almighty bolt of lightning surging through my body, or my heart splintering yet again into a million shards of glass which cut me to pieces inside, all of which left me aching from top to toe for hours afterwards? I wish I knew the answer – my emotions were so raw, so close to the surface all the time. I was an unskilled tightrope walker a thousand feet in the air with a sheer drop below and no safety net - in the blink of an eye I could easily topple and fall into the abyss.

I dug deep, trying to find some of the inner strength which had kept me going thus far and as I concentrated, I began to feel calmer, stronger and more focused. I chanted a mantra in my head, *I can do this, I can find him, I can do this, I can find him*, over and over and over, like I was trying to convince myself it was possible. I had to believe I would succeed otherwise what was I doing here? My all-encompassing love for Joshua was as strong as ever and I knew deep in my heart that no matter where he was, he still loved me too. It was this love, this bond we shared which gave me the strength and resilience to continue searching.

Having reached Matlock, I parked the car, put some coins in the machine then placed the issued ticket on the inside of my windscreen. I checked my map against my list and walked down the street to the first bed and breakfast on the list; I checked again for about the tenth time that I had the photo of Joshua, took a deep breath and walked through the door.

I glanced at my watch, surprised to see it was 4pm. I'd been on the go all day without a break – I'd not even had lunch – and I was beginning to run out of steam. I stopped at a small coffee shop which had a few tables and chairs on the pavement and took the weight off my feet. My legs ached and it was bliss to just sit. I picked up the small laminated menu and was studying it when a young girl of about seventeen approached my table, pad and pen in hand. She smiled down at me.

"Are you ready to order?"

I looked up and saw a pretty face marred by two long scars across one cheek and some smaller ones close to her eye and ear on the same side. I tried not to stare at her disfigurement and returned her smile, thinking what a great shame it was that a young girl with such a pretty face had suffered this mutilation.

"Oh, er yes. I'll have a cup of tea and a blueberry muffin please."

"Certainly," she replied, writing down my order before disappearing back inside.

I looked at my list and was quite pleased with the amount of ground I'd managed to cover – I was slightly ahead of schedule – although I hadn't found Josh yet, I wasn't quite as despondent as I had been in Cumbria and I could only put it down to the fact that I was still running on adrenaline or blind faith. Whatever it was, I was oddly grateful.

The waitress returned carrying my order on a round metal tray. As she set everything down on the table, I noticed a small, embroidered nametag on her uniform.

"Thank you, Bonnie," I smiled up at her.

"You're welcome," she responded, her smile lighting up her face before she turned and left me to eat and drink in peace.

By the time I'd finished the last cup of tea from the pot Bonnie had provided, I found my energy level had increased significantly. I scrutinised my list again and realised some of the establishments still to be visited were only a couple of streets away. I decided to push my luck and get a few more in before returning to my hotel for dinner. I paid my bill and left a tip for Bonnie then set off down the road once more, this time in the opposite direction.

An hour and another ten establishments later I started to flag. I returned to my car, dragging my feet with exhaustion for the last few yards. I sat for a couple of minutes before starting the engine, finding a reserve of energy to get me back to Redow House. I hoped there wouldn't be too much traffic.

My return journey took less than twenty minutes. Trudging up to my room I collapsed on the bed; I was rather tired and a little down, but it wasn't anything I couldn't handle. I closed my eyes ostensibly for a few seconds, but when I opened them again and glanced at my watch, I was shocked to discover I'd been asleep for over an hour and the dining room had already been open for twenty minutes. Jumping off the bed I ran into the bathroom to have the quickest shower in history.

Fifteen minutes later I was dressed and heading down to dinner, my stomach rumbling with every step I took. I would eat well tonight.

After a delicious dinner, I decided to go into the bar and have a couple of drinks. Marcia was serving and I sat and chatted to her for a little while before heading upstairs. Bearing in mind my impromptu nap earlier I was quite surprised at how tired I felt. I began to yawn as

I undressed; my eyes watering with fatigue. Setting my alarm, I ignored my e-reader and climbed into bed. I was asleep as soon as my head hit the pillow.

I was looking through a window and I was sure I'd been here before, the room and its' furnishings looked familiar. Sitting in the room were two women and a man – one of the women was seated alone across the room from the other two, who were seated together – they looked vaguely recognizable yet I knew I'd never met them. Then two more men walked into the room and Joshua was one of them – he looked more handsome than ever.

There was a conversation taking place, but all I could hear was a strange burbling noise – no words or other sounds to try and make sense of – and this was strangely memorable too. The woman seated alone had an arrogant, derisive look about her as if she was taking pleasure in winding someone up. As I watched, her expression suddenly changed to one of fear. At first I couldn't see why she was afraid until I altered my perspective of the room; Joshua railed at her, a murderous fury plastered across his face and I suddenly understood her alarm. His expression was petrifying – I'd never even seen Joshua angry before, let alone in such a rage – he resembled a beautiful yet vengeful dark angel. I worried about what had happened to cause Joshua to react in such a terrifying way; it was so out of character.

The man who came through the door with Joshua had a worried expression on his face and grabbed his upper arm as if to restrain him. Joshua turned to confront him, but backed off when he saw who it was; there was a beseeching look in the man's eyes, but his lips didn't move. Abruptly, Joshua stalked out of the room and out of my field of vision. The man spoke to the couple who also disappeared through the same door – their anxious expressions indicated they were concerned about Joshua. I tried to move to the side so I could see into another room, but all I found was a brick wall, I could only see this room. Now I saw the man, who was obviously the leader, say something to the lone female who'd been on the receiving end of

Joshua's temper; it appeared he was admonishing her big time, but the calculation in her eyes didn't match the contrite expression on her face and then she too left the room.

A series of musical notes interrupted the silence and keeping my eyes shut, I groped for the source of the noise, my hand finding my mobile phone on the bedside table. I pressed a button to silence the music before gradually opening my eyes. I blinked several times, expecting to find myself behind the window looking into the same room, but was surprised to discover I was in my room at Redow House. A small part of me was relieved yet the rest of me wanted to be back looking through that window and waiting for Joshua to appear again.

Something moving in the room drew my attention and I turned my head to see what it could be. My eyes widened to the point of being painful, I craned my head forward straining my neck and a small cry of shock and disbelief flew from my gaping lips. Dancing in the air, as if attached to invisible wires, was my deodorant can.

I clapped my hands over my mouth and stared at the can as it bobbed and weaved back and forth near the far wall. *What the hell? Was I hallucinating?* I squeezed my eyes shut against the vision, willing it to disappear, wishing for it not to be there when I opened them again.

I heard a soft clunk and slowly opened my eyes; my heart pounded with fear as I looked up. My deodorant can was on the dressing table where I'd left it. I shook my head. Had I imagined it? I must have done. Maybe the dream had unsettled me more than I thought and my mind was playing tricks on me. Thinking of the dream once more altered my focus.

Anxious thoughts clouded my mind about what I'd witnessed during my slumber. Was it real or a dream? My perception was that it was scarily real, but how could it be? I didn't know where Joshua was and I'd never met the people he was with or visited the place where I saw him. This was soooo confusing.

I sat forward and hugged my knees to my chest. Perhaps it seemed so real because I wanted it to be. I wanted to know where he was, who he was with and most of all that he was all right. In some ways it made me feel closer to Josh so maybe I was making the dreams appear more real than they actually were. Who knew? It was disconcerting to see Joshua in such a rage – he was normally very placid – so what did it all mean?

I shook my head a little. Thinking about the realistic dream had me totally bewildered and not in the best frame of mind for what could possibly be another difficult day. I had to get my head straight again. I had a sudden epiphany and glancing at my watch to make sure it wasn't too early, I snatched my phone from the bedside table and hit one of the speed dial buttons. I wasn't generally an impatient sort of person, but waiting for the call to connect and be answered took an age. I found myself drumming my fingers on my knee while I waited. Just as I was about to give up and end the call, a beloved voice said, "Hiya hun how's things?"

Just hearing Becky's voice gave me comfort and yet a selfish part of me wished she was here, propping me up as she had before I set off on this . . . quest.

"Hiya Sis, I'm not too bad, considering. You okay?" I tried to sound upbeat, even smiling as I replied, but I should have known with our uncanny twin 'connection' she would see through it.

"Yeah, I'm fine, worried about you though. What's up?" her voice was calm but concerned.

"Have you got time for a chat or will you be late for work?"

"Naw, I've got plenty of time yet – fire away."

I recounted my two dreams and told her how they made me feel after I'd woken up, especially this last one. I decided against mentioning my *hallucination* – I didn't want her to worry more than she already was. She asked me various questions then helped me to get things into perspective.

"I always said you had an overactive imagination," Becky joked.

"Ha, ha. Takes one to know one," I threw back at her, laughing. Boy, it felt good to laugh with her again.

Becky chuckled. "Hey, are you okay now? I really do need to get ready for work now or I'll be late – I can ring you tonight if you want."

"I'm fine now, honestly. Thanks Becks. You get to work and I'll text you later, okay?" I didn't have to make an effort to keep my voice even and upbeat – I really did feel better.

"Okay, Rems, if you're sure. If you need me, call."

"Will do. Have a good day hun and thanks again. Love you."

"Love you too. 'Bye." It was obvious she was now in a bit of a hurry by how quickly she ended the call.

I started to feel a little guilty as I noticed the time and realised I'd probably made her late. I was also running behind schedule and thanks to Becky, I was now hyped up, eager to start the day, so I rushed through my morning routine and hot-footed it down to breakfast.

* * *

I spent my second day in Matlock, going through my list and shortening it with every establishment I visited. In terms of numbers, I'd had another successful day, but still no luck finding Joshua. I was still surprisingly positive despite the lack of result and could only put it down to my chat with Becky that morning. She'd always had the ability to keep me buoyant when I flagged and optimistic when I had an attack of the negatives, which wasn't normally very often. If anything, I was the one who usually propped her up – this role reversal felt very strange.

I stopped at the same coffee shop for a drink and snack about 3pm and Bonnie served me once again. She obviously recognised me from the previous day as she started a conversation with me, asking me how I was, how long I would be in the area and where I came from. I guess she could tell from my accent I wasn't local. I didn't tell her why I was in the Peak District and I was glad she didn't ask.

I ordered a pot of tea and a chocolate chip muffin. It didn't take me long to finish it all off and once again I felt my energy level rise, enough to keep me going for a bit longer. As before, I carried on ploughing through my list for another hour or so, before calling it a day. Exhaustion permeated my being, my eyelids were heavy, and my feet even heavier as I dragged my weary body back towards the car. I wasn't convinced I should even be driving, but I needed to get back to my hotel. I stopped off at a newsagent, bought a high-energy drink loaded with caffeine and drank it so quickly it caused me to belch. I chuckled tiredly before getting back into the car. I rolled the windows down and turned the music up, setting off down the road to return to Redow House.

I wasn't quite as lucky with my return journey as I had been the day before; this time it took me closer to thirty-five minutes and as I pulled onto the parking area, I could feel the last of the effects from the caffeine drink ebb away. I stumbled into the entrance hall; barely able to put one foot in front of the other, and using the banister rail, I literally pulled myself up the stairs.

It was so unlike me to run out of energy to the point of collapse - I was normally so fit. Maybe I'd been pushing myself a bit too hard over the last few days. I reached my room, fumbled to get the key in the lock and once inside, my knees started to buckle and I fell onto the sofa. That was the last thing I knew until 7am the next morning.

Chapter 25 – Remy

I awoke uncomfortable and confused. My back ached and my head felt fuzzy. I sat up and stretched, trying to ease the stiffness in my muscles; the sunlight streaming through the window hurt my eyes and I had to blink a few times until they adjusted. I thought back to yesterday; I remembered driving back from Matlock and pulling myself up the stairs using the banister rail, but after that everything was unclear, like looking out of a window with thick fog obscuring the view. I was surprised I was on the sofa instead of in bed and I didn't remember having dinner. I was still dressed in yesterday's clothes too and I felt all icky and dirty.

I rose slowly and started peeling off my clothes as I walked into the bathroom, dropping them on the floor as I went. After my shower I was feeling more human. I started to get dressed and my stomach growled noisily, testament to not having had dinner the night before. I checked my watch and was pleased to see the dining room would be open for breakfast. I finished dressing and hurried downstairs so I could erase the empty feeling inside. I needed to keep my strength up - after all, I still had quite a bit of ground to cover.

I consumed a much bigger breakfast than normal and even requested extra toast, eating until I was full and the grumbling noises ceased. I pushed my chair back, getting up from the table and strolled back up to my room. I brushed my teeth for the second time that morning and gathered my things for the day ahead. *I could probably finish with Matlock today*, I thought, especially as I was getting an earlier start than normal. I doubled checked I had everything I needed then left and walked out to my car.

As the day progressed my list dwindled. By lunchtime I only had a handful of establishments left to visit, but I was starving again, much to my surprise after my huge breakfast. I wasn't very far from the café I'd been to in the last couple of days so I made my way there again.

The sky had clouded over by the time I arrived and rain clouds gathered. It was also cooler as the breeze became stronger, so instead of occupying an outside table, I decided to sit inside. Entering the café, I was struck by how clean everything was and my nose detected a plethora of delicious aromas. The café was quite busy and much larger inside than was apparent from the street. I managed to find a small, unoccupied table near the back and sat, grabbing the menu as I did so. There were two used mugs and a plate bearing crumbs and a screwed up serviette which had yet to be cleared. It didn't bother me one bit as I concentrated on deciding what I was going to have.

A waitress came over to clear the table and wipe it, muttering an apology. I looked up to tell her it wasn't a problem and was pleased to see Bonnie smiling shyly at me. She told me she would be right back and disappeared through a door carrying the detritus from my table. Within a minute she was back and after exchanging pleasantries, she took my order and once again vanished through the same door.

As I waited for my food to arrive I let my eyes wander around the interior, looking at the décor before making an unconscious decision to people watch. It was a game Joshua and I used to play nearly every time we went out to eat somewhere. We used to try and guess what their names might be, what they did for a living, whether they were local or on holiday. Some of our guesses got a bit wild sometimes as we fabricated fantastically silly existences; in a restaurant one night, there was a man wearing a tuxedo and bow tie, and in our game he became a foreign government agent, a spy, who was packing a handgun or three, had a pocket full of electronic bugging devices and wearing a watch that had a laser beam which could cut through anything. His companion, an elegantly dressed attractive woman dripping in diamonds and rubies, who looked to be a few years older than him, sat opposite. We made up a whole story about her too and as the story got more ridiculous, we started giggling. The rather staid maître d' frowned at our antics, obviously not too impressed – perhaps he thought we were lowering the tone of the establishment by our merriment – which made us laugh even more. When our first course arrived, we quietened down and spent the remainder of the evening enjoying the food, the ambiance and each other's company.

As usual when I recalled pleasant memories of my time with Joshua, my eyes started to fill up and the constant ache in my chest ramped up to about an eight or nine on my pain scale. I grabbed a tissue from my pocket and dabbed carefully at my eyes, not wanting to smudge my mascara and leave black marks under my eyes. Just then, Bonnie approached the table with my order and I tried to conceal my misery by smiling at her as I tucked the tissue into my pocket. When she saw my eyes, a look of concern crossed her face.

She placed her hands on the table and leaned forward toward me.

"Hey, are you all right?" she asked me anxiously.

"Um, yeah, I'm okay. Just had a bit of a . . . *moment*, you know?" I replied, trying to keep my voice even, "but thanks for asking."

She studied me for a minute. "Yeah, I've had a few of those myself," her voice turned a little sour as she ran one finger along the scars down one side of her face and she grimaced. "Are you sure you're okay? You're pretty good at trying to hide it, but I can tell you're not really. It takes one to know one." Her voice had changed, become gentle and now the concern was back on her face.

I hesitated before answering her honestly, my expression showing only a miniscule fraction of the agony I was feeling inside. "Yeah, you're right," I sighed, "but hopefully I will be soon. What about you?"

There was no hesitation in her response. "I will be," she declared. "I'm having plastic surgery soon and then my nightmare will end – on the outside at least. Inside will take quite a bit longer, but I'll get there. I keep telling myself there are people much worse off than me and that helps me to get things in perspective. I have my good days and bad days, but I'm still in there fighting."

"You're in a healthier place than I am right now," I admitted, "things are much too . . . *raw* for me, the wounds too fresh . . ."

Before either of us could say anything further, a voice from behind the counter called her name. She glanced over her shoulder and nodded to the older lady who had summoned her.

"Crap. Sorry I gotta go. Don't let your food get cold." She turned and walked over to the counter.

I watched her for a moment then sighing I picked up my cutlery and began to eat my omelette.

"Poor girl, she's really suffering. I wonder what's happened to her . . ." Bonnie's voice whispered into my ear.

My fork stopped halfway towards my mouth as I looked around for her, but she was nowhere in sight. Was I hearing things? Her voice sighed again.

"She's trying so hard to put on a brave face, but she's not as good at it as she thinks. I can see right through her . . ."

What the hell was going on? How could I hear Bonnie when I couldn't even see her? My eyes roamed the café then I saw her emerge from the kitchen area carrying a large tray of steaming plates. She flicked her eyes in my direction and smiled before crossing to the other side of the room and began serving some patrons.

"I hope she has the strength she needs to get through this, whatever it is." Bonnie's voice breathed again.

My eyes bored into her back as I watched her placing drinks on a table. This was *mental*. What was going on? I watched as she walked to another table then to the counter. It wasn't until I heard a chuckle from a nearby table I became more aware of my surroundings again. I turned my head toward the sound and saw a young boy staring at me. He picked up a fork and did a great impression of me; fork half raised, staring eyes and my mouth formed into a large 'O'.

I looked away from him, embarrassed and put the now cold portion of omelette in my mouth. I chewed the rubbery texture and swallowed it. My eyes didn't leave my plate again until it was clear.

Bonnie was too busy to come and chat to me again. When I'd finished, I walked up to the counter to pay my bill, having already left a tip on the table for her. The woman, who I guessed was either the manager or owner, smiled tentatively at me.

"Did you enjoy your meal, dear?" She sounded quite friendly.

"Yes thanks, it was great," I replied sincerely, handing over a ten-pound note.

She counted out the change in to my hand then surprised me by her next question, "Bonnie wasn't being a nuisance, was she?"

The astonishment must have shown in my face as I considered how to answer. The last thing I wanted to do was get Bonnie into trouble. "Absolutely not!" I stated firmly. "If anything, she was being most considerate and caring – a rare thing these days. It's a pity there aren't more people like her around, willing to offer a helping hand to a stranger."

That took the wind out of her sails and she floundered, searching for a suitable response.

"Oh, er, well, okay. Erm, that's all right then. I just had to check ."

"Of course. I understand. Well, goodbye." I smiled then turned and walked out, giving Bonnie a wink as I passed her. She'd obviously overheard the conversation and mouthed the words *thank you*. I nodded and smiled before continuing out the door.

My afternoon was as fruitless as the morning, and as the previous two days had been. I was feeling a bit depressed as I walked back to the car, but in my peripheral vision I caught sight of the café. Although I couldn't see Bonnie, her scarred face appeared in my mind and her words came back to me with perfect recall. I had to start looking at things as she did. My scars were all inside me – the scratches and bruising Joshua had inflicted were now fully healed and had left no marks – whereas Bonnie's were there for all the world to see. I had to admit she was quite inspiring in her own way. Maybe she'd had longer to wrap her head around what had happened to her – by the looks of the scarring, I would say a few months – but it didn't mean I couldn't aspire to reach the level she had already attained. *I would have to work on it*, I thought, *it sure as hell won't happen overnight.*

I was reasonably pleased I'd managed to cram four days' worth of visits into three. By my reckoning, I still had to allow at least two days to cover Bakewell and another day or so for the villages. I was relieved I'd been able to extend my booking at Redow House from four days to a complete week – I was comfortable there and it would have been a real pain to have to find somewhere else – but I knew I couldn't extend it further as they had new guests arriving the day I was due to leave. However, knowing I had to leave by a certain date did put me under a certain amount of pressure to complete my task in this area, and frankly, it was pressure I could do without. Perhaps I should look at it more as an incentive rather than pressure.

I got into the car, a bit fatigued but not as tired as I had been the last two days, and looked at the clock on the dashboard. I hadn't brought any of the other lists with me and by the time I reached the hotel, there wouldn't be time to go back out again. I could feel anger and frustration winding its merry way through me – if only I'd considered picking up the other lists, I could have fitted in at least one, if not a couple of the villages before returning to Redow House. How stupid was I?

The anger was irrational, nevertheless it gathered momentum and without considering my actions, I slammed my clenched fists down onto my legs, managing to catch the muscles quite accurately. The pain which shot through them caused me to inhale sharply and I cried out "Owww, CRAP!" The incident did serve to dissolve a large portion of the fury I'd directed at myself and I rubbed my legs ruefully. I would probably find two lovely big bruises there tomorrow morning – I only hoped it wouldn't slow me down.

It took another five minutes of me gently massaging my legs before I considered myself capable of driving; I started the engine and had a practice using the pedals to make sure I could cope using them without too much discomfort, then when I was satisfied, I put the car into gear and moved off. My legs were still aching, but not as painful as they had been at first. I remembered I had some Arnica cream back in my room and resolved to massage some in as soon as I got back.

The traffic was much slower than it had been previously and the return journey took me twice as long. It was so typical – 'sod's law' my mum called it – here I was with really aching legs, made worse by the constant braking and changing gear, and the traffic was a nightmare.

Eventually I reached the hotel with some relief. As I got out of the car and stood, the muscles in my legs protested by shooting arrows of pain up towards my groin. I gasped then groaned, holding onto the car door for support. I knew I couldn't remain here; I had to keep the muscles moving, something I'd learned from my years of dancing, so I tried to take a couple of steps. They hurt like hell, but I gritted my teeth and concentrated on moving into the hotel. I made it to the bottom of the stairs then mumbled an expletive. This was going to be a whole new challenge. I took a deep breath through my tightly clamped jaws, moved my foot onto the first tread and, gripping the banister rail for dear life, put my weight onto it, muttering more expletives under my breath. I continued slowly upwards until finally I reached the top. My jaws were now aching too and it was with some relief I found I was able to relax them as I completed the short distance to my room.

Once inside, I quickly located the cream, pulled off my cropped trousers and surveyed the damage. Two large red patches stared up at me –the bruising was already beginning to show a little in the middle where the colour was darker and more purple than red. I moved into the bathroom and over to the sink. Grabbing my face flannel, I turned on the cold tap and placed it under the water. When the water temperature had cooled further, I squeezed the excess out and perching on the side of the bath, gingerly laid it over the redness on my left leg. The respite was instant and I left it in place until the cloth reached the same temperature as my leg. I then repeated the process and draped it on my right leg. When I finally removed the flannel and stood again, they did feel a little better, a little less achy so I massaged in the cream and went to lie down on the bed.

I was determined not to fall asleep and miss dinner two nights running so I grabbed my list for Bakewell and the local map and spent some time planning my route for the next day. By the time I'd completed that task, the cream on my legs was completely absorbed and the skin felt dry to the touch. I gradually manoeuvred until I was on my feet and erect, pleasantly surprised the ache in my legs had subsided enough so I could walk without having to stop myself from crying out.

I freshened up, changed my clothes and grabbed my e-reader from the bedside table before heading down to the dining hall. After a superb meal with a carafe of wine, I headed over to the bar in the guest lounge and had a couple of glasses of Cointreau over ice, immersing myself in The Devil's Kitchen; this wasn't my usual type of book, it was a sub-genre called Steampunk and the second book in a quadrilogy. I enjoyed the first one in the Crown Phoenix series and was gripped by the sequel.

By the time I was ready to crash, I was feeling no pain – not that I was drunk, just comfortably tipsy enough to be mellowed out. I made the trip up the stairs much quicker than I had earlier, that was for sure. I got ready for bed, massaged more cream into my legs then flopped onto the mattress. Within seconds I was dead to the world.

I awoke to my alarm and felt perfectly fine – until I tried to stand up. My legs were lead weights, too heavy for my feet and they ached from the knee to the top of my thigh. I flopped back onto the bed and had a closer look, but with the curtains closed, I couldn't really see very much. I shuffled on my backside along to the head end of the bed until the curtains were within my grasp and pulled it back to reveal a pale blue sky mottled with fluffy clouds and the sun playing peek-a-boo.

I stared down at my thighs, my jaw dropping open at the sight of the humungous bruises which were shades of purple and blue. To my surprise, the marks were much larger than the size of my fist and I wondered idly how they'd got so big. My brow furrowed as I cast my mind back to when I'd thumped them yesterday and all I could think of to explain the size of the bruises was that when my fists had connected with my legs, maybe they'd landed at an angle or slid a bit.

Oh, God. What a *dipstick*. Time wise, this was going to *seriously* set me back. I knew I wouldn't be able to do much today, if anything, but I also knew if I didn't at least try to keep my muscles moving, I would be much worse off in the long run. I found it funny, in a totally ironic sort of way that a momentary reaction to my frustration and anger could have such a profound effect on my ability to function normally.

I started to gently stretch my muscles using exercises learned from my dancing classes. At first it hurt like hell as they had stiffened up overnight, but gradually the pain lessened to the extent I could stand up and start walking around the room without resembling a ninety year old. I carried on exercising for another fifteen minutes before hitting the shower.

The warm water helped soothe my aching limbs even further and by the time I was dressed, I was ready to at least try and carry on with my search – but not until I'd got a decent breakfast inside me. I grabbed my lists, map, photo of Joshua, bag and keys then headed downstairs.

By the time I'd finished eating my muscles had started to stiffen up again, much to my chagrin. I decided to take a stroll around the grounds to loosen them up again. I'd only seen the gardens from the window in my room and whilst I couldn't really afford the time, it was an ideal opportunity.

I wandered around the garden and admired the mature shrubs, the bushes neatly trimmed into various flowing shapes, and the ancient trees. By the time I'd gazed at the proliferation of flowers of different types, colours and scents, my leg muscles had loosened sufficiently for me to consider being able to drive.

Walking to the car I climbed in, wincing a little at the pain which shot through my legs as I sat on the seat. Before starting the engine, I pushed the clutch pedal down with my left foot and a sharper pain caused me to gasp aloud. As I released the pressure on the pedal the same thing happened. This was not a good sign. I tried the brake pedal with my right foot and yet again a searing burn flashed through my muscles, making me cry out. *Crap! Crap! Crap!* There was no way I was going to be able to drive today. This was going to put me seriously behind and, as there was no guarantee I'd be able to drive tomorrow, there was a strong chance I wouldn't even get this area finished before having to check out of my room.

I gingerly got out of the car, flinching as yet another spasm of stinging soreness cascaded down my limbs. I returned to my room and dumped everything unceremoniously on the sofa in a fit of pique. Irritation flooded through me – *how could I have been so damn stupid?* There was nothing to be gained by beating myself up over this – I chuckled to myself at the unintended pun – I would have to do all I could to try and ensure I would be able to continue tomorrow.

I removed my cropped trousers and grabbing the Arnica cream from the bedside table, began to massage it into my thighs using gentle circular movements. Once it was completed, I lay on the bed and started some more stretching exercises, letting my mind drift as I did so. I thought about how I was suddenly so quick to anger – it was so uncharacteristic. Normally I was such a calm and placid person. Maybe it had more to do with my fragile emotional state than an actual change in my personality. That worked – it was a good explanation and perfectly plausible. I actually felt a little better once I'd reached a conclusion; one thing I didn't want was for me to change so much that when I did find Joshua, I wasn't the same girl he'd fallen in love with. I had to make sure I didn't lose *me* along the way.

I deliberately shifted the focus of my musings away from Joshua, as I knew I would end up crying again, so I considered my conversation with Bonnie at the café yesterday. I spent some time speculating on what had caused the horrible scarring on her attractive face. I discounted many theories before I came up with one that could fit, but even this one – a dog attack – was perhaps a little improbable. Maybe if I went back there and she got to know me a bit better, she might even confide in me and tell me what had caused it. *Fat chance of that happening. I haven't got the time, especially now I'm losing today.*

I completed my stretches and lay there, bored stupid. I closed my eyes and slowly drifted into a light sleep. I could still hear the birds singing and calling to their own kind, the breeze rustled the foliage in the nearby trees and I could discern faint sounds of movement and voices from around the hotel.

When I finally opened my eyes, the sun had changed position in the sky and I knew I'd missed lunch. I snuck a peek at my watch and found it was actually late afternoon. I was astounded I'd slept the day away and all my good intentions to get my muscles working to ease the pain had resulted in nothing. I flexed my leg muscles to see how bad it was and was pleasantly surprised to note they didn't appear to be quite as tender as before. I sat up and applied more cream before getting to my feet and walking around the room. It was definitely less painful than before although not completely gone. I did a few more stretches then putting my trousers back on, I grabbed my room key and walked downstairs and out into the garden.

After completing several circuits, I returned to my room, read for an hour then got changed ready for dinner. After a scrumptious three-course meal and a half-bottle of wine, I went back to my room, stretched again, applied more cream and got into bed. I didn't feel particularly sleepy so I turned on the TV and flicked through the channels until I found something worth watching. I didn't remember turning off the TV, but the next thing I was aware of, was the alarm going off the next morning.

My legs were not so painful I had to spend another day

incarcerated at the hotel and was able to continue my search. Over the next two days I managed to complete all the establishments in Bakewell and a few of the villages too. I couldn't help but be quite pleased I'd managed to catch up so well. I still hadn't found Josh and, of course, I was majorly upset by that, but somehow I managed to keep thinking positively. The few villages left were on the way to my next destination so if I checked out straight after breakfast tomorrow, I should have time to complete my list and still make it to Norfolk during daylight hours.

    I packed the vast majority of my stuff before going down to dinner, leaving out my toiletries and fresh clothes for the following day. I limited my alcohol intake to a couple of glasses of wine and went to bed before 10pm as I wanted to get an early start. I rapidly fell into a deep exhausted slumber.

Chapter 26 – Joshua

Joshua had returned from hunting that morning and gone up to his room; he wanted to change his clothes before going out into the grounds. He had decided to explore the numerous outbuildings that day. Although he'd been in them previously when searching for Jasna, he hadn't taken the time to really look around. As Farrell, Erika and Dayna were still unaware he was a daywalker; he waited until they were settled in their rooms before venturing out.

The sun was glorious in the cloudless sky and the heat beat down, causing flowers and plants to wilt. He had an irresistible urge to rest a while and flopped onto the soft grass, singed golden in places by the relentless power and heat of the sun.

Joshua lay prostrate on the lawn, his hands behind his head and his eyes closed against the brightness, contemplating the previous few days. His days and nights had continued as before, roaming the grounds by day and hunting with Farrell and Erika at night. He was worried sick about Jasna as she had still not returned and even Samir had no idea where she was, even with his vamp radar to assist him. *I hope she's alright*, he thought. It was strange – it wasn't until Jasna went AWOL he realised how much of an integral part of his new life she had become, especially his recognition that he had feelings for her. *Talk about rotten timing,* he thought.

Dayna had kept her distance from him, and for once, was quite demure, especially when Samir was around.

After thinking about Jasna for a time, and letting himself get more anxious, he got up and stretched. He meandered at human pace across the gradually browning lawn towards the first cluster of buildings, becoming calmer with each stride. He got a kick out of exploring new places and a sense of excitement began to build within him. As he approached, he noticed they were not as clear in his vision as normal. He was perplexed by this and rubbed the heels of his hands across his eyes as if to remove a layer of film or dust from them. When he looked back at the nearest building, the wall shimmered for a moment like blazing sun bouncing off tarmac, before disappearing altogether and he could see the inside as clearly as if he were standing in it.

He stood motionless, a marble statue, stunned at the tableau before him; his eyes wide and his jaw dropped. He looked at the stable building next to it and again the outside wall vanished, allowing him to see the stalls and the tack hanging on hooks at both ends. What did this mean? Was this another gift? Could he see through walls now? He turned and sprinted towards the main house. As he approached he slowed and found he could see straight into the building as if the walls did not exist.

He rushed straight up to Samir's room and before knocking, looked through the closed door to see if Samir was still moving about. He tapped quietly and Samir opened the door, surprise etched across his face.

"Joshua?"

"I'm sorry to disturb you, but can we talk for a moment please? It's important." Joshua's voice echoed the excitement in his eyes.

Samir opened the door wider and gestured for Joshua to enter. Joshua crossed the threshold and briefly let his eyes flicker around the room; this was the first time he'd seen Samir's quarters, which were much larger and more opulent than his own. However, he was too keyed up to pay it much attention – he wanted to explain to Samir what had happened in the garden. He turned at the sound of Samir's voice.

"So, Joshua, what is all this about? What is so important it can't wait until I've rested?" his voice sounded inquisitive, eager, but his facial expression was more inclined towards impatience and, to a degree, indulgence.

Joshua didn't really notice Samir's expression or tone of voice. He didn't even stop to consider that perhaps Samir would view his knocking on the door as an intrusion into his private time and space. In his excitement, he was as skittish as a puppy and bouncing on the balls of his feet.

"You said you wanted to know straight away if anything else . . . *developed*, with me I mean, and now it has, and it's *amazing* and I just had to come and tell you about it." Joshua babbled in his excitement, talking so fast the words ran together like a continuous note.

Samir's interest was significantly aroused and instead of feeling impatient, he found Joshua's excitement infectious. His expression was more alive and his eyes shone in anticipation.

"So are you going to keep me in suspense, my son, or do I have to try and guess?"

"Sorry," Joshua exclaimed, not sounding at all apologetic, "I can see through walls," he blurted out proudly.

"I beg your pardon?" Samir gaped; his mouth wide and his bottom jaw almost touched his chest.

"Er, I can see through walls," Joshua enunciated much slower than before, but still with pride.

Samir was rather shocked by this announcement, but was at least able to talk coherently. "How and when did you find out?"

"About thirty seconds before I knocked on your door. I was walking in the garden and was going to explore the outbuildings, but as I walked towards them, the outside walls sort of shook and shimmered and then they disappeared and it was as if I was standing inside the buildings, I could see everything, y'know?" in his enthusiasm, Joshua spoke way too fast again, certainly too fast for human ears to be able to pick out the words, but it was no problem for Samir.

Samir sat on the edge of an ancient looking armchair and pondered for a few minutes, his fingers interlaced and supporting his chin. He was completely still – the only things which moved occasionally were his eyes. Joshua became increasingly nervous as the silence stretched into minutes and he became less energised and more motionless as the time went on.

Just as Joshua reached the point when he couldn't stand it any longer and was about to break the quiet, Samir moved at last and raised his head to look at him.

"I'm sorry – I was thinking about the best way to answer you. Obviously there's nothing I can do right at this moment – it's too light outside of this room, for me at least – so will you meet me in the foyer at dusk to discuss this further?"

"Of course," Joshua replied, relieved Samir had spoken at last.

Samir rose from his seat and gently ushered Joshua towards the door. "Thank you for coming to me with this so quickly, Joshua. Please allow me to rest now and I'll see you later."

Joshua nodded and turned towards the door. As he put his hand on the handle, he turned back to Samir about to say something then changed his mind. He opened the door by the smallest crack he could squeeze through and quietly closed the door behind him, leaving Samir in his darkened room to rest, while he wandered back downstairs and out into the sunlight.

As Joshua started to meander towards the outbuildings again, it occurred to him that he would definitely be required to prove his new gift to Samir. He then began to worry. What if he couldn't do it on command? He would look a right plonker and Samir would be disappointed in him, especially as he had interrupted him in his room. He didn't *want* to displease Samir.

An idea suddenly formed in his mind. He would practice. He would make sure that when called upon to demonstrate this new talent, he could do it, and do it well. He stopped where he was and looked back towards the house, staring at the room directly in front of him. At first, nothing happened. A massive streak of horror ran through him as he wondered why it had happened so effortlessly before and now nothing. Did he have to look at it a certain way? Did he have to be in a particular frame of mind?

He recalled the earlier event, analysing his mood and how he'd looked towards the outbuildings. He recognised a sense of anticipation, curiosity and excitement for something new – maybe that was the trigger. He tried to replicate those feelings again as he made another attempt. Again nothing. Was he trying too hard now? He was as tense as a coiled spring so he closed his eyes and concentrated on relaxing.

Two minutes passed before he was sufficiently relaxed to have another go. Still keeping his eyes shut, he allowed the earlier feelings to flood through him before opening his eyes and looking straight at the house again. After about thirty seconds, the wall shimmered as before then vanished, revealing a room he knew well – the library. He cast his eyes around it ensuring he could see every aspect before looking away. Success. *Maybe it was an unfair test*, he thought, bearing in mind how well he knew that particular room. He cast his eyes up to the room above and repeated the exercise. Again the wall disappeared after a few seconds showing one of the guest rooms he'd only seen briefly on his first day at the manor and was not anywhere near as familiar with. He viewed the furnishings objectively and when satisfied, he turned his eyes away.

He moved twenty feet further along his original path and turned back to the house again. Now he had a different view. He repeated the exercise again with different rooms, each time with success. The more he practiced the faster the walls melted away to reveal their contents to him.

He turned his back on the manor and continued towards the outbuildings. In some ways this would be more of a test as they were less familiar to him. As the first one came into view, the wall facing him slid away, like someone moving a scenery prop on a film set, and he examined the contents curiously, before moving on to the next one.

He continued to practice most of the day. He even came across his car and could see into the boot and the interior from quite a distance away. He hadn't even sat in his car since the day he arrived and wondered if the battery had gone flat. *I must turn the engine over and soon*, he thought, *perhaps even give it a bit of a run out. I'll have to remember to mention it to Samir*. As much as he loved to run, especially as he was so damn fast, he did miss his car. He went over to it and ran his hand across the roof as if stroking it. His hand left a clean streak in the patina of dust which covered the paintwork like a shroud, making it dull. He'd never allowed his car to get this mucky before. Still, there were more important things to consider and he turned his mind back to the task in hand.

* * *

As twilight fell, Joshua was waiting in the foyer as requested. Samir descended much earlier than usual – he even beat Farrell and Erika, which was unusual. He smiled at Joshua and gestured for him to follow, leading the way down one of the corridors which were barely used.

Samir suddenly halted outside a door about two thirds of the way along then turned to face Joshua.

"Now, Joshua, do you mind if we test your new talent?" he raised one eyebrow and a small smile flittered onto his lips.

"Fine by me," Joshua was confident and relaxed in his response and waited patiently to discover what his maker had in mind.

"This is one room you have never been shown. Can you tell me what is inside it without opening the door?" Samir challenged him, his smile spreading into a grin.

Joshua matched him grin for grin and positioning himself in front of the door, stared straight at it before replying.

"I can see a huge grand piano set on a dais in the left corner with an upholstered stool in front of it. There are piles of papers on top of the piano. To the right I see a few seats facing into the room with music stands in front of them containing sheet music, I see rows of chairs facing the piano as if ready and waiting for an audience.

"There is a fireplace on the left with a wooden mantel shelf and above is a painting with a country scene and horses depicted. In front of the window on the right is a table – it has crystal decanters sitting on a silver tray and another tray bearing glasses. The window drapes are heavy, green and have tasselled tiebacks. There are three rugs, one in front of the fireplace, one by the table and the other between the music stands and the rows of chairs." He turned towards Samir with a smug expression on his face. Samir's face was incredulous in its astonishment. He quickly recovered and met Joshua's gaze.

"Very well. Let us see if you are correct, shall we?" an amused tone threaded through his voice as he reached for the door handle.

Joshua nodded, supremely confident and eager to be proved right. Samir opened the door wide and walked through, Joshua following in his wake. The room was exactly as had been described. Joshua punched one fist into the air, "YES!" he whispered in jubilation, then catching sight of Samir's amused expression, chuckled. Samir laughed with him and clapped him on the shoulder.

"Well, it seems you have another unusual yet spectacular talent, Joshua," he exclaimed like a proud father, "and I see no reason why we shouldn't share this one with the rest of our coven, although I still want to keep your daywalking abilities to ourselves a little longer."

"Fine by me," Joshua replied, still totally hyped and grinning from ear to ear.

"Shall we?" Samir gestured, smiling.

They left the room, Samir closing the door behind them and retraced their steps to the foyer. Before they entered the library, Joshua advised, "Dayna's not in there but Farrell and Erika are."

"Dayna?" Samir's voice was soft as he called her. He didn't need to shout – she would hear him no matter where she was in the house.

A few seconds later they heard a soft rustle of fabric, too quiet for human ears, as Dayna approached the top of the stairs. Joshua proceeded into the library, greeting Farrell and Erika as he entered. Samir waited in the foyer for Dayna to arrive before joining them. He waited for everyone to settle down before making his announcement. He swept his eyes around the room looking at each of them individually, leaving Joshua for last and winking at him.

"As is our practice and custom in this coven to share important information – I have, or should I say, we have, something to share with you . . ." Samir held his hand out for Joshua to join him. He rose and went to stand beside his maker.

"I think it is better to demonstrate rather than just report this information," he turned to Joshua now and continued, "Joshua, on the table in the foyer at the bottom of the stairs I have placed an object. Can you please tell us about it?"

Joshua grinned before turning his head in the appropriate direction.

"No problem," he said cockily, "it is a porcelain vase with two handles near the top. It has a gold rim and a double gold band beneath. It has some Greek Key symbols on it and is primarily blue with gold figures on it." He looked first at Samir and then at the faces of his coven, a smug self-satisfied expression on his face.

Samir turned to face the others. "Erika? Would you please retrieve the object from the table and bring it in here?"

"Certainly," Erika replied rising from her seat. She cast a sceptical look at Joshua as she passed him then continued into the hall. "Holy crap!" her murmur filtered into the library ahead of her as she entered carrying the vase Joshua had described so accurately.

There was a sharp yet noticeable intake of breath from Dayna, and Farrell whistled through his teeth in amazement. All of them looked incredulously at Joshua, temporarily lost for words. Joshua's smirk turned into a snigger at their expressions. He sneaked a peep at Samir who was also laughing, albeit silently.

Farrell was the first to recover. "Oh, man! So you can see through walls? You've got some sort of x-ray vision?"

"Yeah, it seems that way," Joshua replied proudly.

"So when did *this* happen?"

"Er, as I was going to my room before dawn," he lied smoothly and believably.

Farrell turned to Samir, "So when did *you* find out then?"

"Joshua came to me this morning before I began my rest and told me. Then we met up a little before we came to tell you so he could show me himself what he could do." Samir replied, a smile on his lips.

"Okay, so is it just walls and doors and stuff you can see through or what?" Erika asked nervously.

Joshua looked at her, puzzled at first by her apprehension and then, he guessed what she was referring to and burst out laughing. Farrell cottoned on at the same time Joshua did and his eyes narrowed as he awaited his response. Dayna said nothing, but her eyes glazed in annoyance.

Joshua's eyes raked over them and seeing their reaction stopped laughing at once, although the amusement was clear in his tone as he answered.

"You have nothing to worry about, Erika. I can't see through your clothing."

Her face relaxed, as did Farrell's and Dayna's. Samir found this extremely funny and his loud guffaws echoed around the room; the others joined in as they realised how it must look. After a few minutes, the hilarity had run its course and they all started to calm down.

"There's eons of time to discuss this," Samir chuckled, "but now, I think, it's time to hunt."

Everyone rose and started heading towards the open door to the foyer. Joshua followed them, but grabbed Farrell's arm.

"Can you give me a minute? I need to pop up to my room."

Farrell nodded. "Yeah, sure. We'll wait for you."

Joshua turned and disappeared up the stairs before the others had time to turn their heads. As he walked down the corridor to his room, his eyes flicked towards Jasna's room, as they normally did, hoping against hope she would open the door and walk through it. What he caught in his peripheral vision stopped him cold. He turned to face the room, the walls shimmered and disappeared and he gasped at what he saw. Jasna *was* there, but collapsed inside some sort of cupboard not moving at all. Although he didn't need to, he yelled out for Samir in his urgency and then crashed through the door into her room.

Joshua moved straight to the cupboard and yanked open the door, ripping it off its' hinges. Lying in a crumpled heap at the bottom was Jasna. She was so weak she could barely open her eyes, let alone open her mouth to protest as Joshua scooped her up in his arms and laid her on the bed. Samir, Farrell and Erika had reached Jasna's room by this time and clustered around, aghast at the condition she was in. Dayna stood in the doorway observing for a moment, her face impassive, before disappearing back downstairs and out into the night – she didn't want to be on the receiving end of Joshua's fury again and her self-preservation instinct told her she ought to put some distance between them.

Joshua sat on the bed beside Jasna and stroked her face while Samir bent over and examined her. Her skin looked as fragile and thin as tissue paper, her eyes were dull and her lips colourless. Samir straightened up after a couple of minutes, anxiety written across his features and turned to Joshua.

"She is extremely frail, but the situation is recoverable. She needs to feed immediately to start regaining her vigour yet I fear she is unable to travel. She hasn't got the strength to physically get herself in a position where she *could* feed." His voice echoed the concern.

"That's not a problem," Joshua asserted, "I will carry her and hunt for her and bring her humans to feed on. If Erika and Farrell will help me, we can do it in shifts so one of us stays with her constantly until we're ready to return." Joshua turned towards his friends, but before he could voice his plea, Erika spoke up.

"Of course we'll help you. We want Jasna back to full strength as much as *you* do." She looked him straight in the eyes and smiled gently. Joshua flicked his eyes towards Farrell who was nodding in agreement.

Samir looked at the three of them, awed and proud they would go to such lengths to help one of their own. He masked his disappointment that Dayna had disappeared out alone, seemingly without paying Jasna any mind, but didn't feel inclined to speculate as to why right at this moment. There were more important things to consider.

He turned to Joshua, smiling benignly at him. "That's a wonderful suggestion and I can't adequately express my pleasure and pride in the three of you. Now, there's no time to waste. Jasna's need is urgent so . . ."

Before Samir had a chance to complete his sentence, Joshua gently picked Jasna up and cradled her in his arms, keeping her close to his body; he moved towards the door, Farrell and Erika right on his heels.

"On it." Joshua stated and without giving Samir the chance to utter another syllable, he flew down the stairs and out into the balmy, tropical night.

Samir stared at the empty doorway; a sense of relief flowing through him as he considered the events of the past few minutes. Jasna had been found and three of his coven cared enough to help her recovery. It was incredibly co-incidental Joshua's new talent should reveal itself today of all days – if Jasna hadn't been found for another couple of days, it may have been too late to help her. He shuddered at the thought.

He turned his head and looked at the cupboard where Jasna had been discovered and wondered why it had defied his vamp radar. He moved over to it and examined it more closely. On the surface, it appeared to be a completely normal wooden cupboard, but when he picked up the door Joshua had ripped off in his haste to rescue Jasna, he was astonished by how weighty it was. Not that it was too heavy for him, far from it – he could balance it on his little finger and it wouldn't have been too heavy – but it was certainly not made entirely of wood.

Samir peeled off two panels from the inside of the door and was stunned to find a thick metal sheet sandwiched between the wooden panels. He dropped the panels and stepped inside the large cupboard. He peeled off some more panels at random and found the entire structure was lined with metal. He moved back over to the door and scrutinised the metal more closely. First he sniffed at it then squeezed it between his forefinger and thumb, shocked to find how soft it was. The realisation hit him like a bullet between the eyes – it was lead. No wonder his vamp radar had failed to locate Jasna – it couldn't penetrate lead.

He wasn't aware the cupboard was even in the manor, let alone in Jasna's room. *Of all the rooms for it to be in, it couldn't have been in a worse one*, he thought. If Dayna had kept her mouth shut, he probably never would have known it existed. He had to ensure nothing like this ever happened again, especially as he couldn't trust Dayna not to try and humiliate Jasna in the future. He became a one-man wrecking ball and literally ripped the structure to pieces.

When he was satisfied it was beyond redemption, he gathered the detritus and threw the pieces out of the window so they landed in the courtyard below. He decided to leave the rubbish where it was as he wanted the opportunity to show Dayna the damage she had caused. In the meantime, he needed to hunt, so after casting his eyes around Jasna's room once more to ensure he'd left no trace of the offending cupboard behind, Samir left the manor and headed out to satiate his thirst.

* * *

Farrell, Erika and Joshua elected not to travel too far from the manor with Jasna in such a poor condition. She needed sustenance quickly so it made perfect sense to hunt closer to home than they normally would.

As they sprinted through the countryside, decisions were made as to how they would execute their plan. Erika was going to stay with Jasna while Joshua and Farrell hunted. Joshua would bring a human or two back with him so Jasna could feed then he would stay and help her with it while Erika went to hunt. In theory the plan was sound, but whether it would work that way was another matter. Time would tell.

They reached an appropriate spot to stop and Joshua laid Jasna on the ground, gently propping her upper torso against a tree, her head sagged against Erika's shoulder as she sat next to her. Erika's eyes were wide with fear as she took one of Jasna's hands in her own – it was like picking up an inanimate object. She turned her head towards Joshua and whispered one word, "Hurry!"

Joshua moved faster than he ever had before. He understood from Erika's tone and expression that time was of the essence, let alone her one word instruction. As he flew towards the town, seeming to travel at the speed of light, he knew he would not hunt for himself until Jasna had been fed. She was the priority now – he *had* to save her.

As he reached the outskirts of the town, he found he was in an industrial area surrounded by factories, warehouses and offices, so was surprised when he immediately detected human scent. He scaled the building beside him and skipped across the rooftops towards his prey. He could smell how close he was, besides which they weren't exactly quiet. There were two or three of them, all egging each other on. He heard a small whimper of fear from what sounded like a young girl.

He peaked over the edge of the roof and down to the ground below. With his perfect night vision, he saw every detail and was horrified at the scene playing out before him. Three men aged between twenty and thirty were terrorising a girl of around seventeen. Her blouse had been ripped open revealing her fettered breasts, her face bore evidence that she had been struck more than once and had been crying and her short skirt had also been torn. The men were arguing about who was going to be first to defile her, and as they argued they closed in, surrounding her and cutting off her escape. Hands groped her from all directions, like tentacles; her breasts, her bottom and between her legs – all areas were fair game as far as the scumbags were concerned. She pleaded with them to leave her alone, to let her go, not to hurt her and the men laughed, obviously enjoying her terror.

Joshua dropped silently to the ground behind them, landing so softly on the balls of his feet the rapists didn't hear him. He was right behind them and they were completely oblivious to his presence. In a move faster than the strike of a snake, the three men had been rendered unconscious and lay in a heap on the ground. The girl was completely stunned – she thought there was no way she would get away from them. She stumbled towards Joshua, grabbed his hand and mumbled her thanks over and over. He gently loosened her grip on him, took off his shirt and held it out to her.

"You can't go home in the state you're in – here take this and put it on. Now get out of here, before they start to come round," he ordered gently.

She took his shirt but hesitated. He didn't have time for this – he needed to get these humans back to Jasna. He made his face look more fierce, but not enough to scare her senseless, and growled at her.

"I said GET GOING, NOW!"

That did it – she ran as if her life depended on it and was out of his sight within seconds, although he could still hear her. One of the men started to stir – he must have had quite a hard skull – so Joshua knocked him out again, then grabbing two of them, he threw them over his shoulders in a fireman's lift and sped back to where Jasna and Erika were waiting.

He dropped his prey by Jasna's feet and quickly told Erika what he'd witnessed and where to find the third one as he seized one of them and dragged him closer. He took Erika's place and crooned Jasna's name softly into her ear until he got a reaction from her. He could see she wasn't even strong enough to bite into her food' he laid her down so his knees supported her head.

"Jasna? Can you hear me honey? I'm going to get some blood into you now – can you help me? Can you open your mouth for me?" Joshua crooned, trying to keep the urgency out of his voice.

Her eyelids fluttered and gradually opened. She saw Joshua gazing worriedly down at her and she tried to smile.

"Okay," she whispered her voice hoarse. She opened her mouth and waited.

Joshua used his sharp fingernails to open a slit in the man's throat, straight into the jugular vein. He kept a finger over it until he'd positioned it to drip straight into Jasna's mouth then moved his finger just enough so he could control the flow of blood. Jasna was so frail she barely had the strength to even swallow at first, but as more of the blood got into her body, she began to feel a little stronger and was able to swallow without a problem.

It was a slow process, but eventually the first victim was drained completely. As Joshua monitored her recovery, he noticed her eyes were more alive, a little brighter and some colour had returned to her lips.

"Are you ready for your next course, madam?" Joshua joked with her.

Jasna smiled with less effort this time and said, "Yes please."

He grabbed the other scumbag and repeated the process. By the time this one ran dry, Jasna was able to hold her head up and sit up unaided. She still looked very fragile, but in contrast to how they had found her, it was a huge improvement.

"How do you feel now?" Joshua reached for her hand and held it gently in his as he stared into her eyes, waiting for a reply.

If she had been standing, she would have gone weak at the knees. To see Joshua looking at her this way, to have him holding her hand, it was more than she'd ever dared to dream. She remembered he had asked her a question and she hadn't answered him.

"Still weak and a bit shaky, but definitely better than I was." She squeezed his hand as she continued, "thank you for saving me, Joshua." She lowered her eyes as if embarrassed.

Joshua put his other hand under her chin and raised it, making her look up at him again.

"We can discuss that later. Right now I need to know if you can handle another one," he gestured towards the two corpses which lay at their feet.

"I *think* so. I won't know for sure until I try though." She said.

Just as she finished speaking, Erika and Farrell appeared both carrying an unconscious human on their shoulders. As they approached they were both surprised and delighted by the improvement in Jasna since they'd last seen her, and smiles lit up their faces.

"Thought you might want second helpings," Farrell joked, dropping his catch by her side and grinning. Erika dropped hers next to the other one and crouched down on Jasna's other side.

"And thirds. Or is it fourths?" she chuckled.

Jasna chuckled. "I was telling Joshua I thought I could manage a little more. Thank you both."

Joshua grabbed one of them and pulled it close enough so she could bite into the neck herself. As she drank deeply, a small groan of pleasure escaped from her lips and in no time at all, she was pushing the drained carcass away from her.

"I feel so full now," Jasna stated, "I don't think I can manage another one." She looked so much better.

"Have you fed tonight, Joshua?" Farrell asked, guessing shrewdly what the answer would be.

"Nope," he replied, totally blasé.

"Well, then you're the only person who hasn't and there's a spare one here with your name on it," Farrell gestured towards the other body, smirking.

Joshua turned to Jasna, concern in his eyes. "Are you absolutely sure you've had sufficient?"

"Yes, I'm positive. You go ahead." Even her voice sounded stronger.

"You sure you two don't need it?" Joshua asked, considerately.

Farrell shook his head. Erika rolled her eyes but smiled at him, "Just get on with it."

Joshua chuckled then pulled the man towards him and sinking his teeth into the neck, drank him dry within seconds.

Erika glanced at her watch.

"Hey, it's time we were making tracks people." As she said it she got to her feet and dragged Farrell up with her.

"Do you feel strong enough to walk or would you like me to carry you again?" Joshua asked Jasna softly, not wanting to embarrass her.

"I'm not sure," she admitted, "will you help me up?" she held her other hand out to him. He stood and pulled her gently onto her feet. Her legs were a little wobbly and not yet strong enough. Joshua caught her as her legs gave way.

"I guess that's my answer then" he smiled as he cradled her in his arms, holding her closer than before. She smiled up at him gratefully as they started to head back to the manor.

Farrell and Erika had gone on ahead, but not so far they were out of earshot. As Joshua ran smoothly through the night his eyes barely left the face of the woman in his arms. As they reached the grounds, he slowed to a walk, making the most of his time alone with her. She still looked breakable, but so pretty. He lowered his head and kissed her on the forehead. Raising his head he observed Jasna's face for some reaction. What he saw made his heart sing. He lowered his head once again; this time his lips met hers, once, twice, three times – sweetly and briefly.

Before he had a chance to pull away again, Jasna's arm snaked up and around his neck and pulled his lips back to hers. The kiss was long, gentle, lingering, their lips moving together in harmony and oh so sweet. As their lips drew apart, Joshua gazed into her eyes and saw the love shining out from them. His lips were tingling as if a small electric current had been passed through them and his entire body was aflame with desire. He knew Jasna was probably not well enough for *that* yet and didn't want to push it – it wasn't as if they had a time limit, but having tasted the honey sweetness of her lips, he wanted more and he could tell she felt the same.

In his peripheral vision, he could see the sky lightening on the horizon as the first shades of lavender and pink began to appear. He moved towards the manor at a quicker pace, determined to get Jasna safely out of the sun and knowing Samir would want to see the extent of her recovery before he rested.

"I need to get us inside, now," he murmured to her, his voice a little husky with suppressed emotion.

Jasna's other hand traced the contours of his face with her fingertips, her touch leaving a tingling sensation in their wake. "I know," she sighed softly, letting her hand fall back across her body as they entered through the main door.

Joshua strode straight into the library where Samir was waiting expectantly. When he saw the improvement in her condition, Samir's expression changed from worry to joy. He came over to Jasna, still cradled in Joshua's arms and took her hand.

"How are you feeling, my dear?" the concern still evident in his voice.

She looked directly into his eyes as she replied, her voice stronger than earlier, "I'm still feeling weak and a bit fragile, but certainly much better, thank you."

"Joshua is the one you have to thank – he's the one who found you and came up with the plan to get you nourished once more." Samir said proudly, gesturing towards Joshua.

Jasna's eyes warily swept the room and visibly relaxed when she noted Dayna wasn't there. Farrell and Erika stood together holding hands behind Samir and off to one side. She smiled at them gratefully before turning her eyes back to Joshua.

"Thank you so much, Joshua. And thank you Farrell and Erika for helping me" her eyes flicked back to the couple as she mentioned them, her sincerity heartfelt.

Farrell nodded and Erika smiled. No words were needed.

Joshua turned to Samir, grinning. "I think I'll take Jasna up to her room to rest now, besides, dawn is almost upon us."

Samir glanced at the window and nodded sagely.

"Quite right. You have a good rest, my dear, and we'll see you later." He patted Jasna's hand and placed it back where he'd found it.

"See ya," Farrell called over his shoulder as he pulled Erika through the doorway and into the foyer. He winked at Joshua before his face disappeared.

Joshua rushed upstairs and straight into Jasna's room. He laid her gently in the centre of the massive bed, her head propped up by two enormous pillows. As he went to move away from the bed, Jasna grabbed his hand.

"Joshua? I really don't want to be alone – will you . . . stay here with me for a while? Please?" her voice was timid, as if expecting a rebuff and her eyes hinted at sadness.

Joshua smiled softly. "Of course I will, if that's what you want. Just let me shut the door and I'll sit with you."

Jasna's face brightened. "Okay. Thank you, Joshua."

He closed the door and as he turned back to the room, he noticed the cupboard where he'd found Jasna earlier was missing. He shuddered as he realised they were almost too late to save her. He wouldn't mention the missing cupboard right now – he didn't want anything to jeopardise her recovery – but they *did* need to talk about what had happened at some stage. Now he was content to be here with her.

He moved to the side of the bed and lay down beside her. He drew her into his arms so her head rested against his chest. He heard a sigh of contentment slip from between her lips and he couldn't prevent a huge smirk from plastering itself across his face. His fingers gently stroked her cheek and again the strange tingling sensation flooded through them and up his arm. She tilted her head so she could see his glorious face, a beatific smile danced across her lips when she saw his expression, her face glowed and her eyes sparkled. She looked suddenly radiant, despite her fragility. Joshua bent his head and kissed her forehead. She lifted her face towards him and his lips found hers once more.

Chapter 27 – Joshua

If their lips could bruise and swell, Jasna's and Joshua's would have. They spent all day in each other's arms, their lips exploring the taste and texture of the other's. Eventually they drew apart, but only by a fraction – just enough so their lips ceased to have contact with each other. Joshua kissed down her cheek, from her hairline to her chin, each kiss slow and lingering causing a tremor of pleasure and passion to cascade through Jasna's body. His lips continued to her neck, down her throat and gradually moving up to under her ear.

He pulled back a little and sighed, smiling contentedly.

"It will be dusk soon. We should think about making a move down to the library. How are you feeling now?" Joshua murmured.

Jasna smiled seductively at him. "Wonderful," she sighed dreamily then giggled, as she knew that wasn't what he meant.

He chuckled and bent forward, kissing the tip of her nose. Before he had the chance to say any more, she continued.

"I'm feeling a bit stronger, but until I try to do something I'm not sure *how* strong. Besides, I want to change my clothes before we leave this room."

"No problem. As tempted as I am to keep kissing you, we do need to get you firing on all cylinders again, and that means hunting," Joshua teased, grinning.

"Yeah, I guess so," she sighed in mock exasperation before grinning back at him. "But I'm sure I *could* tempt you," she flirted and blew a kiss at him.

"You're definitely a temptress and a gorgeous one at that," he conceded, "but . . ." he left the sentence hanging.

"I know, I know," she grumbled good-naturedly, "a little help then, please?" She raised herself into a sitting position and held out her hands so he could help her to her feet.

Joshua slid off the bed and grasping her hands, pulled her towards him till her feet touched the floor. Slowly she pushed down into her feet, testing the strength in her legs as she did so, until she was standing upright. Joshua continued to hold her hands, in case.

"Well?" he enquired concern evident in his tone.

Jasna paused for a second before answering. "I feel a bit . . . *wobbly*," she admitted shyly, "but I think I can manage to get changed without help. Not sure about running yet though."

"Don't worry about that. I'm more than happy to carry you again. I'll leave you to get changed – I want to change as well – and then I'll come back and take you downstairs. Okay?"

She nodded. Pulling one of her hands free from his, she stroked his face, feeling the same tingling feeling in her fingertips he experienced when he touched her, although she didn't know that. He leaned in and kissed her then turned and left the room, closing the door quietly behind him.

He was filled with happiness as he glided silently to his room. The past few hours he'd spent with Jasna had been unexpectedly . . . wonderful. He hurried to change, wanting to return to her side once more.

Jasna was ecstatic. As she carefully selected her attire and changed, her mind recalled the previous few hours spent in Joshua's arms, his lips caressing hers in such a way her desire for him had grown exponentially and it had taken all her restraint not to rip his clothes off. The pragmatic part of her knew she wasn't yet strong enough to give herself to him completely, but she knew it would happen – and soon.

She was only too aware he was repressing his desire for the same reason and it only made her love him more. For the first time in any of her lives, she felt desirable and wanted. It was a heady sensation – all the more incredible to her as it was so alien. She was anxious for his presence beside her and hurried to make sure she was presentable for when he returned.

She had just finished brushing her hair when she heard a soft knock at the door.

"Come in," she called softly and turned expectantly, a thrill of anticipation coursing through her. She was not disappointed.

Joshua crossed the threshold and closed the door behind him. In the blink of an eye, he had crossed the room and enveloped her in his arms. She returned his embrace, squeezing him tightly as if she never wanted to let him go. She sensed his gaze and lifted her face up to look at him. The expression on his face was one of joy and matched hers. He crushed his lips to hers, kissing her with passion and longing until she was dizzy.

A soft sound elsewhere in the house broke through their precious moment and they reluctantly ended their kiss.

"I guess that's our cue," she commented lightly, smiling wryly.

"Yeah. Still, we can pick up where we left off later – if you want to," he added as an afterthought, the anticipation evident in his tone.

"What do *you* think?" she replied seductively, reaching up to kiss him once more.

He chuckled as she pulled away. "Walk or ride, milady?"

The temptation to be in his arms again was too much, but she knew she would be for hunting. "I'll try walking and see how I get on, thanks."

Joshua smiled proudly at her determination and offered her his arm. "Shall we?"

She took his arm gratefully and they walked at human pace down the stairs and into the library where the others were already gathered.

As they walked into the room, Samir rushed towards them and took Jasna by the hand.

"How are you feeling now, my dear? You certainly look better." His tone implied concern tinged with a certain amount of relief at seeing her on her feet.

"Thank you, Samir. I am feeling a little stronger, but walking from my room to here was quite an effort." Jasna replied honestly, making direct eye contact.

Samir gestured to a seat next to Erika. "Then sit yourself down and rest. Conserve your strength."

Joshua assisted Jasna to the empty seat and once she had lowered herself into the chair, he took the seat beside her.

Over the opposite side of the room, Dayna sat some distance from the rest of her coven as if she were an outcast. Joshua saw her sneer at Jasna and was thankful to notice Jasna was looking at Samir. He glared at Dayna as he felt the fury begin to rise in him like molten lava in a volcano about to erupt, and a small but menacing growl issued from between his lips.

Dayna looked away quickly. Jasna, startled by his sudden anger, turned towards him and rested her hand on his arm. As he turned his face towards her, he relaxed his features, not wanting to upset her and saw the question in her eyes. He shook his head imperceptibly and smiled to put her at ease.

Samir had seen and heard everything which had transpired and he too felt his anger bubbling under the surface. He would not allow this to continue for a moment longer and resolved to speak to Dayna once the others had departed.

He turned to Joshua. "What are your hunting plans for tonight?"

"Well, I've discussed it with Jasna and she doesn't feel strong enough to hunt properly, so I plan to do the same as I did last night. If Farrell and Erika would care to help again, it would be great, but it's up to them." Joshua replied, obviously not wanting to take his friends' assistance for granted.

Farrell glanced at Erika, who smiled and nodded then turned to face Joshua.

"Of course we'd be happy to help," Farrell confirmed, grinning. "Ready when you are."

Before Joshua had the opportunity to answer, Jasna spoke.

"Thank you both. It's lovely to have *good* friends," her genuine and sincere smile lit up her pretty face. However, no one in the room failed to recognise the subtle barb aimed at Dayna, least of all Dayna herself. She stiffened visibly in her seat and a small hiss escaped through her teeth.

Farrell and Joshua turned their faces away, stifling their chuckles behind their hands. Erika grinned widely and winked at Jasna. Samir had to work very hard to keep his face impassive, but inside he applauded Jasna's little show of gumption.

Once Joshua had regained control enough to speak, he turned to Jasna.

"Are you ready to go now?" he asked politely, his eyes reflecting the hilarity he was trying so hard to suppress.

"Yes," she answered simply.

Joshua gently lifted her out of the chair and cradled her in his arms as he had earlier. He turned to Samir and said, "See you later," before continuing into the foyer, closely followed by Farrell and Erika. As they reached the front door, there was an eruption of giggling which faded as they got swallowed up by the night.

Dayna sat seething. *How* dare *she take a pot-shot at me in front of everyone*, she thought. The fact that she'd committed a much more heinous crime in the first place didn't even enter her head. She was so self-absorbed she failed to hear Samir call her name.

Samir raised his voice, his tone steely, "Dayna!"

She started and whipped her head around to face him, forgetting to smooth her features so her irritation was clear.

"I must talk to you." Samir hesitated to ensure he had her full attention. Once satisfied, he continued. "What is your problem with Jasna?"

This question caught her totally unprepared and she stammered her way through her response.

"I, er, she, um, I don't erm like her."

"Why? What has she done to you?" Samir demanded his features hard and serious.

Dayna was upset to see Samir so cold, especially with her and for a moment she lost her composure, inadvertently letting something slip.

"She's here, isn't she? Ugly cow. Thinks she's so much better than me. Huh! As if . . ." Dayna glanced up and her hands flew to cover her mouth at Samir's expression. She was immediately mortified that she'd let her guard down and allowed Samir to see the real Dayna. Before she could back track, Samir had moved closer so he stood over her, his shock and anger written right across his face. His eyes blazed and his voice boomed in her ears.

"And what makes you think *you're* so wonderful? She was here before *you* and has every right to be part of this coven. She is *far* from ugly – she is beautiful inside and out – unlike YOU. I saw the look you gave her tonight – it was totally uncalled for," his righteous anger spilled over for the first time since becoming immortal.

Dayna recoiled in shock. She'd never heard Samir even raise his voice before.

"Come," he commanded, "I have something to show you."

She hesitated then rose slowly out of her seat. Samir grabbed her arm above the elbow, pulled her across the hallway and out the main door. They turned right and walked around the side of the house to where a pile of timber and metal lay in a heap on the concrete pavement.

"You see this?" Samir demanded his eyes narrowed in his indignation.

Dayna nodded then whispered, "Yes."

"This is a lead lined cupboard which Jasna hid in from you, to escape your humiliation of her. This . . ." he poked at the pile with the toe of his shoe, "almost became her coffin – BECAUSE OF YOU!" he roared.

Dayna looked down at the ground – not because she was ashamed – she didn't want to see the rage in Samir's eyes, the eyes she adored. She bit her tongue and said nothing.

"Your silence condemns you," he spat. "Not *one* word of apology, not *one* sign of remorse. There was a time when I had high hopes for you, Dayna. I even considered one day you and I might be together . .

.." Dayna raised her head and glanced hopefully in his direction. "But after this, after you have demonstrated how cruel you can be, how you can bully someone more gentle than you, and how you are *so totally* unrepentant, there is absolutely *no* hope, no chance I would consider you as a potential partner."

Dayna hung her head in despair. All her hopes and dreams had been crushed *and it's all HER fault*, she thought viciously.

Samir continued, not waiting for Dayna to say anything – there wasn't anything she could say which would improve the situation.

"I'm warning you, Dayna, and you better pay attention. If there is one more incident, one more episode of your cruelty in this house, towards Jasna or anyone else for that matter, I *will* banish you and report your behaviour to Pavel. Do. You. Understand?"

Dayna was motionless and silent at his side. He still had hold of her upper arm so he shook her gently to try and force a reaction from her. She lifted her head slowly, not bothering to hide her despondency.

"I asked you a question. Did you understand what I said?"

Dayna nodded. "Yes, Samir." Her voice was loaded with pain.

Under normal circumstances, Samir would have softened, would have let go of some of his anger in the face of one of his coven being so upset. However, in Dayna's case, she'd brought this down on herself and if he weakened now, she wouldn't take his warning seriously. He meant every word.

"I suggest you go and hunt, and while you're at it, take some time to have a cold hard look at yourself." Samir instructed. Dropping his hold on her arm, he turned and walked away, leaving her to ponder.

Chapter 28 – Joshua

Dayna was fuming, incensed. She couldn't understand why Samir was being so . . . judgemental and nasty. The threat to expel her from the coven and the manor only had an impact because of the depth of her feelings for Samir, but if, as he said, there was no chance of them ever being together, did she really want to be there?

She turned and vanished into the night, wanting to put some distance between her and Samir, hoping against hope he would have calmed down by the time she returned.

As she ran, her thoughts turned to revenge. *That fat, ugly bitch will pay for this*, she thought. She'd had nothing against Farrell and Erika, had even quite liked the quiet couple, until they'd sided with *her*. As for Joshua, if Samir hadn't already captured her heart, she would probably have made a play for him – he was rather gorgeous. But now . . . now he was thick with fatso. What he saw in her she'd never know – it sure as hell wasn't her looks or figure. Dayna chuckled darkly to herself.

She continued on her journey; passing the first village without stopping, she came upon a small town and decided to hunt there. Wandering through the shadows searching for suitable prey, she heard a heated argument between males not far from where she stood. She moved stealthily closer until she could see what was occurring. The situation had escalated into a punch up – blows were raining down at all angles, but funnily enough, the shorter of the two men appeared to have the upper hand. It was all over in the space of a few minutes as th smaller man threw an almighty uppercut, which launched his opponent off his feet, landing on his back unconscious.

Dayna watched as the victor kicked his opponent hard in the ribs and heard a crunch as some of the bones snapped like twigs. He sniggered to himself then kicked him again, this time in the head, before strutting off down the road, towards where Dayna was hiding.

As he approached, she stepped out from the shadows and stood in his path, posing seductively. He stopped in front of her and lazily looked her up and down; appraising her as a farmer would survey his prize bull. He liked what he saw and he could tell by the look in her eyes she was gagging for it. He held out his hand to her and she placed her dainty hand in his. He noticed her skin was very cold, but wasn't particularly bothered by it – he thought it might be quite refreshing on this hot, humid night.

He led Dayna down the road and off into a park surrounded by trees and bushes. They continued into the darkness, moving further and further from the road. He didn't want to get interrupted with this little beauty, especially as he enjoyed roughing them up a little, smack them around and stuff. The sadist didn't want her screams of pain to attract any unwanted attention.

She followed him willingly, matching him stride for stride. Dayna knew he thought she was eager for some of his particular brand of loving; little did he know she had her own agenda and *she* wasn't going to be the victim.

When he considered they were far enough from civilisation, he pulled her towards him muttering, "C'mere, baby. Come see what I've got for you."

He yanked on her arm causing her to crash into him. He wrapped his arms around her and started to kiss her roughly, trying to bite her bottom lip. His fingers entangled in her hair and he pulled it hard as if trying to leave her with a bald patch. To his dismay, she didn't cry out or try to resist. It was the screams and tears which really turned him on.

Perhaps he had met his match. Perhaps she enjoyed receiving pain as much as he relished dishing it out. He grabbed one of her breasts through her flimsy top and squeezed it with all his might. He heard a small snigger and she whispered derisively in his ear, "Is that the best you can do?"

His rage, never far below the surface, reared its ugly head. *How dare this little bitch mock me?* He thought, *I'll show her.* He drew his arm back and punched her hard in the face, expecting to hear the satisfying crunch as her nose broke, but there was no sound and no blood. He couldn't understand it then he heard her voice whisper again in his ear, "My turn tough guy," and she laughed out loud, her voice sounding amused yet triumphant.

He felt a sharp pain in his neck, but before he could react or cry out, his knees gave way and he found himself on the floor. He felt himself growing weaker then everything went black as he sank into unconsciousness.

Dayna got to her feet and without a backward glance, walked away in search of her next victim, unaware he still had a faint pulse.

* * *

Joshua, Jasna, Farrell and Erika couldn't keep their laughter in any longer; although they all tried to wait until they were at least out the door, it didn't quite work. Jasna, surprisingly, had found a large measure of bravery with her returning strength yet her gentle heart prevented her from attacking Dayna directly, despite everything she'd done to deserve it.

The others were absolutely stoked with glee that Jasna had felt she had enough support to be able to make her comment in the first place, especially since she'd nearly perished as a result of Dayna's vicious tongue.

There was a completely different atmosphere during the hunt that night. They followed the same pattern as the previous night with Erika staying with Jasna while the guys went off to hunt and bring someone back for Jasna to feed on, but where there had been an air of extreme urgency in their actions, this night was more relaxed. There was a sense of celebration and hilarity in their endeavours.

Erika was glad to have a little time alone with Jasna; the previous night Jasna had been in no condition to talk and besides, the emotions Erika felt coming from Jasna had only been present since they appeared in the library earlier. Whilst she didn't want to pry, she wanted to ensure her friend was not setting herself up for another huge fall.

"Er, Jasna?" Erika began, hesitantly. Her eyebrows lowered over her eyes and she chewed her bottom lip as she tried to decide the best way to broach the subject without upsetting Jasna.

"Yeah?" Jasna glanced up at Erika and was surprised at the consternation she saw in her friend's eyes. "Hey. What's up?"

"Oh, er . . . nothing's up. I wanted to er . . . talk to you while we're on our own." Erika dropped her eyes, a little embarrassed. She felt she was about to intrude on Jasna's personal space and it didn't sit comfortably with her.

"Yeah? What about?" Jasna was merely curious – she had no idea what was coming, but was a tad perturbed by Erika's body language.

"It's about your emotions. I'm guessing Joshua's got something to do with how you're feeling and I'm a little . . . *concerned* I guess. You've been through a horrendous ordeal with this Dayna business and it nearly cost you your life. Now I can sense some quite powerful emotions emanating from you and I can't help worrying. I don't want to pry into your private life, but I wouldn't be much of a friend if I didn't at least attempt to make sure you're in control of things, would I?" Erika spoke quickly, everything tumbling out in a rush. As she finished she finally raised her head to look Jasna in the eye, a sheepish expression on her face.

"Oh," Jasna exclaimed, taken aback, her eyes wide. She wasn't expecting *that*. She paused for a moment, trying to decide how to answer. The response formed in her mind and a wondrous smile stretched across her lips, her whole face lighting up as if she was seeing daylight for the very first time.

"I don't *know* if I'm in control of things, but . . . well, things have . . . *happened* today which give me a real sense of . . . *hope,* I guess."

Erika could hardly contain her inquisitiveness. "What? What's happened?"

"Well, you know I've harboured feelings for Joshua since he arrived?" Not waiting for Erika's acknowledgement; she carried on. "Well, when we were walking back to the manor this morning, he kissed me," her voice rose with excitement.

"Wow," Erika murmured softly. She unconsciously shifted closer to Jasna.

"'Wow' doesn't even cover it. It was so . . . *electrifying*. We've spent the whole day wrapped in each other's arms. I swear, if my lips could bruise, they'd be twice the size they normally are," she giggled a little shyly at her confession

"Sounds like he's into you as well then. That's great. I knew he was crazy with worry when you disappeared, but I thought he was concerned as a friend. I didn't realise there was more to it – his anxiety masked his other emotions so I couldn't really pick up on those. However, I have noticed a difference in him today. He seems much happier, more content and there's an . . . *excitement* there. Jas, I don't want to burst your bubble or anything, but can I give you a bit of advice please?" Erika's expression changed from being thrilled for her friend to one of wariness.

Jasna shrugged as some of her exhilaration ebbed in the face of Erika's last question.

"What?" She answered, perhaps sounding terser than she intended.

"Please don't be mad at me, okay? Honestly, I don't have any sort of hidden agenda here – my only concern is for your welfare," Erika explained, her voice betraying her underlying emotions, a pleading in her eyes.

"Okay. Let's hear it," Jasna sighed, sounded resigned. Some of the glow had definitely worn off now and in some ways, she felt a little resentful Erika had taken it away from her.

"All I wanted to say was – don't rush it and don't be hurried into anything you're not ready for. Take each day as it comes and don't fall too hard for him too soon. He hasn't been with us very long and he was in a pretty full-on relationship when he was turned. In fact, he was a day or two away from getting married. That sort of love and commitment doesn't go away overnight. He could be on the rebound; he could still have real feelings for her, but be suppressing them.

"I'm not saying he doesn't have real feelings for you – it's obvious he does – but I'm frightened you're going to fall so hard for him and if something went wrong, well . . . it would destroy you. I don't want to see you get hurt, that's all." The heartfelt emotion and sincerity in her voice could not be mistaken. The earnest expression on her face also hinted at the concern for her friend.

Jasna searched Erika's face before replying. There was no doubt in her mind that Erika genuinely wanted to look out for her and was purely being the best friend she could be. Jasna reached out and took one of Erika's hands, holding it gently in her own.

"Hey. I hear what you're saying and I want to thank you for being such a caring friend. As far as my feelings for Joshua are concerned, I've already fallen for him in a big way, but I promise I'll try to rule my heart with my head until I know for sure how he feels about me. Okay?"

"I can't ask for more than that, can I?" Erika grinned at her, a little more tranquil.

"Not really," Jasna confirmed, leaning forward and embracing her friend, smiling softly.

"Just be happy, Jas," Erika whispered in her friend's ear. Then she detected a soft rustling noise coming from behind her and realised the guys had returned. "Ooops, busted," she muttered, a chuckle in her voice.

They pulled apart after Farrell and Joshua appeared with two unconscious humans slung over their shoulders. They looked at the guys' puzzled expressions then at each other before creasing up with laughter.

* * *

By the time Jasna had satiated her thirst, she was feeling much stronger than before – nearly back to normal. Joshua was thrilled to see her so much better. Erika and Farrell had gone off to hunt, leaving Joshua and Jasna alone.

He sat on the ground beside her, one arm around her shoulders as she leaned against him. She felt safe, happy and contented being with him and knowing he was looking after her. He bent his head down and kissed the top of her head.

"How are you feeling, babes?" he murmured in a soft voice.

"Better . . . stronger I think, thanks," she replied, tilting her face up so she could gaze into his caring eyes. A small smile played around her lips.

"Good, I'm glad," he asserted before bending his head to graze her lips with his own. A thrill of desire ran through both of them, taking them by surprise. As they drew apart their eyes met and held for a very long moment.

Jasna was exhilarated beyond words; seeing the longing in his eyes and, maybe, just maybe, something more.

Joshua lost himself in the unfathomable ocean of her loving eyes; a deep well of passion for this divine creature surged through him and it took every ounce of his willpower to keep himself under control. After all, it would be beyond embarrassing if Erika and Farrell returned and caught them in a compromising position. He also wanted to make sure he wasn't rushing Jasna and confirm she had recovered enough from her ordeal.

He reined back his ardour until he was sure he was in control of it before allowing himself to kiss those luscious lips once more. The sweetness of the kiss promised much and he was eager to return to the manor. He cuddled her as they waited impatiently for the others to return.

Thankfully they didn't have more than half an hour to wait before Erika and Farrell returned and they set off immediately for the manor. Joshua insisted on carrying Jasna in his arms for the journey back; they were both acutely aware of the suppressed emotions of the other and a sense of anticipation was building tall as a skyscraper.

Once they had briefly seen Samir and assured him Jasna was making great strides forward in her recovery, they made their excuses and, trying not to make it too obvious they were in a hurry, disappeared up to her room, closing the door firmly behind them.

He swept her up in his arms as soon as the door was shut and carried her to the bed. He gently laid her down and without letting go, climbed on beside her, his lips crushing hers, relishing in the honeyed deliciousness he could taste as her tongue flicked against his. Their kisses became deeper, more ardent as they strived to get even closer to each other.

Joshua moved one of his hands from the small of Jasna's back down to her buttocks and began to massage them, occasionally squeezing them, forcing her hips to gently thrust forwards towards his groin. He could hear her breathing accelerate then felt one of her hands snake around in between them and she started to unbutton his shirt. Within milliseconds her hands were tracing circles on his bare chest.

She broke her lips away from his, lowered her head and began kissing his chest, flicking her tongue across his nipples and causing him to inhale sharply as a frisson of pleasure shot through him. He moved his hands and gradually pushed her cotton top up, caressing her skin and leaving electric tingles in their wake. She pulled away from him and removed her top, throwing it onto the floor and revealing her smooth alabaster skin and perfectly proportioned breasts.

Joshua groaned and lowered his head to kiss her nipples; she moaned with pleasure and reached for the belt on his trousers. His hand stopped her as he murmured, "Allow me." He pulled away from her and stripped off his clothes, leaving them in an untidy pile on the floor. Her eyes marvelled at the god-like creature who stood before her and her desire for him rose impossibly higher. She jumped off the bed and removed the rest of her clothes, watching his eyes and hoping for some signal that he approved of what he saw. She was not left wanting. His eyes traced every curve of her body before gasping with delight. They came together on the bed and sank into a blissfully exciting, passion-filled journey.

Samir sat at the ornate antique desk in his room, his head in his hands, and a troubled expression on his handsome features. Although he hadn't seen Dayna return, unlike the rest of his coven, he could sense she was present in the manor. He felt an overwhelming desire to rest, but his mind was consumed by everything which had occurred under the cover of the purple-black night.

Firstly, his mind recalled the unpleasant experience with Dayna. It had wounded him far more than he initially realised. What he had told her was true – he did have high hopes that one day she would stand beside him as his partner – but in order for that to happen, she would have had to prove she was . . . worthy. Now he knew it was impossible; by her own actions she had excluded herself from that possibility, and he had to move on – to even start afresh.

Of course, he did have some feelings for her. He also knew her affection for him was much stronger than he'd suspected. How would she react to his earlier words, hurled in anger, but nonetheless true? That was his biggest concern. How would she cope with the rejection? Only time would reveal the answer, but he resolved to keep a much closer eye on her in future.

Having exhausted the subject, or taken it as far as he wanted to for the time being, he then re-lived his telephone conversation with Pavel.

After Dayna had sprinted off to hunt, he had returned to the library and stood at the window, looking out but seeing nothing, trying to calm himself. He hadn't been in there for more than fifteen minutes when his mobile phone indicated an incoming call. He pulled the device from his pocket and was relieved to see Pavel's name on the caller ID. He pressed the button to answer and put the phone to his ear.

"Pavel. What a pleasant surprise. How are you?" he didn't have to fake the gladness in his voice.

"Samir, my friend. I am well, thank you, and you?"

"I'm fine, thank you. To what do I owe this unexpected pleasure?" Samir tried to keep his tone even and not give away how troubled he actually was.

"I thought I would call to find out if there have been any new developments with young Joshua."

"As a matter of fact, yes." A sense of pride trickled through him and he was able to inject the appropriate amount of enthusiasm in his voice. "I was about to call you with an update as a matter of fact."

"How fortunate my timing appears to be," Pavel chuckled. "So, my friend, what new talent has been discovered?" He sounded eager for new information.

"He can see through solid objects. He discovered it by accident and rushed to tell me as I was about to rest. As it was too light for me to learn much more, I asked him to meet me at dusk so I could test him." Samir's excitement was infectious.

"Sounds very interesting. So, you tested him? How?" Pavel's thirst for further knowledge was palpable.

"I took him to a part of the house he'd never seen before. We stopped outside one of the rooms and I asked him to describe the contents. He was completely accurate in everything. It was amazing."

"Out of curiosity, which room did you take him to?"

"The music room," Samir responded dutifully.

"Well . . . *another* very unusual talent. This is *not* one I have come across previously – I will have to confer with the rest of the Commissioners to see if they have," Pavel said thoughtfully. "I wonder what else he is capable of."

"What do you mean, Pavel? Is this a problem?" a fearful note came into Samir's voice.

"No. No problem – please don't concern yourself unnecessarily. I meant only that he has at least one more talent which currently lays dormant and I cannot resist the urge to speculate as to what it might be," explained Pavel, trying to reassure.

"Oh. Okay then," Samir sounded somewhat relieved.

Pavel detected an undercurrent, an edge to Samir's voice which immediately rang alarm bells.

"Samir? What is disturbing you? Please tell me so I can help you."

Samir paused, ordering his thoughts before responding. He sighed dramatically.

"There is much that has happened recently and most of it is . . . unpleasant. It will take some time to tell you everything,"

"Time is something we have an abundance of. Please continue," Pavel encouraged, perhaps regretting his flippant retort.

Samir explained about Dayna's verbal attack on Jasna and the subsequent events; he tried to make it more of a report, keeping emotions to a minimum.

When Samir had finished, he nervously awaited Pavel's comments. Pavel was silent as he digested the gamut of information. His voice was supportive as he finally replied yet Samir could hear an element of anger in the timbre.

"That is extremely worrisome and I'm appalled by Dayna's behaviour. I'm relieved to hear Jasna is making a rapid improvement – Farrell, Erika and Joshua should be congratulated for their care and compassion. Please pass that on for me."

"Of course."

"In your position, I would have handled the situation in exactly the same way. Further, I would also have issued that threat to Dayna, so I fully support your actions in every respect. However, you *must* be prepared to follow through should the need arise – you cannot afford to show even a moment of weakness now," Pavel stated firmly.

"I understand Pavel and thank you for your support – I really do appreciate it," Samir's relief at Pavel's reaction and support was a defining moment for him and it was apparent in his tone.

"I want you to keep me updated on a regular basis over the next month or so, perhaps twice weekly, please. Or more often should events dictate. I may even pay you a surprise visit in a couple of weeks. Of course, I will advise you accordingly, but it *must* be kept between us – I don't want your coven to know I'm coming, especially Dayna," Samir could almost picture a plan forming in Pavel's mind.

"No problem. It's always good to see you and of course I can keep your visit secret," Samir confirmed.

"Very good. I will leave you now since you must be anxious to hunt before dawn, as I am," Pavel chuckled, "we will talk again in a few days. Take care, Samir, my friend. Goodbye."

"Thank you, Pavel, you too. 'Bye," Samir returned the phone to his pocket as Pavel had ended the call.

It was reassuring to know Pavel was behind him and he was secretly rather chuffed Pavel was planning a visit. Although he didn't want anything to kick off, it would be helpful for Pavel to see for himself how cruel and remorseless Dayna could be.

Having worked his way through all the subjects plaguing him, he finally felt able to clear his mind so he could rest. He climbed on his bed and closed his eyes, soon achieving a trance-like state.

* * *

A few miles away, a man lay on the grass in a park, quite some way from the road. As he began to regain consciousness, he became aware of a pain which was gradually building within his torso.

He tried to recall what had happened; he remembered getting into an argument with a mouthy git in the pub and then beating seven kinds of crap out of him, leaving him unconscious on the pavement. Then he picked up a gorgeous blonde and wasn't able to get his kicks by hurting her; she didn't seem to feel any pain as he tried to beat her up. He recollected a sharp pain in his neck, but then nothing. Everything spun around and appeared to go black.

He reached one hand up to his neck and found what felt like two small gashes. He tried to explore the wounds with his fingers, but as he pressed on them, the pain became much more acute and he cried out. He curled into a foetal position as the pain accelerated to an unbearable level, closed his eyes and prayed for death to take him swiftly.

Chapter 29 – Remy

I left Redow House around ten in the morning. As I journeyed towards the motorway which would take me first south then east, I stopped off at the villages I hadn't had time to visit, just to be thorough, but I think I already knew Joshua wasn't there. By the time I left the last of the villages on my list it was midday and I still had a good half hours' drive before I reached the motorway.

As I drove, I couldn't help but admire the wonderful scenery. Some of the villages were really quaint and olde-worlde, with cottages that looked to be at least two hundred years old or more. Could I imagine myself living in a little village similar to these? I wasn't sure. I would miss living in a small town where I had access to a plethora of entertainment venues and shops within a twenty-minute drive, but at the same time village life would perhaps be quite a pleasant experience. Of course, everyone would know everyone else *and* their business, but people tended to pull together more and there was a real sense of community.

My grandparents had often regaled Becky and I with stories of the war years and how strong the community spirit was. There were tales of people who took in other families whose homes had been bombed, anecdotes about friends and stories of extreme bravery. The theme which weaved through all their memories was one of helping each other in good times and bad. It was such a rare commodity these days yet these little villages and hamlets sprinkled around the country had somehow harnessed those wonderful old-fashioned values and made them work in today's modern world. It certainly had an appeal.

By the time I'd finished weighing the pros and cons of town living versus village life I was pulling onto the motorway and heading south towards more familiar territory. I still had at least four hours solid driving ahead of me, assuming no traffic jams, the thought of which didn't exactly thrill me. Motorway driving was so boring unless you had a passenger to talk to – but it was a necessary evil.

Two hours later, I could see hazard warning lights and brake lights flashing in the distance. I immediately reduced my speed and put my own warning lights on to caution drivers behind me that there was something wrong up ahead. In less than a minute, I was at a complete standstill, along with the other two lanes on the motorway. In my rear view mirror, I could see the queue of traffic growing exponentially, to the extent I could no longer see the back of it. I also had no idea how far ahead the problem had arisen or what it was. I switched on the radio and caught the tail end of the news. The presenter was talking about police being baffled by the mysterious disappearances of four people in Surrey. The traffic report followed, but there was no mention of the jam I was sitting in so I turned it off again.

After five minutes of nothing moving, I turned off my engine to save fuel and to ensure my engine didn't overheat.

After a further fifteen minutes of remaining stationery, I was beginning to get bored. A few of my fellow motorists had got out of their vehicles to try and see what the delay was and to stretch their legs. After more than two hours of sitting, the idea became rather appealing. As I opened my door and stepped out, I heard the sound of sirens wailing in the distance, coming inexorably closer by the second.

I turned my head to look behind me and could see numerous blue flashing lights approaching, moving extremely fast down the hard shoulder. The sirens became louder and louder as the emergency vehicles barrelled towards me, and then I could see what they were: two police cars, two ambulances and a fire engine.

This must be bad. Really bad. I thought, and my heart went out to the families of those involved. My car door was still open and I stepped up onto the lip to try to see how far ahead the accident had occurred. I knew I was being morbidly curious; in reality I was no better than the rubberneckers who slowed down to gawp at the aftermath of accidents, slowing down traffic flow in the process. How many times had I complained about that very thing? Yet here I was, staring down the road, trying to see what had happened. I felt dreadfully ashamed by my actions yet a sort of sick fascination compelled me and I couldn't seem to stop myself.

I couldn't actually see very much; the blue flashing lights were at least a quarter of a mile further on and there were some high top vans and small trucks obscuring the view. In some ways I was relieved I wasn't able to view the carnage which lay ahead. As I stepped down onto the tarmac, I heard more sirens approaching; within a minute, another fire engine and two more ambulances rocketed past, swiftly followed by two police traffic cars. The crash must have been much worse than I had feared.

I climbed back into the car, leaving my door open. Leaning back into my seat I closed my eyes and inhaled deeply before letting my breath trickle slowly from between my parted lips. A picture formed in my mind, hazy at first as if the edges had been attacked by an eraser then solidifying gradually until it appeared like a photograph - a snapshot in time.

Twisted metal littered the tarmac. A car lay on its roof, one of its tyres still spinning. A jack-knifed truck, a fallen and warped-framed motorcycle lying in a pool of red, a brightly signed delivery van with wisps of smoke drifting from the edge of the crinkled bonnet, another car with the boot concertinaed shortening the car by more than a foot, and a further one which was crushed from all sides.

My eyes snapped open and a gasp flew from my lips. I trembled. The image was so vivid – it had a ring of reality as if I was looking at it through the lens of a camera. My nerves sizzled with adrenalin and fear. I could hear my breath panting rapidly as if I'd just completed half an hour of strenuous exercise and I concentrated on slowing it down, counting out the seconds as I inhaled and exhaled. After five or six minutes, my breathing was normal again and I was able to think more rationally.

Maybe it was my over-active imagination which produced the image, I thought. *Yes, that must be it. I knew there was a major accident ahead and my brain went into creative mode*, I reasoned. I alighted and stretched my legs, chuckling to myself. I must be overwrought if I was letting my imagination freak me out.

There was nothing to do as we waited for the accident to be cleared so I reached into my bag and pulled out my e-reader, immersing myself once more in the fantasy world of Devil's Kitchen.

An hour later the first two ambulances departed, blue lights flashing and sirens howling as they tore down the hard shoulder to the next exit. The third followed a few minutes later, sans lights and sirens, indicating a fatality had occurred. A lump formed in my throat as I realised some unfortunate family would, in the next hour or so, receive the devastating news that they had lost a beloved member. My eyes pricked with unshed tears at the thought of the unknown family's grief – it was a feeling I could relate to, except my Joshua hadn't died.

The traffic on the other carriageway had slowed so much it was easy to hear the screeching of metal as the cutting equipment being used by the fire crews ripped through the framework of a mangled vehicle, desperately trying to free a trapped and probably injured individual. The sound set my teeth on edge and made me shudder.

Another twenty minutes later, the cutting equipment was silenced and the fourth and final ambulance rocketed away, sirens screaming and lights spinning. One of the fire engines followed silently behind; the other left a few minutes later.

It was a further fifteen minutes before any traffic on our carriageway began to move. The outside lane had been cleared and police officers wearing high visibility jackets directed the vehicles around the debris using the free lane and the hard shoulder. I had to wait an additional twenty-five minutes before I was able to start inching forward and another ten before I was able to view the extent of the multi-vehicle pile-up. Three cars, a motorcycle, a brightly painted van and a truck were almost unrecognisable, as their bodywork had been twisted and pulverised with the force of the collision.

One car was missing its' roof, two doors and had nearly been carved in half as the rescuers attempted to free the occupants. A large patch of red liquid had pooled beside another of the cars and by the motorcycle and I realised after half a second it was blood. I wasn't usually squeamish, but my stomach churned and hot bile rose to the back of my throat. An image flashed briefly into my mind and I recognised the position of the vehicles was exactly the same as I'd 'seen' earlier. What on earth was going on? First the dancing deodorant can then hearing Bonnie's voice when she was nowhere near me and now this . . . visualisation. What was happening to me? Was I losing my marbles? I snapped out of my reverie when a horn beeped behind me – I was holding up the traffic. I forced my eyes away so I could focus on the directions given by the officers and swallowed the bile quickly to prevent it from spilling out of my mouth. I concentrated on my breathing, taking deep breaths in through my mouth until the nausea passed.

After what I had just seen, I didn't dare reach for the bottle of water in the holder between the front seats, although I desperately needed to rinse my mouth to erase the awful taste the bile had left behind.

A few miles down the road, I was relieved to spot a sign for a service station; within five minutes I was exiting the motorway and pulling into the parking area.

Even though I was now some two and a half hours behind schedule, I spent an hour in the service station. I couldn't really afford the time, but seeing the aftermath of that horrendous accident, had left me strangely traumatised.

When I switched off the engine and removed my keys from the ignition, my hands were trembling; as I stepped from the car, my legs were jelly – I had to grab the car door to steady myself before I was able to walk.

I couldn't understand why I felt like this – it wasn't as if I'd seen the mangled bodies first hand, although I had seen that strange vision. Maybe it was more to do with my fragile emotional state.

I had a snack and two cups of sweet tea then sat and tried to make myself relax. It took a while, but eventually I was able to continue on with my journey. I stood slowly, making sure my limbs were sturdy and strong then I strode back to where I'd left the car. Two minutes later, I was pulling back onto the motorway.

Just under two hours later, I was travelling on the A146 heading towards Beccles, a small town on the Norfolk / Suffolk border, where Joshua and I had boarded the vessel he hired for us to cruise along the Norfolk Broads. I was nearly there –another ten to fifteen minutes and I would be pulling into the little town.

I was totally shattered, physically and emotionally and couldn't wait to get to the Guest House so I could unwind. I was still tense and uneasy from the earlier accident scene; normally I loved driving, but for the first time since I passed my driving test, I wanted to reach my destination and get off the road as quickly and safely as possible. I still couldn't understand why it had affected me so intensely, even taking into account my sensitive condition.

I turned into another small road and began searching for the house. I saw the sign about another fifty yards up ahead on the right and breathed a small sigh of relief.

The large driveway and front garden area was well kept, with plenty of room to park. The large Edwardian house with its bay windows, hanging baskets and plants in decorative planters looked homely and inviting. I switched off the engine and was happy to be able to get out of the car and stretch. I grabbed my luggage from the car and walked through the bright red door.

After a restless night, I got up grouchy and tired. I borrowed a local telephone directory from the owners after breakfast, took it up to my pretty room and began making another set of lists. This time the lists also included cruise boat hire and holiday companies. By the time I'd finished, it was lunchtime. I looked at the raft of pages in my pad and cringed; there were so many hotels, guest houses and B & B's to check out and what with the holiday and cruiser firms, it appeared I would be in this location for much more than a week.

I tore out the Beccles pages and stuffed them in my bag. I was just checking I had Joshua's photo when I heard a knock at the door. I wandered over, not in any hurry, grasped the door handle and twisted it. As I pulled the door towards me, it was pushed from the other side and a familiar voice yelled, "Surprise!"

I staggered back in shock. Standing in the doorway, with a stupid grin on her face, was Becky.

"Oh. My. God. Becky? What the . . ." I flung my arms around her and crushed her to me. I heard her drop her bag to the floor as her arms encircled my waist. I didn't realise I was sobbing until I heard her whisper, "Shhhh, it's okay hun," in my ear.

She gently manoeuvred me further into the room, kicking the door shut behind her as we cleared it. She led me to the bed and sat beside me. My sobs subsided. I looked up at her through tear-misted eyes; her beautiful smile, which was more an impish grin on this occasion, beamed back at me. I scanned the familiar features on her lovely face, as if committing them to memory – even though it was a face I saw every day in the mirror – and wondered if I was dreaming. It was surreal, utterly unbelievable, that she was here, seated on the bed next to me. Instinctively I closed my eyes and shook my head – I took a deep breath before lifting my eyelids to find her still sitting beside me.

"W-what are y-you d-doing here?" I stammered, still in shock.

It brought joy to my heart to hear her giggle at my stutter, even though I knew she wouldn't be able to resist playing it up until I was ready to throw something at her.

"I missed you and thought that as you were only a couple of hours away, I'd come and spend the weekend with you," she replied simply.

"Really?" I blurted without thinking, my eyes wide and my expression bemused.

"No, I'm pulling your leg and I'm not really here – I'm a cardboard cut-out," she replied sarcastically, smirking at me.

"Oh, har, har, har! Sarcasm is the lowest form of wit you know," my voice was disgruntled, but try as I might I couldn't prevent a small smile from gracing my lips.

Becky burst out laughing at my efforts and suddenly I was giggling too. It was so great she was here – Becky was always able to make me smile and lift my spirits.

"Okay, all joking aside, I thought you could probably do with a hand for a couple of days *and* some company."

"Aw, Becky, you are officially the best sister in the world and I love you to bits." I flung my arms around her again and hugged her tight. "Just don't let it go to your head," I muttered into her shoulder.

Becky chuckled. "I'll try not to."

I pulled away from her a little. "You hungry?"

"Starved. I didn't stop en route – why?"

"Well, I was about to go into town and grab some lunch before I got started, when you turned up and gave me a heart attack."

Becky chuckled again. "Okay. Now you're talking – let's go."

Linking arms, we left the room, closing the door firmly behind us, and trooped down the stairs.

* * *

The weekend passed far too quickly. Becky and I managed to cover quite a bit of ground between us – much more than I would have been able to on my own. It gave me a real boost having Becky with me; not being alone made all the difference in the world. I was stronger, had more focus and less doubt in my abilities; I was only half a person except when Becky was with me though it wasn't until after Joshua vanished I'd had any sense of being incomplete. Too strange for words. But, like all good things, it had to come to an end, and much too soon it was Sunday evening - time for her to leave.

Becky loaded her small case in the car and slammed the boot shut. She turned to me and opened her arms, smiling gently. I slid into them, clasped my hands around her back and hugged her as she embraced me in return.

"I'll text you when I get home, okay?" she murmured into my hair.

"Please."

"Don't forget – if you need me, you only have to call. Take care sis, I love you," she said softly, trying to keep her voice even.

"I know. Thanks for this weekend, Becs. I love you too," I replied simply, also trying hard not to show too much emotion, swallowing back the tears before they could rise to the surface. "Drive carefully."

"Always do." She kissed my cheek then turned and climbed into the car, starting the engine before she'd even closed the door. She pressed the switch to lower her window and I leaned in and kissed her.

I stepped away from the car as she put it into gear; I managed to hold onto the tears until she was driving away from me, waving through her open window as she went. A torrent erupted from my eyes and surged down my face as I waved back. Dragging my heavy feet back into the guesthouse I climbed the stairs to my room. Thankfully I didn't bump into anyone on the way. I entered my room, closed the door, threw myself on the bed and sobbed into my pillow.

This wasn't me. I was a rational, independent woman. Everything had changed in such a short space of time; why was I so dependent on Becky now? Why was I falling apart now she'd left to go home? It wasn't as if I was never going to see her again *and* she was only a phone call away. Perhaps it was the loneliness or Josh's disappearance, or maybe both. *Probably both*, I decided as my tears slowed to a trickle.

I got up from the bed and strolled into the en-suite. I turned on the cold tap and splashed some water onto my face. I glanced at my reflection in the mirror, grimacing as I caught sight of my red, puffy eyes. *God, what a mess*, I thought and splashed some more water on them, bathing them gently for a few minutes until I felt the heat in them dissipate. I dabbed at my face gently with a hand towel, dried my hands and wandered back into the bedroom.

I sat cross-legged on the bed and stared into space. All sorts of things were somersaulting around in my mind, pictures flashed before my eyes like a silent film: Joshua's face the last time I saw him; Becky's face when she surprised me; Joshua's face when he met me at the airport; Grace's face at the police station when we reported Josh missing; my reflection when I saw the bruises and scratches on my body; Joshua laughing; Joshua pensive; Joshua sleeping; Joshua, Joshua, Joshua. The pictures were on a loop, repeating over and over, faster and faster until they became a blur before my eyes.

My head was swimming and woozy, tears were once more flowing down my cheeks, my throat was sore, my mouth parched and my body ached from the muscles spasms of my earlier sobs. I flopped onto my side and pulled my knees up so I was lying in a foetal position. I was still woozy and suddenly I started to feel very hot. Perspiration beaded on my brow and the back of my neck. The last thing I remember was seeing a flash of Joshua's face before I lost consciousness.

When I awoke the next morning, I was really groggy as if I'd taken sedatives. My head was filled with cotton wool and I didn't feel right. I hoped having a shower would wake me up a bit and wandered into the bathroom. I cringed as I peeled off yesterday's clothes and dropped them on the floor. Stepping into the warm water, allowing it to cascade down my face, I began to wake and my head started to clear. I shampooed my hair then massaged the sweet smelling shower gel into my body before I rinsed everything off and turned off the water. As I stepped out of the cubicle I wrapped the too small towel around my damp body and turbaned another around my dripping hair. I certainly felt more human now and my skin tingled as I rubbed it dry. I got dressed, pulled a brush through my hair then went down for breakfast.

An hour later I was in the car and heading down to the Broads. It was a hot and humid day – the sort of day when all your clothes stuck like glue to your body – with no breeze to cool you down. It was going to be a scorcher and I was glad for the wind blowing through the open car windows. I suppose I could have used the Air Con, but I much preferred to smell the myriad fragrances in the country air. Twenty minutes later I pulled into the small car park. I managed to find a space in the shade; left the front windows open a little to let out any heat and locked the car.

It was so pretty and peaceful along the towpath. The grassy picnic area was already littered with mothers accompanying babies and toddlers; some were with their children feeding the ducks with pieces of bread broken into small chunks. I stopped as my eyes were drawn to one particular child – a beautiful girl of around two or three, wearing a bright red sun dress with reins over the top.

She threw a handful of bread into the water and watched intently as the ducks paddled over and dipped their heads to pick up the food, then clapped her hands and giggled; jumping up and down in glee, her chestnut curls bounced and sparkled in the sun picking up glints of red in her hair. The sight brought a smile to my face. I continued to observe for a few minutes; the girl reminded me of Becky and I when we were that age. Thinking of Becky brought a lump to my throat and I turned away and looked back at the scenery to distract me then continued on.

Wild flowers bordered one side of the towpath and reeds edged the water. I wandered down to the offices where the cruisers were booked out, pulling the photo of Joshua from my bag as I approached.

I had no luck in the first two offices. As I walked towards the third one, it looked vaguely familiar. I entered and walked over to the counter. A middle-aged man with a friendly smile looked up as I came closer.

"Hello there. How can I help you?"

I placed the photo on the counter. "Have you seen this man recently?"

He picked up the photo and studied it for quite a while, his brows mashed together in concentration.

"I've seen his face before, but not *that* recently." He stared at me for ages. Just when I began to feel uncomfortable with his scrutiny, he spoke again.

"I've seen you before too," he announced, "and you were with this young man. If my memory serves, it was about May or June time last year. That's right – I remember you both coming here to pick up the keys to your cruiser."

"Really?" I responded, taken aback, "y-you *remember* us?" My eyes had widened at his comments.

"Yes I do. I remember thinking what a lovely couple you were and so obviously head over heels in love – it was so nice to see," as he reminisced, he had a faraway look in his eyes as if he was looking through a window back into the past.

"Oh." His words were a dagger straight through my heart. I felt my face crumple as huge fat tears rolled over my cheeks and dripped off my chin and nose.

He rushed around to my side of the counter dragging a chair behind him. He placed it behind my legs and helped me into it, placing a box of tissues in my lap. I grabbed a couple gratefully and dabbed at my eyes.

"Th-th-thank y-you," I blubbed, not raising my head to look at him. I knew I was making a fool of myself, but I couldn't seem to control it.

I felt an arm snake around my shoulders in comfort and someone kneel beside me. I didn't raise my head, but out of the corner of my eye I saw a female form.

After a few minutes I gained enough control to raise my head. Looking back at me with concern in her eyes was an attractive middle-aged lady.

"Are you alright, my dear?" her voice was soft and caring.

I nodded, not quite trusting my voice, as I wiped the remnants of the tears from my eyes and face.

"Come with me," she commanded gently, getting to her feet and, with her arm around my waist, helped me to my feet. She guided me behind the counter into a small office and deposited me in a comfy chair. She walked over to a small alcove at the end of the room and I heard her fill a kettle with water.

I didn't pay much attention to my surroundings – I stared off into space, seeing nothing – the only thing I was truly aware of was the hollow ache in my torso. Even the passing of time meant nothing. The lady returned with two steaming mugs in her hand – she placed one on the desk beside where my chair was and one on a small filing cabinet close by. She pulled a chair out from behind a desk and sat opposite me, in front of the cabinet.

"I didn't know if you wanted sugar, but I've put some in anyway," she said, scrutinising my face with caring yet curious eyes.

I dragged my eyes back into focus at the sound of her voice and looked at her properly for the first time. Her face was somewhat familiar, but I didn't actually know who she was.

"Thank you," I whispered, lowering my eyes.

"You're welcome. Now then – what's this all about?" she asked in a no-nonsense sort of tone.

"S-sorry?" I stammered, confused by her question. I raised my eyes to look at her.

"Well, it's not every day a lovely young lady like yourself comes into our office and then collapses in a flood of tears," she explained, watching me intently.

I looked down at the floor, totally embarrassed by my meltdown.

"I'm sorry," I mumbled.

"You don't need to apologise - I'm more worried about you," she stated firmly. "Now drink your tea and tell me all about it," the tone of her voice softened.

I raised my head picked up the mug, careful not to spill the contents and put it to my lips to sip the hot beverage. I ran her words through my head again. Did I really want to tell my woes to a complete stranger? I'd found it hard enough to talk to my twin about it at first yet I'd told Pat Kirk, and I didn't know her *that* well at the time. Would it benefit me in any way if I told her? I wasn't sure either way, but I did owe her some sort of explanation for breaking down on her premises. I would give her an abridged version.

If she was puzzled by my pause, she didn't show it. Nor did she prompt me, for which I was grateful. I marshalled my thoughts into some semblance of coherency then took a deep breath, letting it out slowly as I prepared to speak.

"Did you hear what I asked the man and what he said to me?" I asked timidly.

"If you mean my husband, then yes I did," she answered, still studying my face.

"Well, my fiancé disappeared a couple of days before our w-wedding . . ." I hesitated a moment to compose myself, "and I've been searching for him ever since."

She sat completely still as she processed my words then fidgeted a little, picking up her own mug of tea and taking a mouthful. I could tell she was trying to work out what to say to me – she opened her mouth then closed it two or three times before finally responding.

"I'm so sorry to hear that. I also remember when you both came here to pick up your cruiser and I thought the exact same thing as Lawrie - I'm not at all surprised to hear you were getting married. How long ago did he go missing?"

I did a quick calculation in my head. "About three weeks," I replied sadly.

"Oh, you poor thing. What makes you think he's around here though?" she asked a sympathetic expression on her face.

"Well . . . having eliminated family and friends, I racked my brains to think of where he might have gone and at first I couldn't come up with anything. But then I remembered where I'd pulled out a photo for the police and it was one of our holiday albums, so I thought maybe he'd gone to one of the places where he was really happy. I've been systematically visiting places where we holidayed together, calling on hotels and guest houses and anywhere else I can think of in each area, in the hope I can track him down." I explained in a monotone.

Her head was tilted to the side as she listened to everything I said. As I spoke, some of the tension left my body and I started to relax a little. The lady was kind and seemed concerned about me and in some ways it was a bit of a relief to let things out, but I was still really aware I'd made quite a spectacle of myself. I gulped down some more of my tea, abruptly anxious to leave.

She cleared her throat before speaking.

"You must really love him to go to all this trouble to find him – it sounds like you've put your life completely on hold for this," she said, sounding awed.

"I do," I replied simply. "He's my entire life and I know he loves me as much as I love him – that's why I've got to find him," my voice rose an octave and became more impassioned. "His disappearance is *so* out of character. He left to protect me, but it's had the opposite effect. I. Can't. Live. Without. Him . . ."

Sympathy and understanding flooded her eyes. She reached forward and took one of my hands in hers; her expression was serious yet troubled.

"I know you don't know me and I have no right to really comment on what you're doing, but . . ." she paused as if trying to think of how to phrase what was playing on her mind, "I admire your commitment and envy you your love for this man, but in the process of trying to find him, please don't lose yourself in the process."

"What do you mean?" I asked, puzzled.

"This . . . quest of yours is totally consuming you – I can see it in your eyes – it could turn into an obsession and result in you losing everything, your sanity included. You seem a caring, intelligent young woman and it would be too horrible to consider the effect … the toll this will have on you if you fail." Her tone was earnest in her explanation.

I was quite taken aback by her words and her obvious concern for a complete stranger. She was quite insightful too – she was right, it was consuming me, but I couldn't even conceive that I might not find Joshua.

"Thank you for caring enough to tell me what you think and for trying to warn me, but failure is not an option – it's not something I can consider, not now, not ever. I will think about what you've said though and I *will* try very hard not to lose myself. I'm quite lucky in that I have the support of my family, especially my twin sister and if it all gets too much, I know I only have to pick up the phone and she will drop everything to get to my side. Becky won't let me go under. She can tell by my voice if I'm not . . . coping and she'll either give me a pep talk or kick my butt or drive to wherever I am and comfort me. I'll be fine, honest," I tried to explain, my expression as serious as hers.

She nodded, perhaps expecting a response similar to the one she got. As she pondered, I finished the last of my tea then gently withdrew my hand from hers. I got to my feet and smiled down at her.

"I don't know how to thank you for your kindness and I'm sorry to have taken up your time and for making an . . . exhibition of myself in your office, but I need to get going now."

She rose and put her hand on my shoulder as I started to move towards the door.

"You have nothing to thank me, or apologise for," she stated. "Just promise me you'll be careful and remember what I said," she implored, her eyes troubled once more.

"I promise," I vowed solemnly, looking her straight in the eye.

"If you need to talk to someone before you leave, I'm quite a good listener. By the way, my name's Audrey," she grinned at me, her expression a little resigned.

"Thank you, Audrey. Mine's Remy. And thank you again for everything." I patted her hand and walked through the doorway into the front office. Her husband looked up at me and smiled but said nothing. Perhaps he didn't want to embarrass me any further by mentioning my breakdown. I continued to the outer door and pausing for a second before stepping through, I turned my head back to them, smiled and said softly, "Thank you again. Bye."

Without waiting for an answer, I walked out into the bright light eager to make up the hour I'd lost in that office.

Chapter 30 – Remy

The days started to melt into each other as the pattern continued. When I'd made the decision to search for Joshua, I don't think I'd really understood how time consuming it would be to visit all the establishments in each town or village. Nevertheless, I was totally committed to finding Joshua and wouldn't stop – not now.

It took another five days to complete my task in the Beccles area and then another sixteen in the Great Yarmouth area. As I was there for so long, I took a class at a dance school one evening. It was great to get back to dancing – I hadn't done it for a few months. The strenuous exercise and mental distraction sent adrenaline coursing through me. I walked out of the studio with a spring in my step which had been missing for too long and the buzz lasted a few days. Regrettably it didn't last longer. By the time I was ready to move away from Norfolk, I had the weight of the world on my shoulders and was depressed by my lack of success.

I'd had to spend some time in a launderette as I'd pretty much run out of clean clothes and luckily, the landlady at the guest house I stayed at in Great Yarmouth, lent me an iron and ironing board. As I packed my case, I was dimly aware it was taking me far longer than normal, as if I'd run out of steam. My movements were sluggish, lethargic and it had nothing to do with the heat. I wanted to cry and sob and rail at the whole world. I wanted to shut myself away, curl up and die – anything was better than existing in this constant, never ending agony. I had my own personal rain cloud hovering over my head and it was as humungous as it was black. Just like my mood.

I eventually finished packing my case and set about checking all the drawers, wardrobe and bathroom to ensure nothing was forgotten before leaving the room. My feet were heavy weights and I shuffled rather than walked. I picked up my handbag and noticed a folded piece of paper I didn't remember seeing before. Curious, I picked it up and unfolded it. I recognised the handwriting immediately.

Hey Rems,

I decided to leave you a little note in the hope that it will make you smile.

Keep your chin up hun and remember why you are doing this, I know it will be worth it in the end. Call me if you need me, you know I will always be there for you.

Love you loads,

Becky xxx

p.s. if sisters were flowers, I would pick you!

Moisture clouded my vision as I read her note. It was so typical of Becky to think of doing something kind for me – perhaps intuitively she knew that by now I would be struggling with the emotional strain and I would need something to buoy my spirits. The corners of my mouth lifted slightly as I read her post script then they stretched further as I had an epiphany – I had to travel through Essex on my way to Kent, so why not stop off and visit her, Mum and Dad. Even if it was only a short visit, it would be so lovely to see them all. I would surprise them. With new resolve, I hurriedly grabbed my things, eager now to be on my way and within ten minutes was in the car and pulling onto the road.

I closed my car door as quietly as possible before tiptoeing up to the house. I looked through the front window and wasn't surprised to see the room empty, so I turned to the side of the house and crept towards the back. In this weather they were bound to be in the garden. As I reached the end of the building, I peeped around the corner and saw them both.

Mum was lying on a sun lounger reading while Dad was pulling some weeds from one of the flowerbeds. Mum was a very attractive woman for her age, tall and slim with perfectly coiffed blonde hair, manicured and painted nails and flawless make up. Dad, a handsome man despite his receding hairline, had sparkling blue eyes, a physique most thirty-year-olds would kill for and a wicked sense of humour. They had their backs to where I was standing so the element of surprise was definitely on my side. I stepped out further, being careful not to tread on anything which would make a noise then yelled,

"SURPRISE!"

I creased up laughing as my Dad jumped three foot in the air and Mum threw her book up, losing her page in the process. Dad ran across the garden and reached me before Mum had even got out of her seat. He threw his arms around me and gave me a bear hug to end all bear hugs.

"Remy? You little minx," he laughed into my hair before kissing the top of my head. I was still laughing from making them jump. He swung me round literally lifting my feet off the ground then put me down and let go of me so I could hug Mum. She stood patiently waiting till Dad let me go then crushed me to her. We stood hugging for what appeared to be ages, but in reality was only about a minute or so. When Mum eased her grip on me, she stepped back, keeping her hands on my shoulders and looked deeply into my face, scrutinising everything and missing nothing.

"Hello darling," she said softly. "How are you?"

"Hi Mum, I'm good thanks, you?" I replied cheerfully, smiling.

"I'm fine, thank you. How are you really?" she said, disquiet evident in her tone.

"I get by. I have my good days and my bad ones, but I try and stay positive. I miss him so much – it makes me ache all over," my voice changed from even to emotional in one breath. Pain etched into my features and I fought back the pricking sensation behind my eyes.

"Come on inside and let's get you something to eat and drink and we can talk some more," she said, putting her arm around my shoulders. She was good at that – she knew I was struggling to keep my emotions in check and wanted to give me time to compose myself.

We walked together into the house, Dad followed behind. As soon as we got into the cool kitchen, Mum started to bustle around, making sandwiches and cold drinks for us all while Dad and I went to sit at the small kitchen table.

"Do you want a hand, Mum?" I asked.

"No thanks, I can manage," she replied not taking her eyes from cutting and washing the lettuce.

I turned to look at Dad. "So, what've you been up to then, Dad – apart from driving Mum crazy, that is?" I smirked at him.

"Cheeky," he grinned back, then started to fill me in on some trivial things, deliberately skirting away from anything to do with Joshua, for which I was eternally grateful.

Mum brought a large plate of sandwiches to the table then returned with drinks and small plates so we could eat. As we munched, we chatted about their work, friends, neighbours and anecdotes they'd picked up along the way. It was great to catch up and spend a little time relaxing in a known and safe environment.

All too soon, we reached the topic I least wanted to talk about and the one they most wanted to discuss. Mum opened the subject in a typical roundabout way by saying she thought I looked tired. I took a deep breath before bringing them up to date with my travels and lack of success. The disappointment and sorrow in my voice probably conveyed more than the actual words. I must have talked for half an hour straight without interruption and, to my surprise without losing control of my emotions. It was crazy – the one place in the whole world where I could just be me and let everything out, yet not a tear in sight.

Mum and Dad weren't fooled by my bravado. They knew I was in pain. They also knew – possibly more than *I* even realised – how much of a toll this was taking on me, physically and emotionally. Several times when I was talking, I saw their eyes meet, as if they were holding a silent but parallel conversation. It was obvious in their body language and facial expressions they were extremely worried about me and I knew it wouldn't be long before they voiced their fears. I wasn't disappointed.

Surprisingly, it was Dad who started it off. His voice was gentle, but it had a slight edge to it.

"Remy, are you sure this is the right thing to do? I know you miss him, but your Mum and I are worried sick about what this is doing to you."

Before I had a chance to respond, Mum jumped in and backed him up.

"Your Dad's right – we are very worried. You don't look right, we can see you're tired to the point of exhaustion and we can feel your pain. Sweetheart, I know you love him and want to bring him back home, but look at what this is *doing* to you. You're putting a brave face on it and trying to hide what you're really feeling, but we know you so well and you're *struggling*. I think it's wonderful you found someone to love so completely, but how much further are you going to let this drag you down before you wake up to the damage you're doing to yourself?" Mum's face showed her anxiety and her tone, unlike Dad's, was more emotional and less gentle. Her eyes searched my face as she spoke, watching carefully for my reaction to her words.

My brow furrowed at her words and I stared down at my hands. I was trying so hard to disguise my true feelings – I should have known they would see through me. I had to find a way to ease their anxiety without lying to them. Not the easiest of tasks, that was for sure. I sat pensively, while Mum and Dad had another silent, but meaningful conversation with their eyes. An idea came to me – I could be honest with them, but not tell them everything; playing down some of the more negative stuff. Whatever happened, whatever was said, we all knew I would do what I wanted regardless of what it cost me.

I raised my head and looked directly at them both.

"Mum, Dad, I know you're worried about me, but this is something I have to do. I don't *expect* you to understand how I feel, but I would hope you'd respect my decision and give your support. I know I look tired and, to be honest, I am, but it's only because I didn't get much sleep at the last place I stayed – the bed was *awful*, so lumpy and uncomfortable.

"I've been eating properly and looking after myself. Most of the time, I've been sleeping reasonably well. Am I in pain? Absolutely. Am I going to give up? No chance. It's hard to explain, to find the right words, but deep inside me I know Josh and I are *meant* to be together – I know he still loves me as much as I love him – and if the situation was reversed, he would be looking for *me*.

I've come too far to give up and if I quit now, it would be like saying our love didn't mean very much, that our relationship was a sham, that our marriage would never have worked and I *can't* and *won't* do that. Can you understand?" the passion in my voice hit a nerve with them both and I could see, to a degree, they could understand where I was coming from.

"Yes, sweetheart, we *can* understand, but it isn't going to stop us from worrying until you're back home safe and sound," Dad said, showing a little emotion in his voice. His eyes drilled into mine and it appeared as if they were pleading with me.

My eyes swept towards Mum. Her expression was resigned, sad even and I found a lump forming in my throat. I reached towards her and grabbed her hand, holding it tight in mine.

"Mum, trust me. I know what I'm doing and I promise to look after myself. If I need help, I *will* ask for it," I vowed sincerely, my eyes beseeching. I squeezed her hand.

"Remy, darling, you know I trust you and your judgement, but you can't blame me for being anxious or for wanting you close to home. You know we'll support you no matter what and we'll be there for you if you need us. You've made us a promise young lady, and we'll expect you to keep it."

Dad nodded in agreement with his wife, but said nothing further.

"I don't make promises lightly Mum, you know that," I responded tartly, a little put out she would question the validity of the vow I'd made.

"I know you don't, love, and I didn't mean to imply you would."

I smiled at her to let her know she was off the hook, that I wasn't annoyed with her and was glad to see her smile in return. I looked back at Dad and saw a more relaxed grin on his face also.

I glanced at the clock and saw it was mid-afternoon. I still had two-and-a-half-hours worth of driving ahead of me and the Queen Elizabeth II Bridge was notorious for slow moving traffic during the day. I stood and carried the empty plates and glasses over to the dishwasher and loaded them in. I turned back to face my parents.

"I'm going to have to make a move. I don't really want to get caught on the Dartford Bridge and I've got quite a journey still ahead of me. Thanks for the lunch, Mum."

"Why don't you stay the night and travel on in the morning? You know we'd love to have some more time with you," Mum pleaded.

"Sorry, Mum, but I can't. I've already got a booking and if I don't turn up tonight, I'll lose the rest of it. Besides, I've already paid."

"Oh. Okay then, promise to ring us a bit more often, please? Just to put our minds at rest that you're alright."

I nodded. "Of course I will," I affirmed.

I walked over to the table and as I went to bend down to give Dad a hug, he stood to embrace me. I kissed him on the cheek.

"Take it easy, Dad. See you soon. Love you."

He kissed my forehead and nodded. "*You* take care, please. Love you too."

I smiled up at him and nodded then turned to Mum. She stood and was again waiting patiently for her turn. I kissed her and gave her a hug, which she returned, holding me a bit longer than Dad had.

"Love you, Mum. Please don't worry about me – I'll be fine."

She nodded then kissed my cheek.

"I love you too, sweetheart. Don't forget to call me."

"I won't."

I turned and walked out to the car with them following behind me.

I got in and switched on the ignition so I could roll the windows down. Putting the car in gear, I called, "Bye. Love you." through the open window and waved as I pulled away.

Looking in the rear view mirror, I saw Dad had put his arm around Mum's shoulders and she had rested her head against his chest. They stood there, waving, until I was out of sight and then I had to pull over - it was impossible to drive with tears pouring from my eyes.

* * *

My journey to Kent was a little slow in places, but reasonably uneventful and I arrived in Birchington only half an hour later than expected. The little seaside village of Minnis Bay was quiet, relatively unspoilt and not really a tourist place compared with a lot of the Kent coast. I picked up the keys of the small cottage I was renting and nipped to the shops to get some basic foodstuffs to tide me over for a few days.

I found a decent restaurant within walking distance, had a lovely meal and then sauntered back along the beach barefoot. The sand was still damp and it squidged between my toes as I walked. After a short while, I found a small crop of rocks close to the sea wall and went to sit on them. They had mostly dried out, but in a few places little pools of water lay in shallow dips in the rock's surface. I found a smooth dry piece and sat looking out to sea.

Watching water, especially waves, always had a calming effect on me and this night was no different. The tide was ebbing, but wasn't so far out I couldn't see the ripples and small waves which tickled the sand. I watched the sun moving slowly towards the horizon; the sunset was so exceptionally stunning it took my breath away. Where was my camera when I needed it most? I remained there until the sun had all but disappeared before rising and making my way back to the cottage.

It wasn't very far and I was in no real hurry; it was a warm, balmy night with a whisper of a breeze to relieve some of the humidity. There were a few people strolling around – a few even smiled as they passed me. I reached the gate and gazed at the house. It had a rose arch halfway down the long path to the front door and the garden was filled with aromatic plants and flowers. I could smell lavender and lilac, freesia and sweet peas, jasmine and rose; together they made the most wonderful perfume. As I walked up the path I inhaled deeply and smiled to myself. I let myself into the cottage and closed the door behind me.

The interior of the cottage was a little wacky. As you walked through the small front door you were in a tiny hallway and two steps later in a small oddly shaped lounge. Dark wooden beams crossed the ceiling and followed down the walls in an unbroken line, the walls in between having been painted a pale peach. The carpet was an old fashioned patterned one I would have cringed at in any other setting, but here it appeared to fit. The furniture was old fashioned too and made of a heavy dark wood; the seats were covered in flowered chintz and were saggy but strangely comfortable.

The kitchen was through a doorway off the lounge – walking in there was like stepping back in time to the 1920's. The old style cupboards had many layers of paint on and were currently a celery green colour. Quirky wallpaper covered the walls except around the sink where plain white tiles had been decorated with stick on transfers which didn't match anything else in the room. Some of the kitchen utensils also came from the same era and were totally alien to me.

The upstairs had two bedrooms and a bathroom and like the downstairs, had a mishmash of décor styles all from around the same period. However, somehow everything worked together and it gave the cottage a homely feel.

I sat on the sofa with my legs curled to the side. On my lap was my trusty pad and beside me was the local telephone directory. After a couple of hours of working my way through, I still hadn't completed my list for the area and my hand was beginning to cramp from all the writing. I glanced at my watch as I was beginning to get weary and seeing it was almost 11pm decided to get some sleep. I had enough on my list to make a start in the morning and could work on it some more the next evening.

My feet were heavy as I stomped up the wooden staircase. I undressed and got into bed. My eyes closed as soon as my head hit the pillow and I sank into a deep sleep.

I found myself looking through a window into the book-lined room. All the same beautiful people were in the room with Joshua, but something had changed. I searched the room and its' occupants carefully to try and find the anomaly, then realised Joshua was not in the seat I had seen him in before. He was sitting on a two-seater settee, one of the gorgeous women next to him.

I studied their movements and body language. The woman was gazing at Joshua with naked adoration in her eyes; a soft yet slightly smug smile graced her lips as she leaned towards him, her shoulder grazing against his. He turned to glance at her and a gentle smile – a smile I remembered so well – played over his mouth. I didn't like the expression on his face – it was too warm, too open, too loving – and a well of hurt gushed through me.

Joshua turned back to the tall, dark man who always appeared to be the leader. He was saying something to the gathering, but I couldn't hear it. As had happened previously, all I could hear was a weird burbling noise – it was so annoying. A discussion ensued; I could see others talking in turns, some gesticulating with their hands as they spoke, others relying on their facial expressions to get their point across. Only one stayed silent – the tiny blonde with curly hair remained aloof from the debate – she wasn't even looking into the room, preferring to stare out of the window with an arrogant yet bored expression on her face.

My eyes wandered back to Joshua and the woman by his side. The way she had positioned herself was proprietary, as if warning off any of the other females in the room. It screamed of 'he's mine – keep your distance'. I plunged into a deep pit of loathing. How dare this creature think she had any claim to Joshua – he was mine! He would always be mine.

Joshua's attention was totally focused on the leader and, thankfully from my perspective, not on the female. I saw Joshua's lips move and try as I might to read what they were saying, they were too fast; he paused, waiting for a response I guessed then nodded. Some of them got up and started to move towards the door; Joshua turned to the woman and whispered something in her ear, something which made her eyes sparkle and her face light up. They rose together and as they approached the door, I saw Joshua grab her hand.

A pain I'd never experienced before pierced me straight through the heart. It was the sharpest sword followed by the strongest and fastest bolt of lightning, shadowed by a flaming spear tipped with poison, pursued by a strike by the deadliest snake ever to exist, but they all struck at once culminating in an agony so intense I couldn't move or breathe or do anything. My ears were deafened by the sound of my heart thumping unevenly in my chest; my head was about to explode and my lungs seared with the scream that wouldn't or couldn't break free.

I didn't have a chance to recover; I was looking through a different window and this time I appeared to be inside looking out. I was so mesmerised by the scene unfolding before my eyes I failed to notice where I actually was. Joshua and the woman were gliding across the grass towards some outbuildings, but not at a normal pace; they were moving so gracefully yet much faster. I was disconcerted by the way they moved – it gave the appearance of being entirely natural yet was so obviously not. I'd never seen Joshua move that way before and for some reason, it scared me.

I continued observing them, noticing to my absolute disgust they were still holding hands. They rounded a corner and there, gleaming from the house lights, was Joshua's car. Even if I hadn't known the registration plate, I would have recognised it anywhere; hanging from the rear view mirror was a small lucky charm I'd given him when he'd first bought it.

I saw the woman clap her hands together in glee, a huge grin stretched across her face and her eyes widened in astonishment. She turned, spoke to him and he nodded his reply grinning back, his face excited. I was unprepared for what was soon to transpire; the agony I'd suffered previously was a mere pinprick against what I was about to endure. However, I didn't know or realise I would need to protect myself.

Joshua led her to the passenger side and opened the door. Before climbing in, she threw her arms around him, her embrace more than a friendly hug as she pressed her body against his and moulded it to his contours seductively. He returned the embrace with zeal, laughing with her. They pulled away slightly and I watched, horrified, as he placed one finger under her chin, tilted her face up then crushed his lips down on hers.

A hatred more absolute and vicious than I realised I was capable of overwhelmed me as the agony struck the centre of my chest. The sharpest claws were slowly and excruciatingly shredding my heart while pouring acid over it and setting it on fire. Wind rushed past my ears in a roar and then I was falling from the height of a cloud, gathering momentum, speeding down into the blackest bowels of the earth; a scream of unadulterated torture built up and up until I couldn't restrain it any longer and it burst from my lips like a bullet from a gun.

My slumber was disturbed by the strangest screaming noise. It appeared to be worryingly close. My eyes shot open at the same time as I sat up in bed. I scanned the room wildly for a fraction of a second as I tried to see who was making that awful screech. The realisation hit – it was coming from me. I clamped my hands roughly over my mouth and pushed my face into the pillow to stifle the sound. It took all my concentration to inhale deeply and slowly as I tried to calm down and very gradually the screams turned to whimpers and then to silence.

I lay unmoving, trying to remember what had caused me to screech like I was being murdered, but nothing came to me. I had a vague impression it may have had something to do with Joshua, but other than that, zilch. One thing I did know was my lungs ached and there was a fierce pain in my chest. It wasn't exactly an unfamiliar feeling – on the contrary, I'd suffered this since the day Joshua disappeared – it was different somehow, it had an unusual edgy intensity which was different to anything I'd experienced before and fear snaked through my veins.

I rolled over onto my back and stared up at the ceiling. Catching a glimpse through a chink in the curtains, I knew it was much too early to get up yet I found myself too unnerved to fall straight back to sleep. My eyes were unusually dry – not that I was one to cry at the slightest thing – but for something to happen which would wake me screaming so much the walls of the old cottage were almost shaking, it was more likely that tears would also be streaming down my face. This puzzled me greatly. What was so different? What on earth had occurred? Why couldn't I remember? Was my subconscious blocking something, protecting me so I couldn't recall it?

My head started to hurt as I desperately tried to summon the events which remained stubbornly shrouded. My eyelids began to droop; I yawned and turned onto my side. Within a minute I drifted into a deep, but this time, dreamless slumber.

The following three days proved difficult. I had a cotton wool brain; the inside of my head was muzzy. My energy level was much lower than normal and I was quite lethargic. Perhaps I was on the verge of coming down with a bug. I hoped not. I kept pushing myself to carry on, but my progress was slow and I didn't manage to get to as many establishments as I had in other towns.

On returning to the cottage in the evenings, it took a monumental effort to climb the stairs so I could go to bed; my feet were so heavy as if encased in concrete blocks and I had to use the banister rail to haul myself up. Most times, I was too exhausted to undress properly and ended up flopping on the bed and falling asleep instantaneously.

On the morning of the fourth day, I awoke to my alarm and was relieved to discover my head was clear. I rose slowly, testing my limbs, relieved to find I actually felt quite good. I completed my ablutions in record time before skipping downstairs to make myself some breakfast. As I sat at the tiny table demolishing my breakfast, I thought back over the past three days and idly wondered what had caused my symptoms. Had it all stemmed from the nightmare which caused me to wake screaming, but that I couldn't recall? If so, how strange it should affect my health in such a way.

    I cleared up the dishes from breakfast, washed them and left them on the drainer to dry. Anxious to try and make up for lost time, I hurriedly grabbed my stuff and legged it out the door.

Chapter 31 – Joshua

The neophyte prowled through yet another town, hunting for prey and hoping to cross a particular scent. He wasn't cautious and didn't keep to the shadows; no one had taught him – he was acting on instinct and maybe a little from movies. He heard two people exit a pub around the corner; a brief sound of clinking glasses, music and laughter drifted into the night.

He rounded the corner and a couple in their mid-twenties were strolling towards him, hand in hand, chatting and laughing, their eyes full of anticipation as they gazed at each other. He struck with the speed of a King Cobra, incapacitating the man before turning his attention to the young woman. She didn't even have time to scream after seeing her boyfriend hit the pavement – the neophyte pounced, his lips and teeth firmly clamped around her jugular. After draining her dry, he picked up the limp body of the man and sank his teeth into his neck.

It didn't really occur to him that at any given moment, someone could exit the pub or walk around the corner and catch him in the act - he didn't really care either, it wasn't as if he was incapable of dealing with them. When he'd finished with the man, he dumped him back on the pavement, next to his dead girlfriend. He blatantly left them where they fell, making no attempt to hide the bodies, and continued striding along in his usual cocky way.

As he approached the outskirts of the town, he caught the faintest whiff of a familiar scent on the breeze. An excited yet menacing grin rushed onto his face. He inhaled again to make sure he wasn't mistaken and his grin widened further when he confirmed it was the one he'd been searching for.

He set off, following the scent and finalising his plans for revenge.

* * *

Samir sat alone in the library; his coven had left to hunt and he was savouring the few minutes of solitude. A minute or two later, the ring tone of his mobile phone intruded on his reverie. Dragging it out of his pocket, he glanced at the screen to see who it was then answered quickly.

"Hello, Pavel. What a pleasant surprise. How are you?"

"Hello, Samir. I am well, thank you, and you?" Pavel replied.

There was a sound of rushing wind in the background behind Pavel's voice and Samir speculated he was probably travelling.

"Very well, thank you. Where are you travelling to, my friend?

"I'm on my way to you actually – I should be arriving inside of two hours. Now, I hope you haven't forgotten our previous conversation – I want to observe your coven without them even knowing I am around, especially Dayna," Pavel instructed, his voice as even as if he were standing still instead of running full pelt.

"Of course I haven't forgotten, Pavel," Samir replied, affronted by the insinuation, as his eyes tightened.

Pavel immediately detected the change in Samir's tone and realised he'd upset him.

"I apologise if I have offended you, my friend," he said contritely, then continued with barely a pause. "Is there anything else I need to know or consider as I journey?"

Samir paused for a moment before answering, pacified by Pavel's apology.

"Nothing with regards to Dayna. However, it seems Joshua and Jasna have developed a . . . *relationship* I suppose you would call it. The only other thing is that over the past couple of days, I have detected the presence of another immortal in the vicinity. He is not of my making and I don't know where he is from. I must admit I am a little troubled by this - I was about to investigate when you called."

"I strongly suggest you wait until I arrive to investigate the stranger. Is your coven out at the moment? Are they likely to return before I arrive?" Pavel's suggestion sounded more like a command, but Samir was quite happy to acquiesce – he had an uncomfortable feeling about this immortal.

"Very well. Yes, my coven is out and no, I don't expect any of them to return prior to your arrival. I will make my preparations with all speed so everything is ready for you," Samir responded, now in a hurry to organise.

"Excellent. I will see you soon, my friend. Goodbye for now." Pavel ended the call before Samir could say anything further.

Samir replaced the phone and disappeared through the front door – he needed to hunt before Pavel arrived and he *did* have some organising to do and now, not much time to complete it. Driving himself to phenomenal speed, he bolted across the grounds and was swallowed up by the night.

* * *

Samir arrived back at the manor in plenty of time and had completed his tasks only minutes before Pavel arrived. After taking a few minutes to chat, Samir escorted Pavel into the next room and unveiled the one-way mirror with a small speaker attached which would allow him to observe and hear the occurrences in the library without being seen. No one but Samir knew about this mirror, until now, so it was ideal for the purpose. Pavel settled himself and awaited the return of the others, whilst Samir returned to the library and prepared to play his part.

Farrell and Erika were the first to return. They didn't have too long to wait before Dayna walked into the room. She sat far from the others, aloof, not bothering to join in the conversation. Her head was turned towards the window and she didn't even acknowledge the presence of the others – not even when she first arrived.

It was another twenty minutes before Joshua and Jasna walked into the library, and the first time Dayna moved since she sat. Her head turned in their direction as they walked over the threshold, cheerfully greeting everyone, and a glare of contempt and utter loathing shot from her eyes towards Jasna. If the look were daggers, Jasna would have been pierced through her entire torso.

Dayna peeked at Joshua and saw he was talking to Farrell; he wasn't paying any attention to her so she continued to surreptitiously throw hateful looks in Jasna's direction. Samir caught sight of Dayna's expression and frowned. Pavel, watching from the next room, became furious, especially when he observed Jasna flinch as she saw the unadulterated hatred in Dayna's eyes. Erika was used to feeling Dayna's hostility and didn't react to it, but she became aware of another emotion. Someone was angry, very angry. Her eyes flitted around the room to determine whom it was and was puzzled when she couldn't pinpoint them.

Unexpectedly Samir stiffened and became totally immobile. Erika gasped as she felt the emotions pouring from Samir and a look of dread came over her beautiful face, totally distracting her from her previous investigation. Farrell turned towards his partner, grimacing when he noticed her expression. Joshua, who was facing Farrell at the time, moved closer to Jasna, positioning himself between her and the door as he wheeled around to face what he somehow knew was coming. Pavel came out of the adjacent room and began to cross the foyer to the library when there came a loud banging on the main door.

Pavel froze. Samir glanced around the room then proceeded into the foyer towards the door as the banging began again. Farrell and Joshua moved into a protective position, taking Samir's flanks, their expressions calm. Pavel approached and sandwiched himself between them; their expressions were priceless when they saw who stood there. Pavel inclined his head towards the door and stared straight ahead. Joshua complied immediately, as did Farrell and just in time as Samir reached for the door handle and pulled the door open.

The immortal standing on the doorstep was dishevelled and dirty, tramp-like even, but the most disturbing thing was the menacing aura which emanated from him. His eyes were blazing with a murderous rage and his lips were curled back, baring his teeth.

Samir remained calm. His face was expressionless as he spoke to the visitor in a soft voice.

"Can I help you?"

"Where is she?" he snarled, his hands clenched into fists.

"I'm sorry, I don't know who you are referring to," Samir replied honestly.

"The blonde bitch who did this to me," he growled, his anger showing no sign of abating.

"I honestly don't know who you mean," Samir said, his expression and voice demonstrating how puzzled he was.

"Don't jerk me around," the visitor bellowed, "I followed her scent – I know she's here and she's gonna pay for what she did to me." His face contorted and his eyes narrowed to mere slits. His fists were clenched so tight the bones could break through the skin.

"I know nothing of this," Samir stated indignantly. "Perhaps, we should discuss this further."

"What's to discuss? Just hand her over and I'll be on my way," he said belligerently, taking a step closer to the doorway and angling his body forwards in a threatening manner.

Samir hissed through his teeth in warning. He then took a deep breath before speaking again.

"I've already told you, I don't know who or what you are talking about. Would you care to come in and fill in the gaps in our knowledge so we might understand?"

A frightening leer crossed his lips as he realised he would be one step closer to getting his hands on his maker, but as Samir stepped back to allow him entry, he saw the three bodies standing protectively behind and his smirk faded. He walked over the threshold and was shepherded to a room down the hall from the library. After the visitor sat, Samir and Pavel positioned themselves either side of him, whilst Joshua and Farrell sat closer to the door, ostensibly blocking it as a means of escape.

"Now, will you please tell us who you are, your story and what exactly brings you to our home?" Samir requested, trying to maintain a neutral façade.

The neophyte sighed dramatically. Realising he had to give a little to get what he wanted he decided to co-operate, well on the surface at least.

"My name is Liam. I was walking home one night about two weeks ago when I met up with this little blonde piece. Bit of a cracker she was, so I decided to try me luck. We went to a park on the edge of town and started to get to know each other, if ya know what I mean. The next thing I know, I feel a sharp pain in me neck and then everything went black. When I came to, she was gone and I was feeling rough, ya know? Pains all over my body and two bloody wounds in me neck. When the pain stopped, I could hear for miles, my eyes could see the smallest things you could imagine, I was faster than a damn sports car and stronger than Hercules. So, it took me a couple of days to really figure stuff out and then I realised what that bitch had done to me. I had her scent on me clothes so I went searching for it. Came across it last night and now here I am," he explained.

Pavel and Samir's eyes met for the briefest part of a second then Pavel addressed him directly.

"So, Liam, what do you think the woman did to you?" Pavel's face was bland, betraying nothing of his thoughts.

"She turned me into a . . . *vampire*," he spat viciously, his face turning purple with rage, his fists banging down on the arms of the chair, making them groan in protest. Sawdust fell onto the floor, dancing in the air as it journeyed down.

"I see," Pavel said, still giving nothing away, "and have you fed?"

"Yeah. No problem there," he admitted, chuckling in a contemptuous manner.

"Very well. This woman you mentioned – can you describe her please?" Pavel sounded only mildly curious.

Liam's brow furrowed; his thick eyebrows were heavy shades over his tightened eyes.

"Small – petite I guess you'd call it – shortish blonde curly hair, rocking body, gorgeous face – like a miniature friggin' supermodel – and her voice was . . . musical but arrogant. Know her?" his expression changed as he described her. There was a hint of lustfulness and frustration in his eyes and his voice had an edge, like he had unfinished business there.

Pavel didn't miss a beat. "Doesn't sound like anyone I know," he lied smoothly, his face innocent.

Liam's expression changed to one of incredulity. He glared at all their faces in turn trying to read something in the expressions, but all four acted their parts well and gave nothing away. His eyes turned abruptly furious, but his face was perplexed.

"B-but I traced her scent here. She's here – or has been." He growled, defiant.

"It's possible she was attracted by our scent and was curious about us yet not brave enough to make herself known. We are not the only vampires in England – we have met others similar to yourself – but I haven't seen the woman you describe," Pavel turned to Samir. "Have you?" he asked.

Samir was equally as proficient an actor as he replied, "No, I haven't seen anyone who resembles that woman, sorry."

Liam still didn't appear convinced. He turned to look at Farrell and Joshua, the question apparent in his eyes. Both of them shook their heads, their expressions neutral. Liam's shoulders slumped in defeat yet there was a calculating look in his eyes.

"Seems I've had a wasted trip," he sounded resigned, but he wasn't fooling anyone, his acting skills left something to be desired. He got to his feet. "Sorry to have disturbed you. I'll make a move now."

Everyone else rose. Joshua and Farrell moved to the door, ready to escort Liam out. Pavel put one hand on Liam's shoulder in a friendly gesture.

"No harm done. It has been a pleasure to meet you, Liam. I hope we will see you again sometime," Pavel said in a sincere tone, the corners of his mouth twitched upwards in the beginning of a smile.

"Yeah, maybe you will," Liam replied flippantly.

They escorted Liam to the main door, flanking him on all sides and tensed to move in a millisecond should the need arise. Samir opened the door wide then offered his hand to Liam. He looked at it then shook hands with Samir first then Pavel, looking them directly in the eyes, searching for anything to expose the lies he suspected, but saw nothing. Liam walked through the door then rapidly turned back, trying one last time to catch them out, but the expressions were as neutral as ever.

"Bye," he said then took flight without waiting for them to respond.

Samir closed the door quietly then turned to face the others, the blackest fury clouding his features. Pavel put a restraining arm across Samir's chest, anticipating what he was about to do. Samir looked at Pavel, incredulous and defiant in his rage. Pavel's face showed a furious calm; he raised his other hand and put one finger up to his lips to signify they should be silent. He turned to Farrell and whispered in a voice so quiet no human would have been able to hear it, "Get the ladies downstairs, NOW! Hurry."

Farrell obeyed immediately, recognising the sense of urgency in Pavel's tone. Samir turned back to the door and for the first time ever, engaged all the locks and bolts. Joshua, who was never slow on the uptake, flew to the pantry door and did the same then returned to the foyer. Pavel and Samir were waiting for him and together they moved to the hidden staircase and descended into the cellar.

Farrell was waiting at the bottom of the stairs with the ladies for further instructions. No one uttered a sound, but the girl's eyes widened in surprise when they saw Pavel. Samir moved past everyone and stormed down a narrow, unlit corridor passing several doors before opening one. He stepped aside so everyone could file in before following and closing the door firmly behind him.

The walls of the sparse room were heavily padded, similar to cells housing mental patients, only thicker. Half a dozen plain wooden chairs lined the walls, but no other furniture cluttered the room. The floor and ceiling were as thickly padded as the walls; walking across the floor felt a little like walking on a mattress – sort of spongy and springy. It was obvious the room had been seriously soundproofed. It was equally evident that Pavel and Samir believed Liam to be prowling around the exterior of the manor, hoping to catch them out in their falsehoods.

Samir turned to Dayna unleashing the force of his anger and hissing furiously through his teeth, "What. Have. You. Done?"

Dayna gazed back at him totally bewildered.

"What do you mean? I haven't done *anything*."

Samir could hardly contain his rage and it took every ounce of control he possessed not to grab hold of Dayna and shake her till her teeth rattled.

"No? The neophyte who was here – he was created by YOU!" he bellowed, fists clenched tightly at his sides.

Dayna moved her lips, but nothing came out at first; she was genuinely confused by the accusations levelled at her.

"B-b-but I d-didn't – I-I couldn't have," she stuttered, sounding as puzzled as she looked.

"The facts condemn you." Pavel stated coldly, his fury under better control than Samir's.

"The neophyte described you perfectly, Dayna. There is no case of mistaken identity here. You have succeeded in putting the *entire* coven at risk, but yourself most of all. He wants revenge for what you have done to him and he is unlikely to give up. We denied your existence as part of this coven in an attempt to throw him off track and buy you some time, but Samir and I have our doubts he believed us. That is why we are discussing this down here, in case he is watching the manor and listening to our conversations."

Dayna hung her head at Pavel's words. She wracked her brains, trying to remember. Had she been careless and left someone alive?

"Honestly, Pavel, I don't remember creating him," she mumbled sounding contrite.

"Whether you remember or not is insignificant at this point, the fact is that you did and your actions have dire consequences. Something else you are not aware of is I've been observing you, Dayna, *very closely*," Pavel looked at her in disgust as she gasped at this latest revelation. He didn't wait for her to comment.

"Samir told me of your despicable treatment of Jasna and how she almost perished because of you. And then tonight, when you returned from hunting, I was studying you and saw the repulsive looks you were giving her – looks which were totally uncalled for."

Several gasps were heard in the room. Hurt contorted Jasna's face and Joshua clenched his fists in anger, his handsome face distorted in fury. Dayna's head whipped up in shock and anger clouded her features as she realised she had been spied upon. Pavel's eyes narrowed at her reaction, as did Samir's. Dayna, aware she had allowed her mask to slip, lowered her head once more.

"You have become a liability, not only to this coven, but to all immortals. Your behaviour has put us *all* at risk. For now, you will remain under house arrest. You will not leave the manor under *any* circumstances, not even to satiate your thirst. Maybe I can prevail upon the rest of your . . . family to assist you in that regard. However, I wouldn't blame them at all if they elected not to help you after what you have done. If you defy my orders, you will be restrained and held captive like a common criminal. I will summon the Commissioners and together we will decide your fate. Until they arrive, you will not leave your room or make a sound. Do you understand?" Pavel's tone was icy in his fury.

Dayna looked up at Pavel, scared of him for the first time. She didn't trust her voice so she merely nodded. Samir saw red and bellowed at her.

"Pavel asked you a question. You WILL respect his authority and answer him."

"Y-yes, Pavel. I understand," she replied dutifully in a tiny voice.

Pavel turned to Farrell and Erika, his face now calm and his voice gentle as he spoke to them.

"Farrell, Erika, will you please stay here with Dayna until we return? We need to ensure Liam is not hanging around outside before we try to move Dayna upstairs."

"Of course, Pavel," Erika replied solemnly. Farrell nodded his agreement.

Pavel then turned to Joshua, Jasna and Samir.

"Shall we?"

Without another word being uttered, they left the padded room together and traipsed back to the ground floor.

After checking the grounds extensively, they returned to the manor satisfied Liam had left. Joshua stayed outside surveying the area in case Liam returned, while Pavel and Samir returned to the padded room and escorted Dayna up to the second floor.

"We will not lock the door, even though I'm not convinced you can be trusted, but be warned – the slightest defiance on your part and I will take action," Pavel announced harshly, his handsome face once more a mask of revulsion for the vampire in front of him.

"I will obey," Dayna confirmed, entering her room backwards, not daring to turn her back on her superiors.

Samir closed the door on her then he and Pavel returned to the library where the others were waiting. As they entered, Pavel pulled a mobile phone from his pocket and hit speed dial. After a rapid conversation no mortal would have been able to follow, he ended the call and dialled another number. He had the same conversation and then repeated the process twice more. He then replaced the phone and turned to face the others.

"Erika? Would you please ask Joshua to join us?"

Erika disappeared from the room and reappeared with Joshua in tow in less than a second.

"Thank you," he said to her then turned to Jasna.

"Jasna, my dear, Samir has told me all you have had to endure and I'm aggrieved at your suffering. I trust you are back to full health?"

Jasna was surprised at being addressed directly and a little flattered Pavel cared enough to mention it.

"I am completely well now. Thank you for your kind words and concern, Pavel," she said demurely. Her face would have been flushed if it were still possible.

Pavel smiled at her, pleased by her words. He then turned to address the entire coven.

"My dear friends, we have a potentially dangerous situation on our hands. This neophyte could wreak havoc in more ways than one. He thirsts for revenge and is unstable enough to create others to aid his cause. We cannot leave the manor unguarded for even a second, which means hunting in shifts until this . . . problem is resolved.

"I hate to inconvenience any of you, especially as Dayna does not really deserve your support or protection, but this is bigger than just Dayna, and our entire way of life is potentially threatened. The rest of the Commissioners will be arriving tomorrow and will stay as long as is necessary; one of the first tasks will be to conduct a trial to decide Dayna's fate – you are all required to be present. After that, we will have an informal meeting to discuss the neophyte problem. Are there any questions?"

"Will we have time to hunt tomorrow before the Commissioners arrive?" Farrell enquired.

"If you went out as soon as twilight fell and were back within an hour, then I would say yes, but bear in mind you will only be able to go out in pairs, one pair at a time. Any other questions?"

"Er, yes, Pavel, if I may . . ." Jasna spoke hesitantly and softly.

"Of course, my dear, you may ask me anything," Pavel assured her.

"Well . . . I was wondering . . . what is likely to happen to Dayna?" she lowered her eyes as if worried she may have asked the wrong question and offended him.

"The Commissioners have far reaching powers and must exercise them judiciously. The worst-case scenario for Dayna would be death.

Alternatively we could banish her from this coven, this country even if we felt it was wise. She does have a case to answer, but we will be open-minded and consider all the facts carefully before making our judgement." Pavel explained gently.

Jasna nodded, deep in thought, her expression serious.

"Thank you, Pavel." She murmured.

Pavel looked around the room, at each of the vampire's faces in turn. Seeing there were no more questions, he spoke once more.

"I suggest we all get some rest. Dawn is virtually upon us," he gestured towards the window where the sky was lightening rapidly, "I will see you all later and thank you again for your assistance."

Everyone rose to their feet and climbing the stairs, disappeared into their respective rooms – all except Joshua, who followed Jasna into hers. The house fell silent – for now.

Chapter 32 – Joshua

Joshua was first downstairs, even though it was a little early for everyone else. He knew the neophyte wouldn't be prowling around so that wasn't a problem. The sun was beginning to go down and would be safe for the others to venture outside in twenty minutes. He returned to his room and quickly changed his clothes then returned to Jasna. Once inside her room, and after he had kissed her passionately, he asked, "Can you be ready to leave in fifteen minutes?"

"No problem," she answered, smiling. "Are we going first then?"

"I'm going to check with Farrell and Erika then I'll come and let you know. Okay?"

"Yep. I'll get ready. Hurry back," she teased, laughing.

He laughed with her then ducked out of the door and walked up the corridor to Farrell's room. He rapped quietly and waited. Farrell opened the door looking more dishevelled than Joshua had ever seen him – so much so he burst out laughing.

"What's up?" Farrell asked, puzzled.

"Sorry man, but you look like you've been dragged through a hedge backwards," Joshua chuckled.

"Oh," Farrell smoothed down his hair with his hand and smiled sheepishly. "Is that all you came here for?" he grinned.

"Nope. Just wanted to check if it's okay for Jas and me to go hunting first tonight. We're about ready to go now, unlike you," he chuckled, poking Farrell in the ribs.

"Yeah, fine with me. Don't forget we've only got about half an hour each though," Farrell reminded him.

"No probs. See you shortly and don't forget to comb your hair – wouldn't want Pavel to see you like this, would we?" Joshua skittered back as he sensed a kick coming his way, chuckling as he moved.

Farrell pulled his bare leg back into the room, pulled a face at Joshua and closed the door in his face. Joshua could hear Erika laughing behind the door as he returned to Jasna's room.

"Ready?" he called as he poked his head around the door.

"Yep," she smirked, as she was standing virtually on top of him.

"Okay, let's go. We haven't got much time." And with that, he grabbed her hand and they flew down the stairs and out of the house.

Joshua and Jasna returned within their allotted time so Farrell and Erika could hunt. They too were back in the manor within half an hour and the coven was assembled ready to greet the rest of the Commissioners when they arrived. Dayna was still confined to her room, as she hadn't been given permission to leave.

They didn't have long to wait before Samir sensed their impending arrival and he moved towards the main door ready to greet them. Just as he reached it, there was a quiet knock and Samir opened the door widely, ushering them in as quickly as possible then closing and locking the door behind them. Sophia noticed his actions and was somewhat puzzled by it – he'd never reacted that way in the past. Emile was also aware yet said nothing. He knew all would be revealed in good time.

After all the customary greetings had taken place, Pavel suggested they move to the padded room and led the Commissioners downstairs. Samir followed with his coven, bringing extra chairs with him. They all sat in a circle while Pavel and Samir brought the Commissioners up to date with everything which had transpired, from Dayna's bullying of Jasna to the neophyte.

Jasna was embarrassed when she saw the pitying looks she received as Samir recounted the whole sorry tale; her embarrassment turned to pride when Joshua's rescue of her was announced and then astonishment when Samir explained the conversation he'd had with Dayna that same evening.

The Commissioners, on the other hand, were very annoyed to say the least; by the time they had been told about the neophyte, they were livid. Each of them had questions; they had many questions for Jasna, some of which were quite painful for her to answer, but she acquitted herself admirably. Some of them were directed at Joshua - as he was the one who found her, a couple were for Farrell and Erika, but most were for Samir. Once all the questions had been answered and points had been clarified to their satisfaction, the Commissioners were ready to hold the trial.

The seats were re-positioned so the Commissioners were against one wall, the coven against the opposite wall facing them, like spectators, and one empty chair was placed between the two. Dragos turned to Samir.

"Samir, my friend, will you please fetch the accused?" he asked in his heavily accented voice.

Samir bowed and left the room, taking Farrell with him. Less than ten seconds had passed when they returned with Dayna. She was escorted to the lone chair in the middle of the room and sat. Samir and Farrell returned to their seats after closing the door firmly behind them.

Dayna looked at the panel facing her with fear in her eyes. Gone was the perpetual sneer and the arrogance which normally defined her; she wrung her hands and chewed on her bottom lip, a shadow of her former bitchy self.

Luka was the first to address her.

"Dayna, you have been brought before us to answer two main charges. The first charge is that you wilfully and maliciously caused pain and suffering to a member of your coven, on numerous occasions, finally resulting in that member almost perishing. And after said member's recovery, you continued to attempt to cause her more suffering.

"The second charge is that you unlawfully, and without permission, created an immortal which has resulted in your actions putting your coven and indeed all immortals at serious risk. Do you understand the charges brought against you?" Luka's voice was as solemn as a judge in any court in the land. His expression was grave, his brow creased in dismay.

"Yes," Dayna said softly, staring at her hands.

Sophia took over from Luka and she addressed Dayna in the same cold voice Luka had adopted.

"Dayna, on the first charge, how do you plead?"

Dayna hesitated. She was tempted to plead 'not guilty', but it was obvious they knew everything so what was the point? She raised her eyes and looked directly at Sophia.

"Guilty," she replied quietly but firmly, no remorse in her voice. Sophia made a note on a small pad lying in her lap. She looked at Dayna once again and soberly asked, "On the second charge, how do you plead?"

Dayna paused much longer. She hadn't meant to create another vampire – it had been a complete accident so why should she plead 'guilty' to this charge?

"Not guilty," she responded loudly.

Again, Sophia wrote it down, this time a frown marred her beautiful face. Plainly she was not happy at Dayna's 'not guilty' response, and she wasn't the only one. Emile, acting as prosecutor, took charge of the next part of the proceedings.

"Dayna, you have pleaded 'not guilty' to the charge of illegally creating an immortal, despite the evidence against you. Will you please explain your reasoning?"

Dayna looked Emile straight in the eyes, a little of her customary arrogance unwittingly resurfacing.

"I am not an expert when it comes to the law, but I believe the charge hints at some premeditation on my part. This is not the case. I can honestly say it was a complete accident, a lapse of concentration. I didn't mean to do it. Was I careless – absolutely, but am I guilty – no, I don't believe I am." Whilst her diction was formal, Dayna's tone was not as respectful as it should have been and as a result, did nothing to help her case. Emile, not impressed by her attitude, scowled at her. He wasn't the only one – every one of the Commissioners faces was thunderous.

"Be that as it may, do you at least acknowledge your actions have endangered your coven, and all immortals?" The timbre of Emile's voice changed to one of absolute authority.

"Not really," Dayna replied flippantly, "I don't see how it could endanger anyone but me and *I* can take care of myself." She folded her arms across her chest in a defiant gesture, forgetting her earlier fear in her indignation.

Several gasps echoed around the room. Samir hissed in fury and was about to rise from his seat when a look from Pavel stopped him. Samir clenched his teeth and his fists as he tried to maintain some level of control over his anger; Erika visibly blanched at the emotional currents running through the room and laid her hand on Samir's arm in an effort to calm him. He glanced at her and saw the pleading in her eyes – he nodded and worked on calming himself for her benefit.

Emile looked at Pavel, who nodded imperceptibly, so Emile continued.

"Bearing in mind he is untrained, unsupervised and hasn't been given the guidance you have enjoyed, the neophyte you have created may decide to create other immortals in his quest for revenge. We are not convinced he believed Pavel and Samir's attestation they didn't know you and as such, may decide to attack the manor. After that, he could also plan to take revenge on other immortals he finds. Now do you see the danger?" Emile was so irritated his accent became more pronounced than normal. He couldn't fathom why Dayna couldn't see the peril without having to have it explained; she *was* intelligent – Samir wouldn't have given her the gift of immortality otherwise.

Dayna snorted in derision and she sneered at Emile.

"Huh? That sounds a lot of supposition to me. You are hypothesizing he *may* create more immortals, that he *may not* have believed Samir and Pavel, that he *may* attack the manor or other immortals. On the other hand, he *may not* do anything. Maybe he *did* believe I wasn't part of this coven and has gone off elsewhere to search for me. Maybe he *won't* create more vampires. It seems to me that *you* . . ." she glared at all the Commissioners one by one and pointed her finger at Emile in particular, "*you* are looking for any flimsy thread to make your charge stick and I don't see why I should sit here and listen to this drivel." She made a move to get up from the chair when Pavel's voice roared,

"SIT. DOWN!"

His voice was so powerful; an invisible wave hit her full in the chest and forced her to remain in her seat.

"How *dare* you speak to us in such a manner?" Pavel bellowed as Dayna cringed in her seat. "I will *not* tolerate your lack of respect and will not subject the Commissioners to any more of your insolence."

Dayna should have been afraid, but she wasn't. Her earlier defiance had blossomed into a slow burning anger of her own. She stared at the floor in front of Pavel, her eyes narrowing in concentration. Samir was the first to understand what was happening when the first hint of an odour assailed his nostrils; he launched himself at Dayna knocking her off her chair and ruining her concentration. The Commissioners were at first puzzled by Samir's actions until they too detected a faint burning smell. Dragos gazed down at the floor and growled when he saw the scorched area in front of where Pavel was seated. Pavel looked to Dragos in surprise – it was very unusual for him to display any sort of negative emotion – until he followed Dragos's line of sight and immediately understood the reaction. Another couple of inches further towards him and it would have been his feet being burned.

Dayna had gone so far past too far it was unfathomable.

"Samir? Farrell? Take her to the chamber and restrain her, please. Use the metal face mask also – if she's so keen to set light to something, she can do it to her own face," Pavel commanded.

Farrell flashed to Samir's side and they forcibly dragged Dayna out of the room and down the corridor into another padded cell. This one had a solid metal pole in the centre of the room with shackles attached and a shelf housing various restraints and masks. She struggled as they tried to attach the manacles, but she was no match for them; as soon as her hands were restrained, Samir darted to the shelf and grabbed the full-face mask, returning to clamp it firmly over her face. She growled as she whipped her head from side to side trying to stop them. It was no use. The whole process only took ten seconds then Farrell and Samir left the room, a stream of obscenities following in their wake.

The atmosphere was still thick with anger and disbelief when Samir and Farrell returned. The Commissioners had never been challenged in that manner before and they were visibly shaken by it. Samir approached Pavel warily.

"Pavel, I don't know how to apologise . . ." his hands were held out palms upwards, a contrite expression on his face. Pavel didn't allow him to finish.

"Samir, no apology is necessary . . . from you," he qualified. "I know you well enough that if you had suspected, even for a moment Dayna would have turned out this way, you wouldn't have ever considered granting her immortality. None of us hold you responsible, my friend," Pavel's voice was gentle and reassuring. Samir glanced at the other Commissioners and they were all nodding their heads in agreement with Pavel's words.

"Thank you all for your faith in me. I cannot help feeling somewhat guilty though," Samir admitted humbly.

"And it is to your credit you do. However, as I said, it is not necessary." Pavel clapped his hand onto Samir's shoulder and gave it a gentle squeeze then turned to address the Commissioners. "We must deal with the matter in hand. Events have not transpired as any of us expected and we have been subjected to defiance and rudeness from the accused. Despite this, we must make our decision based purely upon the facts and only take into consideration Dayna's behaviour when and if sentencing is appropriate."

As the coven had not been dismissed from the room, Samir returned to his chair and they all sat silent and unmoving while deliberations were taking place. Dayna had already pleaded guilty to the first charge, but her not guilty plea to the second charge was as unexpected as her attitude and this was the cause for the debate.

The decision went first one way, then the other, and then back again. It was funny to watch – the Commissioner's lips were moving so fast and their heads were whipping back and forth like dogs shaking water from their fur. No human would have been able to keep up with the discussion; to them, the voices would have resembled a blending of notes that didn't quite make the rhythm of the music sound right.

After an hour of argument, the decision was split and it fell to Pavel to cast the deciding vote. However, Pavel felt his objectivity was compromised by the all too near attempt by Dayna to cause him harm. The room fell silent as everyone watched and waited for Pavel to make his choice.

Suddenly, he had an epiphany, something totally unprecedented yet utterly brilliant in its daring. Pavel was buoyed by the idea, but he had one small hurdle to overcome first – he had to get the other Commissioners to agree.

He turned to the coven sitting immobile and silent.

"Samir, I need to speak alone with the Commissioners. Would you and your coven mind stepping outside for a few moments?"

The coven rose as one from their seats as Samir replied, "Not at all," and he led them out into the corridor and closed the door firmly behind him, gesturing to the others to keep silent now they were outside of the sound-proofed room.

As soon as Pavel was sure the door was shut, he turned to face his peers.

"My friends, I have to admit I am in a somewhat awkward position here. I cannot be as impartial as is required to cast the deciding vote on Dayna's guilt in respect of the second charge. This is basically because she obviously meant to harm me and, if it weren't for Samir's quick reaction, she probably would have succeeded. I am reluctant to vote when my position is compromised in this way. However, I have a possible solution to this dilemma. It is unconventional to say the least, but I honestly believe it gives us the best chance of reaching a majority verdict," his voice was earnest, as he prepared them for what he was about to impart.

They all sat like sentinels, waiting for him to continue, their expressions eagerly curious.

"Do we have to guess, dear Pavel, or are you going to let us share your thoughts?" Sophia asked a hint of impatience in her tone.

"I'm sorry, I was pausing to give you all the opportunity to prepare yourselves," Pavel smiled without guile, then continued immediately.

"There are five members of the coven, an uneven number. What do you think about them deciding on the verdict? They could cast their votes independent of each other, without debate, and we could then add their votes to yours to reach a binding conclusion to this unpalatable affair."

Pavel watched their expressions carefully as he spoke. Sophia looked amused at his suggestion. Dragos was seriously contemplating the idea; while Luka looked like someone had told a joke and he didn't understand the punch line. Emile's features expressed shock. No one spoke at first – they were all giving Pavel's notion the proper degree of attention. They knew him well enough to know he would not have made this suggestion lightly or without solemn consideration.

Sophia was the first to break the silence, her voice as amused as her expression.

"Well, I think it is a first class solution and I'm happy to endorse it. On a personal note, Pavel, I applaud your honesty and your clear thinking. You have admirably demonstrated why you are the head of The Commissioners, and indeed all immortals," Sophia's tone altered from jovial to sincere.

"Thank you Sophia, for your support and your kind words. I feel I am duty bound to disqualify myself under the circumstances," Pavel replied simply. He then looked at the men and waited for them to declare their decisions.

Emile looked torn. He could see the sense in everything Pavel had suggested yet it grated – it went against the grain. He remained silent and waited to hear what Luka and Dragos would decide.

Dragos was the next to declare; he looked grave as he delivered his opinion.

"This does present us with a solution, albeit an unusual one, but this is not a usual situation. I believe it is the only way forward and as such, I too will support your idea."

"Thank you, Dragos," Pavel acknowledged.

Luka still looked bemused, but knew he could not prevaricate; he had to make a decision. He looked Pavel in the eyes and said simply, "You have my approval."

Pavel nodded. "Thank you, Luka."

Emile was the only one who hadn't spoken. Whatever conclusion he came to was actually irrelevant now - the majority had spoken. Nevertheless, he was honour-bound to share his thoughts. He sighed then turned to face Pavel.

"I have to admit I am uneasy. I can see the sense in what you propose yet it goes against every rule we have set. However, this is an extreme situation and one we have never encountered before. You have never had to disqualify yourself in this way, and like Sophia, I congratulate you for your perspicacity.

"My heart is telling me not to support this, but my head tells me it is the only sensible way to progress. Therefore, I pledge you my agreement, but with reservations." Emile appeared relieved to get that off his chest and some of the tension left his shoulders.

"I fully understand your position, my friend and appreciate your candour. I sincerely regret having to put any of you in this position and value your support. I will call Samir and his coven back in now and explain to them what we have decided – are we agreed?" Pavel asked. Each of them nodded, so he walked to the door, opened it and ushered everyone in.

Pavel turned to Samir's coven; they were all staring at him in anticipation.

"The Commissioners cannot reach a majority verdict on the second charge levelled against Dayna and I have disqualified myself, as I cannot be impartial. We have therefore decided to break all the rules and do something radical but necessary.

"Without debate or discussion, we want each of you to give us your verdict as to whether you believe Dayna to be guilty or not guilty," he explained.

Five stunned, wide-eyed faces gawped at him. Even Joshua, who knew so much less than the rest of his coven, could tell this was huge. Pavel gave them a minute or so to process the bombshell he'd dropped on them before formalising the proceedings once more.

"Farrell? You have heard the charge, the prosecution's questions and statements, and the testimony given by Dayna. Do you believe she is guilty or not guilty?"

Farrell hesitated. Never in his wildest dreams did he think he would have to make a decision of this magnitude and he recognised the gravity attached to his verdict. He had nothing in particular against Dayna, until she'd hurt Jasna yet he'd noticed a significant change in her aura since Jasna was found, and it wasn't for the better. He'd always followed his gut instincts and they had never let him down. He made his decision and spoke clearly and firmly, "I believe Dayna to be guilty."

Sophia made a note while Pavel turned to the person next to Farrell.

"Erika? I ask you the same as Farrell – guilty or not guilty?"

Erika was extremely uncomfortable being put in this position, but she had been given a duty to perform. She too had noticed changes in Dayna's emotions since Jasna had been found in that dreadful cupboard. She was more hostile - even to Samir, which was totally unlike her – and her emotions centred on revenge and hatred. Was it enough to find her guilty? There was no doubt she had created the neophyte. There was also no doubt he was potentially dangerous to them all. With that in mind, there was really only one verdict.

"Guilty," Erika said softly but plainly. She then lowered her head and looked down at the floor, as if regretting her decision and not wanting to face anyone else.

Again the vote was noted as Pavel moved along the line.

"Jasna? What is your vote?"

Jasna had been churning it all over in her mind while Farrell and Erika were making their decisions. The part playing on Jasna's mind was Dayna saying she had been careless, but had not intentionally created an immortal. If there was no premeditation and it had been a genuine mistake, how could she be found guilty?

"My verdict is not guilty," Jasna stated, head held high.

Pavel nodded thoughtfully then called a name out of order.

"Samir, my friend, what say you?"

Samir was startled. He looked up at Pavel questioningly.

"Samir, we both know you had high hopes of Dayna becoming your partner and despite everything she has done, I know you still have some feelings for her. How can I, in all good conscience, put you in the position where you may be forced to make the deciding vote?" Pavel said gently, his eyes filled with concern for his friend.

"Thank you for your thoughtfulness, Pavel," Samir murmured, then shut his eyes to concentrate. He sat silent and immobile while he sifted through everything he'd heard and seen. In some ways he wanted to find her guilty; maybe it was as a result of his disappointment in her behaviour yet Pavel was right, he did still have the vestiges of feelings for Dayna and those feelings were urging him to consider the facts carefully, without letting emotions interfere. Finally, after several minutes warring with the inside of his head, he opened his eyes and looked up.

"I find Dayna not guilty," he stated resolutely, his face calm, all signs of consternation vanished from his handsome features.

Pavel nodded resignedly – he could have predicted which way Samir would vote, another reason why he elected to make Joshua cast the final vote. He turned to the seat next to Samir, expecting to find Joshua looking up at him, but the seat was empty. His eyes darted around the room, but he couldn't see him anywhere and he hadn't heard the door open or close. By now, everyone else had noticed the empty chair and there were a few gasps of surprise, but mostly puzzlement and astonishment.

"Did anyone see Joshua leave the room?" Pavel asked concern in his voice.

Before anyone could answer, a familiar voice piped up.

"I haven't left the room – in fact, I haven't moved. What's going on?" Joshua's disembodied voice drifted across the room.

"*Joshua?*" Pavel called, "where exactly are you?"

"I'm still sitting between Jasna and Samir of course. What's going on?" he repeated, as puzzled now as the rest of them.

Pavel chuckled. "Well . . . we can't see you." Pavel moved closer, slowly reached out his hand until he felt it connect with Joshua's body. He patted around the area until he realised it was Joshua's shoulder then placed his hand on the top and gave it a gentle squeeze. "Well I'll be damned!" Pavel exclaimed loudly, and then began to crease up laughing.

"What is it?" Emile asked, curious yet wary.

Pavel stopped his hilarity to answer the question circuitously.

"Emile, my brother, do you remember the night we first met Joshua?"

"Yes."

"Do you remember what we surmised about his gifts?"

"Vaguely. I believe you mentioned something about two or three major talents, if my memory serves me."

"Absolutely correct. Well . . ." Pavel paused for effect, "it seems young Joshua here, has chosen the most unusual and inappropriate time to reveal another one." Pavel was smiling to take any sting out of his words. He knew very well this was not something Joshua had any control over.

"Are you telling me . . . *invisibility* is one of his talents?" Emile's voice rose an octave in his astonishment.

"More or less," Pavel shrugged nonchalantly. "Although at the moment I'm not sure if it's true invisibility or whether it's more akin to . . . a chameleon can change colour to adapt to their surroundings, perhaps Joshua here can do something very similar."

"W-w-well, er, um . . ." Emile spluttered, lost for words.

"I'm sorry Pavel. I didn't mean to interrupt the proceedings. I didn't know this would happen." Joshua sounded contrite and a little worried. He hadn't got his head around it yet so didn't realise how 'cool' this power was.

"Don't vex yourself, Joshua. Just calm down – no one is angry with you. These things tend to happen at the most inopportune moments. Now, even though we cannot see you at the moment, we do still have the small but important matter of your verdict on Dayna to attend to. Are you ready to cast your vote?" Pavel's voice was calming and reassuring. His face still showed signs of amusement though and he removed his hand now from Joshua's shoulder.

"May I take a moment or two to re-gather my thoughts?" Joshua asked.

Pavel nodded and stepped away from Joshua, not wanting his proximity to create pressure on him. Joshua spent the first few seconds trying to focus on the matter in hand – not so easy after finding out about yet another talent – calming himself, he re-evaluated the evidence. He could understand why Pavel felt it necessary to disqualify himself – he couldn't help recalling his threats to Dayna over Jasna. Would these feelings cloud his judgement? This was such a serious matter – he had to be as impartial as possible – and the pressure this forced on him was unendurable.

The vote was tied and he alone had the final decision. This was both an honour and a curse. Whichever way he voted, someone would be upset with him over it. *Oh crap,* he thought. He felt rather than saw every eye fixed on him (or where he was sitting to be precise), waiting for his verdict. He made his decision and cleared his throat before speaking.

"This has not been an easy decision for me to reach. To a much lesser extent, I can empathise with Pavel's need to disqualify himself, as I too have strong feelings about things Dayna has done. However, I have made every effort to be as impartial as possible and have weighed the evidence carefully. My vote is . . . guilty," Joshua glanced at Jasna, worried he may have upset her by voting the opposite way. Her face was serene; she even had the trace of a small smile on her lips, so Joshua began to relax once more. He had done his part and could now firmly hand back the cloak of authority. As he relaxed, he began to reappear until he was fully visible once more.

Sophia, who had recorded all the verdicts made the announcement.

"The majority verdict on the second charge is . . . guilty."

The Commissioners had been in a huddle for some time while they discussed possible punitive measures they could impose. The charges Dayna had been found guilty of were both extremely serious and would normally call for the maximum penalty to be imposed. But this wasn't their only option. They put two strategies in place before Dayna was brought back before them. Which punishment would be imposed, would depend on her attitude.

Dayna was brought back into the room, still shackled and with the mask over her face. After what had happened previously, they weren't about to take any chances. Once she was secured to the chair, proceeding began again.

Pavel spoke first.

"Dayna. Your plea of 'guilty' to the first charge has been noted. You have also been found 'guilty' of the second charge. Do you have anything to say before sentencing?"

Dayna hung her head as if defeated. She shook her head slowly from side to side.

Pavel then looked to the coven.

"Do any of you have anything to say before we pronounce

sentence?" he asked gravely.

To everyone's surprise Jasna stood. Her lovely face was troubled and a hint of anguish lingered around her eyes.

"May I plead for clemency on Dayna's behalf?" Jasna said concisely. Dayna's head whipped around to face Jasna. Joshua could see the shock on Dayna's face through the mask. Her mouth hung open, her eyes were wide and he detected a hint of hope.

Pavel took a moment to regain his composure before gesturing for Jasna to continue.

"I have known Dayna for many years now. I don't know what changed her into this bitter and vicious person, but she never used to be this way. I hold no grudge now for what she did to me and I truly believe she never meant to create another immortal. I also believe with the right incentive and guidance, she could return once more to the lovely girl I first met. Therefore, I ask that you take my words into account and be lenient. Thank you." Jasna's voice was passionate in her speech and she smiled towards Dayna a little before re-taking her seat.

Silence reigned. Jasna's compassion for her foe had jolted them all.

Sophia was the first to recover.

"Jasna, my dear, it takes great courage to stand up for someone the way you have and I truly hope Dayna appreciates your efforts, even though some here may not be convinced she is deserving of your forgiveness or charity. Your plea will be taken into account as requested."

"Thank you," Jasna acknowledged.

No one else stood or spoke. It was time to pass sentence.

Pavel stood and faced Dayna; although she couldn't see him, she heard his movement and guessed what was happening. This was it. Now she regretted not keeping her temper under better control and not apologising when she had the chance. Not that she *was* sorry, but she could have made them believe she was. The fear returned to her as she realised she could be executed; she wasn't done with this life yet and there were so many things she wanted to achieve. One of those things was to say sorry to Jasna and mean it. She was gobsmacked Jasna would defend her after everything she'd done to her. She knew in her heart she really didn't deserve Jasna's forgiveness, which made it all the more special and astonishing when it came.

Pavel interrupted her musings as he began to talk in a very solemn tone.

"Dayna, the punishment for the crimes you have committed is execution," he paused, letting it sink in before continuing. "However, we have listened to Jasna's heartfelt plea on your behalf and have taken it into account. If it had come from any other source, it is highly unlikely we would have given it such serious consideration, but as Jasna is one of your victims, her plea for compassion is all the more substantial.

"Dayna, you now owe Jasna your life – literally. We sentence you to be banished from this coven and this country. You will be taken overseas where you can build a new life. You must not leave that country for a minimum of five years, this time frame to be reviewed in exactly five years' time, when it may be extended. If you flout our rules, you will be immediately executed without further trial. Do you understand your sentence?"

Dayna raised her head; hope in her heart once more.

"I understand my sentence," she replied softly.

"Very well. You will be escorted to your room so you may pack your belongings and we will leave at dusk. You will not be left alone during this time. When you leave, you will not be given the opportunity to see or speak to any of what was your coven so if you have anything you would like to say to anyone, now is the time," Pavel commanded.

Dayna nodded then spoke, her voice oddly echoed.

"May I speak with Jasna and Samir, separately please?"

"Very well. Farrell, Joshua, Erika, we thank you for your support during this difficult time. Will you please leave us now?" It wasn't a question it was a command, and one which was obeyed instantly. Once they had left the room, Pavel turned to the Commissioners.

"My friends, if one of you would consent to staying here with me, I would be most grateful. Those not required may stay if they wish or retire."

"I will stay with you," Luka announced.

"Thank you, my friend," he turned back to Dayna. "Who would you like to speak to first Dayna?"

Dayna thought for a moment then replied, "Jasna, please."

Pavel beckoned Jasna forward. As soon as she was close enough, he stepped back to give them a little privacy.

Jasna approached Dayna serenely and without fear.

"Jasna, I wanted to thank you for standing up for me and to say how sorry I am for everything I put you through. You've always been decent to me, even when I didn't deserve it," Dayna hung her head in shame but continued, "I hope you and Joshua will be very happy together – you've earned some joy after all I've done." Dayna's voice was full of remorse and she sounded more sincere than Jasna had ever heard her.

"Thank you for your apology, which I accept. Dayna, I wish you happiness in your new life and I hold no grudge against you. I hope you have learned a valuable lesson and will value friendship more in the future. Please don't allow yourself to become bitter – put the past behind you and use this opportunity to start afresh. Take care of yourself. Bye Dayna," Jasna smiled gently, gave Dayna a gentle hug then turned, and without a backward glance, walked from the room.

Pavel gestured for Samir to approach.

"Samir?" Dayna called softly.

"I'm here," he replied.

"I'm so sorry. I've let you down so badly and I wouldn't blame you if you never forgave me. When you showed me the lead-lined cupboard that night and told me of the high hopes you once had for us and how there would be no chance for us, I guess I went a little crazy and didn't pay as much attention as I should have done. I know it won't make any difference now, but as this is my last chance to talk to you, I don't want to leave here without telling you something which perhaps I should have told you a long time ago.

"I'm in love with you, Samir. I've loved you for as long as I can remember, maybe even from the first day you brought me here. I always hoped you would notice me, that one day you would really look at me and see the love in my eyes for you. But you never did. Or if you did, you never showed it. "I'll always love you, and I wish you much happiness. Please don't say anything – my heart is already breaking and if you say even one word to me, I'm not sure I will be able to keep my composure. I wish I could kiss you just once but . . . anyway, I wanted you to know. Goodbye my love and thank you for everything." Dayna turned her back and prayed Samir would do as she asked and walk away. Another part of her prayed he would take her in his arms, rip the stupid mask from her face and kiss her. She wasn't that lucky. She heard him leave the room, and as the door shut quietly behind him, she crumpled into a heap on the floor and sobbed.

None of the coven felt like talking after the dramatic events of the night. When they emerged from the padded room and ventured up to the ground floor, they were surprised to see dawn was upon them. They dared not linger and disappeared to their rooms in a blur of movement.

It took the Commissioners who remained in the room quite some time to calm Dayna enough to be able to move her. As they tried to walk her out, her legs kept collapsing under the weight of her sobs. In the end, Luka picked her up and carried her up the stairs. The light hit them as soon as they opened the door and they scuttled back into the dark, slamming the door shut in their haste. Much more time had passed than they had realised and now they were stuck below ground until dusk.

They returned to the room and Luka laid Dayna gently on the floor.

She appeared totally unaware of anything going on around her; her heart was breaking and she was mourning for what could have been. Luka and Pavel sat and observed her as they waited for the day to pass.

Things hadn't quite worked out as planned. Being confined in the basement all day had put the Commissioners way behind schedule and Dayna wasn't even packed yet. As soon as it was dusk, Pavel and Luka escorted Dayna to her room and with help from Sophia and Emile, packed her items in record time. There wasn't much she wanted to take –some clothes and a few personal items. Pavel was staying a few more days, but the other Commissioners were escorting Dayna to Romania, where she would be kept under the watchful eye of Dragos and his coven.

Pavel descended first. He wanted to ensure everyone was away from the manor – the last thing any of them needed was painful and drawn out farewells. Samir had already ordered his coven to leave the manor to hunt and he was the only one who remained. Pavel found him seated in the library, staring out of the window.

"Samir? Why are you still here?" Pavel enquired approaching him. He stood in front of Samir's chair and looked down at him.

Samir looked troubled which gave Pavel immediate cause for concern guessing Dayna was in his thoughts.

"Pavel, I . . ." he began, but the words failed to materialise.

"I understand, my friend and we will discuss this later, but right now you need to leave. You need to hunt. Go now and don't look back. I will be here when you return and we can talk then," Pavel's voice was as gentle as cotton wool with an underlying edge of authority.

Samir looked up at Pavel's face, a desolate look in his eyes and saw pity staring back at him. He knew he should do as Pavel decreed, but he felt so responsible for what had happened with Dayna; if he had given her a chance, if he had noticed how she felt about him sooner then perhaps none of this would have been necessary. If he had only admitted to himself and her that he was in love with her too. He got to his feet slowly and went to speak, but Pavel interrupted him before he could get the first word out.

"Samir, hear me now. Say nothing – just go. You will make things much harder for all concerned if you remain in the manor. Do you want to hurt her and yourself any further?"

Samir shook his head, sorrowfully. Pavel grabbed his arm and led him to the main door, forcing him across the threshold and out into the purple night. Samir's feet moved sluggishly across the ground – a far cry from his usual graceful flight – but he kept them going until the night absorbed him. He continued across the grounds until he reached one of the large trees on the edge of the property. He stopped there and glanced back at the house. No one was visible so he climbed into the tree and made sure he could observe without being seen and there he waited and watched.

Twenty minutes later, Dayna emerged from the manor flanked by Dragos, Luka, Emile and Sophia. The mask had been removed from her face, but she was shackled to Dragos on one side and Luka on the other. As Samir looked at her face, he saw the beautiful young woman he had first brought to join his coven, and his heart ached for what could have been. He was tempted to go to her, to tell her how he really felt, but what good would it do now? It would only make it that much harder for her.

Pavel appeared on the porch and spoke a few words to them all before the travelling party moved across the grounds. Samir sat and watched Dayna until she was out of sight, his face crumpled in pain.

Chapter 33 – Remy

Three weeks had passed since I'd first entered Minnis Bay; I arrived hopeful and was about to leave in despair. I'd handed the keys to the cottage in to the agent and was back on the road again. I'd felt the dejection descending slowly over the past three or four days and it now weighed heavily on my head and shoulders, dragging me down physically as well as emotionally.

It was peculiar how I left each area engulfed in despondency yet as I pulled into each new town, my spirits lifted once more and I rediscovered the hope and determination to start my search again. Maybe it had something to do with the mere fact it *was* a new area; a new set of chances to find Joshua.

According to the SatNav, my trip to the New Forest would take me three hours; I was somewhat sceptical at that. My depression was probably the reason why I didn't trust the SatNav's calculation. Perhaps I would have a better journey than I was expecting, but then again . . . pessimism was definitely ruling the roost.

The sky, which had begun the day as a cloudless azure sea, was now turning darker as large grey and black rain clouds moved in overhead. It was still hot and very humid – too humid – so a thunderstorm would clear the air quite nicely. I'd never been afraid of thunderstorms, even as a child. I'd always sat by the window counting after each crash of thunder to see how long it would be before the lightning zigzagged across the sky. My dad always told me the number between the thunder and the lightning indicated how far away the storm was and I used to get really excited when the counts got shorter. *Funny the things we remember from our childhood*, I thought.

By the time the first fat drops of water hit my windscreen, I was on the M3. The sky had darkened so much I'd switched on the lights. I had the window wide open so I raised it until there was about two inches gap. I could hear the thunder growling in the distance and as I drove further down the road, it got louder and louder as the rain got heavier and heavier until it was so torrential I could barely see past the front of my car.

I reduced my speed until I was crawling along and switched my lights to dipped beam. Gradually, very gradually, I manoeuvred the car into the slow lane and reduced my speed even further. I couldn't see anything in front of me or any lights behind me – it seemed as if I were the only person left in the world and I was stuck in a vacuum which was chucking water down on me like it was going out of fashion. It was as eerie as I imagined being on an alien planet would be and despite a strange aloneness, I wasn't afraid.

The thunder roared overhead and the lightning streaked across the sky simultaneously. Another flash of lightning forked diagonally down right in front of the car and hit the ground a few yards further than the edge of the hard shoulder. A small bush, desiccated by the heatwave and lack of water, burst into flames shooting sparks into the air like fireflies, only to sizzle and die as the downpour drenched them.

Ten minutes later I drove back into civilisation, but it was one of the weirdest re-entries in history. One minute I was driving through sheet rain and barely able to see three feet in front of me, and the next, I'd gone through a curtain and found sunlight and dry roads. Suddenly there were other cars on the road, all turning their lights off, like me. And everyone was reaching for their sunglasses, like me.

I glanced at the SatNav and discovered I was closer to my destination than I thought and although the storm had slowed me down quite considerably, I wasn't too far behind time. Less than thirty minutes later, I was on the outskirts of Godshill with only another mile or so to go. As I rounded a bend, the familiar sign for Sandy Balls Holiday Complex appeared on the right and I turned in through the gates.

I found my one-bedroom log cabin quite easily; the park hadn't changed since Josh and I were last here. A memory from that time made me giggle; Joshua had come up with a nickname for the place and that first night we raised our glasses and re-christened Sandy Balls as 'Gritty Nuts'. It was silly and frivolous, but what did it matter? We were two young people in love with life and desperately in love with each other. The all too familiar lump started to form in my throat and my eyes glazed as moisture obscured my vision. I shook my head to clear it, wiped my eyes and concentrated on the sight in front of me.

The cabin was beautiful inside and out, surrounded as it was by the stunning parkland and scenery of the New Forest. Although it only had one bedroom, the cabin was quite spacious inside and beautifully yet sympathetically decorated. The furnishings were luxurious and comfortable, especially the large double bed.

By the time I'd settled in and unpacked, there was really only enough time to grab a bite to eat and spend an hour or so making my list for the following day before I'd be ready to crash out on the big comfy bed. However, there was something rather important I had to do first. I grabbed my phone and dialled the number. I managed to catch my boss before he left the office and after a lengthy conversation managed to arrange a leave of absence. That was a weight off my mind – he would hold my job open for me until I returned.

I wandered into the main section of the camp where the amenities were situated and decided to eat at the cosy pub which served only freshly cooked dishes and promised a taste of home with a twist. It didn't disappoint; the portions were large and mouth-wateringly delicious, and after a couple of glasses of wine and a side trip to reception to borrow the local phone directory, I meandered back to my cabin, admiring the cleanliness of the camp and the unspoilt parkland surrounding it.

I'd spent the last couple of hours making my lists and was pleasantly surprised at the number of establishments on it. By my reckoning, I should be finished within a week. The thought pulled me up short. How negative was that? Is that the way my mind was thinking now? Was I starting each new search with the idea in the back of my mind that I would fail? Was I losing hope I would ever be reunited with the love of my life? *NO!* I would not allow myself to entertain the possibility. I *would* find Joshua – I would *never* give up.

I was acutely aware of the fatigue spreading through my body, so I locked the door, turned off the lights and went to bed.

After spending a week in and around Fordingbridge and Lyndhurst with no sign of my beloved, it was time once more to move on. This time my journey was very short compared to all the other ones – it was only forty-five minutes to Stonehenge, and even less to Salisbury where I would be staying.

By the time I arrived in Salisbury, it was way too early to check into my hotel so I decided to go and visit Stonehenge again. When Joshua and I went there, I sensed a sort of magic about the place, even though we had to stay behind the ropes and couldn't get close to the actual stones. There was a spiritual aura which appeared to ooze from the earth and I felt an odd connection to it. That feeling, that connection, stayed with me for several days afterwards, but gradually faded over time. As I approached the parking area, I couldn't help but wonder if it would happen to me again.

I wandered towards the majestic stones in a pensive mood. The wondrous sight took my breath away - as it did last time I saw them – speculating as to how the humungous stones had been moved into place without heavy lifting gear or cranes.

Standing as close as I could to the rope perimeter, I gazed at the monoliths and allowed my mind to drift as I soaked up the spiritual atmosphere. The magic of the stones reacted with my sensitive psyche and a tingle wormed its way through my veins. My acuity sharpened; I closed my eyes enabling me to focus more precisely, my breathing slowed and my consciousness communed with the Stonehenge aura.

I was in uncharted territory. My usual sensitivity to all things supernatural was magnified a hundred fold and I found I was pointing a figurative finger of perception at myself. A quiver of trepidation coursed through me. A picture of a calendar came to mind, one which had multiple months on a single page. I peered at it, forcing it closer so I could make out the date circled in red. It was during my business trip to America, but what was the significance?

Abruptly my eyes opened, my mouth formed a large O and I sank to my knees on the damp grass. I now understood why the date meant something and what my subconscious was trying to tell me. It was the date of my last menstrual cycle and it was three months ago. I had missed two periods. OH MY GOD! My eyes widened, my eyeballs almost popping out of my head as the realisation hurtled through my brain - I must be PREGNANT!

My eyes re-focused and I became aware of people standing nearby staring at me strangely. A tentative and embarrassed smile played across my lips as I got to my feet and brushed the damp grass from my knees. I meandered around the stones not really seeing them. My mind was in tumult. How could I have missed this? Then I recalled some of the strange things my body had experienced over the last couple of months; the fatigue, the strange sleeping fits, even the mood swings – it all fit. Even this morning when I was dressing, I'd found my cropped trousers rather tight around the middle – I just didn't think much of it at the time.

I must buy a testing kit to confirm it - after all, the missed periods and all the other strange symptoms could be a result of stress and emotional turmoil. I'd read about these things in magazines and knew it was possible.

I ran back to the car and drove straight back to Salisbury. I located my hotel and parked the car. Instead of checking in, I strode down the street to a chemist I'd passed a minute or so earlier. I popped in and bought a test, secreted it in my handbag and returned to the hotel.

Once I'd checked in and was ensconced in my room, I retrieved the kit, opened the box and carefully read the instructions. I followed the instructions then paced impatiently while I waited for the result. The two minutes described on the pack seemed hours as I watched the second hand crawl around the dial on my wristwatch. How I didn't bump into anything while I paced was a minor miracle.

Finally the second hand made its final circuit and the two minutes were up. Nervousness crept up my spine and my hands shook as I reached for the wand. I stared at the little window and sure enough, two bright pink lines glared back at me. I squeezed my eyes tight in disbelief then opened them again, only to see the result hadn't changed.

Instinctively my hands dropped to my abdomen and I caressed it without even thinking about what I was doing or what it ultimately meant. I wandered into the bedroom and sat on the bed, dazed, staring into nothingness.

I don't know how long I sat there or what passed through my mind. I came back to the present and it slapped me in the face. I was pregnant. I was carrying Joshua's child. Wondrous joy filled me and a radiant smile lit up my features as tears of happiness pricked my eyes, blurring my vision. Who to tell first?

As I tried to decide, the reality of the situation landed like a brick on my head. Obviously the person I most wanted to tell was Joshua, and as the thought trampled into my brain, it was rapidly followed by an acute pain and longing. The enormity of it all was overwhelming. If it was important to find Joshua before, it was now imperative and I had to hurry. Time would march inexorably on and my stomach would balloon, making it more difficult to move around later into my pregnancy. For now, I would just tell Becky, Jakki, Mum and Dad, and Grace.

As the decision settled into the grey matter, a new thought bulldozed its way to the forefront of my mind. Joshua hadn't answered any of my calls and I didn't know if he was listening to his voicemails, but would he read a text message? It was certainly worth a try and maybe, if he did read it, he would come home to me when he realised he was going to be a father. A surge of positivity thrilled me; he wouldn't ignore his own child.

My mobile buzzed, interrupting my musings. I reached for it and smiled when I saw whose name was displayed.

"Hello you."

"Hi Rems, how you doing?" Becky's voice was normal except for an edge of cautiousness.

"Not bad, thanks, what about you?" I couldn't disguise the excitement in my voice and smiled as I pictured her trying to guess what had caused it.

"Fine thanks, except for a funny twinge in my stomach."

I chuckled. That was twins for you. If one of us cut ourselves, the other would feel it too. She was in for a tough few months, especially when it came to the labour. I laughed out loud as the thought crossed my mind.

"What are you laughing at? It's not funny," Becky pouted.

"Sorry hun, just had a mental picture of something which tickled my sense of humour," I explained, still with a huge grin on my face.

"Sounds dangerous to me," she giggled.

"You have *no* idea," I retorted, deliberately dragging it out.

"So . . . what's up?" Becky couldn't contain her curiosity – she knew instinctively I had some news to impart, but my guess was she would think it had something to do with finding Josh. I would love to have been watching her expression when I told her.

"Erm . . . are you sitting down?" I began, teasing her a little.

"Yes."

"Are there any sharp objects near you?" I chuckled picturing her exasperated expression.

"No. Get on with it," she commanded impatiently.

"Well . . . um . . . I'm not sure how to say it," I prevaricated.

"Oh for God's sake, *tell* me."

"Errr . . . how do feel about . . . becoming an aunt?" I asked hesitantly.

Dead silence.

All I heard was a sharp intake of breath and then nothing. The seconds dragged into minutes as I waited for a reaction. After two whole minutes of silence, I couldn't wait any longer.

"Becky?"

"W-what did you say?" she whispered in disbelief.

"I'm PREGNANT," I yelled.

"W-what? How? Er . . . I mean, *really*?" Becky stammered. The shock in her voice was amusing to me and I giggled.

"Yes, really," I confirmed.

"WOW!"

"You got that right. Wow doesn't even cover it."

"When did you find out?"

"About forty minutes ago, for certain any way."

"Huh?"

"Okay, let me try to explain. It suddenly occurred to me earlier I'd missed a couple of periods so I bought one of those testing kit things and it came up positive. I did the test about forty minutes ago and I've been trying to wrap my head around it. I'd just made the decision to call you and Mum when you rang," I told her simply.

"So I'm the first to know? Cool. Hey babes, that's awesome news," Becky sounded excited now as the idea sunk into her head.

"Thanks."

"Seriously though, how do you feel about it?"

"I'm *ecstatic*. I'm also scared, I mean, it makes finding Josh even *more* urgent and I know as I get bigger, I'm not going to be able to do as much so I'm probably going to get frustrated. I've got so many emotions and ideas running roughshod around my brain at the moment, I think my head's gonna *explode*." I didn't want to entertain the nagging idea I might not find him before the baby was due yet I knew it was a distinct possibility.

"What if . . ." Becky began, but I interrupted her.

"I know what you're going to say, so don't bother. Yes, it has crossed my mind and all I can say is I'll deal with it when the time comes."

"Okay, but you're going to have to register with a doctor, even if it's only temporary, you'll have to get scans done, attend classes. How the hell are you going to fit all that in and *still* look for Josh?" Becky sounded worried now and disbelieving I would consider carrying on with my search under the present circumstances.

"Yeah, I know all that and I'll check into it while I'm here. In the meantime, I *will* carry on with my search for Josh until I can't physically do it anymore or there's a risk to the baby." My tone left no room for argument and Becky had learnt to recognise nothing she said would sway me.

"Yeah, okay," Becky's voice was resigned. "Anyway, hun, I'm meeting the girls in twenty minutes and I'm not ready yet so I'm gonna have to go. You take good care of both of you and I'll ring you in a day or two."

"Okay babes, have fun and say hi to the girls for me. Love you," I replied.

"Okay. Love you too." She disconnected the call.

Tears coursed down my face. I stared at the phone in my hand having disconnected a call to Grace. Telling her she was going to be a grandmother when her son was missing was not exactly the easiest task I'd ever had to perform. I could fully appreciate the mixture of emotions she displayed during our conversation – the joy and the sadness. Hearing the tears in her voice she tried so hard to disguise was what started me off.

Guilt was another emotion trampling through my psychologically battered head. I hadn't spoken to her for weeks; from her point of view, any news at all would have been preferable to silence, even if the news were not good. It was a situation I must endeavour to rectify in the future.

I sat for a few moments before composing the text to Josh, trying to work out what to say. If he didn't want me anymore it would be wrong to pressure him into staying with me for the baby's sake. But at the same time, he had a right to know. I worked out what I wanted to say and tapped in the message:

Hi. Hope u r ok. I miss u so much. Hav important news 4 u – u r goin 2 b a dad! I don't want u 2 feel u hav 2 stay wiv me 4 baby's sake but I do need 2 know if u want 2 play a part in baby's future. Pls call/txt me so we can discuss. Love u. R xxx

I was more settled once I'd sent the message, hopeful even.

I thought back to the conversation I had with Becky. She was right. I *did* need to see a doctor –to check everything was all right with the baby. I was planning to be in this area for a couple of weeks so a side trip to a GP was sensible. I thumbed through the telephone directory and found one in the same street as my hotel. I dialled the number.

I sat in the surgery waiting room and thumbed through a magazine listening for my name to be called. I was lucky to get a same day appointment even if it did mean me sitting here for a while. After twenty minutes my name was announced over the tannoy. I climbed the stairs and entered room two.

The doctor sitting behind the desk had a kind face and smiled as I walked through the door. He gestured to a chair at the side of his desk and I sat in it stiffly. He clasped his hands together on the desk and turned to face me.

"Hello Remy. My name is Doctor Greene. What can I do for you?" His voice was caring – the sort you wanted to hear, especially when you were as nervous as I was right now.

"Well, I took a pregnancy test today and it came back positive. I won't be going back home for a while and my family suggested I see a GP sooner rather than later," I explained.

"Your family gave you some very good advice. Now, when was the first day of your last period?" He picked up a pen and started to make notes on a temporary record card.

I pulled a tiny diary from my bag and told him the date. After adding it to his notes, he pulled a chart from his desk drawer and stared at it, tracing along a line with his finger.

"Is this your first pregnancy?"

"Yes," I answered simply.

"Okay. Hop up there," he said gesturing to an examination table, "and let's have a look at you."

I climbed onto the table and lay down. He pushed up my tee shirt just enough to reveal my stomach and with very gentle hands, examined me. When he'd finished, he pulled my tee shirt back down and gestured for me to return to my seat.

"It all feels normal to me. How have you been feeling?"

I sat and thought how best to answer.

"Well, apart from some fatigue at times and some weird dreams, I'm okay."

"Any morning sickness?"

That question caught me by surprise. I hadn't thought about it before, but actually I hadn't even felt nauseous – well except for when I saw the aftermath of the accident on the motorway, but I didn't think that really counted.

"Actually, no."

He raised his eyebrows, astonished, but didn't remark on it.

"Okay. By my reckoning, your due date is the 15th of March, which makes you . . . nearly twelve weeks. Normally you would have an ultrasound scan at twelve weeks so I think we need to get one organised as soon as possible. How long will you be in this area?" Having written down the due date, he looked at me with curiosity.

"About two weeks and then I'm heading to Bath," I shrugged my shoulders nonchalantly as I replied.

He picked up the receiver on his desk and dialled a number he knew by heart. After a brief conversation, he wrote something down in front of him, said thank you and hung up.

"I've made an appointment for you at Salisbury General Hospital for 10am tomorrow morning. Can you make it?" Dr. Greene asked.

"Yes, that's fine," I confirmed.

"You will need to have a full bladder for the ultrasound. You will also need a blood test," he explained, completing forms while he spoke. "Is there anything you want to ask me?"

"Well . . . yes. You seemed stunned I haven't had morning sickness – is it unusual?"

"Actually, yes it is unusual, but not unheard of. You must be one of the lucky ones," Dr Greene replied, smiling.

"Maybe it's genetic?"

Dr Greene looked puzzled. "What makes you say that?"

I shrugged. "I remember my mum saying once she never suffered from morning sickness when she was pregnant."

"I don't think there's any medical evidence to support that," he said, "anything else you want to ask?"

"No, I don't think so, thanks."

"Okay. Well if you think of anything, please feel free to come back and see me. Also, before you leave, call in to reception and ask for the notes I'm going to prepare for you and you can take them with you for when you see another GP. Here's your form for the Ultrasound and another for the blood test." He passed two white forms to me.

I took the forms, tucked them into my bag, stood and smiled down at him. "Thank you, doctor."

"Good luck, Remy. I hope everything goes well for you," Dr Greene smiled back at me.

I closed the door quietly behind me, walked down the stairs and out into the street.

I got up at eight, had breakfast and drank twice as much tea as normal. By the time I got to the hospital, my bladder was so full I wasn't sure if I could hold it. I reported to the reception desk and was about to sit down when my name was called.

I entered the room and lay on the bed. After exposing my stomach, the nurse squeezed some really cold green goo on me and then placed the probe on my stomach. She moved it around and pressed some buttons on the monitor. I tried to watch but the screen was turned away from me. The nurse pressed more buttons and a printout appeared below the console. She then repeated the process and another sheet popped out. She smiled, turning towards me.

"Do you want to see them?" she asked.

"S-s-sorry? What did you say?" I stammered, sure I'd misheard.

"I said do you want to see them?"

"Them?" I was completely puzzled.

The nurse turned the screen around so I could see it.

"Yes, them. You're carrying twins," she informed me, grinning.

My mouth opened then closed again and no sound came out. My eyes were as wide as saucers and my mouth opened again, my chin dropping almost to my chest. The nurse pointed to the screen and there were two barely distinguishable shapes and two separate blips pulsing.

"See? There's one heartbeat," she pointed to the blip on the left, "and there's the other," she said pointing to the second blip.

"Oh. My. God." I whispered. Even though I was a twin, it never occurred to me I might be carrying two. I stared at the screen. My two babies. Mine and Joshua's babies. Abruptly I was overcome with emotion and tears began to trickle lightly down my cheeks. A sad smile formed on my lips. Yet again, a strange mix of emotions danced through my head – joy and heartache.

The nurse smiled, misunderstanding my expression.

"Would you like a couple of prints of the scan?" she asked.

"Oh, yes please," I replied, enthusiastically.

The nurse pressed another button and a monochrome image appeared from another slot below the screen. She moved the probe a little and repeated the process so an additional picture was printed. She put them into a little folder and handed it to me.

"Thanks." I clutched them to my chest, eyes downcast.

She grabbed some tissues and wiped the green gunk off my stomach, making sure she got it all off then pulled my top back down.

"Go and empty your bladder then come back so we can talk, okay?"

I didn't need telling twice. Still clutching the folder like a lifeline, I nodded and sprinted to the ladies room. I emerged four minutes later, breathing a huge sigh of relief and feeling much more comfortable. I returned to my cubicle where the nurse sat patiently waiting. I glanced at the screen as I entered and the image of my babies was still on the screen, frozen in time.

The nurse pointed out the measurements she had taken, explained why they were needed and what they meant. She agreed with Dr Greene that I was twelve weeks pregnant and reassured me both babies were a normal size for the gestation period. She also explained that as I was carrying twins, I would need another scan at around twenty weeks. She reminded me I needed to get a blood test done before I left the hospital and handed me one of the forms back which Dr Greene had given me. I thanked her and left the cubicle without a backward glance.

After submitting to the blood test I left the hospital, glad to be outside in the fresh air again. I grabbed my phone and wrote a text to go to Becky, Jakki, Mum and Grace.

"Hiya, just had a scan & guess wot – it's twins! I'm in shock. Got pics from scan. Babes r fine. Doc sez I'm 12 wks & I'm due abt 15 March. Talk soon. Luv u all. Remy xx"

I returned the phone to my bag, carefully inserted the folder containing the images of the babies and walked back to the car with a spring in my step.

Chapter 34 – Remy

My search began again in earnest. Time was now against me. It was of paramount importance to find Joshua. No matter what had transpired between us, I truly believed he would never turn his back on his children and would want to play a major role in their lives.

The fact I was carrying twins meant my stomach would grow much faster than with a single baby, resulting in me being incapacitated sooner rather than later. I redoubled my efforts and made up the time I missed from attending the doctor and hospital appointments. By the end of the second week, I'd completed my search in Salisbury and was ready to move on again.

There was a new desperation to my endeavours. At the end of each new day of rejections, my state of mind deteriorated a little bit further so by the end of the second week, I was completely depressed again. I did try to remember Bonnie's courage when despondency set in and it helped to maintain a positive attitude. But I was only human.

As I packed yet again, I caught sight of the folder the nurse had given me at the hospital. I pulled it out and removed one of the images from it. I stared lovingly at the monochrome picture of my twins, tracing their outlines with my fingers. A small smile played on my lips and as I continued to absorb every facet of their perfection, I felt some of the depression melt away, like ice under a tap of running water.

It occurred to me then that by allowing the despair to overwhelm me it was not only harming me, but also my unborn babies. I refused to allow it. These images would be my talisman – whenever I was crushed by my misery in the future, I vowed to look at my babies to give me the fortitude to continue.

I pressed the picture to my lips and kissed it before returning it to its folder. I carefully placed it in my handbag to ensure it didn't get ruined then finished my packing. A few minutes later, I had checked out and was back on the road again.

I arrived in Bath an hour later. I hadn't booked a hotel and needed to find somewhere. I drove into the centre of town, found somewhere to park and stopped by the tourist information centre. The lady behind the desk was a great help, giving me a list of hotels, guest houses and bed & breakfast accommodation. What a result. It would save me making copious lists as I'd had to do everywhere else. I was also given a street map of the area - extremely useful. I took my booty and decided to stop at a coffee house to plan my next move; I remembered passing one as I walked to the tourist office and headed back there.

 I took a seat at the rear of the shop and ordered a latte. I spread the map out onto the table and started marking the hotels on there with an 'X'. I then followed suit with the guest houses and bed & breakfast places while I sipped my steaming coffee. My concentration was broken when I heard a cute giggle from a table nearby. I looked up and saw an adorable young boy of around three or four looking straight at me. As I raised my head a little more he giggled again and put his hands over his mouth. I couldn't fathom the source of his amusement until his mother turned to see what he was laughing at and she chuckled too. I must have had a puzzled expression on my face as the mother pointed to her top lip. I raised one index finger and touched it to the skin just above my lip and then brought it away to look at it. I sniggered to myself as I realised I had a frothy moustache. I started to move my lips and make faces, at which the little boy began to giggle again, as did his mum.

 After a couple of minutes, I got bored and was running out of new faces to pull. I grabbed a serviette from a dispenser on the table and wiped it away. I smiled apologetically at my audience then lowered my head and resumed my task.

 It took me over an hour and another latte to finish marking the map. I worked out exactly where I was and what direction I needed to travel in, then paid my bill and left. As much as I wanted to start looking for Joshua immediately, my most pressing mission was to find somewhere to stay. Perhaps I could combine the two; it *was* a pretty good plan.

I turned down the street, not paying much attention to the shops which lined the busy road. I was more concerned with finding the first establishment marked on my map. After about five minutes power walking, I found the Benson Arms Hotel. I strolled through the foyer and up to the reception desk. A smartly dressed middle-aged man approached me and offered his help. I enquired about a room, but they were fully booked. Before leaving, I also showed him the photo of Joshua and asked if he'd seen him. The man shook his head apologetically. I thanked him and retreated to the street.

I checked the map again and set off to the next nearest. Two hours later, I was without a bed for the night and no one recognised Joshua. I started to get a little concerned. The day was overcast and substantially cooler than it had been - perhaps the heat wave was over – but I was perspiring from the exertion and worry.

Another couple of hours later and I was still without accommodation for the night. Now I was getting a little panicky. I was no longer on foot, having returned to my car an hour or so earlier, and my travels were taking me further from the centre of town.

I turned down a small road lined with careworn houses on both sides. I drove quite slowly, my eyes raking over the peeling paint and crumbling facades. I couldn't imagine Joshua staying somewhere as shabby as this, but I had to be thorough, I had to check under every rock, in every nook and cranny, and every guest house, bed & breakfast and hotel, no matter how seedy and unkempt. I approached a junction and noticed a small B & B on the right.

Pulling over to the curb, I stopped the car and stared at the dilapidated building. With its tatty yellowed lace curtains hanging in the grubby windows, the peeling paint, the broken piece of gutter and the missing chunks of render from the walls, it didn't exactly look welcoming. It looked unloved, uncared for, sad and lonely; in a crazy sort of way, I could relate to that.

I stepped out of the car and carefully locked it behind me. I walked slowly and hesitantly towards the door, stopping on the pavement just before I reached it. The windows were so grimy you could barely see the vacancies sign hanging at the front and up close the building looked even worse.

I reached my hand for the doorknob, twisted it slowly and pushed the door open. I wasn't surprised to hear the hinges creak. I poked my head around and found the interior as shabby as the exterior. The carpet was worn in places, some of the wallpaper peeling from the walls and the paintwork yellowed. I stepped over the threshold and looked around me. There was a patina of dust on everything and cobwebs were strung around light fittings and up around the ceilings. Everywhere I looked, all I could see was grubbiness – I couldn't wait to get out of there.

I approached the reception desk and pressed the bell for attention. I waited for three or four minutes, but no one came. I pressed it again, keeping my finger on it longer this time and waited some more. I heard movement then a door opened and a middle-aged lady appeared wearing an old-fashioned stained apron over her 1970's style dress.

The woman gave an air of being younger than her appearance revealed; her face was lined, her eyes beady yet hooded, her thin lips down turned as if she hadn't smiled in a very long time. She smiled at me, but I could see it took some effort.

"Can I help you dearie?" Her youthful voice certainly wasn't compatible with the face before me and I was momentarily stunned into silence. She gazed at me curiously, waiting for me to reply.

"S-sorry," I mumbled, getting Josh's photo out of my bag to hand to her. Before I had even opened my mouth to ask her about him, she spoke.

"Sorry dearie, I haven't seen your young man."

"W-w-what d-did you say?" I stuttered, flabbergasted. My eyes were out on stalks.

"I said, I haven't seen your young man," she replied patiently. Her calm demeanour was comforting in one way but a little eerie in others.

"How did you know what I was going to ask you?"

She adeptly avoided my question by making another incredible announcement.

"Your twins are going to be wonderfully gifted, but all is not as it appears on the surface. There is something . . . *different* about them."

I staggered back a couple of steps as if the woman had physically struck me. My mouth gaped so wide my jaw ached and my eyes tightened in horrified shock. I was dumbstruck. How could this woman know so much? I couldn't think clearly. My mind was reeling from her words and I struggled to shape a response.

"H-how do you *know* these things? What did you mean by different?" A thunderbolt had struck my brain and I could now reason with it a little. She must be clairvoyant. I didn't give her a chance to answer my last two questions. I had to have my suspicions confirmed. "You're psychic, aren't you?"

She smiled at me enigmatically then nodded.

"I can see so much about your future, but you're not ready to really *hear* it all," she announced softly. It didn't sound as if she was being derogatory, but I failed to understand her reasoning. I decided to challenge her on it.

"What do you mean by that?"

"Please don't take it the wrong way dearie, you've been through massive emotional trauma and you've got more to come. I don't want to overload you," she explained gently. She moved a little closer and leaned forward onto the counter.

"Shouldn't it be *my* decision as to what I can cope with?" my tone was indignant.

"Perhaps," she conceded, "but I have an obligation to my spirit guides and in a strange way, to you too. They tell me things about people, but they also tell me when to talk and when to keep my own counsel. They are telling me you aren't emotionally strong enough to handle all the knowledge they have about you. If I ignore their advice, it'll be me who pays the price – not you."

"If that's the case, why have you told me what you already have?" My indignation had turned to puzzlement. I could sort of understand what she was getting at, but why the hell would she go so far and then clam up?

"It was a test – to see how you would take it." She paused when she saw the furious expression on my face then continued quickly. "It wasn't *my* test, it was theirs. They can see you've been on an emotional knife edge for a while and they are worried if they allow me to impart the knowledge they have, it will tip you into a dark place you will struggle to clamber out of. That's not to say some of their knowledge isn't wonderful for you because it is. All I can tell you is your road is strewn with obstacles and that is where the difficulties lie. Your twins will be a massive source of comfort and joy to you, once you accept them for who and what they are." Her face contorted for a brief moment and she skittered back away from the counter. "I'm sorry, I have to go. I can't tell you anything further. Take care of yourself and those little ones." Pain flashed across her face and before I had the chance to say anything further, she vanished through the doorway from where she had first appeared, closing the door quickly behind her.

"Wait, please," I called after her, puzzled by her sudden departure. I ran to the counter and pressed the bell over and over, hoping she would come back, but the door never opened again.

Dejected, I exited the shabby foyer and as I walked back through the door, the dark brooding sky erupted and the heavens opened.

* * *

I sat in the car for a few minutes. There was no point trying to drive – the rain was so torrential I couldn't see anything around me clearly – besides, my head was a mess. I laboured to make sense of everything the woman had said, and more to the point, what she hadn't said.

My eyes flickered to the clock on the dashboard – it was much later than I thought and I still needed to find a bed for the night. It took an enormous effort to push the tumbling notions to the back of my mind so I was able to concentrate on my driving, but I vowed to re-visit them later.

It took another hour and six establishments before I found a bed for the night. The place wasn't quite as nice as I was used to, but at this late stage I couldn't afford to be fussy. I dumped my case in the room and without unpacking it, went straight out to grab some dinner. I wasn't particularly hungry, but now I had my babies to consider, I knew I had to start taking care of myself. I found a small Chinese restaurant about a mile from my accommodation, had a small meal then returned for an early night, or so I thought.

Once back in my clean, but slightly shabby room and in my lumpy and not very comfortable bed, my mind drifted back to the conversation I'd had with the psychic earlier. I was immensely troubled, not by what she said so much as what she didn't. There was something nagging at me, something the woman said I couldn't quite recall, and it was driving me nuts. Why couldn't I remember it? It wasn't a throwaway comment – it was significant – and I knew it was really important I remembered what it was.

I grabbed my pad and pen from the bedside table and started to write down everything I recalled. I began with her saying she hadn't seen Joshua then there was something about the twins being gifted; there was more to her comment about the babies – what the hell was it? I stopped writing as I wracked my brains, desperate to bring it to the fore, but it eluded me and the more I tried to recall it, the further away it moved. Frustration surged through me, making me uptight. I dragged the nails of my clenched fist across my palm, not paying attention to what I was doing until a sharp edge pierced my skin and caused me to wince. I opened my fingers and found a light trace of blood on my palm; I stared at it mesmerised for a long moment then, with the tip of my tongue protruding from between my lips, I traced it over the tiny wound. The tiny amount of blood tasted uncharacteristically sweet and I wondered if a little of the plum sauce I'd had at dinner had flicked onto my hand.

My brain was hurting from my efforts to recall that one comment so I decided to move on and write down some of the other things the woman had told me. One and a half sides of A5 paper later and I hit another brick wall in my memory. Again it had something to do with the twins; I remembered her saying they would be a comfort and a joy, but that wasn't all of it. What was the rest?

"Crap, crap and more crap." I said aloud as once again, fierce frustration reared at my selective memory.

I made the decision to try and get some sleep. I returned the pad to the bedside table and turned out the light. I spent the next hour tossing and turning, trying to find a comfortable position on the lumpy mattress until I was so shattered I fell into an exhausted slumber.

The next morning I awoke tired and irritable. I'd had a restless night, partially due to the lack of comfort and partially because my brain wouldn't stop churning things over. I knew I shouldn't be lonely, but in truth, that's exactly what I was. Okay, so I could talk to my babies, but I couldn't have a conversation with them, I couldn't hold them in my arms yet and despite having the scan pictures it still hadn't completely sunk in yet.

"Mummy" a soft sighing whispered in my ear. I jerked upright, whipping my head first one way then the other, but I was alone. *Oh, great! Now my mind is playing tricks on me.* I swung my legs around and planted my feet on the floor. As I stood, the tiny voice breathed again, "Mummy". It was a soft caress which I longed to embrace yet there was nobody in the room with me. Was I losing it? Was it tiredness causing my mind to play tricks? I just didn't know what to think.

Yesterday had been such a difficult day I was still suffering the after effects. My emotions were stretched to the absolute limit and I really couldn't be sure how much more I could take before I buckled under the relentless strain. I flopped back on the bed and behind my closed lids I saw Joshua's face. His expression was serious yet gentle, caring and concerned; the sort of look he used to give me when I complained of feeling unwell.

My eyes raked over every feature of the face I adored, from the top of his head to the tip of his chin and from one ear to the other. I could see the small mark on his forehead from when he'd had chicken pox as a child and the small scar on his chin from falling off his bike as a teenager. The more I struggled to hold his face in front of my eyes, the weaker it became until it was shrouded in a mist and his features began to blur and fade. In desperation, I attempted to force it to stay, but it had its own will and began to retreat, moving slowly at first then gaining momentum until he was being propelled along a high speed track with no brakes.

I called his name again and again, to no avail and although I was barely aware of it, the tears which coursed across my cheeks got heavier the further away he moved, until he was swallowed up by the mist and my tears turned to sobs which reached down deep inside me and crushed my heart.

I turned my face into the duvet and cried until I was empty and my tears dried up.

I wasn't really aware of how much time had passed. When I pulled my face up, I was hot and beads of perspiration dotted my brow. I heaved myself off the mattress and lethargically dragged my feet into the bathroom. By the time I'd completed my ablutions I was feeling more human. It took me longer to dress than normal – a lot of my usual clothes were now too tight around the middle. I managed to find some lightweight trousers with an elasticated waistband which weren't too uncomfortable. I really needed to go shopping. After wolfing down an overcooked and tasteless breakfast, I left to get some new clothes and to continue with my search. With luck, I would not only find Joshua, but also locate more suitable and comfy accommodation.

My shopping excursion was infinitely more successful than my search for Joshua or a more supportive bed for the next few nights. I stopped en route for my evening meal before reluctantly returning to my room. I spent another restless night - the lumps and bumps in the mattress disturbing my sleep often – waking fatigued and disconsolate.

Another rubbery breakfast actually made me nauseous and it took me a little longer than usual to depart. At least my new clothing was more comfortable. I still had a large number of establishments on my list and set off in haste.

Two hours later, I'd located a street where practically every building was a B & B or guest house. I parked my car a short way down the road and set off on foot. I made my way down one side of the street and having no luck, started back up the other side. I got about half way up when I spotted a woman marching along the other side of the road coming towards me. I normally wouldn't have thought anything of it, but she looked vaguely familiar. Her head was down as she stormed along and hadn't spotted me. Initially I couldn't place where I'd seen her before then as she came closer, I recognised her. It was the clairvoyant from the dilapidated place I'd been to on my first day in Bath. For a moment I was stunned – I hadn't expected to see her again – then, as if a switch had been flicked in my head, I was galvanised into action. Without thinking or looking to check for traffic, I ran out into the road towards her.

I got about a third of the way across the road when I heard the screech of brakes and a horn blaring. I froze on the spot, scrunched my eyes tightly closed and braced myself for the impact I was sure would follow any second. People say in moments like these, your entire life flashes before your eyes – *mine* didn't. In fact, nothing flashed before my eyes except dots of white light from where I was squeezing my eyes together so firmly.

The noise ceased and it became eerily quiet in comparison. Nothing had hit me – I was still in one piece and unharmed. I slowly opened my eyelids and saw a car had stopped in front of me on the far side of the road. I would have been under the wheels or bounced off the windscreen, if I hadn't frozen in place when I did. Abruptly I realised the stupidity of my thoughtless action; I could have killed my babies or left myself physically unable to care for them. What a moron.

My hands dropped to my stomach automatically as I looked at the woman driver of the car. She was pale and shaking – I hoped she wasn't going into shock. She glared at me with anger and a degree of relief in her expression. I wondered if she was going to shout at me – I honestly wouldn't have blamed her if she did – but I caught sight of her eyes glancing down at the position of my hands and she shook her head slowly. I could picture what she was thinking – how could I have been so reckless as to risk the lives of my twins? I mouthed the words "I'm sorry" then carried on across the road, this time checking it was safe.

When I reached the opposite pavement, I remembered why I was rushing across the road in the first place. I frantically searched in both directions, but the clairvoyant was nowhere to be seen. I ran up the road in the direction she'd been travelling and at each turning, I stopped to see if I could spot her. By the time I reached the very end of the road, I was out of breath, panting like an old dog and I had a stitch in my side. She was nowhere to be seen. The woman had vanished into thin air.

I trudged back up the road, annoyed and dejected, my shoulders hunched and a scowl plastered across my face. I really needed to speak to the clairvoyant again; I firmly believed she had answers for me and I wanted them. I wanted them so bad. If only I hadn't been so impatient to reach her, if only I hadn't run into the road without checking for traffic, I might have caught up and had a chance to talk to her.

Something told me if I turned up at her guest house again, she wouldn't come out to talk to me. So what to do . . . I guess I could sit in my car outside her place and wait for her to come out, but wasn't that stalking? I wasn't sure how to proceed. All I knew was I had to try and encourage her to tell me what she knew. I would have to give it some serious consideration.

In the meantime, I still had two other goals which needed my attention and it was about time I cracked on with them. I stopped and checked to see where I'd got to on my list, then checked the names on the buildings to my left. I was only two away from the last one I called on, so I straightened up, walked up the road to the next one then turned into the drive, a false smile which didn't reach my eyes stuck to my lips.

More dead ends. More crosses on my list with many more still to be checked. The one good thing that had come out of the day was finding somewhere more to my taste to stay for the next few nights. I didn't care that I would have to pay at my existing place as well as the new one for tonight, but it was worth it to have a decent night's sleep.

I returned to the B & B, gathered my things and left, sighing with relief as I drove away.

Chapter 35 – Remy

The small family run hotel was a palace compared with the B & B I'd just left. Not only was the bed comfortable, the entire building was freshly decorated inside and out and was so obviously cared for. I settled into my room and luxuriated on the mattress for a good half hour before being disturbed by my stomach growling.

I got up and walked over to the long mirror sited on one of the wardrobe doors, stopping in front of it. I stood and stared at my reflection for a full two minutes, turning first this way then that and finally face on. Scrutinising my appearance, I was appalled at the sight in front of me. I had to admit the last few nights of lousy sleep had taken their toll. I had dark circles under my eyes, no make-up, my hair wasn't as groomed as normal and as for my clothes – yuck. I'd thrown some things on this morning and not really checked what coordinated and what didn't. I cringed at my mis-matched outfit. *This isn't me. I've really let myself go.* I had a sense of déjà vu; this wasn't the first time since I'd started my search I'd looked in the mirror and found myself lacking. I didn't dare think what Joshua's reaction would be if he saw me in this mess. I was repulsed enough for both of us.

I stripped off and threw my clothes onto a chair in disgust. I pulled my straighteners out of the case and plugged them in. While I waited for them to heat up, I grabbed my cosmetic bag and set about concealing the awful shadows beneath my eyes. After a couple of minutes of careful blending, followed by a light eye shadow, eyeliner and mascara, my eyes looked a hundred times better. I added blusher and some lip gloss to finish it off.

By the time I'd completed the canvas that was my face I set about improving my hair. I picked up the straighteners and got to work. Ten minutes later my hair was sleek and stylish and I smiled at my reflection. *That's better*, I thought. I picked my clothes with a little more care than I had been of late and dressed, pausing to re-appraise my appearance in the mirror. I was pleased with what I was seeing. It was the real me. I snatched my bag off the chair and left the room to go to dinner.

Earlier in the day, I'd spotted an Italian restaurant within walking distance of the hotel. The attractive storefront made me curious to discover if the food tasted as good as the restaurant looked. As it was a pleasant evening, I decided to stroll down and check it out.

I walked in and found the décor tasteful and quite opulent. I was very surprised to find it had a small dance floor and a resident DJ playing a mixture of ballads and disco music from the 80's, 90's and recent chart hits. The music was totally at odds with the ambience created by the lavish decoration yet I liked it because it was different.

The maître d' found me a nice table against the wall where I could see the dance floor and most of the other diners. I studied the menu. There were so many delicious-sounding meals to choose from I had to send my waiter away twice before I was ready to order.

A portion of warm garlic bread smothered with mozzarella cheese was brought to my table – a free appetiser which I thought was a nice touch. By the time I'd consumed it, my main meal had arrived and I tucked into it hungrily. Normally I would have had a glass of wine or three, but due to my pregnancy I didn't want to risk it, so I had a refreshing glass of ice-cold apple juice instead.

By the time I'd finished the main course, the restaurant was eighty per cent full and some patrons were sitting at the bar, drinking and enjoying the atmosphere. A few couples were gyrating on the dance floor and a party mood swirled around the room like an invisible gas, affecting everyone. Everywhere I looked people were laughing, some bounced on their seats in time to the music, while others gravitated to the dance floor.

I enjoyed soaking up the jovial ambience and watching people have fun yet in some ways it was a lonely experience; it was one I would have much preferred to share with Joshua. I pushed the thought out of mind as soon as it landed – I didn't want to embarrass myself by falling apart in front of a restaurant full of people.

A shriek erupted from across the room followed by loud guffaws. My eyes automatically drifted towards the sound and I couldn't stifle the giggle which broke free. A middle-aged man had fallen off his chair and was lying on his back with his legs up in the air. He and his companions were laughing so hard, they were physically unable to help him up and it fell to two of the waiters to rescue him. By now, the whole restaurant was in uproar and the loneliness vanished as I joined in with the laughter that flowed freely throughout the room.

As I watched the fallen man being hauled onto his feet, I was unaware a younger guy at the bar was watching me intently. Now the impromptu show was over, my eyes swept around the room searching for another source of amusement and they briefly met those of a guy at the bar then moved on without lingering. They settled on the dance floor where a group of people were dancing and mucking about. Their antics amused me and I chuckled repeatedly, not noticing the guy from the bar had strolled over to my table and was now standing opposite me.

The guy bent towards me and said, "Excuse me," very close to my ear.

His voice startled me and my head whirled around to see who it was. I met a pair of the most mesmerising eyes I'd ever seen; they were such an unusual shade – turquoise. I sat back in my chair leaning away from his proximity, my eyes wide in astonishment.

"I'm sorry," he said, "I didn't mean to startle you." His smile caused his eyes to twinkle and the colour became more defined.

"Oh, er, that's okay," I replied, the corners of my mouth turned upwards a little.

"I couldn't help noticing you appeared to be alone and I sort of wondered if you'd mind if I joined you?" His cheeks flushed a dark pink and he lowered his eyes in a shy way.

It had been an extremely long time since another man had approached me – it was unsettling yet also flattering that I was still attractive enough to invite interest from the opposite sex. I stared at him for a long moment. He was quite handsome in a rugged way with a muscular build and certainly not unappealing at first glance. He was fashionably yet smartly dressed and he carried the clothes well. However, just appreciating his good looks was tantamount to being unfaithful to Joshua to my mind and I diverted my eyes as I answered him.

"Thank you for noticing, but I don't think it would be a good idea."

"Why not? You're alone, I'm alone, we could keep each other company, no strings," his voice was persuasive and I could feel his eyes boring into me.

I lifted my head to meet his gaze, steeling myself to be firm yet kind in my rejection. I pointed to the engagement ring still in its' rightful place on my left hand.

"I'm engaged," I responded waggling my ring finger at him, "and I'm meeting my fiancé later," I lied straight-faced.

His face fell as disappointment clouded his eyes.

"Oh, okay. Sorry I bothered you," he mumbled then with slouched shoulders, he turned his back on me and trudged towards the bar.

I watched him for a few seconds as he retreated. I must have hurt his feelings if his reaction was anything to go by and a sense of guilt swept over me. I knew I hadn't done anything wrong or deliberately set out to cause the guy pain, but I'd never deliberately hurt people – it's part of who I am. By the time he reached the bar, my eyes were diverted to the dance floor once more.

Half an hour passed and I began to grow tired. I checked out the bar area in my peripheral vision and was relieved to see no sign of the guy who'd approached me earlier. I called for my bill and paid with my debit card. I left a tip on the table, got up and left.

The night outside was quite mild. I strolled down the road heading back to my hotel enjoying the night air. The sky wasn't black, more a mixture of grey and lilac hues with a smattering of clouds dotted randomly. The waxing gibbous moon had hints of pink around its edges and a glowing silhouetted ring shadowed it. It was a beautiful sight and I marvelled at the majesty of it.

A sound behind me interrupted my admiration of the night sky; footsteps approached, getting nearer all the time. I continued walking, but increased the speed of my steps, not daring to turn around. The pace of the footsteps matched mine and I could tell by the sound of them it was a male. There was nobody around apart from the occasional car and I started to get scared.

I kept increasing my speed and my shadow followed suit until I was close to breaking into a full on sprint. I'd gone from scared to terrified; my stomach was tying itself in knots, my heart was pounding vitally in my chest beating its' own mantra in desperation to keep from being silenced, the blood charged through my veins like an out of control steam train going downhill and the sound was so loud, I could hear it rushing in my ears.

I kept my eyes straight ahead – I wasn't far from the hotel now – I hoped and prayed I could make it there in one piece. I knew he was much closer to me now, his breath tickled the back of my neck, an icy tentacle snaking its way down my spine. Then I remembered I had my mobile in my bag. If I could extract it without him seeing, I could call the police. As I continued to walk faster still, I gradually moved my bag around so it was across my burning chest. I partially opened the zip, put one hand inside and fished around for the phone. It was hard to do this covertly whilst maintaining my speed and concentrating on where he was.

My frantic hand movements in my bag aroused his suspicions. Perhaps he thought I had a can of pepper spray in there. His breathing became more rapid on my neck and he cleared his throat. My throat constricted and a scream started to build from deep within my core, but before I let it rip, a vaguely familiar voice said, "Please don't be afraid - I won't hurt you," his voice was breathless and came out more as a whisper.

With a degree of courage which came out of nowhere, I stopped dead, spun around to confront my shadow and was astounded to see the guy from the restaurant. All the terror which had been building and consuming me, exploded into cold fury as I ripped into him.

"What the bloody hell are you *playing* at? You scared the crap out of me and I was about to phone the police." My voice was so cold one could have expected to see ice around my lips.

"I'm really sorry," he said, his voice full of contrition. "I didn't mean to frighten you – I just wanted to make sure you got back home safely as you were on your own," he explained. He stared down at his shoes and looked miserable.

"What's it to you? You don't even *know* me? Did it not occur to you to ask me, or even say something much earlier, you moron?" I spat the words at him, my indignant rage spurring me on.

He took a step away from me as if I'd physically struck him. His expression was thoughtful as he decided how to answer.

"Please let me try to explain –hear me out, okay?" he begged. His eyes were filled with a deep sorrow I found disturbing. I nodded.

He took a large breath to steady himself.

"Seeing you sitting in the restaurant all alone, I thought you looked . . . *vulnerable* and you reminded me of someone I used to know." The melancholy tone of his voice struck a profound chord inside me. He continued after another noticeable intake of breath.

"Just over three years ago, my girlfriend Tamara had been out with friends one night and was walking home alone when she was . . . attacked. She fought back, but there were two of them and she was no match for their strength. They dragged her behind some bushes where they brutally . . . ," he took another deep breath to control the raging emotions surging through him as his voice broke on the last word.

". . . raped her repeatedly, beat her to a pulp and robbed her of everything she had. They even ripped the earrings from her ears," his voice rose in righteous indignation and he was shaking all over, reliving the horror once again.

My hand flew to my mouth in shock; my eyes wide as saucers and my mouth gaped open.

"Oh my God," I whispered from behind my hand.

He continued as if I hadn't spoken his voice softer than before, but still loaded with mournful inflection.

"Tamara wasn't found for about sixteen hours by which time she'd lost a great deal of blood. She was a complete mess; those thugs had beaten her so badly her face was unrecognisable, her clothes were torn so most of her body was exposed to the elements and what was left of her personal belongings were strewn over the ground nearby.

"We had over fifty volunteers working alongside the police trying to find her; it was actually two of her best friends who located her and it was so traumatic for them they both needed counselling afterwards. Tamara was rushed to hospital where she underwent surgery for more than eight hours, but the head injuries were so severe she was in a coma. The specialists spent a couple of weeks running test after test after test on her before they finally told us she was clinically brain dead and there was no hope for recovery." His voice trailed off to a whisper at the end and he closed his eyes to conceal the wetness there.

I yearned to reach out a hand of comfort to him. There was no way I could disbelieve his tale – the timbre of his voice, the expression on his face and the tears in his eyes were too real for this to be some elaborate lie.

"I'm so sorry," I said. The words were inadequate to ease his obvious suffering. He nodded, his eyes still shut tight then continued.

"When I came out of the men's room and saw you'd left the restaurant, I had a strange sense of déjà vu. It was a peculiar panicky sensation and I knew I had to try to find you. I left and looked both ways up the road then spotted you strolling along. All I wanted to do was keep you safe, make sure you got to your destination unharmed so I followed you," he explained then opened his eyes to watch my reaction.

I hesitated, weighing his words. I couldn't be angry now if I tried and what little ire remained quickly dissipated.

"Well, er, I guess I should thank you – even if you did nearly give me a heart attack," I grinned to soften the words.

He grinned back. "Yeah, sorry. I suppose I could have gone about it differently," he admitted.

"Yeah," I agreed. "By the way, my name's Remy."

"Kyle," he replied, holding out his hand. I took it and we shook.

"Hi Kyle. I hope you don't mind me asking, but did they catch them?" I cringed inwardly as I asked the question.

"Yeah, the police got them," he confirmed, his voice bitter, his expression darkening as he resumed. "One of them was only sixteen, the other was nineteen. The sixteen-year-old got two years in a youth offenders place and the other bloke got ten years. With good behaviour, he'll be out in about six years. SIX BLOODY YEARS!" he ranted, "he should have got LIFE for what he did."

I sympathised with his pain. However, how could I respond to what Kyle had said? Everything which came to mind sounded so trite and I was sure he would have heard all the platitudes a hundred time or more. I held myself tense as I waited for him to calm down. I watched, remaining silent, as he struggled to compose himself. His fists clenched and unclenched as he tried to slow his breathing.

After a couple of minutes, his face began to relax, his hands stayed open at his side and he was able to raise his head and look at me once more. An impish and somewhat embarrassed smile crossed his lips.

"Um, sorry about that. I tend to lose it a bit when I get started on that subject," he admitted, a sheepish look on his face.

"I can understand why. You okay now?"

"Yeah, thanks. So, what's your story then?" he asked.

I shrugged, nonchalant. "I don't have a story really. My fiancé is late returning from a business meeting so I came out to have some dinner and now I'm returning to our hotel." I lied, my voice smooth and convincing – or so I thought.

Kyle stared at me, an incredulous look on his face. He sniggered in disbelief.

"What kind of bullshit was that?"

"I *beg* your pardon?" I wore my indignation like a cloak, my tone as sharp as a butcher's knife.

"Look, I don't mean to offend you, but that sounded pretty lame. I'm usually rather good at sussing people out and it seems to me you're in a lot more pain than I am right now." He explained in a very natural voice.

"Well, I don't know where you got that idea from. I'm absolutely fine. The only pain you can see is from the ache in my chest and the stitch in my side from walking too fast when trying to get away from, what was at the time, an unknown stalker," I responded getting annoyed.

"Wow. *Very* defensive. Me thinks the lady protests too much." Kyle was mocking, but he did so with a small smirk on his face.

My eyes tightened and my mouth pinched into an unflattering pout. There was no way I was going to admit the truth to Kyle, especially as he was now being a little smug, thinking he'd sussed me out. My earlier sympathy for his devastating loss hadn't disappeared; rather I'd pushed it to one side. I had a desperate urge to end this conversation and get back to the hotel as rapidly as possible. How do I extricate myself from this situation without hurting his feelings? After all, he was trying to be gallant and keep me safe so I do owe him something for that. An idea flew into my head.

"Look Kyle, I'm really grateful to you for trying to keep me safe, but I'm really tired and need to get back to my hotel now. I guess being pregnant has that effect on women." I really *was* tired – in fact I was exhausted – so it was no lie.

Kyle stared at me for a moment, taken aback, wide-eyed his eyebrows rose in an arc.

"You're *pregnant*?" he asked, the surprise evident in his tone.

"Yep. Carrying twins too." I grinned with pride.

"Wow," he whispered. "Okay then, let's get you back."

"You don't *have* to escort me," I said, trying to give him an out. He was having none of it.

"You're kidding. That's even more reason to see you safely back to your hotel," he stated, his voice firm.

I could see there would be no point in arguing so I set off in the direction of the hotel, only this time he walked beside me. Within five minutes we'd arrived at the main door.

"Thank you, Kyle." I said, smiling, sincere gratitude in my voice.

"My pleasure Remy. It was lovely to meet you," he replied, returning my smile.

"Yeah, you too."

Kyle fumbled in his pocket and pulled out a tiny notebook and pen. He scribbled something on a sheet of paper, folded it and pressed it into my hand.

"If you need to talk, or want an escort, give me a call. Who knows? You might decide you want to get some of the pain you're suffering off your chest and I'm a good listener." He was trying to be nonchalant, but his tone was a tad too earnest.

I opened my mouth to deny his claim, but he put one finger up to my lips to quiet me.

"You may be able to lie to yourself, but I can see through you – it takes one to know one and your eyes are a dead giveaway. All I'm asking is you consider my offer. Goodnight Remy." He turned and started to walk back the way we came.

"Goodnight Kyle, and thank you," I called after him. I was astonished he'd been able to see my pain – I thought I was doing a bang-up job of hiding it, but obviously not if a complete stranger could pick up on it with such ease. That notion depressed me and I barely registered him raising his hand in farewell as he was consumed by the darkness.

I strolled up to my room, my brain going over his last couple of comments. Upon reaching my room, I lay on the bed, my head propped up with pillows deep in thought.

Chapter 36 – Joshua

Samir remained in the tree all night as motionless as a statue, mentally berating himself for all the mistakes he'd made with Dayna. He saw the rest of his coven return to the manor, but still he didn't move. Pavel appeared on the portico, his concerned eyes searching the grounds. He stared at the tree where Samir was concealed for a long minute before going back inside.

The sky began to lighten and the first streaks of lilac and pink could be seen on the horizon, but still Samir remained where he was. Pavel came out of the manor again, this time accompanied by Joshua. Pavel pointed to the tree where Samir was ensconced and Joshua set off, reaching it within a second. Without pausing, he climbed into the tree and sat beside Samir. Joshua put his hand on his maker's shoulder and gave it a gentle squeeze.

"Samir? You need to come with me." Joshua's voice was gentle and full of compassion.

Samir turned his head so he faced Joshua; his eyes were glazed and his face was a mask of agony. He didn't answer.

"Samir, you need to come NOW!" Joshua said his tone urgent. He shook Samir's shoulder when he got no reaction to his words. Still nothing. Joshua glanced towards the horizon and saw he only had mere minutes to get Samir into the house before it would be too late. It worried the hell out of Joshua that Samir was so unresponsive – it was so out of character.

Joshua made his decision in a split second – he knew he didn't have time for niceties or subtlety – he grabbed hold of Samir and hauled him out of the tree. They landed hard on the ground; Samir just lay there so Joshua picked him up, slung him over his shoulder and took off, arriving back at the house in less than a second.

Once through the door, he took Samir straight up to his room and laid him on his bed, Pavel followed right on his heels. Samir didn't move from the position Joshua laid him in, he stared up at the ceiling, his face still betraying the anguish Joshua had witnessed in the tree.

Pavel put his hand on Joshua's shoulder.

"Thank you Joshua. I will stay with him now – you go and rest." The concern on Pavel's face matched Joshua's.

Joshua looked at Pavel, a question in his eyes, but Pavel just nodded. Joshua turned and with a final glance at Samir, walked out of the room, closing the door softly behind him.

Joshua didn't go straight to Jasna's room as he normally would have done instead he wandered down the stairs and back out into the daylight. He stared at the horizon and watched the sun rise higher in the sky. It scared him to think of how close they had all come to losing Samir and it worried him to see Samir in such an unresponsive state.

Joshua sussed out long ago that Dayna had strong feelings for Samir, but didn't realise those emotions were reciprocated. He also understood, to a certain extent, why Samir might have chosen not to reveal them yet he couldn't help but wonder if Dayna would have been less disruptive if she'd known Samir *did* have feelings for her, or even if he'd shown them.

For the first time in quite a while, his thoughts drifted to Remy and he wondered how she was and what was happening in her life. How had she coped with his abrupt disappearance and the on-going silence? Had she moved on or was she pining for him? He knew the answer to the last question. He knew her well enough to know she would be going through hell, even after all this time and an intense wave of remorse came crashing over him.

He closed his eyes and Remy's face appeared behind his eyelids; the expression on her face made him gasp – it held the same devastating agony he had observed on Samir's face a short time earlier and a new fissure of unendurable anguish ripped through his chest. A sob escaped from between his inflexible lips and he shoved his fist into his mouth to stifle the noise. A physical ache settled in his torso welding itself to his bones, he scrunched his eyes tight and bowed his head with the crushing weight.

Locked away in his heart, eternally potent, was the everlasting love he held for her. Even though he loved Jasna, there was no comparison. He was torturing himself and if he wasn't careful, Jasna would notice and he didn't want to hurt her. He had to bolt Remy back into his heart again, but seeing her face once more, even sharing the same distress as Samir's, was better than not seeing it at all.

He meandered through the grounds, aimless and distraught; he missed Remy so much and it had taken Samir's plight to bring this forth from the depths of his heart where he had buried it. He needed to examine it, to rationalise and reconcile the pain and the love so he could submerge it once and for all time. He would never be able to move forward in his immortal life otherwise, this life which was far beyond anything he dreamt existed, this life his darling Remy could never become part of.

He glanced up noticing he had wandered over to the outbuilding where his car was garaged. He sped up, walked over to his car and sat in the driver's seat. The keys were in the ignition where he'd left them the last time he used it. He fired up the engine and listened to it purr; filled with an abrupt urge for a change of scenery, he backed the car out of the building, drove down the back drive, turning onto the road at the end. As soon as his wheels found purchase on the tarmac, he floored the accelerator and rocketed down the road.

He never would have attempted such speed down the twisting country lanes prior to becoming a vampire, but his new, faster reactions were more than up to the task. He had no idea where he was going and didn't really care; he lowered the windows and let the wind caress his hair like sensual fingers massaging his scalp – like Remy used to do when he had a headache or was tense.

It was a good job his vampire senses allowed him to process many thoughts at once; Joshua, haunted by Samir's expression and Remy's face, was still able to cope with driving safely at high speed. He had no idea where he was heading and didn't much care, he needed some alone time to work through all the unresolved issues he was carrying like excess baggage.

After driving for about an hour, Joshua came to a wood which had a picnic area and a small car park. He pulled in and shut off the engine. He got out and locked the car before setting off into the trees. He meandered through the undergrowth, not paying much attention to where his feet were taking him – he was too wrapped up in the contents of his mind.

Joshua was oblivious to the thinning of the trees until the light changed in quite a dramatic fashion and he found himself in a small clearing. There was no defined shape to it; neither square nor circle, and the grass in the middle had been fried to a golden straw by the sun. He sat on the dry ground and leant against a tree at the edge of the glade. Even though his skin no longer detected heat or cold, he enjoyed the fact he could sit in the sun, unlike his contemporaries.

Another set of faces appeared as a photograph in his mind and new fresh guilt overwhelmed him. He hadn't given his parents or brother a single thought since he became immortal – this was something else to beat himself up over. What must his poor mum be going through? Leaving Remy was one thing – he'd made his decision for her own protection and before he knew the reasons behind his obscure behaviour – whereas his parents were a whole other matter entirely.

Joshua put his head in his hands as devastating grief consumed him. What to do? He didn't want anyone to suffer because of him, least of all his parents, but there were a lot of things to consider before making any decisions.

His first instinct was to call and speak to them, allay their fears and reassure them he was fine, but was it really the best way to deal with it? Would a letter or postcard be preferable? Or would it be kinder in the long run to maintain the silence? All these alternatives ploughed back and forth through his brain yet making a decision was proving impossible whilst he allowed his emotions to interfere with methodical approaches to problem solving.

He raised his head and peered up at the sky. Clouds of white and pale grey were beginning to build in the east and a brisk breeze had sprung up – it wouldn't be long before the sun would play peek-a-boo before being completely concealed. This small act distracted Joshua long enough to gain a little perspective and he began to think more clearly, looking at the positives and negatives of each possibility.

One of the biggest difficulties in making his decision was knowing how close Remy was to his parents, and if he contacted them in some way and not her, how much more would it wound her? Or, would it be unfair of him to swear his parents to secrecy when he knew their first instinct would be to reassure Remy he was okay?

Was it such a bad thing for Remy to have some peace of mind or would it give her false hope? Could he count on his parents' loyalty to him first and foremost? He wanted to think so. And then there was Todd. Would it be better to contact him? Joshua had always been close to his brother – there had never been any sibling rivalry between them and they were good friends as well – perhaps he *would* be the better choice. In fact, the more he thought about it, the more he was sure this was the path he should take.

It was hurtful knowing he would never see any of them again and the contact would have to be a one-hit wonder, but it was infinitely better than leaving them fretting about whether he was alive or dead. Joshua chuckled at the words that had come to him – alive or dead – interesting choice, all things considered.

With the decision made, Joshua found a modicum of peace. There was still the Remy issue to reconcile, but first things first. He pulled his phone from his pocket and was about to craft a text message to Todd when he noticed a message in his inbox. He vaguely wondered how long it had been there, but he didn't have to open it to know who had sent it. His instincts told him it was from Remy. The question was – should he open it?

He was torn between curiosity and self-preservation. By opening and reading the message it could seriously set him back. He had worked so hard to stifle his feelings for Remy and start moving on with his new life – was he going to risk it all for the sake of one message? He guessed it said how much she missed him and wanted him to come home. He'd had a couple of those already and really didn't need to read anymore. He resolved not to allow a text message to ruin everything he'd achieved and hit the delete button.

He opened a new message and began pressing keys.

Hey bruv, 1st I'm sorry 4 disappearing & 4 not contacting u. I can't tell u wot's gon on & sorry but this is last time u will ever hear from me. It has 2 b this way 4 u & mum & dad's protection. Can't explain but I'm ok. Pls tell mum & dad I'm sorry. Hav 2 ask a favour – pls don't tell Remy u hav heard from me, its 4 the best. Luv u all so much. Don't worry abt me. Take care. Josh x

It took several attempts to arrive at something he was close to being satisfied with; Joshua read it one final time before hitting 'send' and then it was gone. Knowing Todd as he did, he anticipated receiving a message from him within the next few minutes; regardless of what it said, Joshua knew he wouldn't reply and that went against the grain, but it was necessary. Besides, he'd already written he would not contact him again. He switched the phone off and shoved it back in his pocket.

Now he had to deal with Remy, or rather his love for her. Hadn't he already been through this when he was trying to make the decision about whether or not to start a relationship with Jasna? The simple answer was yes and all his reasoning at the time was as relevant now as it had been then – the only things which had really changed was he was closer to Jasna now and his feelings for her were deeper and stronger. However, Joshua also knew the love he felt for Jasna paled in comparison to the love he still held for Remy. Then again, he *had* been with Remy much longer and maybe, in time, the love he had for Jasna would rival that of Remy's.

The one thing troubling him was why his brain had made the link between Samir's agony and Remy. He had no doubt whatsoever that Remy had been existing in her own distressing version of hell since he left and he still suffered an incredible amount of shame for the physical and emotional injury he'd inflicted on her. Nevertheless, deep inside, he knew the decision to leave had been best for her, especially once he realised she could never be part of his new life, and given identical circumstances, he would do the same again.

Still, it didn't explain the link with Samir. Maybe it was the fact that Samir was broken-hearted about Dayna, and Joshua imagined it was how Remy had been about him. Or was there something else going on? Having already gained all these amazingly cool talents, was there more to come? Was there a particular reason behind this? Was there a message trying to reveal itself to him? It would be beyond simplicity to drive himself crazy attempting to answer all the questions flying around his brain like protons in a hadron collider, but that would be rather counter-productive.

Joshua knew he had to be pragmatic and torturing himself yet again about Remy was not going to solve anything. He couldn't shake the notion there was a particular reason why she escaped the locked box he'd placed her in. There was no point in trying to force something that may, or may not, be lurking in the ether, so at least for the time being, he would have to be patient and see what developed, if anything.

With a supreme effort, he shoved all his emotions, ideas and everything else even remotely connected into the Remy box and bolted the lid shut. As he figuratively removed the key from the lock, he experienced a lightness of being which brought tranquillity on swift wings. Joshua closed his eyes and let his mind drift for a while until a drop of water landed on his cheek. His eyelids opened and he gazed at the sky, which had altered to a dirty grey. The rain didn't bother him in the slightest so he remained in his place a while longer.

It was strange to be out in the daytime again – it was the first time since he and Jasna had become a couple he'd ventured out alone in daylight – and he realised he'd missed the freedom of it. He assumed Jasna thought he was with Pavel and Samir, in which case, she wouldn't be upset by his absence. But – would she get suspicious if he was gone all day? Regardless, he found he didn't want to be away from her all day; he missed her arms around him, holding him tight, he missed her lips, her body curved against his. In short, he missed *her*.

He stood and raced back to the car, reaching it in under five seconds. After starting the engine, he turned the car around to face the way he came and flooring the accelerator, took off like a rocket.

Chapter 37 – Joshua

Pavel sat beside Samir's bed, worry etched into his features as he stared unblinking at his friend. Samir was catatonic with grief and hadn't uttered a word since Joshua had laid him on the mattress. Pavel had never seen Samir this way; he knew he had to somehow pull him out of this all-consuming depression, but how? He believed that pointing out Dayna's faults would not help the situation as Samir would only blame himself more than he already was for the choices Dayna had made. Perhaps he should focus on other aspects of the coven and try to draw him out that way. Pavel searched through the events of the last couple of days and had an epiphany.

"Samir?" Pavel's voice was soft and he worked to smooth the worry from his features.

Samir did not respond to Pavel's voice and gave no indication he even heard him. Pavel tried again.

"Samir, I think we need to have a discussion about Joshua," he said a little louder, his tone ringing with authority.

Whether it was the mention of Joshua's name or the firmness in Pavel's voice, he wasn't sure, but for the first time in hours, Samir responded by turning his head towards his friend and mentor. Samir still didn't appear to be fully cognisant of his surroundings or in full control of his faculties, but any reaction was better than the catatonic state he'd been immersed in.

"Did you hear what I said, Samir?" Pavel asked, trying to draw him out further, the timbre of his voice demanding a response.

Samir sat up and stared at Pavel for a couple of minutes before the glazed expression cleared and his eyes focussed on Pavel's face. Samir started, as if he wasn't expecting to see anyone in the room with him, let alone his friend and mentor.

"Pavel?" Samir enquired his voice husky as if he hadn't spoken in a very long time.

"Yes Samir, I'm here," he replied, as if speaking to a child, his voice soft. His face showed his concern once more.

"I'm sorry, Pavel, were you saying something before?" Samir asked sounding and looking puzzled.

Pavel was exasperated by Samir's demeanour – he was more used to Samir being as sharp as a samurai sword – yet he hid it well, knowing the situation had to be handled with quite a degree of care, lest Samir slip back into his catatonic state, which Pavel wanted to avoid at all costs.

"Yes, actually I was," he admitted, "I was saying we need to have a discussion about Joshua."

"Joshua? Why?" Samir asked, even more puzzled than before. His brow was furrowed over his eyes as he leant forward. Pavel hesitated to marshal his thoughts; the slightest slip on his part, the wrong words and Samir's tenuous grip on normality could shatter like a rock thrown through a window.

"Well, in case you haven't been paying attention, Joshua has now displayed *three* tremendous gifts, two of which even *I* haven't encountered before. He is the most talented immortal in our long and distinguished history and I can't help but wonder if there is more he is capable of, if there are still *more* gifts he hasn't displayed yet. What do you think?" Pavel managed to inject quite an amount of enthusiasm in his voice to disguise how carefully he was choosing his words; in truth he didn't have to try very hard. His face had become more animated than usual and his eyes were twinkling with excitement.

"Three? I can only recall two, so what is the third one?" The surprise and curiosity was evident on Samir's face and in his voice.

"Well . . . some might call it invisibility, but I believe Joshua to be a chameleon," Pavel responded.

Samir's eyes widened, his eyebrows arched in astonishment and his mouth gaped open. He wasn't faking – he honestly didn't remember seeing Joshua disappear from view. How could he fail to recall something so . . . so . . . enormous and significant?

"A . . . a *chameleon*? I've never seen him demonstrate this talent and I'm sure something as monumental as this would not slip my mind," Samir stated, his voice was firm yet there was an undertone of ambiguity.

Pavel had to think rapidly. He hated the idea of lying to his friend yet he didn't want to cause Samir any further anguish. He decided the best course of action was to be a little vague about the specifics and hope Samir didn't press for further details.

"It was in the last couple of days, perhaps you were absent from the room at the time or otherwise distracted," Pavel said, his tone nonchalant enough to convey it wasn't of particular importance exactly when the event had taken place.

"Oh. So what happened then?" Samir's curiosity was peaking.

"Joshua was sitting in a chair and he spoke to me. I turned around to reply and I couldn't see him at all. I asked him where he was and as soon as I heard his voice, I realised what had happened." Pavel explained.

"Do you think Joshua knew about this gift before the event occurred?"

"Not that I'm aware of. In fact, his surprise was absolute. It took him a while to transform back and I'm wondering if this gift is triggered by strong emotion," Pavel replied. He worked hard to keep his expression neutral.

"What makes you think that?" Samir asked.

Internally, Pavel cringed. Again he had to be so careful with the next few words which came out of his mouth. These thoughts flew through his head in a millisecond and there was no perceptible pause to make Samir suspicious.

"By the tone of his voice, I would say he was agitated about something, but I don't know what." It was only half a lie, Pavel reasoned, and done with the best of intentions. He gauged Samir's reaction and was amazed to see disappointment etched into his features. However, he kept silent and waited, somewhat uncomfortably, to hear Samir's response.

Samir's expression had betrayed his thoughts. He *was* disgruntled; perhaps he thought Pavel would provide much more understanding and insight into Joshua's apparent new gift, rather than a vague notion of Joshua's perceived state of mind. He sat, pensive, thinking not so much of what Pavel said, but what he didn't say. He couldn't believe Pavel would deliberately hide things from him about his own coven yet Samir had a vague inkling there was something Pavel wasn't saying.

Samir also sensed Pavel was uncharacteristically uneasy; as Pavel repeatedly shifted his gaze away in contrived boredom, highlighting a state of turmoil. But what reason would he have?

Like a truck going down a steep hill with no brakes Samir realised why Pavel was being so . . . casually careful in his words and actions – Pavel was being sensitive to his feelings, not wanting to mention Dayna for fear of upsetting him even more. Samir was touched by his friend's compassion, but the thought of Dayna caused him to start sinking slowly back towards the depression which had enveloped him before.

Pavel scrutinised Samir's reaction surreptitiously and noticed immediately when Samir reached his conclusions. He was saddened to see Samir's expression drop and realised the direction he drifted towards, but before he could re-open dialogue, Samir turned to him and, in a quiet voice, said, "Thank you, Pavel, my dear friend. I know what you have tried to do and I'm overwhelmed by your consideration. I can assure you I'm in control now, but you must recognise I need to reconcile the Dayna situation in my own way."

Pavel nodded sagely. "No thanks are necessary, Samir, and of course I appreciate you need to work through your emotions, but I have to be sure it will not be at the expense of your coven. You are fortunate to have a family who cares and will support you through this dark time, but you also need to realise that Joshua still requires some guidance from you, especially with his new talent. I think it caught him as unawares as the rest of us and he must be uncertain about it. You will not be able to effectively support him if you allow yourself to sink into the near comatose state you were in earlier," Pavel responded, his voice gentle but with an edge of firmness. He allowed Samir to witness the concern in his eyes in the hope it would have the desired effect.

Samir pondered Pavel's words carefully for a few moments before responding.

"I understand and concur with your assessment regarding Joshua and you need have no fear that I will slip back. As I said, I'm in control of myself now." Samir's tone was a little too formal, cold even, and had lost the friendliness it usually held when speaking to Pavel.

Pavel was perturbed by the turn of events. He failed to comprehend the abrupt change in Samir's attitude. What had he said which offended Samir to such an extent? He had been compassionate and sympathetic, probably more so than with any other immortal, so why had Samir turned cold? This wasn't something he could ignore.

"Samir, I have to ask, what is with your tone?"

"My tone? What, may I ask is wrong with my *tone*?" Samir snapped.

Pavel frowned. His tolerance level dropped several notches.

"*Excuse* me? I don't much care for your attitude, Samir. You would do well to remember whom you are addressing." The timbre of Pavel's voice left no room for misinterpretation. His expression was grave and his eyes narrowed.

"Well I don't much care for *your* attitude. Just because you're one of the Commissioners, you think the rest of us immortals should bow and scrape and lick your boots, well I'm sorry *Sir*, but you're no better than the rest of us, so don't think for one minute you have any *power* over *me*. And, what's more, if you don't approve of the way I talk, then get the hell out of my home," Samir shouted in anger, springing to his feet.

Pavel, caught completely by surprise, visibly shuddered at the verbal onslaught. Abruptly, he became furious by Samir's attack. His eyes narrowed to slits so his eyebrows became hoods, he pursed his lips and his handsome face transformed into a mask of fury.

"How *dare* you speak to me that way?" Pavel bellowed.

Samir was way past noticing as the events of the previous couple of days tumbled down on his head like boulders in a landslide. He took one pace towards Pavel and, bringing his arm back as far as his shoulder joint would allow, he snapped it forward, his fist hitting Pavel in the mouth. Pavel was totally unprepared for the physical assault and he staggered back three steps with the force of the blow. Before he had chance to recover, several more punches rained down on him, forcing him to his knees. Pavel instinctively brought his arms up to protect his head as still more blows crashed down from above.

Samir had completely lost control of all sense of reason as he allowed his emotions free reign. He didn't think about what he was doing, he didn't even really see who he was attacking, he was a blind man lashing out as his agony became too much to bear.

As Samir's violent assault reached its height, Joshua arrived back in the manor and ascended the stairs. He heard the commotion coming from Samir's room and was disturbed by it. He approached the door and knocked quietly, calling Samir's name. There was no response except for the alarming sounds within. Joshua knocked louder and heard a muffled voice from the other side of the door – it sounded like a plea for help.

Joshua didn't hesitate. Thinking his maker was in distress, he flung back the door and leapt onto the back of the assailant, pulling him away from the figure crouched on the floor. He threw the attacker across the room and heard rather than saw the crash as he hit the wall with such velocity the brickwork bowed outwards. Joshua bent to the figure on the floor and inhaled sharply when he realised it was Pavel being assaulted. He helped Pavel to his feet then turned to face Samir, who strode toward them like a demented animal.

Joshua was horrified to see Samir in such a condition. His maker had obviously lost his senses. Samir's face was contorted with rage, his hands were balled into fists and his lips were curled back over his teeth. As he got closer to Pavel and Joshua, a deep animalistic snarl emanated from the back of his throat.

Joshua knew he had to at least try and distract Samir and he had to think of something fast. It was obvious from his stance that Pavel was ready for the attack this time; his eyes were narrowed, his expression stern and his mouth set in a grim line. Joshua really didn't want to see them brawling . . . or worse. An idea popped into his head. It wasn't a particularly good one, but it was all he had. Joshua stepped forward into Samir's path his hands held forward, as a cop would approach an armed gunman.

"Samir?" Joshua said, in a voice loud enough to carry over the snarling. He tried his best to appear helpless in the hope Samir would respond, but Samir kept on coming. Joshua tried again.

"Samir? Please – I need your help." Joshua injected a note of pleading in his tone. It was as if Samir were deaf, he was so consumed by his rage. Joshua decided to give it one last try – it was about all he would have time for.

"SAMIR, PLEASE . . ." Joshua begged, but to no avail. Samir continued stalking towards them. Joshua flicked his eyes over to Pavel and for the briefest moment their eyes met; Joshua could see his own anxiety reflected in Pavel's eyes, although Pavel's expression remained unchanged. Samir raised his fists in readiness to strike, but both Pavel and Joshua were prepared. In less time than it takes to blink, Pavel ducked low and charged, his head butting into Samir's abdomen, causing him to stagger back several paces.

With Samir temporarily off balance, Pavel brought one of his feet up and tried to hook it behind Samir's knees; Joshua saw what was happening and moved to the other side of Samir to copy the move. Samir's growls were vicious as he realised what they planned and he began to swing his fists indiscriminately, not caring who or what they connected with. He attempted to counter their defensive moves; he stepped forward and tried to twist around, half succeeding in his efforts. However, Joshua changed his tactics at the last moment, managing to catch one of Samir's legs from the front causing Samir to trip. If he had been human, Samir would have landed flat on his face, but with the agility of a cat, he managed to stay on his feet and regain stability.

The three immortals began a deadly dance, circling around each other, two against one. Snarls issued forth from all of them. Using clever choreography and teamwork, Pavel and Joshua started to herd Samir towards a corner. If one of them started to get too close, Samir would lash out, but never with just one fist. He was in fight mode and was using his feet as well as one of his hands hooked into a claw, his long nails sharp enough to gouge flesh.

All of them were crouched, ready to spring at the first lapse in concentration. Samir never took his eyes from his adversaries, little realising they had no desire to hurt him. The hatred in Samir's eyes unnerved Joshua, but he maintained his façade, continuing to complement Pavel's movements as Samir was driven ever closer to the spot where they would launch their counter-offensive.

Pavel moved a little too close and Samir kicked out, catching him in the knee. Pavel stumbled but kept his footing; his menacing growl would have made the bravest of humans cower. Joshua moved a little nearer, taking advantage of Samir's momentary distraction. Pavel copied the move, forcing Samir further back. Samir swiped a clawed hand in Pavel's direction, but Pavel was prepared and neatly dodged the blow.

Samir attempted to move to one side, but found Joshua blocking his exit. A look of deranged desperation flickered across Samir's face, replaced as rapidly by a contorted grimace. The end game was upon them.

As one, Pavel and Joshua executed a pincer movement which pushed Samir close enough to the corner to ensure he could not escape. They pounced at the exact same time, pinning Samir against the wall. Using their bodies in conjunction with their hands, Pavel and Joshua restrained Samir so he was unable to defend himself. A cry, like that of a wounded animal spewed from between Samir's lips, as he was forced to concede defeat.

Pavel and Joshua held their positions. After about an hour, Samir's anger began to diminish; his rigid body started to slump and his expression slowly altered from pure unadulterated rage to that of a broken man. If the process had been speeded up, Samir's face would have resembled wax melting, the change in his expression was so dramatic.

It took another hour before Pavel was convinced enough to ease his grip – loosen but not release it. When there was no reaction from Samir, Pavel glanced at Joshua and inclined his head towards the bed. Joshua understood and together they dragged Samir's now limp body over to the bed and laid him down. Samir offered no resistance and didn't make a sound; he lay unmoving with his eyes closed.

Pavel watched Samir intently, as a jungle cat sizing up its prey. He couldn't be positive Samir wouldn't suddenly attack again and wanted to be prepared in case this was a ruse.

Joshua also studied Samir, but for different reasons. Now it appeared the crisis had passed, Joshua pondered the traumatic events which had unfolded and couldn't help but wonder what would have happened if he had failed to arrive when he did. He had no doubt in his mind Pavel had not been expecting the attack and would have fought back. How deadly would that confrontation have become? These two immortals were probably evenly matched and even though Joshua believed Pavel would only have tried to defend himself rather than wound his friend, would the situation have exploded out of control?

While Joshua understood Samir's anguish over the Dayna situation, he failed to comprehend the attack on Pavel. What had occurred in this room to make Samir react so violently? What had been the trigger point? What had Pavel said or done to provoke such a response? Joshua knew he wouldn't ask Pavel for an explanation, but hoped he might offer one just the same.

After another thirty minutes and Samir still hadn't twitched so much as an eyebrow, Pavel pulled his phone from his pocket and dialled a number. He whispered into it, his lips moving so fast it appeared they were merely vibrating. No human would have been able to decipher even a single word – it would have sounded like he was hissing into the phone – whereas Joshua understood every word Pavel said to Iskra, including his request for reinforcements.

When Pavel ended the call, Joshua forgot himself for a moment, and without thinking blurted out, "Do you really think that will be necessary, Pavel?"

Pavel understood what Joshua was referring to and nodded, his expression sad.

"Unfortunately, yes," he answered simply, "I cannot take the chance of another violent outburst." He turned his head back towards Samir, watching him for any sign.

Joshua studied Pavel's face for a long moment; he saw through Pavel's controlled expression and observed the underlying concern and sadness for what had happened with Samir. Joshua noticed something else about the set of Pavel's features, but he wasn't sure what it meant. There was definitely another emotion lurking below the surface, he couldn't put his finger on what it was.

He continued to analyse Pavel; for some reason Joshua had a strong intuition it was important for him to discover what he was missing here. If asked, he wouldn't have been able to tell anyone why he felt that way, he just did.

In a flash of inspiration it came to him – Pavel was assuming responsibility for Samir's breakdown. Further, Joshua recognised Pavel was also suffering a certain amount of guilt. In two ways Joshua understood this; firstly, with Pavel being head of The Commissioners, he was responsible for passing sentence on Dayna, and secondly, he was probably thinking if he'd handled things better Samir would not be in this state now.

A pang of guilt shot through Joshua as he recalled it was his final vote which condemned Dayna to her fate. Was he as guilty for Samir's meltdown as Pavel, or should he shoulder a greater portion of the guilt?

Joshua leant forward, putting his head in his hands. If he *was* ultimately responsible for this, what sort of man did that make him? Did he make his decision for the right reasons or did he seek revenge for what Dayna had done to Jasna? Was he as hurtful as Dayna or worse?

No, he decided, he made his choice based on the evidence against her. He sat up straight then stood and started pacing the floor. He had to get his head clear – he would be no good to Samir, Pavel, or Jasna for that matter, if he allowed this situation to screw *his* brain too.

Pavel glanced at Joshua and was disturbed by his pacing. The expression on Joshua's face was of a man warring with himself. Was Joshua cracking up too? Joshua raised his head and noticed Pavel peering at him. Joshua raised the corners of his mouth in an approximation of a smile, but it didn't quite reach his eyes. Pavel's brow furrowed as a look of consternation marred his features.

"Are you alright, Joshua? You look troubled," Pavel's voice was barely above a whisper.

Joshua hesitated, debating whether to be honest or not. He didn't want to increase the pressure on Pavel, but at the same time, Joshua knew by the expression on Pavel's face he was worried Joshua was about to crack too. Joshua returned to his seat, making his decision en route.

"I was wondering if I was partially responsible for what's happened here," Joshua replied, gesturing to Samir with his hand.

"What makes you think that?" Pavel's expression had changed to one of curiosity.

"Well, it was me who cast the deciding vote on Dayna which set everything else in motion." Joshua explained his voice also soft.

Pavel nodded sagely. He understood where Joshua was coming from and empathised. After all, it was the same decision he would have made if he hadn't felt the need to disqualify himself. The question in his mind was should he tell Joshua? He knew in his heart there was no decision to make – of course he should.

"If it's any consolation, I would have voted exactly the same way," Pavel admitted, keeping his voice hushed. His expression confirmed the truthfulness of his confession.

Joshua realised he wasn't altogether surprised by Pavel's admission, but before he'd thought of how to respond, a howl of such unbearable agony it chilled both Joshua and Pavel to their core, ripped through the room.

Chapter 38 – Joshua

Movement could be heard from other rooms within the manor, tiny sounds which would not have been detected by human ears. It was too early for the rest of the coven to emerge, but they had been disturbed by the wounded animal sounds blasting from Samir's room.

Joshua and Pavel stared at Samir in horror. He was writhing on the bed, his face again contorted in the agony which pierced his very soul. His eyes were open so wide it appeared they would burst out of their sockets and the depth of excruciating anguish which blazed from them appeared to have been dragged up from the innermost fire pits of hell.

Pavel had never, in his eight hundred plus years, seen an immortal react in such a manner and really had no clue how to handle the situation. He hated feeling powerless; it gave him a sense of vulnerability and he hadn't been vulnerable since becoming an immortal. He was glad Joshua was in the room with him although he *was* concerned at the possible effect the situation might have on him. He would certainly feel more in control when his reinforcements arrived. He didn't have much longer to wait.

Joshua, on the other hand, could empathise with Samir in a way he would never admit; he remembered only too clearly the anguish he felt leaving Remy and the reasons behind it.

Despite the dreadful noises coming from Samir, a different cry of pain could be heard from further along the corridor. It was a higher pitched and softer keening which would have set a human's teeth on edge. Pavel and Joshua exchanged glances, wondering what had happened now.

"It's Erika," Joshua explained to Pavel, "she's reacting to Samir's anguish."

"Ahhh, of course. The poor girl must be really suffering. At least she has Farrell to comfort her," Pavel responded. His expression was rather bland, removing the sincerity from his words. Joshua stiffened and became aware of a slow burn of anger creeping through his veins.

He flexed his hands into fists and relaxed them again as he tried to maintain a calm façade.

"Pavel, with respect, I'm not sure you fully appreciate how devastating this is to Erika. She's in as much pain as Samir, maybe more. Don't you understand she's also sharing your emotions, plus mine and everyone else in the manor as well?" Joshua's tone was as sharp as a butcher's knife, his expression dark and brooding.

Pavel started, taken aback at being spoken to in that sort of tone and by the usually respectful Joshua. However, he did recognise Joshua had a valid point and his comments weren't as considerate as they should have been. He turned to Joshua looking suitably contrite.

"I apologise, Joshua. You're absolutely right. I wasn't thinking straight. Of course, Erika *must* be in terrible agony and I do sympathise. I wish there was something I could do to ease her pain, but regrettably it's something I cannot control. If we can calm Samir then hopefully it will ease Erika's torture, or at least allow her to cope better." This time, Pavel was absolutely genuine in his concern; both his voice and his expression convinced Joshua of this. Joshua's anger began to dissolve.

Then Samir spewed forth a guttural moan which echoed up from a bottomless well of emotion and, at last, he became quiet.

The silence in the room was a welcome relief in many respects. What wasn't so welcome was the frozen expression of torture on Samir's face. Further down the corridor cries of anguish could still be heard emitting from Erika and Farrell's room.

It was getting close to dusk; the rest of the coven would soon be venturing from their rooms. Within an hour or so, Pavel's reinforcements were due to arrive. Joshua was concerned that if he left Samir on his own with Pavel, Samir might get violent again, so he reluctantly remained where he was. A sour expression lay on his perfect features.

He'd missed being with Jasna more than he expected and his arms ached to hold her. Despite his earlier meltdown surrounding his lingering love for Remy, Jasna was part of his future, a big part, and he felt incomplete when he wasn't with her. In his core, Joshua knew he would never stop loving Remy and suspected he would experience further episodes of regret. Part of him worried that, in some ways, he was being unfaithful to Jasna by thinking about Remy, let alone still loving her.

Joshua looked through the walls and watched as Jasna paced back and forth in her room. She had a worried expression on her face and was no doubt wondering where on earth he was. As much as he wasn't comfortable lying to her, he *did* have the perfect alibi. It wasn't a lie really, just a stretching of the truth. He continued to observe her movements, a soft smile playing on his lips.

Ten minutes later, Joshua saw Jasna leave her room and walk up the corridor to his. She knocked on the door, and getting no reply, turned the handle and poked her head around the door. She scowled when she saw the empty room. Joshua's smile widened a little and wondered how long it would take her to figure it out.

Jasna stood and thought for a second and then resolutely marched down the corridor to Samir's room. She hesitated outside the door before tapping gently on the polished wood. Pavel raised his head and looked questioningly at Joshua, who mouthed Jasna's name before arising and walking over to get the door.

Joshua yanked it open and smirked when Jasna took a step back, her lips shaped into a perfect O. He stepped into the hallway but left the door ajar, in case things kicked off again with Samir. He enveloped Jasna in his arms and pressed his lips against hers. He felt her shoulders drop as she relaxed. Joshua reluctantly withdrew his lips and moved them to her ear.

"Sorry about today, love. Pavel's had some serious trouble with Samir and I had to step in and help him. I've been stuck in there *all* day," he whispered, giving her a squeeze.

"That's okay. Of course you had to help Pavel. I thought something was going on with all the noise earlier and then the wailing. How's Samir now?" she whispered back.

"Not too good. He's actually in a really bad way. Pavel's called in reinforcements. I'm not sure what's going to happen – Pavel's not giving anything away."

"Oh. So what are we to do now? Do we go hunting? Do you have to stay here?" Confusion was evident in Jasna's voice.

"Don't do anything until I've had a chance to ask Pavel. My guess is he'll want me to stay here until his coven arrives. In the meantime, do you want to go see how Erika is? She's suffering so much and I'm sure Farrell would appreciate the help." Joshua's whisper was firm yet caring.

"No problem. See you soon, I hope," her voice was full of promise. She kissed him once, briefly then sashayed down to Erika and Farrell's room, feeling his appreciative eyes following her. She paused at the threshold and glanced back at him. She smiled and blew him a kiss before tapping on the door and entering.

Joshua re-entered Samir's room, irritated at being confined when he wanted to be with Jasna. He closed the door behind him, flopped into the chair and angled his body towards Pavel.

"The others want to know what they should do. Can they go hunting or do they have to stay here until your friends arrive?" Joshua's tone highlighted his frustration and his sour expression did little to convince Pavel that Joshua was content to remain there with him.

Pavel empathised with him; he didn't relish the thought of being stuck in this room for much longer either. He wanted time to clear his head and reconcile everything which had occurred during the last six hours, and it wasn't likely to happen while he had to watch Samir's every move.

"Actually, I need to talk to the rest of the coven. I think they should understand what's happened – I don't want to leave them in the dark. Do you think you can look after Samir for a few minutes?" Pavel asked, his eyes beseeching.

Joshua saw the sense in Pavel's words and could not, in all good conscience, deny him.

"No problem. I'll shout if I need help," a small grin crossed Joshua's face as he tried to make light of the situation.

"Thank you," Pavel replied then rose and left the room, closing the door silently behind him.

Pavel strode down the hallway and knocked on Farrell and Erika's door. Jasna opened it expecting to find Joshua standing there, so was shocked to find Pavel before her. Pavel smiled and said, "Hello Jasna. Can you three meet me in the library immediately please?"

"Of course. I'll get Farrell and Erika and we'll meet you down there," Jasna replied, surprise colouring her voice.

Pavel smiled, turned on his heel and strode off. Within mere seconds the coven, minus Joshua, were seated in the library; an air of expectation filled the room. Pavel took a deep breath, looked at each of them in turn then began.

"My dears, I'm sorry to have to tell you this, but Samir has suffered some sort of mental breakdown. He has been uncommunicative for several hours, which makes it extremely difficult to help him. I have called for members of my coven to join us so there are more carers available. Whilst Samir is . . . *incapacitated*, this coven is like a rudderless ship. Samir will consume my time so I will have to appoint a temporary leader.

"I have thought long and hard about this. Farrell, although you have seniority, I'm very aware of how much Erika has been affected by Samir's emotional state and you've had your hands full trying to look after her. As this situation is not likely to be resolved for a few days, I would rather you spent your time helping your partner. As a result, I have elected to appoint Joshua as temporary leader.

"Please do not see this decision as a slight against any of you, as Joshua hasn't known Samir as long as you all have, he is less . . . *emotionally* involved and therefore, able to make unbiased decisions. I trust you will work with Joshua and give him your full support."

They all looked at each other then back to Pavel. They all knew it didn't matter what they thought – Pavel's word was law – but they did appreciate being apprised of the situation. Farrell was the first to respond.

"Pavel, I understand your reasoning, but with all due respect, Joshua is so new to immortality. Do you really think he's the right person to step into Samir's shoes – even if it *is* only temporary?" Farrell's tone was respectful. He looked Pavel direct in the eye and his face was smooth and bland.

"I have thought about this *very* carefully, Farrell. I agree Joshua is still very young in terms of this life, but the coven needs a strong leader. You were naturally my first choice, but when I heard the distress dear Erika was suffering, I knew you would be fully occupied caring for her.

"My decision is not sexist either – in case you're wondering Jasna – with the recent troubles and potential threat which still exists from Dayna's creation, I felt having a male at the head of the coven would help protect all who dwell here." Pavel's hands were outstretched towards them and his voice held no sign of guile. He sat silent and immobile as he waited for their next reaction.

Farrell stared at Erika for a very long moment. It was as if he were weighing up whether or not to speak and defend his claim. He made his decision and returned his gaze to Pavel. He was pretty annoyed at Pavel's decision. As the oldest vampire in the coven after Samir, he was being denied his right. Whilst he was forced to admit that Erika would need more of his time and comfort than usual, he was more than capable of running the coven as well.

Despite Pavel's reassuring words, Farrell was totally against the decision and wanted to fight for what he felt was his. Farrell sat forward in his seat, his expression animated, voice earnest in its persuasiveness.

"I'm sorry Pavel, but I'm not happy about this at all. I'm . . . angry and disappointed you think so little of me, that you believe I can't cope with running the coven AND caring for Erika. Besides which,

Erika has other people who I believe would be more than willing to step in and help her if she needed it and I was otherwise engaged.

"In terms of seniority, it's my right to take over leading this coven if Samir is too . . . incapacitated to do so. I'm the next oldest immortal here and Samir's second in command. I should be allowed to prove myself," his voice was passionate and full of yearning, yet with a subtle sharp edge to it.

Pavel was appalled at the accusation levelled at him. What he'd deliberately neglected to tell them was the other reason he'd chosen Joshua – his gifts were so powerful and useful and no one could equal him. The Commissioners and Samir had decreed that, for the time being at least, the coven should not be told about Joshua's daywalking abilities. But how could he explain this to Farrell and the others without giving too much away?

Pavel knew Farrell had a valid point. He *had* to reassure Farrell – he needed him on side. If he backed down now and gave Farrell what he was by rights, entitled to, he would lose face and his authority over this and every other coven. If he stuck to his decision, he would alienate Farrell and probably Erika too. What to do? Whilst his expression was inscrutable, Pavel's eyes were burning with indecision and a degree of anxiety. If he were still human, he would most likely be wringing his hands and his stomach would have been churning.

As if a little voice had whispered in his ear, Pavel had an idea, one which could possibly solve the dilemma without him appearing to back down or Farrell being upset. For the first time in several minutes, Pavel moved his body and leaned forward toward his audience.

"Farrell, I have to concede you have a valid point and by rights, you *should* lead this coven. However, there are . . . *circumstances* you are unaware of and which I cannot reveal at present. The last thing I want to do is upset you and I ask your forgiveness if you feel I have slighted you. It was not my intention to make you think you were seen as not capable.

"I believe the most prudent way to resolve this is by compromise. What do *you* think, Farrell?" Pavel's thoughts were a tad on the smug side, although it didn't show in his expression. He believed he'd planted Farrell in such a position that the girls would see him as unreasonable if he didn't at least consider what Pavel had to offer. A shrewd move on his part.

Farrell was suspicious. Pavel had him backed into the proverbial corner and he was certain it had been done quite calculatingly. He had only one course of action open to him, but he was damned if he was going to make it easy for Pavel. He mirrored Pavel's posture, his expression and eyes as hard as granite giving nothing away.

"That depends on what you have in mind," Farrell said, his tone cold. He sat unmoving, scrutinising every move, every expression and every flicker in Pavel's eyes, His shoulders were hunched and he was wound up tight.

"Well, I'm pleased you are at least . . . *willing* to hear my suggestion," Pavel retorted, a hint of sarcasm in his voice. He was actually quite annoyed, and also perturbed. He wasn't used to being challenged and this was the second time in this house, in a very short space of time, it had happened. What had changed? It couldn't be because he was here without his entourage or fellow Commissioners – he'd been here alone before and had always been shown the utmost respect.

Whatever was happening, he didn't like it one little bit. This situation would have to be addressed, and firmly, very soon. But now was not the time, not with Samir having some sort of breakdown upstairs plus he was very conscious he'd left Joshua alone with him. Whilst it was a relief to be away from that room, he felt obligated to get back up there as soon as possible. Besides, it wouldn't be too much longer before help arrived. His reflections were interrupted by Farrell's voice.

"I'm listening."

Realising he couldn't prolong this any further, Pavel answered immediately, hoping it may disarm Farrell somewhat.

"My proposal is an either or situation, or maybe you can combine the best of the two." Pavel continued without waiting for Farrell to comment. "I need to have Joshua in a position of authority, in case you *are* occupied with Erika. Therefore, you can either share the responsibility of the coven with him, as in head it together or you take it in turns, one day about. Your choice." Pavel's tone was as firm as his expression and brooked no other alternative being offered.

Farrell sat and thought for a moment. He had nothing against Joshua, in fact he'd become like a brother, so he believed Joshua had nothing to do with this and was as much a pawn in this as he was. However, if he agreed to head the coven jointly with Joshua, his experience would put him in a much stronger position and as such could 'guide' Joshua down the path he wanted to take. In truth, the coven didn't really need anyone to head it as such – not unless something kicked off – so there wouldn't really be that much to do. He made his choice.

"I am happy to share the responsibility of the coven with Joshua." Farrell announced.

Pavel stood and clapped his hands together once.

"I'm glad that's settled. I will now inform Joshua. We will be having visitors arriving soon, so I would appreciate it if you could wait until they arrive before heading out, then Joshua can accompany you." Without waiting for a response, Pavel turned and exited the room.

His timing couldn't have been more perfect – as he exited the library, there was a knock at the door. They had arrived.

* * *

Samir hadn't moved a muscle and had remained silent since Pavel left the room. Joshua was going stir crazy. He began pacing around the room like a caged animal desperate for freedom. As he paced, Joshua started talking to Samir, although he was sure he would get more sense from the wall than from his maker.

It didn't matter to Joshua – in some ways it was cathartic talking aloud about all the things which were cruising around his brain at breakneck speed. He made sure to keep his voice low bearing in mind how acute the hearing was in the house and babbled to himself.

"I'm so conflicted. I can't forget Remy. I love her more than anything and I miss her every day. But she *can't* be a part of my life now. I've already hurt her too much – physically, emotionally – nearly every way a man *can* hurt a woman. In my mind I see her face every time I close my eyes and I want to reach out and touch her . . ." unconsciously his right hand stretched forwards and his eyelids drooped heavily with his words as emotion overcame him.

"I dream of kissing her lips, of holding her body against mine. I have conversations with her in my head . . . or am I reliving past discussions? Oh, I don't know. I try to put her out of my mind but she keeps on creeping back in. I keep thinking about things we did together and places we visited, her cheeky giggle, how sweet she looked when she was sleepy, how she screwed her nose up when she was mad, how she stuck the tip of her tongue out when she concentrated on something . . ." Joshua ran his fingers through his hair and a small sob escaped from his throat. His eyes were downcast and squinted, his lips turned down at the ends, his brow furrowed and his shoulders slumped. He was a troubled man in a great deal of pain.

It seemed he'd all but forgotten Samir was in the room with him and failed to notice Samir had opened his eyes and was leaning up on one elbow.

Joshua continued to drift around the room, not really seeing anything, but managing not to bump into any furniture. His panther-like pacing had diminished in line with the rise in his emotions. He began to mumble to himself again.

"And what about Jas? Am I being totally unfair to her by thinking about Remy and wishing I was with her? But I don't think about Remy when I'm *with* Jas so does it mean it doesn't count? How do I really feel about Jas? Do I care for her – absolutely. Do I love her?" Joshua stood absolutely still, his eyes rolled up as if trying to see into his own skull. Sometimes he thought he did – when he was with her.

She *did* make him feel special and despite his lingering feelings for Remy, he knew he *did* have very strong feelings for Jasna. But how could he *love* Jasna when he still had such strong feelings for Remy? Was it possible to love two women at once?

"Oh, I don't know. I'm so confused." He sank into the nearest chair and put his head in his hands. Samir started to push himself into a sitting position then stopped as he heard the barest brush of feet ascending the stairs. Samir didn't want Pavel to know Joshua's murmurs had penetrated his stupor so he lowered himself back into a prone position and closed his eyes. Joshua had just enough time to sit upright and lower his hands before Pavel strode through the door flanked by Iskra and four of his coven.

Pavel looked calmer and more confident than he had when he left the room earlier. He and Iskra were holding hands, clearly delighted to be reunited. The four members of his coven clustered behind their master, not in a protective way – they somehow knew no threat existed – rather they were awaiting instructions.

Pavel turned to Joshua, who had risen upon catching sight of Iskra. Joshua reacted before Pavel spoke.

"Madam Iskra, it's a pleasure to see you again. I hope you are well," Joshua gave Iskra a small bow.

Iskra smiled benevolently. "Thank you Joshua, I am very well. It is good to see you also. I have been hearing interesting things about you. Perhaps we will have some time to converse before I leave." She inclined her head to the side as she watched his reaction.

"Thank you Madam Iskra, it would be my pleasure," Joshua replied, sincerity ringing in his voice. He genuinely liked the statuesque woman and would enjoy getting to know her better.

"Joshua!" Pavel commanded his attention. Joshua dutifully turned towards him. Pavel gestured for his companions to approach then turned back to Joshua. "Firstly, please meet my friends, Anya, Cora, Mattias and Kristophe." Pavel pointed to each person as he named them and Joshua shook hands with them in turn. With the niceties out of the way, Pavel was keen to address other matters. He put one hand on Joshua's shoulder and steered him across the room – not to exclude the others, rather to ensure he had Joshua's undivided attention.

"I wanted to briefly advise you on my conversation with the rest of your coven. You and Farrell are jointly in command of the coven during Samir's incapacity. I will explain this in more detail later, but for now you need to hunt. They are waiting for you in the library. Come and see me on your return." Pavel's lips moved quickly, but the gentle authority in his voice was unmistakable.

Joshua nodded, turned and moved to the door. He stopped to bow to Iskra then raised his hand to his new acquaintances before walking into the hallway, closing the door behind him. He raced down the stairs, a huge grin spread across his face as he found the others waiting in the hall for him. Jasna's eyes twinkled like sparklers as soon as she caught sight of him and her smile was glorious. As Joshua reached the bottom step, Jasna rushed into his arms and they embraced lovingly; his hungry lips sought hers and the passion which was always lying directly beneath the surface, ignited. Jasna unconsciously moulded her body into his as she automatically responded to him. They seemed to forget they weren't alone until an exasperated voice piped up.

"Get a room you two."

Jasna and Joshua reluctantly pulled apart and turned to see Erika laughing at them. Farrell had an indulgent smirk on his face and his hands were placed firmly on his hips in a Peter Pan type pose. Jasna glanced at Joshua at the exact same time as he turned his head back to her and as their eyes met, they burst into laughter.

"C'mon, let's go and feed," Farrell said between chuckles. He glided through the door and out into the rainy night. The others rapidly followed.

Chapter 39 – Joshua

In Samir's room, Pavel began to recount the events to his coven. He explained about Samir's breakdown in minute detail, reliving the unexpected attack and how Joshua had intervened, little realising Samir was listening to every word, and seething.

Pavel sat in the chair he'd occupied earlier, but he'd turned it around to face his coven. His eyes were hooded and his face troubled. He leaned forward, shoulders hunched as he continued in a perturbed voice.

"I have to admit I'm rather concerned about the behaviour, or should I say disobedience, of certain members of Samir's coven. Earlier, I was subjected to an outburst from Joshua. I have to concede he *did* have a valid point and as such I understood why he reacted as he did. However, he still shouldn't have spoken to me in such a way. I'm embarrassed to admit I was distracted and showed a lack of consideration towards another member of his coven so Joshua was justified in reprimanding me. I can also make allowances for him because of the stressful situation preceding it with Samir's breakdown and violence plus how new he is to this life."

Pavel's voice took on a different quality; there was a perceptible tone of annoyance as he explained further.

"I am much more concerned with Farrell's behaviour. I made the decision that Joshua should temporarily lead the coven while Samir is . . . indisposed. My reasoning behind this was two-fold. Firstly, with Erika being an empath, she has been suffering tremendously through Samir's misery and I knew Farrell would need to allot most of his time to support and comfort her. Secondly, Joshua is extremely talented and with his daywalking abilities, he is ideally placed to protect the coven.

"While I left Joshua here guarding Samir, I gathered the rest of the coven in the library and told them my decision, giving them my reasons. I made it clear I was concerned about Erika and that it was the biggest single influence on my edict, but Farrell questioned it." Pavel clenched his fists tightly and his tone became more vehement as his anger flared.

"Farrell is old enough to know how to behave, to show me the proper respect and should never have questioned my orders. I gave him a sound reason, a *caring* reason for passing him over and he *should* have accepted that.

"I was forced into a compromise to protect my authority whilst ensuring I didn't alienate Farrell so he, in turn wouldn't alienate Joshua. I am trying to fathom whether Samir has lost his grip on the coven, or if Farrell is taking advantage of Samir's condition. The thing is I don't see what else I could have done." Pavel shrugged and held his hands out in front of him, palms up as he made his last comment. He was still angry, but his concern also blazed through his eyes.

Iskra approached and crouched down in front of him, taking his hands in hers. Her eyes reflected anxiety at her partner's consternation.

"Darling Pavel, you couldn't have done anything else under the circumstances and I wholeheartedly agree with your decisions. I would have done exactly the same in your position so please do not vex yourself. I suggest we keep a close eye on the situation though." Iskra's voice was gentle and reassuring. Pavel searched her eyes. Satisfied by what he found, he nodded.

Another voice entered the moment of silence. It was tentative yet musical.

"Pavel? May I make an observation?" Anya tilted her head to the side as she waited for permission, her expression carefully neutral. Pavel nodded, inclining his head towards her as he did so.

Anya's face became animated as she spoke, an underlying excitement in her tone.

"I've listened carefully to everything you've told us and it seems to me Joshua should be applauded for having the strength of character, not only to stand with you and assist with Samir, but also to chastise you when it was, by your own words, necessary. If you think about it for a moment, how can you lead effectively when you don't have all the pertinent facts? Joshua made sure you *did* have all the relevant information so you could do what you needed to."

Pavel remained silent for a long moment, his head down staring at his hands still resting within Iskra's, digesting Anya's words. He could see the sense in what she said and had to agree with her.

"Wise words, my dear. Thank you for voicing your thoughts. You know, I believe Joshua will make a great leader one day."

Samir bristled at Pavel's suggestion that he had lost his grip on his coven. He was incredibly close to a retort, but bit it back at the last second. He remained silent and unmoving. He wasn't yet ready to reveal his hand.

* * *

Two villages north of the manor, Joshua and the others were scouting for prey. The atmosphere was different to normal. Gone was the carefree camaraderie they usually enjoyed and Erika wasn't the only one to notice. Jasna slowed down and gestured to Erika to do the same. They allowed the men to get far enough ahead of them so Jasna could whisper to Erika without alerting them.

"I think the boys need to talk things through. How about we hunt together and let them go off on their own?" Jasna whispered so fast her lips were a blur of movement.

Erika looked into Jasna's eyes for a fraction of a second then nodded in agreement. Farrell and Joshua suddenly realised the girls weren't with them and turned around to see where they were. Erika and Jasna were a few hundred feet behind them. Farrell took one step towards them, but Jasna held up her hand, palm towards him. He stopped a puzzled expression on his face and looked from Jasna to Erika and back to Jasna, searching their faces for some clue as to their behaviour.

"Jasna and I are going off on our own tonight," Erika announced, "we'll meet you back here in a couple of hours." And with that, the girls disappeared into the night without further explanation and before Farrell and Joshua could react.

Farrell and Joshua stood and looked at each other open mouthed, nonplussed by the girl's sudden departure. It took them a couple of minutes to recover from the shock. Joshua turned and glanced back to the spot where Jasna had stood.

"I wonder what the hell that was all about," he muttered, still flummoxed. His brow crinkled hooding his eyes.

"I was thinking the same," Farrell stood with his hands on his hips, clearly as bewildered as Joshua.

Joshua turned back and started walking at a slow human pace in the direction they were originally taking. Farrell followed and quickly caught up. They set off at their normal breakneck speed both absorbed in their own thoughts.

It wasn't long before they came across a couple of victims and satiated their thirst. As they began to make their way back, at a slower pace for them, but still super speedy by human standards, Farrell brought up the subject of the earlier meeting with Pavel.

"Don't know if Pavel's told you yet, but we are jointly sharing responsibility for running the coven. He was quite the pompous ass in *my* opinion. Kept going on about how the coven needed a strong leader while Samir is *unwell* and how, by rights, it should be *me* in charge, but he didn't want you to feel excluded and how he'd thought long and hard before making his decision. He went on and on for what seemed bloody ages. The girls and I weren't asked for our opinions – he'd decided and that was *it* as far as he was concerned.

"Anyway, I just want you to know your age won't go against you and I'll do everything in my power to guide you in how to handle a coven, okay?" Farrell's voice betrayed some of the bitterness he felt towards Pavel, although he tried to disguise it. He barely looked at Joshua while he was recounting the episode and only turned his head toward Joshua at the very end.

"Pavel mentioned it to me briefly when he returned to Samir's room, but as Iskra and the others had arrived, I got the impression he wanted me gone so he could talk to them in private. I have to admit I was concerned you might be angry with *me* over Pavel's choice, even though *you* knew about it before *I* did – I'm really glad you're not.

"I think we could work together quite effectively. I reckon I can manage pretty well without much guidance though – I guess most of it is common sense really. You know, I *would* understand if you felt the need to place more of the burden on my shoulders so you can support Erika more. I can see she's been struggling with the emotional atmosphere in the manor and I heard her cries earlier. You only have to say . . ." Joshua replied. He was scrutinising Farrell's expressions in his peripheral vision as he spoke and became troubled by what he saw. Joshua tensed his powerful muscles, ready to react physically if necessary although he hoped things wouldn't develop in that direction.

Joshua caught a glimpse of movement from Farrell and turned his head to look at him directly; Farrell's expression was as black as the night sky. Farrell's fists were clenched so tight by his side the bones were in danger of breaking through the skin; he stopped dead in his tracks and not waiting for Joshua to halt, hissed venomously,

"I can rule the coven *and* take care of Erika and I certainly don't need *your* help."

Joshua came to an abrupt standstill, completely astounded by Farrell's whole demeanour. He couldn't understand why his friend was displaying such rancour towards him – he'd only offered to help. Was that so wrong? Farrell had become like a brother and Joshua was wounded by the unprovoked acrimony. Making a swift decision and keeping his hands carefully flat by his sides, he answered.

"I think it best if we go our separate ways now. Tonight has been stressful enough already and maybe we need to calm ourselves. I'm going to return to the manor – perhaps you wouldn't mind informing Jasna so she knows where to find me." Joshua deliberately kept his voice formal and as bland as possible in an effort not to inflame the situation further. He stared at Farrell, working hard to keep his expression neutral and not let him see the hurt.

Farrell nodded stiffly in agreement but remained silent. Without further ado, Joshua turned away and rocketed through the damp and cloudy night, only slowing when he was sure Farrell was far enough behind him.

* * *

A groan from Erika forced Jasna to whip her head around; Erika was sitting on a low tree branch with her head in her hands, shaking it slowly from side to side. Jasna, who was perched on the other side of the trunk, scooted over to her friend's side.

"What's the matter?" Worry was etched into Jasna's features as she reached a hand forward and rested it on Erika's arm. She'd thought they were far enough from the manor that Samir's emotions wouldn't affect Erika.

"It's Farrell. Look Jas, I'll explain everything in a few minutes, wait here for me and I'll be right back, okay?" Erika slipped down off the branch, landing lightly on the balls of her feet and took off into the trees.

Erika picked up Joshua's scent and intersected his path some ninety seconds later. Joshua could smell her fragrance and heard her approach yet was not perturbed, only curious as to why she was alone.

"Erika?" His voice was soft, his face displaying puzzlement.

"Hi Joshua. Look, I haven't got long so just listen, okay?" Her lyrical voice rushed through the words as if to emphasise them.

Joshua could see the conflict in her eyes and wondered what had caused it. He nodded and waited for her to continue.

"I'm really worried. When you were talking to Farrell a few minutes ago, I sensed some really dark and angry emotions emanating from him. He's not handling the shared leadership thing very well – he's really angry Pavel originally wanted *you* to lead the coven . . ."

Joshua interrupted her, an incredulous expression on his face. "Wait. Did you say Pavel wanted *me* . . . that's *not* what Farrell said," his confusion was superseded by his rising anger at being lied to.

The worry lines on Erika's glorious face deepened markedly.

"Yes, Pavel wanted you to lead us," she confirmed. "He was worried Farrell was going to have his hands full supporting me and that's one of the reasons he decided you should be in charge. If Farrell hadn't challenged him on his decision, I'm sure Pavel would have stuck to it. Anyway, I think Farrell is hoping to manipulate you into doing what he wants so he's effectively leading the coven.

"It may seem I'm trying to sabotage my own partner, but I'm honestly not. You need to do what you can to block his attempts to control you, for *his* sake as much as yours, otherwise this whole situation could destroy him and I couldn't *bear* it if I lost him." Her voice had become more impassioned as she explained.

Joshua reached out a hand and grabbed one of hers. He gave it a gentle squeeze to comfort her. He knew she could feel the conflict of emotions running rampant inside him; the anger at his so-called friend's betrayal and lies, the hurt that Farrell would treat him in such a cavalier fashion, his sympathy for Erika's plight, and a certain amount of pride that Pavel thought him worthy to lead the coven. However, he didn't want to add to Erika's burden and tried hard to calm himself. He took a couple of deep breaths, knowing time was running out for both of them as Farrell was probably approaching the area where they were supposed to meet the girls.

"Look, I'll do the best I can, okay?" he continued without waiting for an answer. "Don't tell him about our conversation – you don't want him to turn on you too. If you get the chance, tell Jas to meet me at the manor. You'd better get back – Farrell will be at the meeting place in a couple of minutes. I'll see you at the manor later. Now GO."

Erika turned and raced back in the direction from which she'd come. Joshua heard her whisper "Thank you" as she disappeared. He took off like an angel being chased by demons and arrived back at the manor in record time.

* * *

Joshua walked through the front door and was amazed to find Pavel waiting anxiously in the entrance hall. Pavel was relieved to find Joshua had returned alone.

"We need to talk – come with me, quickly," he commanded then set off down a familiar corridor. When they reached the soundproofed room, Pavel ushered Joshua inside and closed the door behind them.

"We don't have long before the others return which is why I've brought you down here. I wanted to tell you everything that happened earlier in the library." Both men remained standing facing each other, neither uncomfortable in that position. Pavel raised his lips into a brief smile designed to put Joshua at ease then continued.

"I'm going to give you the condensed version as I don't want Farrell to know we've been discussing things behind his back. I announced to your coven *you* were going to lead them until Samir had recovered and I gave them my reasons for choosing you. One of those reasons, which you brought to my attention, was poor Erika is enduring unspeakable pain and *will* need the support of her partner until this episode has run its course. However, your particular talents are also a major factor and, although you still have some things to learn about our immortal existence, I believe you to be the best candidate to take on this role.

"Farrell on the other hand didn't like what I had to say. He pointed out *he* was the most senior member of the coven after Samir and should be in charge. Farrell became somewhat . . . *abrasive* and particularly disrespectful. I feared a mutiny and, as I hoped he would support you and give guidance if required, it was important to keep him on side. I was forced to compromise and agree to joint leadership, but it went against my better judgement. I could not allow Farrell to claim a complete victory, as it would diminish my authority as well as hurt Erika and you.

"The compromise I've had to make does not sit comfortably on my shoulders. After Farrell's testosterone-fuelled display earlier, I have serious misgivings about his ability to even lead the coven jointly with you." Pavel sank into one of the few chairs in the room. His eyebrows jutted over his anxious eyes. His expression was one of a seriously troubled man.

"I spoke to Farrell when we went hunting. He told me you wanted *him* to lead the coven alone, but was worried about upsetting *me* and that's why you made your decision. He made noises about guiding me, and my age not going against me – he was a bit patronising to say the least.

"I told him I didn't think I would need much guidance and I would understand if he needed me to shoulder more responsibility so he could care for Erika. His reaction was vicious in his denial of my offer and he told me point blank he could run the coven and look after Erika without *any* help from me. I'd braced myself for a physical attack but it didn't come. I told him I was returning to the manor and left him to calm down." Joshua's expression turned sombre as he recounted the earlier events. He watched Pavel's face and wasn't surprised to see the anxiety make way for anger.

"There's something else you need to know," Joshua continued, not giving Pavel the chance to comment. Joshua began to pace slowly to and fro across the room as he marshalled his thoughts.

"On my way back, I ran into Erika – or should I say I was intercepted by Erika. She told me she's incredibly worried about Farrell's emotional state. She could feel his anger and dark emotions when he and I were talking, and knows Farrell wants to lead the coven alone. She told me what you said to them in the library and was shocked when I told her Farrell's version of events. She asked me to do what I can to restrict Farrell's control over me – she's petrified his desire for his new position will destroy him and she doesn't want to lose him." Joshua's voice betrayed some of his inner turmoil concerning Farrell's behaviour and Pavel was quick to detect it.

Pavel decided to keep his own counsel about Farrell's betrayal. He was surprised and delighted to find Joshua so capable and willing considering the circumstances. He rose and stood in Joshua's path to stop his pacing. He put his hands on Joshua's shoulders in a fatherly fashion.

"Joshua, you never cease to surprise and impress me. You are still so young to this life, but you act as though you are much older. It is as if you were born to be an immortal. I too am concerned about Farrell and I promise you now, I will do whatever you need to help you deal with this situation. You have my full support.

"My coven will shoulder the bulk of the responsibility of caring for Samir which will leave you free to concentrate on the coven. I will expect you to come to me with any concerns or problems which may occur." Pavel's voice rang with sincerity and conviction.

"Thank you Pavel," Joshua responded humbly. "If I may make a suggestion? I can do my fair share of helping with Samir during the day so your coven can rest, and it would prove a useful cover as my coven are still unaware of my daywalking abilities, but we might want to keep it as a backup for when Farrell starts to get out of control. Sending him to do a stint of night-time guard duty as it were, should give him time to calm down."

"I think that is an excellent idea. However, you need your rest too – admittedly not as much as the rest of us – but I really appreciate the offer. Maybe one or two days a week would be good. We'll see how it goes and I'll let you know."

Joshua nodded then froze. He had been unconsciously monitoring the vicinity and detected someone was close by. His senses ranged outwards and as the walls disappeared in front of his eyes, he could see Farrell and the girls appearing at the very edge of the property line. Moving his lips so fast it appeared they were vibrating, he warned Pavel of their imminent arrival.

"Thank you. I am returning to Samir's room now. Spend a little time planning before returning upstairs. I'll see you later." Pavel's voice was as hurried as Joshua's had been. Once he'd said his piece, Pavel turned and disappeared through the door leaving Joshua alone with his thoughts.

* * *

The next evening Farrell and the girls were in the library awaiting Joshua's arrival; the girls sat chatting while Farrell stood by the window staring out. He wasn't paying much attention to the conversation behind him until he heard Jasna mention Joshua's name. He began to listen in the hope of picking up something to use against him.

Erika shuddered as her senses became aware of a change in the atmosphere, but kept her own counsel.

"I think Josh is coping really well with the shared responsibility of the coven, bearing in mind the short amount of time he's been with us, don't you?" Jasna said.

Erika nodded. "Absolutely. He's doing a great job."

A derisive snort from across the room caused both girls to look up. Farrell had turned around, his lips contorted into a sneer.

"Yeah, Mr Wonderful is doing a *perfect* job, without any guidance from me of course. He wouldn't know his butt from his nose if I wasn't helping him *all the time*. If there's any credit being handed out, it should all go to *me!*" His sarcastic tone only served to highlight the anger bubbling below the surface. He turned his piercing gaze on Erika; she gasped at the loathing in his eyes. He pointed his index finger at her.

"You are meant to be *my* partner and supporting *me,* not a fully paid up member of the Joshua fan club. Whose side are you on?" he accused.

Jasna reached a hand towards her friend as Erika's face crumpled in pain.

"Does it have to be that way? I'm *not* taking sides, Farrell." Her voice shook with emotion and matched her trembling torso.

Before Farrell could respond, the door opened and Joshua walked in, immediately spotting Erika's pain and sensing the atmosphere. Farrell strode over to Erika and grabbed her hand, pulling her upright. Without a word, he tugged her from the room and slammed the door behind them.

Joshua turned to Jasna who had a shocked expression on her face and rushed to her side.

"What's going on? Are you okay?" he sat beside her and placed an arm around her shoulders. Jasna recounted the events verbatim and included tone of voice and expressions in the telling. He scrutinised her face as he listened and could see the anxiety this episode had caused.

"Wait here for me – I'll be back in a minute." He stood and after giving her a peck on the cheek, dashed up to Samir's room. He knocked on the door and entered immediately. Pavel glanced up in surprise – Joshua normally waited to be invited in.

"Pavel, I'm sorry to disturb you, but I need to talk to you immediately. It's about Farrell." There was an urgency in Joshua's tone Pavel had never heard before. It grabbed his attention.

"Of course, what is the matter?" Pavel gestured to one of the empty seats. Joshua sat and explained what occurred in the library and what Jas had told him.

"I want to give Farrell some time to think about his actions and have him guard Samir tonight. I also think Erika needs a break from Farrell, especially after his behaviour a few minutes ago. I wondered whether Anya would be prepared to stay with him – her gift could definitely help this situation. We need to move quickly, if you agree to my suggestion, before Farrell leaves the house." Joshua had never spoken so fast – it was a good job he didn't need to breathe any longer or he would have turned cyanotic.

Pavel stood and nodded thoughtfully. "I concur with your suggestion. I will go and tell Farrell while you brief Anya."

As Pavel was about to leave the room, Joshua placed his hand on Pavel's arm to stop him.

"Pavel, may I suggest you let Farrell believe this was your decision? I don't want to inflame the situation any further."

"Very wise." Pavel replied then shot downstairs to find Farrell.

Joshua walked down the hall stopping two doors down. He knocked, and this time waited for it to be opened. Kristophe opened the door and ushered Joshua inside.

Joshua briefed Anya quickly and explained why he had suggested she keep tabs on Farrell.

"It was my turn to sit with Samir tonight anyway," Anya chuckled. "I'm flattered you thought my gift would be of use in this situation though. I'll do what I can to calm the situation."

"Thank you, Anya. Now, the thing is, I can't leave this room until I'm sure Farrell is firmly ensconced in Samir's. He can't know I'm involved in this."

"No problem." She glanced at Kristophe, a question in her eyes and he nodded. "Kristophe will come with me to Samir's room, stay a couple of minutes so it doesn't look suspicious then return here so you can leave. How does that sound?"

"Perfect. Thank you both." Joshua was relieved. He hoped Jas was still waiting for him.

Anya and Kristophe left immediately, closing the door behind them.

Ten minutes later Joshua was back in the library, he gathered the girls and they all left together.

Farrell was in a foul mood. He resented having to 'babysit' Samir and was still hacked off with Erika and Jasna. He'd barely spoken to Anya and was deliberately ignoring her, preferring to sit and sulk.

Anya sat and surreptitiously observed Farrell. He had a face like a smacked behind and his anger was rolling off him in waves. This went on for over an hour before Anya decided to break the silence.

"Are you alright, Farrell?" she asked gently.

He whipped his head round to face her, surprise etched into his features. She had a concerned expression on her face which Farrell didn't expect. Before he had time to think about it, he had a bad case of verbal diarrhoea.

"No, actually I'm not. I resent being stuck in this room watching someone who doesn't move or talk. I want to be out hunting. But even more than this I'm so angry I've had to share leadership of this coven with our neophyte. He's only been with us a few months and he's being treated like some prodigal son who can do no wrong. I've been in this coven for over a hundred years and I have to *share* responsibility with the young pup. It's not fair. And now, NOW I'm told if my attitude doesn't improve, he will be leading the coven over ME! I've done an exemplary job leading this coven, even better than the old man here. There's been no trouble with the neophyte Dayna created and now that bitchy miserable cow has gone, the atmosphere in the manor has been pleasant and calm.

"He struts around the manor thinking he's so bloody special just because he can see through walls, he's got Samir wrapped around his little finger and he's now trying to turn my girl against me. He's the golden boy around here, Samir and Pavel's little favourite who can do no wrong. He's not fooling me though. I can see what he's up to. He might have hoodwinked everyone else, but not me. But what I don't understand is why no one else can see through him and why he's suddenly favoured above me . . ." Farrell ran out of steam and slumped into the chair. He didn't expect an answer from Anya so was astounded when she replied.

"Farrell, can I be blunt with you?" she asked. He hesitated, searched her face minutely then nodded warily.

"To be honest, Farrell, you haven't exactly done yourself any favours, especially where Pavel is concerned. You challenged his judgement and showed a total lack of respect." Anya paused and Farrell jumped in before she had a chance to continue.

"Hang on a minute. Joshua argued with him too . . ."

"Yes, he did, but on that occasion he was quite right to do so. Pavel made a mistake and Joshua was merely correcting him. You, on the other hand had no reason to attack Pavel, you were so . . . *fuelled* by your own ambition you didn't even really consider Erika and her suffering. Is it any wonder you've gone down in Pavel's estimation?"

Anya explained.

Farrell was too angry to speak, but this time, the anger was directed as much at himself as Joshua. He sat there steaming; as clothes in a tumble dryer, myriad thoughts rolled around his head. He'd played his hand badly, he could see that now. He would have to be more careful how he handled Pavel in future.

Anya could see the anger and connivance in his eyes and resolved to change the immediate situation for the better. Farrell was so distracted he didn't notice Anya staring intently at him. Suddenly he felt his hair ruffle as if someone has opened a window and a breeze had blown through the room. As it subsided, so did his anger. He became calm and stopped conspiring against everyone, slumped further in his seat and relaxed.

Samir had heard every word Farrell uttered and was fuming. The lack of respect Farrell had shown not only Pavel, but himself, was out of character and not how he was taught. He wasn't ready to take the reins back yet, to pull himself out of the depression which surrounded and consumed him. But when he was ready to take over again, he was going to deal with this situation decisively.

It was several uneventful days later that Joshua found himself back in Samir's room. There had been a tense atmosphere in the manor and Joshua couldn't help but speculate if it was a lull before the tempest. Farrell had been distant and more reserved than usual, but he hadn't caused any real trouble, other than an edge in his voice when addressing Joshua, and had shared responsibilities fairly. Joshua wondered if Erika had been influential there or whether Farrell had climbed out of his tree momentarily and could see the sense in them sharing the leadership. Whatever the reason, Joshua was still wary yet grateful.

Joshua took the daytime shift caring for Samir, accompanied by Cora. Joshua positioned his chair at the foot of Samir's bed, but didn't sit immediately. He'd managed to acquire a dropper and bags of blood from a hospital the previous evening and now used it to siphon blood from a goblet on the bedside table and trickle it into Samir's mouth. He was very conscious that Samir hadn't fed for many days and was concerned he would be growing weaker. Samir did look quite frail; his bones were more clearly visible through the opaque skin stretched taut over his frame, his eyes appeared sunken and he had markedly aged.

Joshua spent over an hour sucking the blood from the vessel and squeezing it past Samir's lips. When the goblet was empty, Joshua refilled it and repeated the process. By the time Joshua had finished with the second glassful, Samir wasn't as gaunt and fragile-looking. Joshua made a mental note to talk to Pavel about the whole feeding regime.

Glancing over at Cora and noting she was preparing to rest, Joshua returned to his seat. Cora smiled at him warmly.

"Okay if I rest up for a while?" She asked a hopeful edge to her voice.

"Yeah, sure. I'll soon let you know if there's a problem." Joshua chuckled then continued in a more serious tone.

"Oh, and Cora? Don't be surprised if you hear me talking to Samir – I like to think he can hear me and the sound of my voice gives him some comfort, even if he doesn't respond."

"Awww, that's so . . . *sweet*. You're such a sensitive and caring guy." There wasn't a trace of disingenuousness in her tone. She smiled then settled her diminutive frame onto a large two-seater couch, closing her eyes as soon as she was horizontal.

Joshua spent the first three-quarters of an hour brooding about how Remy was coping; his eyes firmly fixed on Samir. As dawn broke, Joshua found himself staring not at Samir, but at Remy. His eyes widened in shock and his jaw dropped; Remy was in a tortured sleep, writhing on the bed with pain etched into her beautiful features. Joshua stared at her for several minutes, his own agony climbing the scale exponentially until he could bear it no longer. He slowly closed his eyes, squeezing them tight against the haunting vision, but it stayed with him. He snapped his eyes open and to his consternation - or was it relief? - all he could see was Samir laying on the bed.

Joshua sat there stunned. Was it a premonition or his imagination working overtime? Was it a message of some kind? His brain was scrambled egg – he didn't know what to make of it. Maybe it was his subconscious planting further seeds of doubt about his relationship with Jasna.

Joshua leaned back in his seat and stared blankly in Samir's direction, lost in the myriad workings of his mind as he tried to make sense of it all.

Chapter 40 – Remy

I didn't realise how restless my sleep had become as my dreams flitted from one scene to another, the one common theme being Joshua. As the sky turned to shades of pale lilac, gold and orange and the edge of the sun peeped over the horizon, the scene of my dream changed once more.

Joshua was sitting at the end of a large old-fashioned bed. He was staring down at someone with a tortured expression on his face. I could see he'd changed from the last time I saw him; his complexion was much paler, his bone structure was more defined as if he'd lost weight and, impossibly to my mind, he was even more handsome. I noticed all of these things despite the agony etched into his features.

I stared into his eyes, which were much closer than I'd first realised. Instead of the usual warmth, Joshua's eyes were colder and so deep it was like peering into a bottomless chasm. In my peripheral vision I could see parts of the room he was in, but then it blurred into my room and back again. The room Joshua sat in was gloomy with dark masculine furniture – it wasn't a room I recognised.

I saw his lips move; he mouthed my name and I realised with shock he was looking down at me. Instinctively I reached out to him, calling his name. I could hear the joyous surprise in my voice followed by an agonised sob as he vanished along with the room and all that lay before me now was a grey canvas of nothingness.

I could hear someone crying in the distance, the sound gradually moving closer until it appeared they were right next to me yet I couldn't see anyone. Abruptly a stab of pain shot through my chest leaving a searing heat in its wake. My eyes flashed open and then I understood, it was me weeping, my heart was shattering all over again. My pillow, face and hair were damp from the tears surging from my eyes; I turned my face into the bedclothes to quieten the wailing spewing from my lips. I was having trouble catching my breath; my lungs were painfully constricted and my chest appeared to have a huge red-hot boulder sitting on it, weighing me down.

For a brief moment I was so overcome with grief I considered pushing my face deeper into my pillow until I could no longer breathe. Then a fluttering in my stomach followed by two sharp prods reminded me that I couldn't wallow or allow my misery to overwhelm me. I had responsibility for two precious lives. I pushed myself up and wiped the tears away with the heel of my hands. Clasping both hands around my swollen abdomen, I crooned my apologies to my unborn twins before slowly raising my eyes.

I gasped and shivered as a trickle of ice singed my spinal cord. Several items flew, spun and jigged around the room; a deodorant can, hairbrush, my watch, various cosmetic items and my mobile phone danced on puppet strings in mid-air. It was like something out of a Disney animation and I half expected to see a cartoon wizard pointing his magic wand at the items. I slapped my hands over my eyes to block the vision, but when I slowly peeled them away nothing had changed.

My brain lurched and reeled. What was happening to me? I didn't want to believe what I saw. Hadn't I been through enough without this too? Was this someone's idea of a cruel joke? Was I losing my mind?

As I sat doubting my own sanity I saw my phone and hairbrush move toward each other until it appeared they were waltzing around the room. A cackle escaped my lips; hints of hysteria could be heard in the tone. I was mesmerised by the strange sight yet I could hear my pulse quicken, my breathing become faster and shallower and perspiration beaded on my top lip.

I shook my head in denial, screwed my eyes up tight and a vehement "NO!" blasted from my throat. A smaller voice in my head chanted a mantra, "Please make it stop, please make it stop, please make it stop."

Time has a strange way of changing; sometimes it moves much faster than you want it to and at other times barely a minute can pass yet it seems hours. I don't know how long I sat before finding the courage to open my eyes once more, and when I did, everything was back to normal again.

I rose and walked slowly to the dressing table, staring at the objects which had been swirling around the room. They looked normal enough; I reached my trembling hand forward and touched some of them with my fingertips. I half expected them to move when my fingers brushed against them, but of course they didn't and this made me doubt my sanity even more.

I turned away, sighed dramatically and padded to the bathroom.

* * *

I was running out of places to search and time in which to do it. I was now very obviously pregnant and in full maternity wear as none of my clothes fitted me any longer. I wasn't able to move as quickly and found myself exhausted much sooner in the day.

Standing under the shower, I reflected on the previous few weeks. Much to my annoyance and despite my best efforts I hadn't been able to converse with the clairvoyant again in Bath. I'd wasted several precious days in that pursuit; I would have been better off if she'd not said anything in the first place, but as it was, her words haunted me on a daily basis.

I was coming to the end of my stay in Perranporth; it had been as unsuccessful as all the other areas I'd visited and as lonely, frustrating and heartbreaking. This was my penultimate stop in what had been the hardest few months of my entire life. I was no less committed to finding Joshua as I had been at the beginning of my journey yet now I was weary and I missed my family.

The holiday Josh and I had shared in Cornwall was one of the longest and happiest in the UK. Maybe that was why I'd left it till last. I was sorely tempted to revisit Land's End, St Michael's Mount, Pendennis Castle and some of the other wonderful attractions we'd spent time at, but I knew I would pay a hefty price emotionally as well as wasting precious time.

I stepped from the shower and began to dry myself, taking extra care around my baby bump. My thoughts turned to the dream which had woken me. I couldn't quite wrap my head around how real it seemed. Seeing Josh staring down at me felt so . . . natural regardless of how different his face looked. It shocked me to see him so pale – he had a year round tan and never looked white – and I couldn't stop myself from worrying as to the cause.

I shook my head slowly and cursed under my breath. It *was* only a dream after all. Or was it? I strolled back into the bedroom, so preoccupied I didn't really take much notice of the clothes I pulled on. Was it possible there was some sort of tenuous psychic link between us? Was it a premonition of some kind? I was tempted to dismiss both notions and yet . . . I vaguely remembered snatches of other vivid dreams I'd experienced since Josh disappeared and they all appeared uncannily real too, although this was the first one where I hadn't been watching Josh through a window. Perhaps that was why this one had perturbed me so much, because it was so very different from the others.

I happened to glance in the mirror as I passed it on my way down to breakfast – boy was I glad I did. My clothes were completely mismatched and clashed horribly. Anyone would be forgiven for thinking I was colour-blind, I'd made such a hash of things. I giggled softly and set about looking more like a mum-to-be than a bag lady.

I reflected on the change of seasons as I rearranged my clothing. Gone were the shorts, strappy tops and dresses from the beginning of my journey, now it was trousers, jumpers, boots and waterproof coat.

My birthday had been and gone with no fanfare and no celebration of any kind. I did get phone calls from Becky and my parents, but although it was lovely to speak to them, they only served to highlight how lonely and homesick I was. In fact, it was the most miserable birthday of my entire life.

I glanced in the mirror once more and satisfied with my appearance, headed downstairs for what should be the last day of my search in this area.

Hours later, I returned to the guesthouse. The soles of my feet burned with all the walking I'd done. I shivered uncontrollably from where the strong icy wind had ripped through my clothing and the driving rain had soaked through and chilled me to the core. Droplets of water trickled from my hair, running down the back of my neck and down my face. I was so exhausted it took all my effort to put one foot in front of the other to get me to my room and once there, I could barely muster the energy to strip off my wet clothes and dry myself.

My brain was like overcooked vegetables which had been pushed through a sieve. The months of traipsing around different streets in different town and villages had left me spent – emotionally and physically. I still had one short stop on my way home and knew I would have to dig deeper than ever to find some hidden reserve of strength to keep me focused a little longer.

I was at an extremely low ebb. I would *never* give up on Joshua, but I didn't know how much more rejection I could take. Seeing the expressions on the faces of all the landlords, landladies and managers of the establishments I'd visited, the pitying looks as they shook their heads and told me they hadn't seen him – it had all taken a heavy toll. I'd suffered some meltdowns on my travels, but this was, in some ways, worse.

As depression dug its claws into me and dragged me down into a spiral of lethargy, I was grateful for the little nudges and kicks which reminded me I had something worth fighting for other than my lost love.

I slowly peeled the wet layers from my quivering torso and wrapped the duvet around me. Pulling my knees towards my chest I rocked back and forth and very gradually the shaking ceased as I warmed. I knew I had to eat something, if not for me then for the twins, but I wasn't sure if I could garner enough energy to get dressed and get my backside downstairs.

As I considered my limited options, I heard a knock at the door. Dragging the duvet tighter around me, I shuffled to the door fully expecting to find someone was at the wrong room. I opened the door just enough to peer out and was astonished to find a waitress holding a covered tray.

"Miss Harman?" she asked.

I nodded mutely, confused.

"The manager noticed how tired you looked when you came in and was worried you might not make it down to dinner so he asked me to bring you up a tray," she explained, nodding towards the door in the hopes I would open it so she could divest herself of the heavy tray.

"Oh, er . . . sorry. Come in," I mumbled pulling the door wider and shuffling back carefully so I didn't get my feet tangled in the duvet.

If the waitress was surprised by my appearance, she gave no sign. She walked in and put the tray on the small round table by the window. Turning back to me she smiled again, revealing perfectly straight teeth – the product of many years of braces.

"If there's anything here you don't like or would prefer to change, tell me and I'll sort it out for you." Her Cornish accent was quite endearing although she did sound like a country bumpkin.

"Thank you." I walked slowly and carefully to the table as she removed the heavy cloth covering the dishes. There was a bowl of minestrone soup, a plate warmer in the centre of the tray supported a dinner of roast chicken with roast potatoes and a selection of vegetables, and a dessert plate decorated artfully around the edges with icing sugar and raspberry coulis framed a vanilla cheesecake adorned with two curls of chocolate. Finally there was a glass of apple juice to wash it all down.

I gaped at it, tears springing irrationally to my eyes. The waitress, who had been watching my reaction became alarmed then flustered.

"I-is anything wr-wrong with it?" she stammered not knowing quite what she should do.

"No, it's wonderful," I assured her, smiling through my tears. "It's been a rough day and I'm . . . blown away by the manager's thoughtfulness. Please thank him for me."

She looked relieved and headed back to the door.

"I'll pass on your message Miss Harman."

"Thank you," I called after her, but she had already left the room and closed the door behind her.

I sat at the table and found I was actually ravenous. I devoured the delicious meal in record time then sat back in the chair to stretch out my full stomach. The babies had woken, probably as a result of all the energy I'd ingested, and were having their own disco dance inside me. Their tiny feet and hands were everywhere; their movements so lively I wondered if I would end up covered in bruises. I placed my hands on my stomach, smiling when the little darlings managed to kick or punch them.

An overwhelming desire to have Joshua here, with his hands on my stomach feeling his children kicking, crashed over me like a tsunami. My eyes pricked and huge fat tears rolled down my cheeks. The urge to sob and rail vociferously against the forces that had separated us was too hard to resist. I clapped my hand over my mouth as I felt my throat close around the wail which was straining to burst forth.

I held my breath until my head swam and my vision blurred. Taking a huge gasp of oxygen into my lungs the pain in my chest eased, but not the agony caused by Joshua's continued absence. I stumbled over to the bed and flopped onto it, dragging the duvet over me. My breathing sped up and became ragged as the emotions, never far from the surface, spilled over. Tears fell in torrents down my cheeks as the past five months caught up with me. Five months of holding myself together with the most tenuous of threads. Five months of rejections and disappointments. Five months of keeping hope and faith alive. Five months of the most excruciating heartache known to woman.

My torso throbbed as the wracking sobs ripped through me. I was aware the babies appeared agitated by the movements they made in my abdomen yet I couldn't stop. Sure I'd cried many times over the period of my search, but this was the culmination of all the emotions I'd suppressed.

I think I knew this would happen if my search proved fruitless, I was sort of expecting it, but I really thought I'd be able to hold it together until I got home. Maybe this was 'round one' and there was more to come. I really didn't know. I'd lived with the pain for ages now; it was relentless, unending, unyielding. It was a constant but unwelcome companion, a consummate bore at a party who attaches themselves to you and follows you everywhere you go not taking the hint to sod off and leave you alone.

Fatigue washed through me. The tears slowed and the wracking sobs gave way to sporadic heaves as my body ran out of energy. A wave of blackness crashed over me and I sank into oblivion.

* * *

My eyes opened reluctantly. I felt groggy and my aching head was filled with cotton wool. I heard a rumble of thunder swiftly followed by an almighty crack as lightning speared across the stormy sky. The sound was so loud it startled me and as my body twitched, the babies awoke and gave me a few solid kicks.

I caressed my bump lovingly, crooning to my little angels in a soft singsong voice. They grew more excitable and I was sure it was due to the sound of my voice. I rolled up into a sitting position then carefully stood. I wobbled a little then finding my balance, walked into the bathroom.

The warm water from the shower eased the knots in my shoulders which hadn't quite disappeared during my slumber. I briefly turned the water cool for a few seconds before cranking it back to warm; it had the desired effect and by the time I climbed out of the shower, I was much more awake.

Eager to be on the road, I dried quickly and threw my clothes haphazardly in my case, not bothering to fold them. I ate a hearty breakfast, gathered my belongings and checked out, making sure to thank the manager for his thoughtfulness the previous evening.

I pulled out of the car park without a backward glance. Within fifteen minutes I had reached the A30 and headed east. Being a single carriageway, I couldn't speed, but it did allow me to appreciate the picturesque hamlets I passed through, even though the dirty grey sky was throwing a serious amount of wet stuff down to the already sodden earth.

Around seventy-five minutes further along, I noticed the Dartmoor National Park on my right. In summer the scenery was breathtaking, yet even though the rain caused the moors to be obscured by a fine mist and most of the colours were dark shades of green and grey, they had a kind of desolate beauty.

Close to Exeter, I picked up the M5 and was able to pick up speed, although not as much as I normally would – the slick road surface and spray kicked up by the trucks made driving conditions hazardous. I had to concentrate harder than normal with the reduced visibility; I could feel my eyes straining with the effort and I began to feel tired. The rain lashed against the car, driven horizontal by the gusting wind. My hands tightened on the steering wheel as I struggled to keep in the centre of my lane.

A brief glance to the side and my eyes caught the sign for a service station two miles ahead. I debated whether to pull in now or press on to the next one. A massive lorry and trailer about fifty yards ahead of me was also having trouble with the wind. The trailer was swaying from side to side across the lane and I had a . . . *hunch*, a feeling of impending doom. I experienced a flash of a picture in my mind and a sizzle of fear snaked down my spine. I slowed further and crossed into the far left lane. The off ramp approached and I signalled my intention to pull off. In my peripheral vision I saw the lorry driver still having problems keeping his trailer under control. I somehow knew what was about to happen and as I pulled off the motorway, I heard brakes screeching, horns blaring and the awful high-pitched keening of twisted metal scraping on the tarmac.

I parked the car, hurried into the building and up the stairs to the walkway which crossed over the motorway to the other side. I only had to take a few steps along the gantry to see the devastation sprawled across all three lanes of the carriageway. My shaking hand grabbed my mobile phone from my bag and I dialled 999.

Reporting the accident to the emergency services, my stomach churned uneasily. I stared at the carnage below me and realised it was exactly the same as the picture which had careered into my mind. How did I know what was going to happen? My spine turned to ice. My shaking legs wouldn't hold me up any longer and I slowly sank to the ground. I couldn't seem to wrap my head around it.

I could hear multiple sirens approaching fast. Turning my head slightly I could see down the motorway in the direction I came from. Red and blue flashing lights tore down the hard shoulder, their sirens heralding their arrival. I watched with morbid fascination, breathing a sigh of relief every time I saw someone get out of their mangled vehicle and walk away from it.

After a while I realised I was rather uncomfortable. I stood up and steadied myself before making my way back to the main area. After a quick nature stop, I returned to the car. Starting the engine, I pulled out of the parking area and re-joined the motorway clear of all the wrecked vehicles.

The rain had tapered off to a drizzle, but there was still a substantial amount of surface water on the tarmac necessitating keeping my speed moderate. As a consequence, it took me much longer to get to Surrey than I'd planned. By the time I found my turn off, street lamps were on and the sky was inky black. I was exhausted – much too tired to do anything but get to a hotel and crash out. I'd got past the stage of being hungry even though I knew I really should eat something.

About a mile further down the road I noticed a sign for a hotel which had a restaurant attached. I signalled and pulled into the large parking area. As I got out of the car I realised how stiff I'd become. I stretched gently, easing the knots from my muscles then wandered into the reception. As luck would have it, they had rooms available so I booked in and after retrieving my luggage and dumping it in the room I strolled over to the restaurant and found a table.

Because I was so tired, I knew I wouldn't be able to eat much. I settled for grilled salmon with vegetables and a glass of sparkling water – something which wouldn't lay too heavy and prevent me from sleeping. I didn't linger. As soon as I'd finished I headed back to my room. The only thing I unpacked was my pyjamas. I pulled them on, got into bed and was asleep as soon as my head hit the pillow.

I ambled down the high street, glancing in store windows brightly decorated with tinsel and fake snow, the occasional display making me stop to look closer. The sky was overcast, but not dark enough for rain. The wind blew my hair in all directions; the cold didn't really bother me. As I carried on, I came across a shop with an array of beautiful figurines artfully positioned on glass shelving. I paused to gaze at the pretty pastel coloured fairies in various poses and the porcelain dragons, some with wings spread, some prone and others seated as if surveying the land for their next prey.

The majesty of the dragons struck a chord within me yet I couldn't for the life of me explain why. A movement in the glass diverted my attention. I looked to see what it was and realised it was a reflection. Ordinarily I would have shrugged it off and returned my attention to the wonderful creatures on display yet there was something about the way the person moved which piqued my interest.

I watched the reflection as the man moved slowly yet as gracefully as a dancer along the pavement. I couldn't see his face at first, hidden as it was by a hood, but then a blustery gust of wind dislodged it and I could see his profile. I gasped in recognition; it was Joshua. Or was it? It looked so much like him, but his complexion was not the light tan he had all year round, it was alabaster white. His lips, in contrast, were cherry red as if he was wearing lipstick. His cheekbones and jaw line were more pronounced – all serving to make him even more handsome. In fact, he looked so ...beautiful; the type of beauty most male models would kill for.

All my observations took place within a millisecond or two when my brain abruptly kicked into gear as I realised it really was him. I turned and called his name, excitement evident in my tone. I saw his head incline slightly in my direction and his expression changed to that of a wounded man yet . . . there was a sparkle in his eyes – the sort of sparkle I used to see when he was thrilled about something. It was short lived. He turned his head back and began to move much faster along the pavement.

I called to him again, louder and with desperation in my voice, unconsciously reaching one hand towards him, but he didn't stop. I started trying to run after him, but the extra weight I now carried hampered my efforts and I could barely manage a slow jog. I kept calling to him until I was screaming his name, but he didn't turn or stop, he kept moving faster until he was nearly a blur.

I could feel the tears running down my face as he disappeared from view yet I continued trying to follow him. I didn't see which way he went yet I was spurred on, another reserve of inner strength appearing from somewhere in the depths of me. I still cried his name as I moved as quickly as I was able; my breathing now coming in short gasps, there was a pain in my lungs from the extra exertion and I was aware of some discomfort in my abdomen.

A loud banging noise broke through my thoughts and my eyes snapped open. I looked around, disorientated to see I was in my hotel room. The banging was coming from the door. I got up, walked over and opened it a crack; an irate man wearing a bathrobe stood there, his fists clenched and his face purple with rage.

"Do you realise what time it is? Some people around here are *trying* to sleep. Keep the bloody noise down or I'll get you thrown out," he hissed vehemently at me.

"I-I'm really sorry," I mumbled, "I had a nightmare."

The man must have discerned a note in my voice or noticed the tracks my tears had made on my cheeks, or maybe even both and his face began to turn back to its normal colour. He paused a moment, staring at me then made a noise in the back of his throat and without another word, turned and strode to the room next to mine. He didn't look back as he entered his room and closed the door a little noisier than he probably intended.

I closed the door, noticing my hands were shaking and returned to the bed. I flopped onto it, desolation coursing through me. My dream appeared so real, but then again, so had some of the others. I sat there for ages running the dream through my mind until I felt tired and cold. I climbed back under the covers and lay down. I was asleep within minutes.

Traffic noise filtered through my unconsciousness and brought me back. I stretched gently then opened my eyes. I was still weary but had no idea why. I thought I'd slept quite well; the dream or nightmare was, for the time being, forgotten.

As my brain started to wake and function, a thrill of excitement trickled through me. By tonight I would be home, my family would be close by and I would be reunited with my twin. I hadn't seen Becky since she surprised me in Norfolk – it was the longest separation we'd endured since birth and I felt a part of me was missing when I was away from her.

Eager now to complete this last destination, I dressed hurriedly and dived into the restaurant attached to the hotel for some breakfast. Less than an hour later, I was in the car and headed towards Esher town centre. I chuckled to myself at the thought of describing it as a town centre. It was a little too large to be considered a village, but way too small to be a town. I entered the outskirts and kept an eye out for the car park sign I vaguely remembered was a little further on and to my right.

I soon spotted it and drove in, parking my car close to the exit. I bought my ticket and displayed it in the front windscreen. Following the signposted footpath, I strolled down a small alley and found myself at the bottom end of the main street.

The blustery wind whipped my hair around my face. I glanced up at the overcast sky; it was gloomy and miserable, but not dark enough for rain. I began strolling down the road, glancing in shop windows adorned with sparkling baubles and other Christmas decorations, stopping every once in a while if a particular display caught my attention.

The cold didn't really bother me; my hands were a bit chilly so I shoved them into my deep pockets. Further down the street I came across a storefront which drew my attention immediately. On layered glass shelves was an exhibit of exquisite china fairies, their faces almost lifelike, their colours a range of pastels and earth tones. I gazed at each of them in turn, admiring the delicacy and skill which created them.

Once my eyes had feasted upon each fairy, my attention was drawn to the other half of the window; on this side were a range of glorious dragons – some with wings extended, some prone, some seated with fierce eyes that appeared to be searching for their next victim.

A strange sense of déjà vu came upon me. I didn't remember seeing this shop when Josh and I had stopped here before yet I couldn't escape the notion that this was all very . . . *familiar*. I also failed to shake the feeling that something was about to distract me. I continued to scrutinise the dragons, but when I reached one entitled 'Freyedar the Fearsome' a reflection in the glass caught my eye.

I looked up to see the reflection of a hooded man on the other side of the road. He moved as gracefully as a dancer as he slowly glided along. A sudden bluster of wind dislodged his hood and I was able to see the profile of his face. The skin was albino with prominent cheekbones, a strong jaw line and lips that were ruby in colour. He was beautiful, even angelic. In fact, he looked a great deal like Josh. Then with a gasp of recognition I realised it *was* him, but he had changed . . . subtly. I whispered his name and saw his head incline slightly towards me. An excited sparkle gleamed in his eye, but his face was agonised. He turned his head away and proceeded down the street quicker than before.

I spun around and called his name expecting him to halt, but he continued on. I began to follow him, trying to run but only managing a fast walk. I screamed his name, desperation and frustration in my tone, but he just moved faster.

"Joshua. Please stop," I begged. Hot tears coursed down my cheeks. I was oblivious to the stares of people I passed. I caught my foot on an uneven paving slab and just managed to regain my balance so I didn't land on the floor in a heap, no mean feat being over five months pregnant. I looked up again and there was no sign on him anywhere. I continued along the road, my breath now coming in gasps from the exertion; my lungs protested, my chest hurt and there was a certain amount of discomfort in my abdomen.

I arrived at the spot where I last saw him and looked in every direction. He had vanished. Disappointment flooded through me, and more. Why didn't he stop? I knew he recognised me by the look in his eyes, so why did he walk away? Had his feelings for me changed? I shook my head at that one. No. I knew with every fibre of my being that he still loved me – the agonised expression on his face had given him away. But still the question remained unanswered. What had caused him to flee?

My heart beat erratically and my core turned to ice. My face was wet and now cold. My head began to swim so I reached out and put my hand on the wall for support. My brain turned to mush and I couldn't think straight. I didn't know what to do. An elderly couple approached me, worried expressions on their kindly faces.

"Are you alright, dear?" the lady asked. She rested her hand on my elbow as if trying to keep me upright. I looked at her blankly, not knowing how to answer. She glanced at her companion and he shrugged. Turning back to me, she squeezed my arm and repeated her question.

I tried to focus on her. "I-I'm not sure. No, I'm not. I-I'm . . ." my reply was choked off as fresh tears clouded my vision and a sob caught in my throat.

Without reference to her husband, she put her frail arm around my waist and steered me back the way I'd come. Her husband came to the other side of me and grabbed my arm above the elbow. Together they walked me back down the street and into a nearby coffee shop. They found a fairly secluded table and sat me down. He disappeared to the counter while the woman remained at my side.

I was numb and in shock. I could feel myself begin to tremble yet it was nothing I could control. The lady stroked my hair, holding my hand with her free one. I failed to notice her husband's return. He carried a tray holding three steaming mugs. He placed one in front of me and before I could protest, put three heaped teaspoons of sugar into it. He stirred it well and pushed it closer before placing the other mugs into position.

"Drink it," he commanded gently. "It'll help." My eyes flickered to his face and I noted the concern etched into his wrinkled skin. I looked at the woman and she nodded soberly.

I couldn't find my voice to thank them at that moment. I looked down at my hands, confused. I wasn't sure I could remember how to pick the cup up. My body felt alien and there was an empty space in my head where my brain should reside. Something in my expression must have given me away; the woman moved my hands to the mug and positioned them around it.

I managed to lift the drink to my lips without spilling any and took a sip from the steaming liquid. It was still too hot and much too sweet. I carefully set it down and tried to voice my gratitude, but I didn't hear a sound. My lips formed the words – well I thought they did – yet nothing came out.

I lifted the mug once more and took another few sips. The too-sweet liquid scalded its way down my throat and began to warm me. Gradually, it did the job it was designed to do and the trembling ebbed. My brain reappeared in my head yet I couldn't make any sense of it – it was still mush. I heard the woman whisper to her husband.

"Look Harry, she's getting some colour back in her cheeks."

"She does look less pale than when we found her, that's for sure," Harry whispered back.

I continued to sip the sweet tea, not daring to let go of the mug in case I forgot how to pick it up again. I knew it was a ridiculous thought – as if I could forget – but I was so fuzzy headed rational notions eluded me. I looked at the woman again, this time making eye contact with her. She smiled gently, her kindly eyes full of concern.

"Are you feeling a bit better now dear?" her voice betraying the disquiet I saw in her eyes.

My head tipped to the side as I considered the question.

"I ... *think* so." My voice sounded ethereal and weak. I tried to smile back at her.

"You had us worried there," she announced, "I thought you were going to pass out or something."

I nodded. "Yeah, so did I for a minute," I admitted. "Thank you for your kindness – both of you."

"You're very welcome," Harry responded, his tone sincere. "By the way, this is my wife, Winnie, and I'm Harry."

"Pleased to meet you," my reply was automatic, "I'm Remy."

"That's a pretty name and quite unusual too," Winnie muttered.

We sat there in companionable silence while they finished their beverages. My brain was functioning again and I had a plan of action. I wondered if I could make my excuses and leave without offending them, but before I could plan what to say I noticed Harry glance at his watch and grimace.

"I'm really sorry Remy, but we have to leave. Winnie's got a doctor's appointment and we're going to be late," he apologised. He still looked worried only now I couldn't decide if it was about being late for the doctors or me. I had to convince him he could leave me without worrying.

"Don't worry Harry. I'm okay now, honestly." I tried to sound positive. I reached into my bag and withdrew my purse. Before I could unzip it, he placed his hand on top of mine.

"No need for that, it's already paid for."

"But you must let me . . ." He shook his head, looking a little offended at my gesture. Not wanting to upset him I nodded and returned my purse to my bag.

"Thank you, so much," I said sincerity evident in my tone. He nodded and smiled. I got up from the table and slung my bag over my shoulder. Hanging onto the strap, I leaned forward and placed a kiss first on Winnie's cheek and then Harry's.

"You take good care of yourself and your baby now, Remy," Winnie ordered, mock sternness in her voice. Her warm smile took the edge from her words.

"I will and thank you again. Bye." Without waiting for them to say anything further, I turned and walked from the café without a backward glance.

I returned to the car as quickly as I was able. I pulled onto the road and headed in the direction I'd last seen Joshua. From the last spot I'd seen him there was only two directions he could have gone, straight ahead or right. My instincts told me to turn right, so I followed them. I drove slowly up the road, passing a sign which showed Clavemount Hall was five miles ahead. The name didn't mean anything to me so I dismissed it. I scrutinised each man I passed, but none of them were Joshua.

I continued to drive until I reached Clavemount Hall, but I failed to spot Joshua again. My stomach had a large gaping hole as did my heart. Had my eyes been playing tricks? Did I really see Joshua or someone who resembled him? No. I shook my head. I knew what I saw. I saw Joshua. A question flitted into my mind and I cringed. It wasn't one I wanted to ask myself let alone answer.

I pulled over to the side of the street and switched off the engine. Crossing my arms over my chest, I grabbed my shoulders and buried my face in the crook of my elbow. The question bounced around in my head demanding I answer it, but I didn't want to – I was scared of the answer. Scared of my reaction to the answer.

I tried to divert my thoughts along a different path, thinking about home, Becky, Mum and Dad, but the damn thing kept nudging away at me. I would have to face it sooner or later, but was I strong enough right now to face it alone?

I squeezed my eyes shut. No. I wasn't tough enough, yet . . . if I didn't confront it, would it impair my driving home? Almost certainly, yes. Was it a risk I was willing to take? No. I took a deep breath and held it in as I allowed the question to gallop rampantly through my brain.

If Joshua still loved me, why did he run away?

My head began to swim and I realised I still held my breath. I released it and my soul fractured opening an immense fissure as the most obvious answer, wearing concrete boots, did an Irish jig on my heart. A pulse of agony ripped through me and I thrust it away denying the answer with an intense fervour.

Joshua *did* still love me. I just knew it. The way his eyes sparkled when he saw me reinforced what my shattered heart held true. But even knowing that, I still couldn't fathom why he fled.

I rocked gently back and forth in my seat, my brain spinning on a peculiar axis as my thoughts bounced in all directions. The more I tried to find an explanation, the more confused I was. The beginnings of a headache nibbled at my temples and I screwed my eyes up, trying to force it to dissipate. If anything, it made it worse. I relaxed my face and massaged my temples, my fingertips travelling in small circular movements.

After a few minutes the pain gradually eased. I removed my fingers from my head and opened my eyes. I sensed I was being watched, but after looking around and seeing no one, I shrugged it off. I gazed at the mansion which lay beyond the low stone wall and iron railings, admiring the architecture and what little I could see of the landscaped grounds. Once again I got a sense someone was looking at me yet I couldn't see anyone.

I started the engine and turned the car around. As I started to drive back the way I'd come, I glanced at the mansion once more then concentrated on the road. I was going home.

Joshua

Joshua observed from high up in a tree on the edge of the grounds. As Remy drove away, a sad longing clouded his features and his agonised eyes turned liquid. He remained sitting in the tree until long after Remy's car had disappeared from view then dejectedly made his way back up to the house.

* * *

Upstairs, Samir sat up. His eyes snapped open and his face became animated for the first time in several days. He had a new purpose – the hunt would soon begin.

Chapter 41 – Remy

The two hour drive back to Essex was uneventful yet tiring. Water lay on the tarmac throwing spray onto the windscreens of the cars and, in some places, vehicles aquaplaned. As I turned off the motorway, I began to relax a little. Only another twenty minutes and I'd be home.

I tried not to think that home was going to be an empty shell, devoid of the love it once celebrated. The notion was too painful to be considered whilst driving. Besides, I had to start thinking more about my twins and their needs. I'd been so focused on finding Joshua, so bound up in my own emotions I hadn't really considered what effect it might be having on the babies. *They need me to be serene, happy and rested not an emotional wreck chasing around the country*, I thought. As if to reinforce my thoughts, a few small nudges in my ever-growing stomach served as a timely reminder and I chuckled aloud. I took one hand off the steering wheel and caressed the area where the gentle kicks had landed, smiling to myself.

The time had flown past since I'd first found out I was expecting. Despite my midriff ballooning like it was its own continent, I still marvelled at the prospect of becoming a mother. It was certainly in the back of my mind for some time in the future – I'd always wanted children – but it wasn't meant to be for a few years yet, not that I would change this for the world, except for one thing. I'd never planned to be a single mother. All my plans had been swathed around my future with Joshua – a future I still believed in and wanted so badly I could almost taste it. But, for now, I would have to muddle through as best I could. I sighed then took a couple of deep breaths as my eyes began to prick with unshed tears. *Not now*, I thought, *there will be time for that later.*

I knew, without having to be told, I'd neglected myself too much in the preceding months and, by so doing, had also not given my babies the best of care. I had to rectify this. I would have to make arrangements to see my GP in the next few days – after all, it was several weeks since I'd had a check-up and my next scan was overdue. I had to start eating healthier too and get more rest – I was absolutely exhausted, physically and mentally.

I turned a corner and was in my street. Eight seconds later I pulled onto the driveway. I was home.

I paused at the threshold, took a deep breath then turned the key and pushed the front door open wide. As I struggled through the door with my case, my nostrils were assailed by the most delicious smell of home-baked bread and roast chicken. I glanced back to the road and realised Becky's car was parked by the kerb in front of the house. A smile lit my face. I should have guessed she would be here to welcome me home and my heart pounded with joy. I'd missed her so much.

As I dropped the case onto the hall floor Becky came flying into the hall and enveloped me in a massive hug. I clung to her so tight, as if gripping a lifeline, and didn't realise I was crying until I tasted the saltiness of the tears on my lips.

"Welcome home, sweetheart. I've missed you so much," Becky said softly, her voice breaking on the last few words. I heard her sniff then she loosened her hold and stepped back a little to look at me. Her eyes were glassy, as I knew they would be and she giggled when she saw her own expression mirrored on my face. The only difference was she'd succeeded in holding her tears back whereas mine trickled down my face.

"I've missed you too – more than I can tell you," I whispered in response, not quite trusting my voice.

Becky led me into the lounge, helped me take off my coat and sat me on the sofa. On the coffee table was a steaming mug of tea and hot buttered toast – she timed everything perfectly.

"Don't let it get cold," she ordered, her expression tried for stern, but there was an impish smirk on her face which gave her away. I chuckled then bit into the toast.

"Yes Mum," I mumbled sarcastically with my mouth full. Becky poked her tongue out at me then disappeared into the kitchen. As I continued to consume the snack, I could hear her open the oven and place a tin on one of the shelves. By the time she returned to the lounge, I'd finished the tea and toast and was feeling a bit more human. She walked over and grabbed my hands, pulling me to my feet.

"I've got a little surprise for you – come on…" the excitement in Becky's voice was infectious and curiosity surged through me. I eagerly followed her up the stairs. She led the way past my bedroom to the spare room at the end of the landing. The door was closed. She turned to me as she reached the threshold.

"Close your eyes." Becky demanded.

I raised my eyebrows and stared at her.

"Aw c'mon, don't spoil it. *Please?*"

A false sigh flew from my lips and I slumped my shoulders in mock defeat. I didn't fool her for one second – she knew me too well. She giggled then came behind me, placing one of her hands over my eyes. I heard her open the door and she guided me into the room.

"You ready?" Becky asked excitedly.

"I guess so," I replied, pretending to be resigned to whatever fate awaited me in the room. She giggled again then removed her hand from my face. I opened my eyes, blinked and then gasped. I staggered back a couple of steps in astonishment as I gazed open-mouthed at the tableau before me.

The room had been completely refurbished. The walls were now a pale lemon with murals of Disney characters on them, two white cots were positioned against one wall, each with a brightly-coloured mobile hanging over it. Against another wall was a white cabinet with a changing mat laid neatly on the top, two white drawer units next to it with a large teddy bear on each. In the centre of the room was a double pram with a big lemon bow on the handlebars.

My eyes pricked causing my vision to blur. It was all so . . . *perfect*. It was *exactly* how I would have done it myself. I turned to face my twin; moving my mouth to try and express my gratitude yet nothing came out.

"Do you like it?" Becky asked nervously, chewing her lip.

I couldn't answer. I flung my arms around her and hugged her tight.

"Can I take it that's a yes?" she chuckled. She loosened my hold and moved back a little so she could see my expression. I nodded, smiling broadly. Just then, I heard a rustling sound behind me and to my left. I turned around and gasped again as my parents stepped out from behind the bedroom door.

Seeing the warm smiles on their faces stripped away the years and I was a little girl again. I rushed over to my mum and dad, tripping over my feet in my haste to reach them, and was immediately enveloped in a double embrace. The tears freely cascaded down my cheeks as, in that instant, the long lonely months of my heart-shattering search caught up with me.

A gentle hand stroked my hair as I buried my face into dad's shoulder and I became aware of another set of arms around me – Becky had joined us in our group hug.

"Shhhh. It's okay now, sweetheart," Mum crooned in a soft melodic tone. The ghost of memories past was paying me a visit; I'd heard those words said in that exact same voice so many times when I'd scraped my knee or hurt myself as a child. I heard Dad clear his throat – he always got a bit choked up if Becky or I cried – but as usual, he remained silent until I was calm enough to talk.

I didn't know how long we stood there while I cried myself out, but I *was* aware of Becky whispering about going to check on dinner and her arms disappearing from my torso. Maybe it was the trigger for my tears to subside and I finally lifted my head from Dad's shoulder, guiltily noting the wet patch on his shirt.

Mum wordlessly handed me a tissue and I took it gratefully. I dried my face and blew my nose, noting both were a little on the tender side. Dad reached out and enveloped one of my hands in one of his and led me from the room.

"Let's go see if Becky's managed *not* to burn dinner shall we? I'm famished." Dad smirked, his eyes twinkling with devilment. My stomach growled in response and we all snickered as we trooped down the stairs following the source of the delicious aroma wafting through the house.

Chapter 42 – Joshua

Joshua sat in his favourite chair in the library deep in thought. He was glad of the solitude – he didn't want to be around people right now – he needed space and time to marshal his thoughts.

Seeing Remy was as unexpected as it was agonising. And having to run from her, when all he really wanted to do was rush over and sweep her into his arms, was equally as unbearable. His heart was as heavy as lead. Wretchedness filled his veins as he recalled the misery etched on her face when she couldn't find him. What was she doing here? Had she somehow found out where he was? He dismissed the notion as soon as it entered his head; of course she couldn't have found out – nobody knew where he was – it must have been one of those weird coincidences. She must have been here for another reason.

Joshua stared out of the window and watched the purple-grey storm clouds gather over the gardens, changing the land from jade to a dark green which was almost black. It seemed fitting the weather became turbulent in tandem with his mind. He was shaken to his core. For the first time since becoming immortal hatred coursed through him for what he had become and for his maker. A small part of him recognised the futility of these emotions – he couldn't turn back time and undo what had been done – his intellect was telling him one thing, his heart another.

This wasn't the first, or even the second time he'd castigated himself for the pain he knew he'd caused Remy. It wasn't the first time he'd tormented himself by allowing his love for Remy to ride thundering from the box he'd imprisoned it in. It wasn't even the first time he'd sat in this chair and refereed between his emotions and what he knew to be right and proper. But it *had* to be the last.

Joshua knew he couldn't continue to live a life of half-truths any longer. He wasn't being fair to Jasna or himself. A deep frown creased his forehead, his eyes obscured under heavy brows. He inhaled deeply, closed his eyes and held it for a few seconds then let it out slowly. Joshua opened his eyes, his features smoothed as his muscles relaxed yet his mouth was set in a determined shape.

Enough was enough. Remy had to be permanently locked away in his heart if he was to find any kind of peace. He had to resist the temptation to peek into the box for to do so would be his undoing. He had hundreds, if not thousands of years stretching before him; Joshua knew he would not survive if he wasn't strong enough now to do what had to be done. He closed his eyes and allowed himself one last gaze upon the adored face in his mind before he pushed it into the box in his heart, firmly locked it and threw away the key.

The sky was deep ebony when Joshua and Jasna strolled hand in hand into the library. Farrell stood in front of the fireplace, his arms folded and an unfathomable scowl marred his handsome face. An obviously perplexed Erika sat by the window, casting surreptitious glances at her beloved. Before Joshua and Jasna had the opportunity to greet their friends, Farrell turned on them.

"We've been waiting ages for you two – I will not tolerate tardiness, you should have come down over an hour ago," Farrell snarled, leaning forwards in an aggressive stance, his hands curled into claws.

The abruptness of Farrell's attack shocked Joshua – shocked and angered him. Jasna stiffened at his side then wordlessly moved across the room to join Erika. The two women held hands, united in their discomfort; the atmosphere in the room so tangible they could taste it.

Joshua planted himself directly in front of Farrell, defiantly placing his hands on his hips, top lip curling into a sneer.

"Come again?"

Farrell growled at Joshua, his face a mask of fury.

"How dare you question me? *I* lead this coven while Samir is indisposed – you *will* obey me and treat me with the same respect you would him."

An incredulous expression momentarily flitted across Joshua's face before being replaced by a glare as icy as his voice.

"Are you suffering from memory loss, Farrell? Pavel decreed we were to *jointly* lead the coven and as such, I will *not* be spoken to in that tone."

"*I* am the most senior member of this coven after Samir and you *will* recognise my superiority," Farrell's voice thundered through the room, causing the light fittings to quiver. Erika and Jasna cringed into their chairs, not in fright but disbelief. Erika was in agony as the emotions assaulted her body in blows, but Farrell was too far gone to even think about his partner.

"The hell I will," Joshua retorted, his tone causing a blizzard of air to blast through the room. His hands balled into fists so tight his bones jutted through his skin.

Farrell's expression contorted once more, rearranging his features into that of a deranged psychopath. Erika cried out as the torture assailed her in waves and Jasna put her arms around her friend's shoulders to try to comfort her. Farrell was completely oblivious. With a shriek of pure rage, his hands moved faster than a cobra's strike to encircle Joshua's throat.

Joshua reacted instinctively. He knew Farrell had the strength to literally rip his head off and it would be the end of him. One hand streaked up to grab Farrell's throat while the other grabbed one of Farrell's wrists and gripped it in a crushing vice, a guttural growl ripping from his throat. Joshua brought his knee upwards connecting with the area between Farrell's legs then used the same leg to swipe at Farrell's ankles, sweeping his legs from under him. Farrell snarled like a savage wolf as both men fell on the floor in a tangled heap, neither willing to let the other have the advantage.

Farrell was the first to recover, using his strength to manoeuvre himself on top of Joshua he released the free hand from around Joshua's throat and punched him in the face. Joshua roared, not in pain but in fury. He pushed against the floor with his feet, leaving a divot in the wood and dislodged Farrell who fell onto his side. The two men wrestled for several minutes, both snarling and growling as they tried to gain advantage over the other. Joshua eventually gained the upper hand, positioned himself over Farrell and pinned him against the floor in an effort to restrain him. Farrell struggled like a madman, roaring and snapping. A whimper from across the room distracted Joshua's focus; Farrell was quick to seize the opportunity and in the blink of an eye, had Joshua prone under him once more. He thumped Joshua in the face again and as he brought his arm back to repeat the blow, a new and unexpected voice ripped through the room.

"FARRELL!"

Farrell froze in shock. Two strong hands grabbed his shoulders and yanked him backwards; Farrell released his hold on Joshua and found himself flat on his back, staring up into Samir's furious face. Pavel, who had walked into the room directly behind Samir, went straight to Joshua and helped him to his feet.

"Are you alright, Joshua?" Pavel's concerned voice matched his eyes.

"Yeah, I'm okay, thank you," Joshua replied, absentmindedly rubbing his throat. Bloodlust ignited by anger still coursed through his veins. On a very basic level, he knew if he so much as glanced at Farrell now, he would lose control and attack him so Joshua was careful to keep his eyes firmly on Pavel's face.

Pavel flicked his eyes towards Erika and Jasna. He could immediately see Erika's distress. He put his hand on Joshua's shoulder and gave a gentle squeeze.

"Get the ladies out of here – now," Pavel demanded in a quiet but steely voice. "Take them hunting – Samir and I will deal with this. We will speak to you upon your return."

Joshua nodded and took a step towards the distraught women. They heard Pavel's command, and immediately complied. Within three seconds they had left the manor and were swallowed up by the bitterly cold night.

Their feet moved so fast across the terrain they barely touched the ground. Erika had Joshua on one side, Jasna on the other and they each held one of her hands. They didn't stop until they were over twenty-five miles from the manor house, although the journey only took them a handful of minutes.

Halting in a wooded area on the outskirts of a small town, Joshua steered them to a copse surrounded by majestic oaks which appeared to be hundreds of years old judging by the girth of their trunks. Jasna pulled Erika down to sit beside her while Joshua crouched in front of her.

"How are you feeling?" Joshua asked his worried eyes boring into hers.

Erika leaned back against the tree and hesitated as she struggled to find the words. The others patiently remained silent.

"The . . . *pain* has lessened, but not the memory of it . . ." Erika tilted her head to one side, brows knotted in concentration as she tried to articulate in a meaningful way. "Trying to deal with my emotions on top of everyone else's is enough of a challenge, but when it's intensified to the level it was in the library, it becomes unbearable. It causes me physical *and* mental pain. And even though it eases the further I am removed from it, the echo of it remains for much longer. That's bad enough under normal circumstances, but today . . ." her voice tapered off as her mind recalled Farrell's behaviour. Anguish filled her eyes and she pressed her lips together so tightly it appeared all she had was a thin slash for a mouth.

"I'm so sor . . ." Joshua began, but Erika cut across him.

"Joshua, *stop*. You have nothing to apologise for – unlike Farrell." Erika's voice broke over her partner's name and it came out sounding more of a sob. Her face crumpled and she buried it in her hands, pulling her knees up as if to hide further. Her body heaved with the tears she couldn't shed.

Jasna wrapped her arms around Erika and held her close, crooning softly to her until she began to calm down. When her body was still, Joshua reached forward and gently pulled her hands away from her face. Gazing at the anguish in her eyes, he knew he had to be extremely careful what he said. Holding her hands in one of his, he placed one finger under her chin and softly tilted her face upwards so she had to look him directly in the eye.

"Erika, listen to me and please don't interrupt until I'm done, okay?" Joshua's voice had a soft, soothing quality, bordering on hypnotic – the type of voice one might expect an angel to possess. Erika nodded mutely so he continued.

"I can't honestly say I know how you're feeling because I don't. However, I *can* imagine how the situation with Farrell earlier impacted on you. I can only apologise for my part in that, even though I didn't start it. I have no idea why . . . actually no, that's not quite true – I *do* have an inkling why Farrell felt he should exert his authority.

"I can't fathom why he would *dare* go against Pavel's instructions or what possessed him to start on me, but I'm sure he didn't mean for you to get hurt by it. He loves you so much and he wouldn't deliberately cause you pain. I can only guess he was hurt by Pavel's edict that he share leadership of the coven with the *new boy* and I can understand that. But it doesn't excuse his behaviour.

"Now Samir appears to have recovered enough to regain control, this shouldn't happen again, but . . . I *will* be keeping out of Farrell's way for a while – at least until I'm convinced he's calmed down and put this whole episode behind him.

"Jasna and I will be there for you whenever you need us and we'll help you all we can. I think it would be . . . *prudent* to keep my distance. Just promise me you'll come to us if you need help – please?"

Erika was touched by Joshua's sincerity and compassion. Joshua was far more generous towards Farrell than he deserved. She smiled sadly and nodded.

"Thank you, Joshua. You have been far kinder than most immortals would in your position." She turned towards Jasna so she could address them both.

"I don't know what finally triggered Farrell's outburst today, but I've sensed something was brewing for a day or two – I'm so . . .

mortified you paid such a heavy price. I promise I'll come to you both if I need help or to . . . escape for a while. I'm not sure what else I can say right now except, thank you – both of you – for your support. You really are true friends and it means *so* much."

Jasna gave Erika another hug then got to her feet.

"I'm so thirsty. Feel up to hunting?" Jasna held out her hands to both of them and smiled a mischievous twinkle in her eyes.

Erika giggled as she watched Jasna waggle her eyebrows then reaching for her hand, allowed Jasna to pull her up. Joshua chuckled, got to his feet and then he too took Jasna's hand.

Silently they set off towards town to find sustenance.

* * *

Joshua and the girls returned to the manor well before dawn; the cloudless velvet sky had caused the temperature to plummet and the land was covered with a thick frost, not that they felt the cold. As they reached the main door, Joshua halted in front of them then turned to face Erika.

"Are you okay?"

Erika took a deep breath and let it out slowly through her nostrils.

"Yes thanks. I'm a bit apprehensive – I can still sense an undercurrent, but compared with the atmosphere earlier, it's manageable."

Joshua scrutinised her exquisite face, but saw nothing to indicate she was telling anything but the truth.

"Are you sure?" Jasna asked, concern dripping through the words.

Erika looked Jasna directly in the eyes and nodded a small smile on her lips.

When the girls turned back to Joshua he had his back to them, both arms stretched out to the sides to stop them from entering. He peered through the walls to survey the terrain – he didn't want them to walk into any nasty surprises.

"Samir is waiting for us in the library. He *appears* to be quite calm and thoughtful . . . Pavel is in the room two doors down to the right of the library with Farrell."

Before Joshua had a chance to continue his report, Erika butted in.

"How does Farrell look?"

"How does Farrell feel?" Joshua shot back at her without altering his position.

"There's still some anger there, but nowhere near as . . . *fierce* as before. It's more of a slow burn now. But there's something else . . . I'm trying to get a handle on it . . ." Erika faltered, narrowing her eyes in concentration. She bowed her head; unconsciously her shoulders dipped forwards until she appeared hunched and her thumbs stroked along the tips of her fingers as if crushing something into a fine powder.

The others waited in silence for Erika to continue; Joshua maintained his observation of movements within the manor, particularly Farrell – he was trying to get his *own* handle on him.

"He seems sort of . . . *resigned* to whatever has happened in our absence yet there's an edge to him – I can't quite nail it," Erika spoke in a low voice.

Joshua snorted – an uncharacteristic sound for him.

"Try defiance – I've just seen a flash of it in his eyes. This isn't over yet, I'm sure of it." He turned around to face the girls; a grim expression marred his handsome features. "I don't know when we'll get another opportunity for the three of us to talk freely and we can't stay out here much longer – Samir knows we're back.

"Erika, I want to assure you I hold no grudge against Farrell for his actions earlier – I *still* look upon him as a brother. BUT, I *will* be keeping my distance for a while. I'm not going to put either of us in the position where something could kick off again.

"I don't think for one minute Farrell would turn on you of all people, but . . . if you get worried or you need to put some distance between you, well . . . we're here if you need us, okay?"

Erika dropped her eyes for a moment. When she raised them again, they shone with gratitude. She turned to Jasna, threw her arms around her and gave her a hug, whispering "Thank you" in her ear. Erika then turned to Joshua and took a step closer to him.

"Joshua, you're a better friend to Farrell than he deserves right now. Thank you for your kind words and your support – it means more to me than I can say," Erika said in a humbled tone. She hugged him quickly then stepped away.

Joshua smiled warmly at her then reaching for Jasna's hand, said, "We'd better go in. Ready?"

Both girls nodded. Joshua opened the door with his free hand and they stepped inside.

"Farrell has been severely rebuked for his attack on Joshua earlier. He has been out hunting with Pavel and myself and is now with Pavel down the hall. He has been very forthcoming about the reasons for his behaviour and they basically stem from his inability to accept joint leadership of the coven. He believes as the most senior member of our little family he alone should have been appointed leader while I was . . . *indisposed*. I *can* appreciate his point of view. However, as Pavel decreed both Farrell and you, Joshua, were to jointly lead, I would have expected him to look for ways to achieve a status-quo rather than attempting to thwart your efforts and over-assert his authority.

"Farrell informed me the reason the fight started was as a result of your defiance and attitude, Joshua. I would very much like to hear your version of events before I make any further judgements." Samir stared directly at Joshua and waited for a response.

Joshua recounted the entire episode with complete accuracy; his face a mask of tension and sobriety. He even imitated the voice and tone Farrell used so accurately that Jasna looked to see if he'd entered the room. As he reached the end of his account, Joshua's face softened a little around the eyes and mouth. He leaned forward in his seat, an earnest yet contrite tone in his voice.

"Samir, I'm so sorry if my part in this has displeased you in any way. I allowed my temper to get the better of me when perhaps I should have shown restraint, but I wasn't . . . *prepared* for a verbal attack as soon as I walked into the room or to have Farrell talk down to me the way he did. As far as the physical fight is concerned, I only tried to defend myself and restrain Farrell – I certainly didn't start it and wouldn't have done so."

Samir stood silent and thoughtful; his hooded eyes stared towards the window seeing nothing, his lips pursed. Joshua's statement conflicted somewhat with Farrell's account; Samir didn't want to think either of them would lie to him or distort the truth, but clearly that wasn't the case. He considered asking the girls, but would they each take the side of the one they were partnered with?

Samir let his mind wander along a different path – who had the most to gain by not being completely honest? In some ways it could be Joshua; he was the newest member of the coven and, from what he'd seen of him so far, wouldn't want to be alienated. However, Farrell was desperate to cement his position as number two in the coven. He had already admitted he was aggrieved at having to share responsibility with Joshua, but was he desperate enough to twist the truth?

He turned his mind back to the conversation he'd overheard between Farrell and Anya and replayed it. He recalled the bitterness in Farrell's voice, his anger and the disrespectful way he spoke about Pavel and himself.

Samir's musings led him to one conclusion yet he couldn't prove it. How could he get to the truth? Did he have to engineer another confrontation to get proof – one he could observe unseen and, if necessary, be close enough to control should the need arise? Could he take the risk? Was there another way? He flicked his eyes briefly towards Joshua and away again. With his decision made, Samir turned back to Joshua and the girls.

"Thank you for the information, Joshua. I've heard all I need to . . . for now. You may go if you so wish – I need to confer with Pavel. Excuse me," Samir's tone was more formal than usual and his expression aloof. He didn't wait for comments, he turned and swept from the room, leaving the others gawking after him.

Chapter 43 – Remy

As I lounged on the sofa nursing a steaming mug of tea, I watched huge fluffy white flakes float past the window, landing on the already frozen ground. I was glad I didn't have to go out – I hated driving in snow. But sitting in the warmth of my lounge, I loved watching how the landscape changed and was made Christmas card pretty.

Christmas had long since passed and my due date of 15th March had been and gone. I was now five days overdue – extremely unusual when carrying twins, or so I was told. It would be just my luck to go into labour now while there was over a foot of snow on the ground, I was alone and an ambulance would have difficulty reaching me. Although I was excited, impatient even, to actually see and hold my babies, the thought of raising them without Joshua still filled me with an all-consuming aching grief. I thought of him every day and every day I lamented his absence. I hadn't given up hope of finding him, but in my current condition there was little I could do. It was as frustrating as it was agonising.

Many strange things had happened since I returned home. My dreams had become so vivid I believed I was actually there – until I woke up. The weird dreams I had when I was out searching for Joshua were quite tame in comparison; back then I appeared to be looking through windows watching things unfold – I was on the outside looking in – whereas now I was on the inside, *actually in the room*. I could detect very sweet yet unusual scents, the memory of which stayed with me for a few hours after I awoke. Sometimes I was touched by the emotions of others in the rooms. Occasionally I woke up screaming, but I could never remember why. I only knew that when this happened, I awoke with pains so acute in my chest I could readily believe I was being repeatedly stabbed through the heart.

Why were these dreams so much more realistic? Why could I detect aromas and be affected by emotions? Why did I sense a tenuous connection to the strangers? Why was I having them at all?

Every dream featured Joshua, always surrounded by stunningly gorgeous men and women with alabaster skin and fierce mesmerising eyes. It was always the same crowd involved; sometimes there was only one or two with him, other times the whole group. One girl in particular was always there, close by his side; she looked at Joshua with adoration and this angered me beyond description. *He was MINE, not hers!* Sometimes their movements were so rapid, I would blink and find someone across the other side of the room, or sitting when they had been standing, or one of them had left completely. The maddening thing was I still couldn't hear conversations – maybe things would've made more sense if I could. The strangers, and Joshua's lips moved so quickly it was impossible to try to make out the words; all I could ever hear was either a gushing sound as if I were in a wind tunnel or the type of burbling noise you hear in your ears when you are under water. More frustrations. How the heck could they move so fast? Why could I never hear any dialogue? Perhaps more to the point, why were they always with him? Who were they? Did he live with them?

So many unanswered questions. *Too* many.

I struggled to get to my feet – if this went on for much longer I'd need a block and tackle to get me in and out of bed and off the sofa. As it was I didn't dare take a bath if I was alone in the house. I waddled into the kitchen to refill my mug then returned to the lounge. The snow still fell thick and fast, passing the window like a billowing white sheet; it all but obliterated the houses on the opposite side of the road. I was in a cocoon, the only thing disturbing the absolute silence was my pounding heart.

Weariness seeped through me – ridiculous considering I'd done naff-all most of the day. I placed my half-drained mug on the coffee table, lay back and closed my eyes. As I began to drift on a cloud of sleepiness, a number of sharp twinges in my lower back, followed by two sharp kicks in my humungous abdomen startled me.

My eyes opened in a flash. All traces of drowsiness instantly vanished. I was on high alert. My bag for the hospital had been sitting packed and ready in the hallway for over a fortnight. My phone was within easy grabbing distance. Was this the start of labour? I lay motionless, not daring to move, waiting for something new to happen. The babies were moving around, or trying to; my stomach sort of . . . undulated as tiny fists, elbows, knees and feet caused bumps to temporarily appear.

I stroked my hands over my belly and crooned softly to the twins.

"Pretty babies. I'm sorry you haven't got room to move. It shouldn't be too much longer now. I can't wait to meet you and hold you both in my arms. I love you so much, my little ones."

Two little nudges against my hand caught me by surprise. Could they really hear me? Could they understand what I was saying to them? One way to find out . . .

"Can you hear my voice, little ones?"

Two more nudges against my hand confirmed it. At first I was too stunned to speak then as I recovered I let out a whoop of joy and excitement.

"Wow. You can hear me!" I yelled. The loudness of my voice must have startled the twins and I received two hefty kicks for my trouble. I chuckled to myself then mumbled "Sorry my darlings," in a whisper as soft as a summer breeze.

When I finally glanced up at the window, the sky had changed to a dark, dirty grey colour. Either we were in for one hell of a storm or it was later than I realised. I turned my head to look at the clock – it was a little after 4pm – Becky would be here in a few minutes.

I gradually heaved my bloated torso off the sofa and turned towards the kitchen. As I took my first steps, a peculiar tingling sensation ran from the base of my skull down to the bottom of my spine and I sensed I was being watched. I whipped my head around towards the window and I saw a pair of eyes staring back at me. In the time it took for me to blink they disappeared. How odd. I was rooted to the spot, gazing at the exact same place on the window waiting for the eyes to reappear. My brain tried to assimilate what I'd seen and it swerved between incredulity and dread. Suddenly, in my peripheral vision, I saw movement in the bottom right corner of the frame. My eyes zeroed in, but whatever it was had gone. I hesitated then shuffled to the window and peered out. Visibility was poor through the unrelenting snow, but the light from the streetlamps helped a little. I scanned the vicinity but saw no one. I looked for footprints in the front garden – there were none.

Shaking my head, I turned and made my way back to the kitchen. I could have sworn . . . I couldn't shake the feeling though and cold fear snaked through me, making my hands tremble. I was in no position to protect myself, I couldn't run. Moving on autopilot I filled the kettle and put it on to boil. My eyes swept around the room looking for something, anything I could use as a weapon.

The noise of a car engine interrupted my search. Relief blew through my veins like a shot of adrenalin – Becky was home. I hurried to the door as fast as my bulk would allow and flung it open, not considering for one second that whoever was watching was still out there. Becky trudged up the path, fighting her way through the snow which reached the top of her boots. She stomped on the mat dislodging snow from her wellies then stepped through the door, closing it quickly behind her.

I flung my arms around her; it wasn't until this very moment I realised part of my reaction to my unseen voyeur was because I was subconsciously worried sick about Becky driving in these awful conditions. Now she was here, safe and sound, my earlier fears began to drain away. Perhaps it was my imagination playing tricks on me. Perhaps my anxieties for Becky's safety caused me to see things which weren't really there. But then again, I still had a nagging awareness that I really *did* see those eyes.

"Well hello you. This is a lovely greeting," Becky chuckled. She kissed the top of my head. I let her go and took a small step back.

"You complaining?" I raised one eyebrow at her, put my hands on my hips and scowled, pretending to be peeved.

She looked at my expression and cracked up. "Hell, no."

I couldn't help but laugh with her. It was therapeutic after the afternoon I'd had.

Becky removed her boots, coat, scarf and gloves and put them in the hall cupboard then followed me into the kitchen where I was pouring cups of tea.

She perched on the worktop and watched me.

"So, how've you been today? How're the little ones?"

I didn't raise my head to look at her when I answered – pouring scalding tea over my hand was not my idea of fun.

"We've been okay. I had some sharp twinges in my back earlier, but nothing since. Oh, hey, you'll never guess what else . . ." I continued without waiting for Becky to answer. I turned towards her, excitement twinkling in my eyes. "They can hear my voice," I blurted out breathlessly.

"Yeah? How do you know?" Becky tilted her head to the side.

"Well, I was talking to them and they nudged my hand. So I asked them if they could hear me and they nudged my hand again, as if they were saying 'yes'. It was *amazing*." I bounced on the balls of my feet with delight.

"Wow," Becky said softly. She reached for her tea and took a sip, wincing as the hot liquid scalded her tongue.

I grabbed my mug and headed to the lounge, Becky following behind me. I'd only taken three steps when a spear of agonising pain shot across my stomach. The mug slipped from my grasp shattering on the floor, the hot liquid splashed my feet, but I didn't notice. As my hands flew to my abdomen, another wave of agony pulsed through me and I inhaled sharply.

"Remy? What is it? Are you alright?" Becky came around to stand in front of me, worry etched into her features. She placed her free hand on my arm.

"Yeah," I panted breathlessly. "Just a couple of major twinges, but much sharper than before."

"Can you make it to the settee? I'll help you."

I nodded. "I *think* so."

Becky moved and put her mug onto the coffee table before returning to my side. She placed one arm around my back and guided me further into the room. As I reached the sofa yet another spasm hit, only this time it was accompanied by a warm, wet feeling between my legs. I gasped and looked down to see a damp patch appearing on the carpet.

"Oh, OH!" I gasped again.

"Remy, what is it?" I could tell Becky was scared by the tone of her voice.

"Um, I think my waters broke. Becky, I think I'm in labour." My voice rose with each word – a combination of fear and excitement.

"Okay babes. Don't panic. Let's get you on the couch and then we'll phone the hospital." I stifled a snigger. I could tell she was close to panic herself and here she was telling *me* not to panic.

I sat on the sofa and she gently lifted my legs on so I could lie down. As she reached for the phone another contraction hit – this one made both me and Becky cry out. Becky tried to press the keys quickly and only succeeded in punching the number in wrong. She ended the call, cursing under her breath and using a word our parents would definitely frown upon. She tried again, pressing the digits slower, making sure she did it right.

After a brief conversation with the maternity department, she hung up.

"This is definitely *not* the best time to be a twin – I'm getting twinges every time you have a contraction! Anyway, they're sending a 4x4 ambulance," she reported. "They don't want to risk me driving in this weather, especially as you're carrying twins and you're overdue. We've got to start timing the contractions too."

"O-kay. Anything else?"

"I've got to get some blankets or something warm to wrap you in for when the ambulance arrives. Will you be alright for a minute while I go and fetch some?"

"Course I will, silly," I chuckled then gasped as another contraction arrived. Becky checked her watch making a mental note of the time then dashed upstairs. I reached for the phone. I needed to let Mum know I was in labour – as Becky had apparently forgotten. I hit speed dial and waited impatiently to hear an answering voice.

"Hello darling. How are you?" Mum's voice answered.

"Hi Mum. I'm okay thanks. I can't chat for long – I just rang to let you know I'm in labour. My waters broke and I'm waiting for the ambulance," my words tumbled out in a rush.

"Are you there alone?" I could hear the concern in her voice.

"No, Mum. Becky's here. Don't worry – everything's under control. Anyway, I'll get Becky to ring when your grandchildren finally make an appearance. I've got to go - I think I've got another contraction coming."

"Okay, darling, take care. Hope it goes well. We'll be thinking of you."

"Thanks Mum. Love you." My voice sounded strained as I felt the contraction beginning to build in intensity.

"We love you too, darling. Bye."

I couldn't speak and didn't want Mum to hear me cry out so I pressed the button to end the call moments before I yelled in pain. Becky returned carrying a double-size fleece throw as the contraction came and she checked her watch again.

"I hope the ambulance doesn't take too long – your last two contractions were only ten minutes apart," she announced.

By the time the ambulance had negotiated the snow-encrusted roads, my contractions were nine-minutes apart. The paramedics walked through the door all bundled up in heavy fluorescent jackets, hats, gloves and boots. One carried a folded chair, the other a large green holdall-type bag.

After giving me a brief examination, they wrapped me in blankets and the fleece throw, helped me into the chair and got me into the ambulance at an impressive speed considering how slippery it must have been on the pavement. Becky grabbed my case from the hall and followed us out making sure the door was locked firmly behind her. She climbed into the ambulance and the paramedic closed the door behind her.

As the ambulance pulled away from the kerb with its blue lights flashing, Samir emerged from the shadows disappointed and cursed his bad timing. The venom was flowing over his tongue in anticipation – she was another special one – his desire to taste her and bring her to the fold was all encompassing. He watched until the ambulance disappeared at the end of the road before turning away. He wasn't overly concerned – he knew where she was now and it would be only a matter of time before she joined him. He would have to be patient. He always acquired what he sought and this special one would not escape him. Time was on his side.

* * *

Four minutes into the Vernal Equinox, the first of the twins entered the world announcing their arrival with a loud wail.

"Congratulations Remy, you have a beautiful boy," the midwife's smile lit up the room.

A boy? I wasn't expecting *that*. Isn't it strange how we get certain notions in our head and when reality doesn't match up, we're totally taken aback by it. I'd convinced myself I was carrying twin girls, maybe because of Becky and me. A boy!

Before I could think about it any further, another wave of contractions cleared all rational thought from my mind and all I could hear through the pain was the midwife telling me to push – again. I was so exhausted – all I really wanted to do was sleep – but somehow I found a reserve of energy and pushed with all my might, letting out an almighty yell in the process.

Just when I felt I couldn't push any more, a different wail echoed around the room and I huffed with relief.

"Oh, Rems, it's a girl and she's *exquisite*," Becky cried her voice full of emotion.

"Are they . . . are they both alright?" I asked hesitantly. It was the midwife who answered.

"They are both perfect, Remy," she reassured me.

My tired eyes filled with tears as my babies were brought over to me and laid in my arms. Becky dabbed at my eyes with a tissue and I smiled at her gratefully. I looked in awe first at my son's handsome face – his cerulean eyes were open and gazing up at me – and immediately I could see Joshua in some of his features. I then turned my attention to my daughter. *Becky's comment was bang on,* I thought as I looked at her exquisite face. Her eyes were also open and the exact same shade as her brother's.

"Have you chosen any names yet?" the midwife asked.

I looked up and smiled, nodding.

"Aidan and Ashley."

Chapter 44 – Remy

The twins were a constant source of joy for me. They were always smiling and content. Between Mum and Becky I had plenty of help in the early days; coming to terms with being a mother was daunting enough, let alone being a mother to twins. Trying to raise them without the support of their father still shattered my heart into a gazillion pieces every single day.

At the beginning it was a sharp learning curve; learning about their everyday needs, learning to listen to each noise they made and decipher what it meant, learning to juggle my time – at the end of each day I fell into bed and was asleep as soon as my head touched the pillow. I really don't know how I would have coped without Mum and Becky's help.

There was only one other dark cloud in my azure sky. They seemed normal babies . . . except for their development. Within four months Aidan and Ashley were sitting up unaided and had several teeth. They were smiling, chuckling, communicating with each other in their own special way and grabbing hold of any object within their reach. They knew instinctively whether it was food they held or something to throw or play with, as only the former ended up in their mouths. My amazement at their rapid development hit a new high when I was least expecting it.

I awoke to the sounds of giggling from the nursery. I didn't get up straight away – my children's laughter was more tuneful for me than any bird song – so I lay there and listened for a while. Turning my head, I glanced at the clock on the bedside table and my heart became a huge heavy lump in my chest. Next to the digits showing it was time I got my rear end out of bed, was a date – one I'd been unconsciously dreading – today was my birthday. Joshua had been missing for sixteen months.

Hot tears poured across my cheeks and into my hair. I chewed my bottom lip to keep the sobs locked inside – I didn't want Aidan and Ashley to hear. I buried my face in the pillow and cried until there were no more tears left inside me then got up and went to the bathroom to bathe my eyes in cold water. By the time I was ready to face the babies most of the evidence from my mini meltdown was absent.

As I walked across the landing toward the nursery, the giggles morphed into full scale laughter. This was new. I crept up to the partially-open door, peeped into the room and became immediately frozen to the spot. My jaw hit the deck, my eyes bugged out so much it hurt and I couldn't say a word. Some of their brightly-coloured plastic bricks were bobbing and weaving in the air, creating weird jerky dance moves as if they were puppets on strings.

Ashley was pointing her fingers at them and swaying her little arms like she was conducting an orchestra. Her cherubic face was more alive at this moment than I'd ever seen it; her eyes sparkled with delight and her mouth stretched into a wondrous smile. Aidan was looking up at the bricks laughing and clapping his hands. *Clapping his hands? He's not even seven- months old yet. What the hell IS this?*

My eyes flew around the room searching for a rational explanation to what I was seeing, but there was nothing – absolutely nothing to account for it. My limbs unfroze and I took a hesitant step further into their room. Ashley had her back to me so didn't see me enter; Aidan, although not looking directly at me must have perceived movement in his peripheral vision and turned his head in my direction.

Aidan grabbed the bars on the side of his cot and pulled himself up into a standing position – something else I'd not seen him do before. As if that wasn't shocking enough, what happened next caused me to collapse in a heap on the floor as my legs turned to jelly and gave way beneath me.

It's okay Mummy, don't be scared. This little voice came from nowhere – I didn't even see his lips move. Ashley turned her head then and saw me gawking at the pair of them, but instead of letting the bricks fall as most children would have done, she carried on directing them while throwing me a proud grin.

My head was full of mush. I couldn't make sense of anything – it was like someone rode a lawnmower across my brain and shredded everything in its path. *What the hell was going on here?* I didn't trust my legs to hold me up so I crawled on all fours over to the twins' cots. I turned to Aidan first – his shy smile melted my heart.

"Did you talk to me, Aidan?" I tried very hard to keep my voice low and even, but a slight quiver crept in.

Aidan looked me straight in the eye and without moving his lips I heard, *Yes Mummy.*

"But your lips aren't moving . . ."

I'm talking with my mind.

"How?" My voice raised an octave.

I don't know I just can. He shrugged his tiny shoulders and pursed his lips. *Is it . . . wrong?*

I reached up and stroked his cheek, stalling while I tried to find the right words. "No, my darling, it's not wrong, it's . . . well I didn't know it was really *possible*. I've read and heard about it, but I never took it seriously." I paused for a second while my brain tried to catch up. "The trouble is not everyone will understand how you can do this and they will be frightened by it, so I need you to promise me something – promise you won't talk to anyone else this way unless I tell you it's okay."

Aidan's expression turned solemn. He placed his hand on mine and I heard, *I promise, Mummy.*

"Thank you, sweetheart." I turned to Ashley who was still orchestrating the bricks; they were now spinning as if caught in a whirlpool. "Ashley, can you talk with your mind too?"

Her face looked a little sad as she shook her head.

"But you're making these bricks dance about, aren't you?"

Her lovely face lit up and she giggled, nodding her head so her blonde hair flapped around on the top of her head. There wasn't much point in me asking her how she did it –like Aidan, she wouldn't know.

"Will *you* promise not to do this in front of anyone else unless I tell you it's okay?" I placed my free hand on her cheek, as I had with Aidan. Her expression turned serious and she nodded. "Thank you, sweetheart. Now then, who's ready for breakfast?" I sing-songed, endeavouring to keep the building panic from my voice. I picked them up, one in each arm and walked downstairs. The main thought running through my mind was *how in God's name was I ever going to explain this to Becky, Mum and Dad?*

* * *

Samir sauntered down the street at a normal human pace. Even though it was dark, he didn't want to draw attention to himself. The majority of the gardens were devoid of trees and large shrubs so concealing himself was out of the question.

He turned the corner and saw lights still on in the house; anticipation gripped him – it was akin to an electric current running down his spine. He sniffed the air – the unmistakable scent was even stronger now – and he savoured the taste of the venom as it coated his tongue. Hopefully there would be a much sweeter flavour to moisten his palate tonight.

By the time he reached the house, the street was deserted. It wasn't so late other people wouldn't appear and he could hardly risk being seen peeping through the window. He stood two doors down weighing his options. It took a fraction of a second before he was moving again, his decision made.

Samir deliberately strolled past the house he sought keeping his eyes straight ahead. He checked around to ensure he was alone in the street before darting up the neighbours drive and scaling the wall up onto the garage roof. With the agility of a cat, he silently clambered over the roof and dropped into the back garden.

He stood as motionless as a statue. He knew his landing would have gone unheard by human ears, but there was always the one-in-a-million chance of someone thinking they saw movement in their peripheral vision and going to the window to investigate.

He waited patiently for five minutes before daring to move towards the kitchen window. He glanced down at the patio and made a mental note of where obstacles were; after all his preparation, he would be mortified if he blew this by kicking a plant pot or knocking over a garden chair. His movements were stealthy, sure and unhurried. Reaching one side of the kitchen window, he slowly moved his head until he could see into the house.

Samir was delighted when he saw his target appeared to be alone. If he had been a younger vampire, he probably would have made his move immediately, but decades of experience had taught him to be cautious. As he watched, a shudder passed through her body and she rubbed the tops of her arms as if cold. She stood and walked toward the lounge window. Cupping her hands around her eyes she peered into the gloom. Was she waiting for someone?

His eyes never left her and so was able to detect the slight movement indicating she was about to turn around. Samir bobbed down and moved to conceal himself behind a large wheelie bin. From this viewpoint he could see the window without being seen. His instincts had been spot on – she switched on an outside light then came to the window and looked out. Samir was relieved he didn't have a shadow to give him away.

The garden light remained on for three minutes before being switched off, but Samir wasn't going to chance repositioning himself – he was more astute than that. He waited a further five minutes before returning to the window then slowly raised his head until he could once more see into the house. She was still alone in the room, but then he heard her voice.

"I keep getting the feeling I'm being watched and it's creeping me out."

Was she talking to herself? Another female voice answered and then Samir saw an older couple walk into the room; the man cradling a sleepy infant in his arms. Disappointment began to course through Samir's veins, but he stopped it in its tracks. It was getting late and they would most likely be leaving soon – he would bide his time until she was alone again. The appearance of an infant disturbed him a little. Was the one he sought a mother? He mentally shrugged it off. It didn't matter to him one way or the other; when he wanted someone as much as he wanted her, his morals were non-existent.

Samir tuned out the inconsequential chatter from inside the house; he moved away from the window and settled down to wait.

An hour later Samir heard the occupants saying goodnight to each other. Once more the anticipation quickened him. He waited to hear the front door open and close, and a car engine starting, but instead three sets of feet climbed the stairs. The realisation hit him like a physical blow – the visitors weren't leaving, they were staying the night.

Anger and disappointment surged through him. He was *so* close. . . There was no point in him remaining there – he couldn't risk gaining entry to the house and being caught. He sprang noiselessly back onto the garage roof and off again, landing back on the drive.

"I *will* be back for you," he whispered in a voice softer than a breeze.

Samir took one last wistful look at the house before running off down the road at a speed most race car drivers could only aspire to.

* * *

The twins were in their high chairs in the kitchen, munching on sliced banana from small plastic bowls in front of them. It had been a relaxed morning. As it was a warm sunny day with a hint of a breeze we'd gone for a walk to the park. I'd wheeled them over to the small lake where they'd watched the ducks with fascinated expressions on their faces, until it was close to lunchtime. We'd then strolled back, they had a play on their activity mat and then I'd given them their lunch.

I decided to begin preparing ingredients for the evening meal. Becky and my dearest friend, Jakki, were coming to dinner and we had planned a real girlie night. I couldn't remember the last time I'd had one of those and was so looking forward to it.

I diced some onions and sliced some mushrooms, putting them into the waiting casserole dish on the worktop. Opening the fridge, I pulled out the fillet steak and had just begun cutting it into strips only to be interrupted by the doorbell. I hurriedly rinsed the blood from my hands under the tap, grabbed a towel and began drying them as I rushed to the front door. I took delivery of a parcel for my neighbour, set it down in the hall and made my way back to the kitchen.

As I walked through the door, I glanced at the twins as was my habit and stopped dead. *What on earth?* All around their mouths and across their cheeks was something red. I turned to get a cloth to clean them, but as I did so, I noticed the steak was missing from the worktop.

I turned around slowly, suddenly filled with trepidation; Ashley and Aidan had the raw steak in their hands and mouths and were ripping chunks out of it with animalistic savagery, like lions shredding a carcase.

My scream echoed around the house just before blackness swallowed me whole.

[TO BE CONTINUED IN HEART SEARCH: FOUND]

More Exciting Titles from Myrddin Publishing Group

Tower of Bones by Connie J Jasperson

Crown Phoenix Series by Alison DeLuca

The Ring of Lost Souls by Rachel Tsoumbakos

Emeline and the Mutants by Rachel Tsoumbakos

Silent No More by Krista Hatch

The Other Way Is Essex by Writebulb Writers Group

The Infinity Bridge by Ross M Kitson

Darkness Rising 2 – Quest by Ross M Kitson

Chinese Lolita by Lisa Zhang Wharton

A Simpler Guide to Gmail by Ceri Clark

The Body War by Kathleen M Barker

Ednor Scardens by Kathleen M Barker

Land of Nod, The Artifact by Gary Hoover

Land of Nod, The Prophet by Gary Hoover

Hearts & Minds by Maria V A Johnson

After Ilium by Stephen Swartz

Yum by Nicole Antonia Carson

Sons of Roland by Nicole Antonia Carson

Hired by a Demon by Gypsy Maddon

The Last Guardian by Joan Hazel

What the Heart Sees by Joan Hazel

Dark Places by Shaun Allan

Check www.myrddinpublishing.com for new titles coming soon.

Other Thrilling Books

The Sheol (The Wanderer Trilogy #1) by Mia Hoddell

YA Paranormal Romance

Being a trained killer, Kala can handle most things the world throws at her. However, when she murders her fiancé, Kala's life is thrown into chaos. Forced to leave everything behind, she runs from city to city, in fear of her psychotic boss who is seeking her death. If that wasn't enough, she also has to cope with the re-appearance of her dead fiancé who is struggling to keep a hold on his sanity as he strives for revenge.

The Flawless (The Wanderer Trilogy #2)

A battle is going to arise soon; The Sheol and The Flawless will come together but only one can survive to continue their manipulation of humankind. The Wanderers have to decide whether to summon the courage to fight so they can save themselves from eternal unrest or whether they like being lost, immortal souls. Nachtmahr is upgrading his Sturmmen to create more ruthless and efficient killers due to interference from The Sheol, while Kala is becoming darker; her rage consuming her as she strives to fulfill her own personal mission...Kill Nachtmahr.

Available from: Amazon, Smashwords, iBooks (ebook)
Lulu (paperback)

Made in the USA
Charleston, SC
07 December 2012